The

DANCE

of the

SHARKS

Best Wishes
Russ Pelton

The
DANCE
of the
SHARKS

RUSSELL PELTON

outskirtspress
DENVER, COLORADO

The Dance of the Sharks
All Rights Reserved.
Copyright © 2014 Russell Pelton
v1.0

Outskirts Press, Inc.
http://www.outskirtspress.com

ISBN: 978-1-4787-2247-2

Outskirts Press and the "OP" logo are trademarks belonging to Outskirts Press, Inc.

PRINTED IN THE UNITED STATES OF AMERICA

*Dedicated to my family and friends who
encouraged, prodded and cajoled me into writing
and finishing this book, made valuable suggestions,
and in the process proved that you can, indeed,
teach an old dog new tricks.*

Part 1

BLOOD IN THE WATER

Chapter One

—∿∿—

"Robert, help your father out of the cab. Careful now--don't let him fall."

The taxi had jerked to a stop in front of the Emergency entrance at Blessed Trinity Hospital, and Bertha Roosevelt quickly gave the driver two five-dollar bills and pushed open the left rear door without waiting for change. She almost lost her footing on the slick Chicago street, but caught the door handle to keep her balance, slammed the door shut, and ran around to the other side, where her twelve-year-old son was struggling to help her husband out. Sam was standing in the street, leaning up against the cab's open door, holding his head and sagging back toward the cab. Robert, still mostly inside the cab, was propping him up, trying to keep him steady, but Sam was a big man, and the light rain that was falling didn't make things any easier.

Bertha threw her left arm around Sam's back and grabbed the open door with her right hand for support.

Robert scooted over to his father's left and kept him from falling sideways.

"Can't you please help?" Bertha pleaded to the cabby, a chunky Hispanic wearing a White Sox cap.

He merely shrugged. "Hey, lady, I got you here. Ain't that enough?"

The hospital doors swung open, and two young men in white jackets rushed out, pulling a gurney.

"What's the problem?" the tall one asked.

"It's my husband," Bertha shouted in near panic. "He's had a stroke or something. His left side's all weak. And his head hurts."

"Terrible headache," Sam mumbled, holding his head with his right hand, his left arm around Robert.

Within seconds the two orderlies were wheeling him into the hospital. They rushed him through the lobby while the receptionist began to coax the information she needed from the distracted Bertha. Sam worked for the Chicago Public Schools, Bertha told her, so they had full medical coverage. Bertha scribbled her signature on a series of forms and began fumbling in her purse for the insurance card, her eyes darting back and forth trying to keep track of Sam. Robert, unsure of what was happening, stood close beside her.

"Here it is." She pulled out the card and slammed it down on the counter. "Come on, Robert." She turned and began running down the corridor where Sam had been wheeled. She knew her husband needed her. She could hear the receptionist calling to her, but Sam was all that mattered.

A stout nurse with graying blond hair stepped through a set of steel-covered doors a few yards down the corridor and held up her hand.

"Can I help you?"

"Yes. My husband was just taken in there. I am trying to get to him. I need to be with him."

"I'm sorry, but I'm afraid you can't go in," she said, firmly but kindly. "At least not right now. They're giving your husband some tests. He shows some weakness on the left side, which may indicate a stroke or a hematoma, and the doctor wants him to have a CT scan."

"A what?" Bertha's mind was swimming. She had heard the woman but didn't quite understand.

"A CT scan," the nurse repeated. "It's like a giant X-ray of the entire body, and it'll show the doctors exactly what's wrong and where the problem is. Don't worry. Your husband is getting the best care there is." She put a reassuring hand on Bertha's arm and gently pushed her back. "Please go back to the reception area and wait. We'll let you know as soon as we have any results. That's the best thing that you can do for your husband right now."

Bertha, feeling overwhelmed, searched in vain for an alternative. She nodded, looked pleadingly at the nurse for a moment, then with a deep breath turned toward her son and said, "We'll wait up front, Robert. Like the lady said."

She walked slowly back down the corridor and dropped heavily onto one of the green plastic-covered couches. A dozen other people were sitting around the room, some reading, some dozing, others just staring emptily into space. Her son followed her, unzipped his Bulls jacket, and sat quietly at the opposite end of the couch, looking at her. After a few minutes, he gathered his courage to ask, "Mom, is Dad going to be okay?"

Bertha took a deep breath, exhaled, then took another. She could feel her heart racing. The antiseptic smell of the hospital was reassuring. She sat back, shut her eyes, and tried desperately to pull herself together.

"Yes, your dad will be all right. Whatever has happened to him, we got him here in time. This isn't County Hospital; this is a *good* hospital."

When she and Robert had returned from the teacher's conference at Abraham Lincoln Middle School that afternoon they'd found Sam lying on the living-room floor. His left leg had given way, he said in alarmingly slurred speech, he couldn't get up and his head hurt, he told her. Bertha was shocked. It was the first time in twenty-six years of marriage that she had seen Sam helpless. He was the head janitor at Crane Tech, the same school where he had played football as a kid, and always took pride in being in good shape. A few pounds overweight now, maybe, but still able to lift a hundred-pound crate with no trouble at all. He was her pillar of strength.

Bertha had instinctively called 911, but when she couldn't get an answer after several rings, she sent Robert down to find a cab. She knew that might be difficult; it was raining, and even in good weather few cabs cruised the inner-city neighborhoods. But luck was with them;

Robert found one within a few minutes. It was not easy getting Sam down the four flights of stairs, but he was a proud man and he did what he could, taking the steps one at a time and gripping the railing with his right hand. Finally, they had made it to the street, and with agonizing slowness they'd gotten him into the cab.

Now, waiting, eyes closed, she was still mad at the cabby for not helping them with Sam. She shook her head when she thought of that again.

"Mom?"

She opened her eyes to Robert's voice and saw a young man in a white smock standing in front of her. He was tall, with thinning brown hair and bloodshot eyes. The kind blond nurse was standing behind him and off to one side.

"Mrs. Roosevelt," he said, "I'm Dr. Chivers, the emergency room physician. We've taken a CT scan of your husband, and the radiologist, Dr. Rashdani, says it shows a large hematoma, a blood clot, on the left side of his head." He glanced at the clipboard he was holding and continued. "We've called in a neurosurgeon, Dr. Michaels, and it may be necessary to operate. We wanted you to know. And we need to have you sign some additional papers." He handed Bertha the clipboard and she stared at several sheets of paper with yellow Sign Here stickers attached.

She was numb. *Operate? On his head?* She didn't know what to say. Finally, she forced herself. "You say he has a blood clot?"

"Yes, ma'am," the physician responded politely. "It's on the left side of his brain, on the surface. If Dr. Michaels concurs, we'll operate immediately. Fortunately, you got him here quickly. Time is critical in these cases. With any luck, we'll be able to clean that blood out, and your husband will have a good chance to make a full recovery. Here's my pen."

Bertha slowly took the pen, still in a daze. As she began scribbling her signature, the nurse stepped forward and leaned close to Dr. Chivers. "Did you say the *left* side of his brain?" she whispered, loud enough for Bertha to overhear.

"Yes," he snapped. "Dr. Rashdani said the CT scan clearly shows the hematoma on the left side."

"But the hemiparesis is on the left side."

He turned and looked at her for a moment, then replied brusquely, "This is one of those cases where pressure on one side of the brain causes a false lateralization, and the hematoma is on the same side as the hemiparesis. They're rare, but not unheard of. I suspect they don't teach that at nursing school." He glared at her, waiting impatiently for Bertha's last signature. She'd barely finished writing when he snatched the clipboard, wheeled around, and walked away.

The woman looked at Bertha and shrugged her shoulders. "I'm only a nurse," she said. "What do I know?"

Bertha was uncomfortable. *What were they arguing about? Was it important?* She turned and looked at Robert and beckoned him over. He slid up next to her on the couch and she wrapped her arm around him. *Sam will be all right. Sam will be all right.*

Dr. Leonard Michaels had performed this operation hundreds of times before. The patient's CT scan clearly showed a subdural hematoma on the left side of the brain, on the surface. His skull had been shaved and was marked for surgery at the site where the films showed the hematoma to be. Their job was to open up the head, locate the blood clot, drain it, stop the bleeding, then close him up again. It should take about three hours, and the patient had about an eighty-percent likelihood of recovering fully. There were seven masked people in the operating room, and Dr. Michael's choice of music, Verdi's *Aida,* was playing quietly in the background. Michaels turned to his right and nodded to the resident holding the craniotome, an electric side-cutting drill.

Forty minutes later, however, Leonard Michaels began to have doubts. The head was open and he was looking into Sam Roosevelt's brain, but there wasn't any clot. The only blood was the blood from the incision. Everything looked perfectly normal except for some swelling.

He administered some Mannitol, then stepped back and looked at the CT scan film again. Could he have opened the wrong side of the patient's head? No, the CT scan was clear; the hematoma was on the left side. Dr. Michaels knew that the Walbrook CT scan machine automatically imprinted "left" and "right" on the correct sides of the print, so that an error in labeling couldn't occur.

He looked again for the clot, then finally gave up. There was nothing there.

"Radiology must have given us the wrong patient's films," he said to the young man standing beside him. "Check with them immediately, every minute counts." As the intern stepped to a phone and began punching in numbers, Dr. Michaels turned to the head nurse. "And if they can't resolve it right away, have another CT scan taken. This man's obviously got a serious problem, but we can't deal with it if we don't have good films."

"The CT scan machine's down," the nurse quickly replied. "I heard that just as we came in. They're working on it and it won't be operable before the morning, at the earliest."

"Damn!"

"Radiology insists that we have the right patient's films," the intern said, speaking up through his surgical mask and holding the phone off to one side.

"Damn!" Dr. Michaels repeated. He took a deep breath. "Well, there's nothing we can do till we get some new films. Sew him up and put him in ICU till morning."

"Here's our new policy covering hospitals and their medical staffs, Chester. Every insurance agent in the

United States will have it in his hands by the end of the year. We expect to totally co-opt the market."

Gordon Hawke pushed the bound sheaf of white papers across his polished desk and leaned back with a smile. "We'd like your firm to be involved with us from the beginning on this one. We expect it to be lucrative, very lucrative indeed. And if you chaps can give us a hand in running the program and in handling the claims, you could do rather well."

Chester Melrose couldn't suppress the little smile that crept from the corners of his mouth. His years of cultivating the London market had finally borne fruit. This wasn't going to be an isolated case, like everything else his law firm had handled for London over the years. This sounded like more, much more.

He picked up the insurance policy. It had blue binding and a dark red seal with a lion's head imprinted on the front page. He thumbed through the pages slowly, both because of the arthritis in his hands and because he liked the feel of the heavy bond paper.

"It sounds very interesting, Gordon," Melrose responded as casually as he could. "But tell me, what's so innovative about this particular policy?" He laid the document on the desk between them.

Gordon Hawke pulled his half-glasses from the left front pocket of his blue pinstriped suit, slid them on, then flipped open a folder on his desk. He was tall and angular, with high cheekbones and black hair graying at the temples--an imposing figure even seated behind his desk.

He began talking about underwriting principles, gesturing confidently and occasionally referring to specific language in the policy.

Melrose tried to follow him at first but quickly gave up. He sat back with a fixed smile, nodding from time to time. He just couldn't focus. He hadn't actually read a policy in years, and the late-afternoon sun glistening off the distant Lloyds Tower kept drawing his attention.

Chester Melrose had been coming to London for years, seeking out bits and pieces of work for his Chicago-based law firm. He had been modestly successful and had come to know some of the underwriters well. The relationships were basically social, built around lunch, tea, cocktails, dinner, theater. From time to time, usually after a particularly lavish evening's entertainment, one of them would send Melrose's firm, Wilson Thompson & Gilcrist, a case to handle. But Melrose knew, and his partners suspected, that the net cost of his trips to London far exceeded the fees that they generated. Since Melrose was chairman of the firm's finance committee, he had been able to bury most of his expenditures, but lately some members of the management committee had been openly asking questions, and he needed some major new work from London to placate them and to quash the firm's growing feeling that, at seventy-six, it was time for him to retire. Gordon Hawke's new hospital malpractice business was the perfect answer.

Hawke was one of London's new breed of underwriters, more aggressive than the traditional Lloyds insurers.

He and his company, the Imperial Insurance Syndicate, had started out in the early 1980s on the fringe of the Lloyds market, snapping up insurance opportunities that the old-line syndicates were hesitant to write. His aggressive underwriting over the next two decades had made him a force to be dealt with in the London insurance world.

"And so you see, Chester, by underwriting the policies in Bermuda and reinsuring them one hundred percent in Munich, we reduce our reserve requirements to virtually zero." Hawke leaned back as he closed his folder. "The result is that we can offer this insurance to hospitals for half of what any other carrier will charge--the few carriers, that is, that still write this line of insurance. What your domestic carriers don't understand, and what we've carefully calculated, is that your medical liability market is about to make a dramatic recovery, with all the so-called tort reform initiatives that have been adopted in recent years. Our Bermuda company is now licensed in forty-seven of your states, as well as in three Canadian provinces, so we're positioned to take the medical liability market by storm, just as its profitability soars."

"That's remarkable," Melrose nodded in agreement, oblivious to everything the Englishman had been saying for the past few minutes. "Now exactly how does Wilson Thompson & Gilcrist fit into the picture?"

Hawke looked at him quizzically. "As I mentioned, we'd like your firm to administer the program in North America, and handle the defense of any suits that are filed against hospitals or physicians we insure. You can see from the draft of the policy there that Wilson Thompson & Gilcrist is named as the party to whom all claims and inquiries should be directed. We took a bit of liberty in including your firm's name in the draft. Hope you don't mind."

"No, no, of course not," Melrose laughed. Actually, he was elated. He knew that when a law firm's name was written right into a master insurance policy it was almost impossible to change legal counsel during that policy's life. This was sounding better and better.

"Fifty percent of the net premiums received," Hawke continued, "will be deposited into an escrow account in your firm's name. You'll have full discretion to apply those funds to pay your fees and expenses as well as to settle cases."

"And the reserves to cover any large losses...?" Melrose's voice trailed off; he was having difficulty envisioning the arrangement.

"That's the beauty of this program." Hawke smiled again as he stretched back into his black leather chair. He opened his hands and spread them wide. "We really don't have to maintain any reserves. Nothing of consequence, anyway. That's the concern of the reinsurer; they'll be responsible for everything over a million dollars per claim."

Melrose wasn't sure he understood what Hawke had just said. But then, that didn't matter; the underwriting of this program was Hawke's concern, not his. Still, he wondered if he should have one of the firm's younger partners take a look at all this before he made any commitments. Maybe Cal Cizma; he did a lot of insurance work. But Cizma would then surely claim some of the credit for the business, and Chester Melrose wasn't going to let that happen. *This is going to be all mine.*

Hawke leaned forward, peered at the old Yank over his glasses, and tapped the folder on his desk. "Our plan," he said, lowering his voice slightly, "is to test-market the new policy in Chicago and two or three other major cities this spring. Our agents tell us that they've got a dozen hospitals ready to sign up as soon as we give them the go-ahead. If it goes well, we'll take it nationwide and into Canada later this year. We intend to refinance the program in the fourth year. At that point we'll be able to measure quite accurately the funds needed to cover the losses coming down the road, and we'll reserve the entire program accordingly. And your firm's job, in a nutshell, is to get us to that four-year mark without having to pay out any excessive sums for patients that our hospitals foul up. If you handle it prudently, and keep a tight grip on the purse strings, you should do very well. What say, Chester, are you with us in this one?"

What a beautiful turn of events. Melrose had to meet with the rest of the management committee when he returned to Chicago. Its chairman, Barton Thompson, had told him pointedly before he left that they'd be expecting a full report on the results of his latest trip. Melrose feared that if he came back empty-handed he'd be told to retire. With Gordon Hawke's hospital program in his pocket, he'd return in glory, his next four years assured.

"Of course we're in on it." Melrose stood up with some effort and extended his hand. Hawke rose too, returned the smile, and shook his hand, sealing the pact.

"Excellent. We'll advise our agents to proceed immediately. Oh, and by the way…" He paused. "Our man in Chicago would like to have the policies retroactive to the first of the month. You don't have any objection to that, I presume?"

"Of course not. Why would I?"

"I didn't think you'd mind. This should be an exciting four years for us, Chester. I like doing business with you. You're my kind of solicitor."

—*mm*—

Bertha Roosevelt sent Robert home by taxi. She wasn't going to leave the hospital until she knew how Sam was doing. She'd been told by Dr. Chivers that they'd done a "preliminary" operation, but that another surgery would be necessary in the morning after a new CT scan was taken. She was allowed to visit Sam in Intensive Care, but he was unconscious and probably didn't know she was there. He was hooked up to a couple of electronic machines with flashing lights, tubes stuck in both his arms. He looked terrible. After a while she went back to the reception area and collapsed onto a couch, exhausted and afraid. She dozed there fitfully through the night, without really resting.

The waiting room was almost empty when Bertha awoke in the morning and went to the ladies' room. She picked up a copy of the *Daily Defender* from a chair when she returned, but was too distracted to read. She was putting it down beside her on the couch when the doors swung open and two men who looked like doctors entered, talking excitedly. When they neared her, she could see from his nametag that one of them was Dr. Michaels. He was the one who had operated on Sam.

"That was *your* responsibility, not mine," she could hear Dr. Michaels snap at the other. "That's why I want you here when we explain to her what happened." The other doctor--Dr. Rashdani, his nametag read--was looking down as they neared.

Bertha stood up as they reached her.

"I'm afraid we have some bad news, Mrs. Roosevelt," Dr. Michaels said. He hesitated for a moment and went on. "We took another CT scan of your husband this morning…"

"Yes, I know," she interrupted. "What did it show?"

"That's the problem, Mrs. Roosevelt. It shows a major hematoma, a blood clot, on the *right* side of your husband's brain, very similar to the one that we saw in the film on his *left* side last night."

"Oh, my God," she said, feeling the strength drain out of her. "Another one?"

"Well, no, actually not," Dr. Rashdani answered defensively. "I'm afraid that it's the same one we saw before. We can tell by the location and shape. It's larger now, of course. Much larger. But it is definitely the same one."

"I don't understand," Bertha said, confused.

Dr. Michaels responded and looked angry. "It appears, Mrs. Roosevelt, that the CT scan film was mislabeled. Somehow the left and right sides were reversed. We operated on the left side of your husband's head last night, relying on that CT scan, when the clot was in the right side all the time. I don't know how that happened. The radiology department insists"- he glared intently at Dr. Rashdani - "that the machine imprints the 'left' and 'right' labels automatically, so that there's no possibility of human error. But somehow an error did occur." He took a deep breath. "We're terribly sorry, Mrs. Roosevelt."

Bertha Roosevelt felt ill. She eased herself back down onto the couch, unable to focus on anything.

"What we want to do now," Dr. Michaels went on, "if you concur, is to operate immediately on the right side of your husband's head. The chances of recovery are admittedly small, after all this time, but it's the only chance he's got."

Bertha leaned back and shut her eyes. Her whole world was collapsing around her. Sam would never walk out of that hospital; she knew that.

"Mrs. Roosevelt, did you hear us?"

"Yes," she whispered. "I heard you." Eyes still closed, she sighed deeply, a single tear rolling down her cheek. "You do whatever you think you should do."

Tony Jeffries walked into Ditka's bar, paused for a moment to adjust to the din and the muted lighting, and began working his way through the crowd.

"Hi, Tony." Lillian, the buxom blond waitress, smiled as he passed the service end of the bar. "Your usual?"

"You bet."

Ditka's was busier than usual that night. Probably a convention in town; he remembered how difficult it had been to find a cab that afternoon to get back to the office from the Sears Tower. At five-nine he couldn't see over the crowd, but he knew where he was headed: the round table in the corner. Yes, he concluded as he sucked in his gut to squeeze between two overdressed matrons wearing nametags--definitely a convention in town.

"Evening, fellas," he said, pulling up a chair. He was the last to arrive.

"Evening, Tony," Cal Cizma responded, nodding, as Curly Morgan and the others raised their drinks in greeting. Lillian brought Tony's Chardonnay, Grgich Hills; they stocked it especially for him. He raised his chilled glass to his friends, then savored a sip of the mellow oaken wine.

The five of them had been meeting like this after work on Fridays for longer than they cared to recall. Maybe sometimes another attorney from the firm would join them, or one or two of the quintet would be gone, on a business trip or a vacation. Otherwise, it was a ritual: if you were in town after work on Friday, you headed to Ditka's for a drink.

At first they had met upstairs at the Italian Village, the old bar and restaurant near their office on LaSalle Street. When the firm outgrew that space fifteen years ago and moved to the Hancock Building on North Michigan, changing bars was more wrenching than moving their files. But once they'd surveyed their new neighborhood, and found this haven, one block to the west on Chestnut, they knew they had a new Friday home. It was called Cricket's, until the old Bears coach bought and renamed it a couple of years later.

They'd all been fresh-faced young lawyers back then, hired by the firm along with so many other fresh faces. Most of those had drifted away, some voluntarily, others, otherwise. But these five had stayed, and stayed together, had helped one another through their growing pains as young lawyers, and now, in 2003, were all partners in Wilson Thompson & Gilcrist.

"Did you hear that Tony is about to become a medical mal expert?" Cal Cizma asked as he reached for some cashews.

"Is that the new book of business that Melrose brought back from London?" Rasheed Collins asked.

"Yeah." Tony laughed. "Chester asked me today to start clearing my schedule. He expects cases to start coming in next month, and he wants my group to handle them. We may hire a couple of new associates, depending on the volume." He took a sip of his Chardonnay, then gestured across the table at Cal. "It's not just me, though. I've got the litigation, but Cal has the administrative side of the program. It sounds like a pretty big deal."

"That's great," Rasheed answered. "Does this mean that we'll have to start addressing you two as 'Doc'?"

"Absolutely. It also means I'm taking Wednesdays off from now on."

"Here's to Docs Jeffries and Cizma," Pete Spanos toasted laughingly, raising his beer. "By the way, Doc, I've got a severe pain back here," he said to Cal, patting his butt. "Do you want to take a look at it?"

"No, just shove two cashews up your ass and call me in the morning."

Tony laughed with the others, as Lillian, who always kept a close eye on their table, brought them a fresh round of drinks.

These were Tony Jeffries's closest friends. He and Cal Cizma had reported for work the same week in 1983, right after their judicial clerkships. They soon learned that they'd grown up only a few miles apart in the western suburbs, even run cross-country against each other in high school. They enjoyed comparing notes about their teenage haunts, especially the places where they'd been able to get drinks without too many questions being asked.

Pete Spanos had been hired about a month later. His family, with its rich Greek heritage, was from the South Shore. He was thin and wiry and one of the brightest people Tony had ever met.

Tony, Cal, and Pete were all avid Cubs fans, even though Pete was a South Sider. In their early days at the firm they'd sneak off to catch games on hot summer afternoons, all claiming to be at the Cook County Law Library. Now that they were partners, their trips to Clark and Addison were made less deviously, and usually enjoyed the sanction of entertaining clients. For the past half-dozen years, they had shared four season box seats above third base as well as membership in Wrigley Field's Stadium Club. They were all anticipating the season opener next week, confident that this would be "the year."

They were all married when they joined the firm, and their wives and children became close friends too. In fact, Tony Jeffries was the proud godfather of the Cizmas' first child, Lenny.

Rasheed Collins had arrived in '84, straight out of UCLA Law School. He was tall and handsome, a Denzel Washington look-alike, and immediately became the target of every young woman in the office. He'd warded them off successfully, at least as far as any permanent relationships were concerned, and now lived by himself in a comfortable condo overlooking the Oak Street Beach on the near North Side.

The last of the group appeared in '85, Jack Morgan. Nicknamed "Curly," he'd been bald as Michael Jordan since his late teens. His record as a high-school debate star in Lawton, Oklahoma, earned him a scholarship to Northwestern, which in turn led to the University of Michigan Law School. Like Tony Jeffries, Curly Morgan was a litigator; and like many litigators, he drank hard, lived hard, and never was reluctant to speak his mind.

When he got going, Morgan was a bad drunk, and everyone knew to steer clear when they saw it coming.

All five men now headed practice groups at Wilson Thompson & Gilcrist; in terms of seniority, they ranked just below the seven men who comprised the firm's management committee. They liked to make cracks about management, as though they were outsiders. But they weren't, and all of them were well aware of their strong positions within the firm. Their common goal--first just a fantasy, but now a real objective--was that someday they'd be the ones running the show.

As they talked, the large flat-screen TV on the bar's west wall prattled on. Suddenly Cal, who'd been glancing at it from time to time, raised his hand.

"Wait a minute!"

Tony turned to follow Cal's line of vision. Up there on the screen, a gray-haired man in a dark overcoat was being escorted into the Dirksen Federal Building. His collar was turned up and he was trying to avoid the probing eye of the camera and the questions of the crowd of reporters. It was hard to hear the announcer above the bar din, but the noise slowly eased. Within seconds, everyone had an eye on the screen.

The announcer's voice was clearer now. "...arrested by FBI agents." And then a still photo flashed onto the screen. It was a face the five men knew well.

"...Informed sources report that prominent Chicago attorney Henry Gilcrist will plead guilty to charges of securities fraud, insider trading and tax evasion. A former president of the Chicago Bar Association, Gilcrist . . ."

Tony turned and looked at the others. No one spoke a word. The noise in the bar was picking up again, but the five of them just stared at each other. "Jesus Christ," Tony muttered. "Henry Gilcrist! Unbelievable!" Then he paused, lowered his voice, and added, "What's this going to do to the firm?"

"It's survived for a hundred years," Rasheed answered. "I'm sure it'll survive this."

"Well, I'll tell you one thing this incident's going to do, gentlemen," Cal said, leaning forward. "It's going to open some doors. There's already a vacancy on the management committee since Ed Stepanovich died. Now there's going to be another. There's no reason why a couple of us shouldn't be appointed to those spots."

Tony let out a deep breath. "Cal, let the body cool before you start picking at the bones."

"Sorry, Tony," Cal answered. "No one admires Henry Gilcrist more than I do. At least until this. That was just a gut reaction."

"Cal raises a good point, though." Curly leaned forward and lowered his voice. "This may put at least one of us on the management committee. The five of us have been through a lot together. Regardless of who makes it, I hope it's understood that we're all going to cover each other. The firm of the future is sitting around this table right now."

"Absolutely." Pete raised his glass. Tony and the others nodded and toasted in agreement.

"Well," Cal said quietly after a moment, "I don't have any intention of just sitting back and waiting to see what the tooth fairy brings me. I'm going to try to make something happen. This is too big an opportunity to let pass." Tony and the others stared at him. "For all of us," he added.

Cal finished his drink, dug a twenty out of his pocket, and threw it onto the table. "Look," he said as he stood up. "I've got some odds and ends to clean up back in the office. And this news has certainly put a damper on the evening. So if you don't mind, I'm going to go back and get some things done. See you all on Monday."

"Or at the indictment," Rasheed answered. "Whichever comes first."

Chapter Two

———

"Come in, Tony, have a seat." Barton Thompson gestured toward one of the two black leather chairs in front of his oversized desk.

Tony Jeffries took the seat closer to him and sat down without comment. Even though he'd been in the firm for twenty years, he was still uncomfortable around Barton Thompson, and had instinctively put on his suit coat before responding to the summons.

Nothing about Thompson or his office was designed to put a person at ease. He was tall and formidably distinguished, with sharp features and flowing white hair. His charcoal-gray three-piece suit was impeccably cut. The décor was equally intimidating: the thick Oriental carpet centered on a dark oak floor; the paneled walls with their half-dozen original Renaissance oils; the leaded glass windows. None of this was what one expected to encounter on the eighty-eighth floor of the Hancock Building. The polished mahogany desk was bare except for a closed black leather folder and an onyx-and-gold desk set.

"What a terrible thing to happen," Tony said after an uncomfortable silence. "To both Henry and the firm. Who would have thought . . .?" He shook his head as his voice trailed off.

"Yes, it certainly is," Thompson answered coldly as he opened the folder. "But Henry was either greedy or stupid, or both. He resigned from the firm yesterday, but that was a mere formality since he's going to be disbarred. However, life goes on, and we have to make our adjustments." He took a sheet of paper from the folder and glanced at it, then looked up. "We'll have to change the firm name, of course.

"This incident has also forced me to rethink our management structure, Tony." Thompson leaned back in his chair, put the fingers of his hands together, and swiveled to look out over Lake Michigan. A low cloud bank was rolling in off the lake, far below them.

"We've had a seven-man management committee for years," he continued. "There's nothing magic about the number seven; it goes back to the 1974 agreement, when we had only forty lawyers. Before that, as you may know, for about fifty years a committee of three ran the firm." He paused, still looking at the lake, then continued. "We already had one vacancy. Now we have two. And soon we're going to be losing Roscoe Blackwell, who plans to retire this year. You probably didn't know that, did you?" he asked, swiveling back toward Tony.

"Why, no." Tony was indeed surprised. Blackwell,

who headed the firm's trusts and estates practice, was one of the older members of the management committee, along with Chester Melrose, but no one had ever mentioned his retirement.

"Yes. His wife has talked him into moving to Florida. I always knew he wasn't in it for the long haul," Thompson snorted. "In any event, I've concluded that with the growth we've experienced the past few years, it's time to expand the management committee to nine, and to add some younger partners."

Thompson took a long look straight at Tony. "I'm recommending that you be named to the management committee, along with four others. You appear to have good judgment. You're well regarded by the other partners, and your background as chair of the hiring committee may very well prove useful."

Tony was stunned. This was the last thing he expected to hear from Barton Thompson. His surprise quickly gave way to elation, as the enormity of the announcement sank in. Being promoted to the management committee had huge implications, both financially and professionally.

"That's great," Tony stammered, fumbling for words.

"Changing the number on the committee to nine will require an amendment to the partnership agreement, of course. But I believe I can convince the other managing partners, as well as the firm in general, of the wisdom of that, as well as of the individual appointments."

Tony knew that was Barton Thompson's little joke. The only debates on firm policy were among the members of the management committee. The partnership as a whole never debated, let alone refused, an action that the management committee recommended.

"Of course, we're going to look to you men to provide some leadership in terms of developing new business for the firm." Thompson continued. "That's important. In fact, at the end of a year we'll review the situation to see whether everyone's been providing that leadership or not, and if we find that someone hasn't been contributing significantly, we may make some further changes."

Tony Jeffries felt a warm sense of euphoria. He was confident that he could produce enough business to maintain his position. While Thompson went back to discussing the mechanics of implementing the changes, Tony reclined into the soft leather chair, more at ease than he'd ever felt with the old patrician. He realized just how much he owed the man.

"Barton, I'm very flattered," he said. "And I'm not unappreciative. I want you to know that I'll certainly look to your advice on important matters. You can count on that."

"I have no doubt of that, Tony," Thompson added dryly. He handed Jeffries the piece of paper he'd been holding. "And to make *sure* we never have any differences of opinion, I'd like you to sign this, if you don't mind."

Tony didn't understand what Thompson was saying until he glanced at the paper. It was an undated letter of resignation from the firm. His euphoria was swept away in an instant, replaced by confusion, then anger.

"What the devil is this?"

"As I said, Tony, it's just your assurance that there'll never be any serious disagreements between us."

"I've never heard of anything like this!"

"I rather suspected that," Thompson replied in measured tones. "But you're not being singled out here, Tony. I have similar letters from all the other new members of the management committee." He tapped the black leather folder in front of him and smiled slightly. It was the first time Tony had ever seen that particular smile, and it sent a cold shiver up his spine.

"Who else has signed a letter like this?" Tony pressed, raising the paper slightly.

"Well, let's see." Thompson reopened the folder, adjusted his glasses, tilted his head back, and stared down his nose as he began flipping pages.

"Cal Cizma…Jack Morgan--Curly, as you call him… Pete Spanos…" He paused. "Oh, and Rasheed Collins, of course. I thought it might look good to have a black on the management committee. Hate that damn name, though," he muttered.

The whole gang. We've all being named to the management committee. Competing reactions swirled within Tony. This is what they'd always dreamed about: running the firm together. But not under these conditions; this was a sham. Why had the others all signed the letters? That made it very difficult for him to refuse. *But have they actually signed?*

"I'd like to think about it overnight, Barton," Tony

said. "This letter really bothers me."

"Tony, you accept my proposition now, or you can forget about it." There was a steely tone in his voice as he leaned forward. "I'd like you on the management committee, with the rest, but only if I know I can count on you one hundred percent."

"Are you saying that my signing this letter right now is a condition of being named to the committee?" Tony asked, looking Thompson hard in the eye.

"That's exactly what I'm saying," Barton Thompson answered softly as he leaned back in his chair, his eyes never leaving Tony's.

Tony took a deep breath, paused, pulled out his pen, and scrawled his signature across the bottom of the letter. He knew he had no alternative. He also knew that at that moment he despised the old bastard, and maybe himself too.

Thompson reached forward, picked up the letter, and placed it in the black leather folder. He looked pleased with himself as he pulled another piece of paper out and glanced over it.

"Here's something else you may be interested in," he said. "Cal Cizma has taken the trouble of compiling a list of all Henry Gilcrist's clients, and assessing which of our partners would be best suited to handle their matters. I've reviewed the list and concur in his thoughts. I'm going to have this distributed to all the partners this afternoon."

Tony scanned the list. The clients were assigned entirely to their group of five. Cal had worked fast; he was taking care of them. Then Tony noticed something else. While each of them had been given about the same number of clients, most of the big hitters had "Cal Cizma" written alongside.

"I could handle some of these other clients, Barton," Tony protested. "For example, the American Medical Society. I've handled some big cases for them and know some of those people very well."

"I'm aware of that, Tony. But Cal tells me that you're going to have your hands full with the new medical malpractice book of business that Chester Melrose brought in. I don't want you to bite off more than you can chew."

There was, or course, some logic to that. But Tony also knew that anyone's long-range position in the firm was greatly influenced by the amount of business that he *controlled*. The medical malpractice work was considered Melrose's, not his. He was uncomfortable with the way this allocation issue was being handled.

Barton Thompson stood and looked at his watch. "I've really got to run, Tony," he said, taking back the list of reassigned clients. "I'm meeting Judge Cornish at the Union League Club at noon. In any event, I'm glad to have you aboard."

"Yes, thank you," Tony said, slowly rising to his feet. There were still things he wanted to discuss. But he knew there wasn't time; not now, anyway. As he turned toward the door he wondered if there'd ever be.

Chester Melrose was very pleased with the way his medical malpractice book of business was developing. Gordon Hawke had kept his word, and dozens of new cases were coming into the office every week. Talk of his retirement had ended.

His satisfaction with the new business was offset by his dismay over the arrest of Henry Gilcrist and Gilcrist's sudden withdrawal from the firm, now renamed Wilson & Thompson. They had been colleagues for forty years, if never close friends. He was shocked by the depth of the government's case against Gilcrist; new details were appearing in the press daily. Some of the evidence seemed to be confidential data from Gilcrist's private files, and it was difficult to conceive how the FBI had obtained it without the cooperation of someone in the firm. He shook his head and focused his attention back on his growing London business, a far more pleasant matter.

Hawke had sent him a long letter discussing the arrangements, but it was impossible to understand; he'd spent two frustrating days trying to decipher it before finally giving up. But he didn't want to write back with any questions that might reveal just how little he really knew about insurance. If that happened, they'd probably pull the business, which would be a disaster. Nor did he want to discuss it with any of his partners; if they sensed he wasn't fully in command of the relationship with Imperial they'd be elbowing right in. Hawke's letter was still in front of him, unanswered. In a sudden burst of resolution he grabbed his pen and scribbled his signature across the bottom of the last page. He folded the original into an envelope to be mailed back to Hawke, as requested, and stuffed his copy into his desk drawer.

He had asked Tony Jeffries, one of the firm's best trial lawyers, to be responsible for the litigation, and Cal Cizma to handle the program's administrative side. That was very clever, he concluded, since he had now delegated all the substantive work to others while retaining overall control. *The key to being a successful senior partner is knowing how to delegate effectively.*

Jeffries's chief lieutenant, Carol James, had hired two new associates to help her and was now working full time on the malpractice cases. She's a good lawyer, Melrose thought; she'll make sure that the cases are all handled well. If any of them end up going to trial, though, Jeffries will be the trial lawyer. That arrangement worked well for Jeffries and James; she was the "set-up" person and he was the "closer." Chester Melrose was very happy that this proven team was handling his cases.

Cal Cizma was working with the accounting department daily to monitor the premiums being deposited in the firm's escrow account as well as the fees and settlement vouchers being applied against it. Melrose knew that he could never handle that on his own. And with the fund beginning to accumulate nicely, he also knew that this was going to be a very profitable account, both for the firm and for him personally.

He was especially happy that both Jeffries and Cizma had been named to the management committee; that had been his idea. He knew he was slowing down, and getting a couple of new allies on the committee would be a prudent move. He'd been good to Jeffries and Cizma and he knew they'd be supportive if any confrontations developed.

Barton Thompson had had other candidates in mind. But he finally agreed to a compromise that expanded the management committee to nine, and brought aboard all five of the men being considered.

Someday he'd have to sit down with Jeffries and Cizma and explain all of this. Melrose chuckled as he anticipated their surprise. Machiavelli himself would have trouble surviving at Wilson & Thompson, he mused.

But this wasn't the day for that talk. The chimes of his wall clock alerted him that it was three p.m. He'd have to leave soon to catch the 3:35 home. That would give him time for a nap before dinner.

—*mm*—

The Grand Temple of Islam towers over Chicago's South Side like India's Taj Mahal dominates the crowded and depressing community around it. The complex's centerpiece is the marble Tabernacle, originally built as a Greek Orthodox church in the forties and acquired by the Nation of Islam in the early sixties as the community's character changed dramatically. The Elijah Wing, constructed during the seventies, runs a full block north from the Tabernacle and houses the temple's university, the largest Islamic school in the country. The Muhammad Wing, dedicated in 1994, runs a full block in the opposite direction and is the nerve center of the temple's international network of newspapers, publishing companies, radio stations, and more recently, television stations. Although never listed among Chicago's major corporations, the temple's billion-dollar annual income and four thousand full-time employees place it high on the list of the City's economic forces. But more importantly to Wilson & Thompson, its substantial legal fees placed the Temple of Islam very high indeed on the list of the law firm's most valued clients.

Rasheed Collins paid the cabby, turned, and began walking up the Tabernacle's great stone steps. What a beautiful day, he thought, as the spring breeze off the lake tossed his tie over his shoulder. He put it back in place and buttoned his suit coat when he reached the top of the stairs, then entered the small doorway to the left of the fifteen-foot wood-and-iron main doors that brought to mind a medieval cathedral. The familiar musty smell merged with a hint of incense and enveloped him as he shut the door and began walking down the long corridor to the temple's administrative offices. The sound of his footsteps on the marble floor echoed ahead, announcing his presence. The hallway was empty at the moment, but Rasheed knew that behind the closed wooden doors he was passing were hundreds of young people earnestly teaching and learning the true meaning of the Holy Qur'an.

Rasheed had been General Counsel of the Temple of Islam for three years, succeeding to that position when its in-house counsel, Rasheed's uncle, Lucius Collins, who knew the value of having the temple's growing business handled by a major downtown law firm, dropped dead of a stroke at sixty-eight. For ten years prior to that, Rasheed had handled most of the temple's nuts-and-bolts work under his uncle's aegis, and came to know everyone in the temple's hierarchy, from Minister Habib Lund (son of the founder) to Andre in the copy room.

It was through his work for the temple that Rasheed first met Aliza Lund, the minister's daughter. She was in her early thirties, a bit on the plain side, and taught Qur'an lessons to preschoolers. She lived with her parents in the Sanctuary, a marble building just east of the Tabernacle.

They became occasional dinner companions, then escorts for each other's social functions, and finally, good friends. The senior Lunds encouraged the relationship, and last year on Muharram, Islam's New Year's Day, the minister took Rasheed aside and told him he'd be honored to have him as his son-in-law someday. That wasn't exactly what Rasheed had in mind, but he was well aware that having the minister as a father-in-law wouldn't hurt his career as the temple's General Counsel.

He smiled as he walked past Angela, the minister's secretary, without waiting to be announced. "Good to see you, Mr. Collins," she said, returning his smile.

"Good morning, Habib," Rasheed said as he walked in and shook the older man's outstretched hand.

"Good morning, Rasheed. Good to see you."

They chatted about the temple's current business affairs for a few minutes while they sipped some ice water that the minister had poured from a crystal pitcher on his credenza. Things were going well for the temple; revenues from their real estate holdings were up; they'd completed the acquisition of a chain of newspapers in Florida; and the Chicago City Council had approved their petition for a zoning variance to build a new dormitory just west of the university. That last little accomplishment, the minister laughed, came with a price tag: they had to agree to name the alderman's brother to the university's board of trustees. The fact that he was a Southern Baptist seemed to be only a minor consideration.

"There's something that I'd like you to take a look at, Rasheed." The minister put down his glass and pushed his intercom button.

"Angela, ask Wallace to come in here with the Peru proposal."

While they were waiting, Minister Lund turned to Rasheed. "Aliza tells me that you're thinking of joining us on the temple's pilgrimage to Mecca next year. I think that's wonderful."

Rasheed smiled in response. "Well, I'm certainly considering it. I've never been there. I know that Aliza has; she never stops talking about her trips there with you. I'd love to see it with my own eyes, and I know that someday I'll have to make that trip. The only question is whether I'll be able to take the three weeks off."

The door opened and a young man in a dark suit walked in and handed the minister a thick folder. Rasheed nodded to Wallace; he had met him before. The minister asked Wallace to briefly explain the proposal to Rasheed; he did, then excused himself.

As his office door shut, Minister Lund turned to Rasheed and raised an eyebrow. "Anything about that young man look funny to you?" he asked.

"Wallace? Why, no. Why do you ask?"

"There's something about the way he walks," the minister said, half to himself. "I wonder if he's queer. That would be quite a scandal, wouldn't it? A homo on our staff?"

Rasheed winced. The one thing that he disliked about working for the temple was Minister Lund's arcane social views. This was just one example; there were others. But he knew he couldn't change the minister's prejudices; the best he could do was simply to ignore them.

"He looked perfectly fine to me," Rasheed answered as he sipped his water. "I wouldn't worry about it."

"Well, then, I won't. I certainly trust your judgment."

—*mm*—

"Cal, I like it here in Broadview. I have no desire at all to move to the North Shore." Sandy Cizma pushed the *Sunday Tribune* real estate section back across the couch toward her husband.

"We've been through this before, Sandy," Cal replied

testily. "A person's image is based, more than anything else, on where they live. Success breeds success; and the most important components of success are image and contacts. From a career standpoint, it's essential that we establish ourselves on the North Shore. Somewhere like Wilmette, or Winnetka, or, ideally, Kenilworth. We've been too long in the western suburbs."

"But this is where my mother lives, Cal. I enjoy being able to stop by and visit her every afternoon. That's important to me. It really is."

Cal took a deep breath, trying to control his anger. They'd been having this same argument for ages, over and over, and he had always given in. In the meantime years had slipped by; important years. And they were still mired in Broadview.

"Maybe that's part of the problem. Your parents were never able to rise above the middle class, and you seem determined to make sure that the same thing happens to us, too!"

"That's not fair, Cal," Sandy answered, her eyes filling with tears.

"Not fair? Are *you* being fair to *me*? I've spent years trying to establish myself in the firm, with very little help from you." He stood up in frustration and began pacing back and forth in front of the couch.

"Look at Tony and Karen," he said, turning and pointing accusingly at his wife. "They grew up in the west suburbs, but had the sense to move to the North Shore years ago. When Tony takes the train to work in the morning he talks to federal judges, senior partners in other firms, and presidents of companies. When I ride the train to work I talk to people who report to those people. You don't understand, Sandy, how important that is in terms of career development."

"But, Cal..."

"And as long as we're talking about supportive," he interrupted, "look at Karen. She got herself elected State Representative three or four years ago. Everyone on the North Shore knows who Karen Jeffries is. While you're having afternoon coffee with your mother, she's having coffee with the Governor or the Attorney General. That's bound to have a tremendously positive effect on Tony's career; I can see it happening already."

Cal shook his head as he continued his pacing. It was maddening that Sandy hadn't a clue how important these things were, maddening. He had let this issue of where they lived slide too long. Now that he had been appointed to the firm's management committee, he had to do something about it.

"You used to like it here," Sandy said. "And you used to like the neighbors. I remember when Lenny was in Cub Scouts, and you and Mike Wiznewski ran the Pinewood Derby. You used to be good friends. What happened?"

"Nothing *happened,* Sandy," he said, taking a deep breath. "It's just that we were at a different stage in our lives then. That was a long time ago. By now, I thought we'd..." His voice trailed off in frustration.

Cal walked over to the picture window and looked

out. The lawn looked great; resodding it last year was a good idea. Across the street Doug Bednarek was washing his pickup truck in the driveway. A *pickup truck!*

"Sandy, do you know how much money I made last year?"

"A lot," she answered quietly. "I know that."

"Three hundred and fifty thousand dollars, as a matter of fact. And this year it'll be more, maybe much more, now that I'm on the management committee." He turned back toward her. "And who do we have as neighbors? A high-school teacher, an insurance salesman, and a bank teller." He shook his head.

"They're all good, decent people, Cal. Do you remember how much they helped when I was sick a couple of years ago? Someone brought us dinner every night for almost a month. And Marge Wiznewski went shopping for us every week. My mom couldn't have done all that, even if she'd been healthy."

"I'm not saying they're bad people. They're not at all. But how much business can they give me? Nothing. Nothing that I'd want, anyway. What I'm saying is that we can do better than this - a lot better. And now that I'm on the management committee, I'm going to be in contact with our senior partners and important clients on a regular basis. What if I brought one of them here for dinner," he pointed out the picture window, "and they saw pickup trucks parked on our block?" He shook his head again.

"Think about the kids," Sandy pleaded. "Their friends are all here. They've got all their activities at school.

Lenny has a chance to be a starter on the basketball team next season. They don't want to move." She fumbled in her pocket for a hankie; found it, and dabbed her eyes.

Cal hated it when Sandy cried. They could never have a serious discussion without Sandy crying.

"I'll tell you what I'll do, Cal," she said. "Why don't we wait until Stephanie is out of high school and goes off to college? That's only three years away. I'd be willing to move then."

"Three years? I'll be almost ready to retire."

Cal turned and strode to the front hall closet. He pushed the coats around until he found the corduroy jacket he was looking for.

"I'm going to take a drive. I need some fresh air."

"Okay, but be sure you're back by six. Mom's coming over for dinner."

Right, Cal muttered to himself as he slammed the door and walked quickly down the steps to the driveway. Why don't we ask *her* what she thinks about our moving out of the neighborhood?

He got into his Cadillac Seville, the only sign of success that Sandy hadn't vetoed, backed out, turned, and sped toward the expressway. He wouldn't be back by six, or even seven. He knew that. It was an hour's drive to Kenilworth, and by the time he found a house, signed a contract, and returned, it would probably be close to eight. Sandy's mother would be gone by then. Whether Sandy liked it or not, the Cizmas were going to be moving.

He drove east on the Eisenhower Expressway, through

the western suburbs where he and Tony Jeffries had grown up, past Cicero and the remnants of Western Electric's Hawthorne Works, where Cal's parents and thousands of other Poles and Czechs had made telephones for the world in the fifties and sixties, into Chicago and past its Lawndale neighborhood, where his grandparents and countless Eastern Europeans had settled and first dared to dream of success in this New World. He sped around the Circle Interchange and headed toward the North Shore. That dream was going to be realized today.

mm

"But Mom, I kinda like my trumpet lessons. And Mr. Rees says I'm getting better and better."

"I know, Robert," Bertha Roosevelt sighed. "But since your father got sick we just don't have the money we used to have. And trumpet lessons are expensive--*very* expensive. You're just going to have to practice on your own for a while."

"I don't think I can get to be as good as Wynton Marsalis practicing on my own, Mom," Robert protested, his eyes getting moist. "Mr. Rees tells me things every week about how to play better. Things that I don't think I'd learn on my own, even if I practiced a lot."

Bertha Roosevelt couldn't recall a more painful moment. Robert's trumpet was supposed to be his key to getting out of the ghetto. That's what she and Sam had always planned, or at least hoped for, and now she was taking it away from him. But she didn't know what else to do; she was absolutely desperate. After Sam's second brain operation they told her he'd never regain consciousness--and they were right, he never did. When his disability checks began arriving, she'd been told that she had to turn them over to the home where they'd put Sam. The checks were meant to pay for Sam's expenses, not hers. She'd signed some papers, and now Sam's checks went straight to the home.

Last week she did something she'd sworn she'd never do; she applied for welfare. The lady at the welfare office said it would take three or four weeks to complete their investigation, and arranged for her to get a hundred-dollar grant in the meantime. That, plus the small amount that Bertha earned from cleaning two homes in Kenwood once a week, would have to hold them.

She opened her purse and unfolded a ten-dollar bill. She could see that all she'd have left was a five and some change.

"Here," she said, taking a deep breath and handing the ten to Robert. "Give this to Mr. Rees for today's lesson, and tell him that you're not going to be able to come for a while. Tell him that we just don't have the money right now."

"Okay, Mom," Robert said quietly, carefully tucking the bill into a pocket. He picked up his black leather trumpet case, a gift from Sam last Christmas, and slowly walked out, chin on his chest. Bertha turned away; she didn't want him to see the tears.

Once she heard the door shut, Bertha let herself go, crying quietly for several minutes, standing right in the middle of her kitchen. She wiped her tears away and fished around in her purse for a Kleenex. As she did, she saw something she'd forgotten about. It was a lawyer's business card; someone had handed it to her at the hospital. She took it out and looked at it.

Maximilian J. Greene, Attorney at Law, it read, along with a phone number and an address. On the back were some initials she couldn't make out.

Yes, she said to herself. I'll see a lawyer. *This* lawyer. I'll sue them for what they did to Sam and me and Robert. *I'll sue them real good!*

Chapter Three

~~~

Maria Spanos pushed back her chair at the head of the table, grabbed her glass of roditis firmly in her right hand, and rose to her feet. In an instant the room hushed, and all fourteen heads were turned toward her.

"I'd like to propose a toast," she said in Greek, raising her glass. "To my son, Petros, who is now the manager of his law firm."

They all clinked their glasses, smiled, and turned to Pete, who smiled and raised his glass in return.

"Thank you," he responded in Greek. "Thank you very much. But Mama's too generous in her praise. I'm on the management *committee,* not the sole manager. It *is* an honor, though, and I appreciate your best wishes."

Pete Spanos smiled at his mother's oversimplification; he didn't really mind. There weren't many Greeks on the management committees of major law firms in Chicago, and he was proud of what he had accomplished. And to have that acknowledged here, with his family around him, gave him a deep sense of satisfaction.

This was the first Sunday of the month, the traditional day for the whole family to gather at Mama and Papa's for dinner. Pete's wife, Lucy, and their two sons were there, along with his sister, Sofie, and her family. Uncle Ed, Mama's brother, was with them today, although his attendance was less predictable than the others'. Uncle Ed was a very successful businessman, a produce wholesaler.

Pete took a bite of his dolmades and savored the delicate taste of its creamy lemon sauce. The grape leaves were fresh, which made all the difference in the world. "But who is *in charge,* Petros?" Mama asked after she sat down. "A committee cannot be in charge. Who is the boss?"

"There is no boss, Mama. On the committee we're all equal. There are nine of us. We discuss things, then we vote. What the majority decides is what we do."

"Nine?" Mama exclaimed. "A committee of nine? So many?"

"It's not so many, Mama. Not for a firm of over two hundred lawyers. Believe me. Some firms our size have management committees of twelve or fifteen."

He was being defensive now. Pete realized that he had disappointed Mama; he should have said that the committee had only three members, or even five. and that he was in fact the boss. But Lucy and the boys knew the difference, and he didn't want them to see him lying to his own mother.

"On a committee it is never equal," Mama said as she

picked up the big wooden salad bowl and handed it to her grandson Chris. "Not among nine. Not even among two. Someone makes the decision and the others go along." She wagged her finger at Pete as she continued, "The man who can say, 'Give ten thousand dollars to my church,' and it is done, that is the man who is truly in charge."

"It's not that simple, Mama," Pete answered in frustration. "Besides, the firm doesn't give money to anybody's church. We leave donations up to the individual partners."

"Your glass is empty, Petros," Papa said quietly. He leaned forward with the bottle of roditis and refilled Pete's glass, then Sofie's and his own. "How's your friend Tony doing?" he asked.

"Fine. Just fine, Papa." Pete took a sip of his wine, conscious of the silence that had fallen on the room. Everyone was focused on their salad. "He's been appointed to the management committee too," Pete added. "Along with three other good friends of ours. It's very exciting for all of us."

"I'm sure it is." The old man nodded to his son. "And I'm proud of you."

"Thank you, Papa."

"Well, we're all proud of Petros," Mama said. "But maybe he should get some business advice from Ed." She gestured toward her brother. "He knows all about partnerships. You tell him, Ed." Having issued her directive, Mama went into the kitchen to check on her pastitsio.

Uncle Ed finished chewing on a hunk of feta cheese he had speared out of the salad. He was a tall man, with

47

graying black hair, a bushy mustache, and a deeply lined face. He looked across the table at Pete as he washed the cheese down with a mouthful of roditis.

"I was in a partnership once," he said, his eyes fixed on his nephew. Pete sighed and quietly sat back. He'd heard this story at least a dozen times; did he really need to hear it again?

"When I opened my restaurant on Odgen Avenue in 1967, I had a partner," Uncle Ed said, pointing his fork at his nephew for emphasis. "George Patronis. That was two years after we came over from Athens. I put every penny I had into that business. Patronis and I lived upstairs. We had one bed. The restaurant was open twenty-four hours a day, and we were there all the time. We worked hard, and did well. Only Patronis and I handled the money, and only the two of us knew the combination to the safe. Everything we made went into that safe."

He paused and emptied his glass, then set it down heavily in front of him and stared at it for a moment. Lucy took the bottle and poured him a refill. The children were all transfixed by Uncle Ed.

"And then one day," he went on, "I found that Patronis was stealing from me. I had counted the money in the safe and knew how much we had. And when I counted it the next time, I found that a thousand dollars was missing. A thousand dollars! It had to be Patronis. And the worst part was that our bank note was due and we couldn't pay it. We had a terrible fight over that, and I vowed that day never to have another partner. Never! It's not good business."

He nodded to his nephew and took another deep draft of roditis.

"A law partnership is different, Uncle Ed," Pete answered. "We have bookkeepers and accountants and banks, and know exactly where our money is and how it's all spent. If someone stole from us, we'd learn about it pretty quickly, and that person would be out of there. And there's no way that someone could steal enough money to put the business in jeopardy. It just couldn't happen."

"I didn't think it could happen to me, either, but it did. And it happened because I had a partner. Never again!"

Pete wasn't going to argue with him. Uncle Ed had no idea of the sophistication of a modern law firm's accounting system. Wilson & Thompson had an accounting department of twelve people, headed by a CPA, which kept very close track of the firm's assets. They wire-transferred funds at the close of every business day to banks all over the world to ensure the highest interest on the firm's overnight deposits. Comparing Uncle Ed's simple two-man partnership to the complex business of a major law firm was like comparing the Wright brothers' flying machine to a stealth bomber.

Mama's pastitsio was as good as ever. Pete could count on her to serve either moussaka, baked lamb, or pastitsio as the main course for their Sunday dinners, but Mama's pastitsio had been his personal preference for as long as he could remember.

Over dinner they decided that this was definitely the year for the Cubs to make a run for the National League pennant. It had been ninety-five years since the Cubs won their last World Series, in 1908, and the 2003 season had started well. Papa had become a real Cubs fan since his retirement, and Pete took him to several games every summer. He made a point of sharing his tickets with Tony Jeffries at least once each year when Papa would be with him. Papa and Tony had struck up a friendship over dinner several years ago, and Pete enjoyed nurturing that relationship.

After baklava and coffee Papa led the men into the living room while the women and the girls followed Mama into the kitchen. The four younger boys, free at last, ran outside.

The house was one of those fine old homes in South Shore built before the turn of the nineteenth century. It was made of brick and stood two and a half stories tall, with a grand old elm on the parkway. When Pete and his sister were growing up, there had been two, but the other had fallen victim to Dutch elm disease in the seventies. In fact, there were only a few trees left on the street now. A generation earlier, you could walk from one end of the block to the other on a bright summer day and never leave the shade.

Like the trees, the neighborhood had changed, too. When Pete and Sofie were young, South Shore was a worthy rival for its sister neighborhood to the north, Hyde Park; some even claimed that, with its Lake Shore Country Club, it was the better of the two. No one would say that today. The old families had moved out, one by one, until only a few remained. On every block, stately old homes had been turned into rooming houses or divided into flats. Pete could measure the deterioration of the neighborhood by counting the number of cars parked on the street every night. When he was young, there were only a few. Now it was nearly impossible to find a parking place.

But inside the Spanos home, nothing had changed except for the extra locks on the doors. The living room, with its heavy drapes flanking curtained windows, its overstuffed sofa and chairs, and its large fireplace at one end, still made a comfortable den for men to retire to after dinner. On the oak mantel were more photographs than he could count, of people both living and dead; old country and New World. Most of those pictures had been there all of Pete's life.

Papa put a bottle of Metaxa on the coffee table, and Uncle Ed lit up one of his Cuban cigars. No one knew the source of Ed's cigars; he just smiled whenever anyone asked. Sofia's husband, Tom, poured four glasses, one for each of the men, then took one and sat back in the couch opposite Uncle Ed. They raised their glasses silently to each other.

"Ed, how's the market treating you these days?" Tom asked after taking a sip.

"Better than I'm treating the market," Ed laughed. He took a deep draw on his cigar, leaned back, and released a slow a stream of smoke high into the air. He bent slightly forward to tap his ashes into a tray, and chuckled to himself.

"Tell us about it, Ed," Papa said. "The boys need to know how the world operates."

Ed nodded in agreement.

Pete smiled to himself. He was forty-four and Papa still thought of him as a boy. Some things would probably never change.

"You know my business," Ed said to Tom and Pete as he stretched back on the couch. "I buy produce from shippers and resell it to distributors. If I'm lucky, I'll make 15, 20 percent on the resale. Of course, the grade of the produce we deal with is very important. The way I make real money is what I did today." He emptied half his glass of Metaxa, and capped it with a puff on his cigar.

"Today," he continued, "I brought a carload of class C tomatoes at seven o'clock and resold them at eight-thirty as class B tomatoes. I made my usual 20 percent on the resale, plus 50 percent on the markup. It was a hell of a deal."

"I don't understand," Tom said. "How could the class of the produce change?"

Ed chuckled again as he took a deep drag on his cigar. "Five hundred bucks," he said after a moment. "For five hundred bucks to the FDA inspector, my carload of class C tomatoes became a carload of class B tomatoes. And I made ten thousand bucks."

Pete was amazed. He'd never even suspected that aspect of Uncle Ed's business. "Weren't you concerned about getting caught?" he asked.

"No. Not at all. Remember, I've dealt with these

people for years. If anyone gives me trouble, I'll bring them down too. And they all know that."

He looked hard at Pete and went on. "What you've got to remember, Petros, is that there's no such person as an honest man. Everyone's got his price. *Everyone.* It's usually money, but not always. Sometimes it's something else. And once you find what a man's dreams are made of, you've got the key to that man's soul. If you remember that, you'll be a wiser man tonight than you were when you woke up this morning." He raised his glass to Pete with the smile of someone who'd just divulged the secret of the universe.

—*mm*—

"You *what*?" Sandy Cizma crumpled the newspaper into her lap and stared at her husband. Cal knew this was going to be tough, but he also knew that he'd done the right thing.

"I signed a contract for us to buy a house in Kenilworth," he said firmly. "I found the house and signed the contract last Sunday when I went out for a drive. I didn't want to say anything about it until I knew we had the financing. That came through today. We'll close on June thirtieth." He hesitated, then added, "It's a lovely house, Sandy."

Sandy sat on the couch, her mouth agape, and slowly shook her head, still staring at her husband. "I can't believe you did this," she whispered. "And without even letting me see it?"

Cal could see the tears welling up. He knew he had

only a few moments before she'd be crying full-tilt and become completely irrational. He sat down on the other end of the couch and tried to keep his voice calm.

"I'm sorry, Sandy. But it was something that was too important from a career standpoint to put off. I knew you were all hung up on the subject, so I just had to make the decision for both of us." He smiled, then added, "Believe me, you're going to love this place. It's only two blocks from the lake."

"No!" she shouted, tears trickling down both cheeks. "I won't do it! It's *my* home *too,* and you can't make me move like this!" She dug into her pocket for a hankie. "Besides," she said defiantly, "I won't sign anything. This house is in my name, too, and if I know you, you're going to need every penny you can get out of this house to buy your *mansion"*-- she spat out the words--"in Kenilworth."

"Sandy, be reasonable."

"No, *you* be reasonable. I *won't* cooperate with you in selling this house! I *won't* sign anything! I won't let anyone in to see it, and any realtor who shows up, I'll have them arrested for trespassing!"

Cal knew she'd be angry; that was predictable. But he'd never seen her *this* angry before. Still, he had anticipated resistance and was prepared to deal with it.

"Well, if that's the position you take, Sandy, then we're going to go into bankruptcy. It's as simple as that."

"What are you talking about?"

He could tell that her self-confidence was shaken. There was confusion in her eyes. He was counting on that. "We're legally committed to purchase that house in Kenilworth on June thirtieth," he replied. "And you're right, we need to clear at least two hundred thousand from the sale of this place to close the deal. Without it, we're in default. Not only do we forfeit our down payment, but we also owe the sellers their damages, which will probably be considerable. They've taken their house off the market now. If we default, and they can't sell it soon for the same price, they can come after us for everything we have." He gestured around them.

"How much of a down payment did you make?" There was fear in her voice now. Cal knew he had her on the defensive.

"Eighty thousand dollars." Actually, the down payment was only half that, but he wanted to put as much pressure on her as he could.

"Eighty thousand!" she moaned, leaning back and shutting her eyes. "That was most of the kids' college money! How could you do that?"

"Houses in Kenilworth aren't cheap, Sandy. Besides, with the contacts we'll make there, I'll make that back within two years, believe me."

She raised both hands to her eyes and began sobbing, softly at first, then in spasms punctuated with muffled moans, her head slowly shaking from side to side. Cal watched her for a moment, then got up and walked into the family room to get a drink. He'd beaten her. She'd sign the papers he had in his briefcase before the night was over. *We're moving to Kenilworth!*

"Tony, look at this," Carol James said as she pushed open the door to his office and walked in. "Nine new medical mal cases in today. We're absolutely swamped already--how in the hell are we going to handle these?"

Carol dumped the stack of files on Tony's desk and stepped back with her hands on her hips. She was an attractive brunette, wearing a tailored dark-blue business suit, jacket unbuttoned, over a white blouse. After him, Carol was the senior attorney in Tony's group, and she wasn't smiling. Tony knew her well enough to know that she was really upset.

"The new people, Driscol and Kratovil, are they already loaded up?" Tony couldn't believe that they were; they'd been with the firm less than a month.

"They've each got over twenty cases, Tony. I don't think they can handle what they've got now, much less take on anything new. And some of these are big cases," she said, gesturing toward the pile. "They're going to need someone who can spend a lot of time on them real fast."

Tony's mind was swimming. It had been this way for the past month, cases pouring in every day. He thought he'd solved the staffing problem by having Carol reassign all her other work and concentrate entirely on Chester Melrose's medical mal book of business. He had her hire two new lateral associates, which gave her a staff of four attorneys. Apparently that wasn't enough.

"How many of these new cases are filed in Cook County?" he asked, groping for a solution.

"Only two," she answered as she sat down in the up-holstered chair across from him. "The rest are all in the L.A. area."

"Well, then maybe the firm's got to open that L.A. of-fice we've been talking about," he said, shaking his head. "With these, we've got over forty cases we're defending out there. Maybe it's time to stop hiring local counsel and trying to run those cases from here." He paused for a moment, then added, "I'll bring it up at the management committee today; let's see what kind of support we can get. I know that Cal likes the idea of an office on the West Coast. In the meantime, leave these new L.A. cases here until I figure out what to do with them."

"What about the other new cases?" she asked. "The two that are filed here. Someone's got to get on them."

"I'll ask Charlie Dickenson to handle them," he an-swered. "At least for the time being. That's not his area, but he can cover them. He told me he can handle a couple of files if we get in a bind, and it sure looks like that's where we are. And I'll go through those resumes again and see if there's anyone else we want to invite in for interviews. It looks like you could use another person."

Carol nodded, then leaned forward and thumbed through the pile of cases on Tony's desk. When she found what she was looking for, she pulled it out and sat back. She leafed through the file for a moment, then looked up.

"This one's especially bad," she said. "*Bertha and Samuel Roosevelt versus Blessed Trinity Hospital.* This guy's family brought him in after what looks like a relatively minor hematoma, a blood clot in the head. He had a couple of brain operations and ended up permanently comatose. I've read the hospital records, Tony, and they don't look good. Seems like they somehow screwed up the CT scan and opened up the wrong side of the patient's head. Nobody figured it out, and they sewed him up and just stuck him in Intensive Care. The next day they did another CT scan and found the hematoma, on the other side. By the time they got to it, it had jellified half his brain. Looks like a lot of liability here."

"How in the hell could they cut open the wrong side of his head? That's terrible! Was somebody on something?"

"Damned if I know," Carol shrugged. "All I know is that it's a real bad case, and someone's going to have to get a handle on it real fast."

"Why don't you keep this one yourself, Carol, and give the other new Cook County case to Charlie. I know your plate's pretty full, but this sounds like one that we need to keep close tabs on."

"Okay," Carol said, letting out her breath. "Bill and I were going to go up to Wisconsin for the weekend, but I guess that's out. These new cases are taking a serious toll on my love life, Tony." She gave him enough of a smile to reassure him that he hadn't pushed her too far. Still, he knew he'd better get her more help.

After Carol left, Tony gathered some papers and headed out of his office for the noon management committee meeting. It was being held on the north side of the eighty-sixth floor, in conference room A. He walked up the big spiral staircase from eighty-five, where his office was located, and was a few minutes late. But it was a luncheon meeting, and they never began discussing business until about twelve-thirty.

By the time Tony arrived, everyone else but Curly was already there, seated in their leather swivel chairs around the fifteen-foot polished oak table. A small buffet had been set on a separate table to the left of the door. Tony nodded to the others, dropped his papers on the table in front of one of the empty chairs, made himself a ham and Swiss, grabbed a Diet Coke, and sat down next to Rasheed Collins.

The men were clustered in two quite obvious and distinct groups. Barton Thompson, at the head of the table, was chatting quietly with Chester Melrose to his right and George Lazenby and Ralph Stritch to his left. All of them were on the gray side of seventy. They were speaking in that subdued tone of voice which Tony was convinced came only from years of discussing important business in the Union League Club's main dining room. Unless you were within two feet of them, you couldn't pick up a word they were saying.

At the other end of the table, although there weren't any empty seats between them, were the newer members of the management committee. Cal Cizma and Pete Spanos were talking about the Cubs' loss the night before.

"I couldn't believe it," Cal was saying. "Prior strikes out sixteen and has a three-run lead after eight. Then

Baker pulls him, puts in Borowski, and they blow it in the ninth."

"Unbelievable," Pete agreed, shaking his head.

"Hey, guys, don't sweat it," Tony said, picking up his sandwich. "The season's half over, the Cubbies are in first, and Prior and Wood are both on a pace to win twenty. The playoffs are a lock."

"Tony, the eternal optimist," Pete said, shaking his head again as Curly walked into the room and shut the door behind him. He filled a plate with lettuce salad and took the last empty chair, across form Tony. Curly's eyes were bloodshot; he looked like he had a hangover.

"By the way, Cal," Barton Thompson called from the head of the table, "I read your memo about moving to Kenilworth. Congratulations. If I can help you get established there, or perhaps sponsor you at Indian Hills, I'd be happy to do so."

"Why, thank you, Barton," Cal Cizma responded with a smile. "I just might take you up on that. Sandy really loves Kenilworth."

"Well, she and Flora will have to get to know each other better if we're going to be neighbors." Thompson nodded to Cal rather grandly, then returned to his conversation with Chester Melrose.

A few minutes later the meeting began in earnest. "I'm pleased to report," Thompson said, "that the firm has retained all of Henry Gilcrist's clients, due in large part to Cal Cizma's work." He gave Cal another deferential nod. "And since Henry has pleaded guilty to all the federal charges, and his name extricated from the firm's, the less said about him in the future, the better." The others unanimously concurred.

Chester Melrose, as chairman of the finance committee, then reported on billings and receipts, both of which were up. The firm's arrangement with the Imperial Insurance Syndicate was off to an excellent start, he said. Since they were able to bill all the new medical malpractice files on a monthly basis, and write checks to themselves out of the escrow account, there was no lag time at all in being paid. Thus far, after less than three months, they had charged that account $230,000 in fees, settled a few small matters, and still maintained a healthy balance of $1,100,000 in the fund. It looked like this was going to be a very lucrative book of business.

Tony raised the issue of the need for West Coast offices, particularly one in the L.A. area, and after some discussion they agreed that the firm would pursue merger negotiations with two small firms that they had dealt with in the past, one in Los Angeles and the other in San Diego. Wilson & Thompson's concentration of medical malpractice cases in both of those cities would provide the lifeblood for the new relationships. Cal volunteered to handle the negotiations with the other two firms and promised to get the mergers put together as quickly as possible.

Pete Spanos, moving on to a new subject, then said, "Gentlemen, the firm has done very well recently, and this year seems headed toward record profits. I think it would be appropriate for the firm to establish a policy of regularly making contributions to appropriate charities. That could generate some very positive PR for the us. It would send the right message to both our staff and the business community, and would show that we're a responsible civic organization. I also think it's the right thing to do."

Tony nodded his assent, as did most of the others. He wasn't surprised by his friend's remarks. Pete had approached him earlier that day and enlisted his support for the proposal.

"Very commendable, Pete," Barton Thompson said. "I've always had that view. Unfortunately, it hasn't always been shared by everyone on this committee. Perhaps with this new blood, we can revisit the issue."

Only Lazenby and Stritch expressed reservations. But when they saw that they were outnumbered, they acquiesced, and it was unanimously agreed that the firm would adopt a policy of donating fifty thousand dollars a quarter to a selected charity.

"Pete, since this was your proposal," Barton Thompson said with one of his grand gestures, "I believe you should have the honor of designating the first recipient of our donations. Have you any suggestions?"

"Thank you. Well, as a matter of fact, I do have something in mind. Saints Peter and Paul Greek Orthodox Church. It's my family's church and they're engaged in a fund-raising drive right now. This would be timed perfectly, and would be greatly appreciated."

"Fine," Thompson answered. "Call the church this afternoon if you'd like to. Tell them that we're contributing fifty thousand dollars to their campaign. Try to get something in the press about it too." Thompson collected his papers, then rose to his feet. "All right, gentlemen, this meeting is adjourned."

Pete's proposal was a good one, Tony thought as he pushed his chair back--but hadn't it passed a bit too easily? He wondered what commitments Pete had made, perhaps even unwittingly, in order to get it approved. It went through too quickly. Tony followed the others out into the hall, but stopped when Rasheed Collins, just ahead of him, was approached by a young associate.

"Mr. Collins," he said, "this just arrived by messenger from Mr. Brent at the Mid-Central Bank. The note on it says that it's about an important meeting this evening and that we should give it to you immediately. "

"Really?" Rasheed laughed nervously. "That's strong language for a banker. Well, I'll take a look at it." He took the sealed envelope and walked toward his office. Tony turned the other way, toward the stairs, still wondering about Pete. What kind of bargain had he struck with Thompson to get his way?

Chapter Four

~~~~

The Skyline Club is one of Chicago's most interesting yet least-known dining establishments. Originally an eighteenth-century British country inn, it was dismantled, shipped stateside, then reassembled atop the Republic Insurance Company Building when it was constructed on Michigan Avenue after the First World War. A comfortably furnished den with a fireplace, a small dining room with a dozen heavy wooden tables, and an even smaller private meeting room provided a genteel and urbane luncheon environment for the club's hundred or so members. Accessible only by a winding staircase ascending from the top elevator floor, the club is rumored to have been an executive speakeasy during the city's legendary Roaring Twenties.

Pete had been introduced to the club by Tony back in '97 or '98, and when, just recently, they both made the management committee, he'd asked his pal to sponsor him for membership. He needed a quiet place to entertain clients and friends; and since the firm paid downtown club dues for all the management committee members (a fact unknown to the other partners), the Skyline Club was a natural and convenient choice.

Pete's guest that day was Frank Donatelli, an old high-school buddy from South Shore and now a claims supervisor for the American Union Insurance Company. For years, during an endless series of dinners, drinks, and ball games, they had discussed sending American Union's legal work to Pete and his firm, but the problem was always the same: Wilson Thompson & Gilcrist wasn't on the list of "approved" firms at American Union, a fact Donatelli seemed powerless to change.

But that was then, and now, with the firm's new name and new configuration, Pete was up for giving it another try.

Luis, the maitre d', seated them at a corner table and served an appetizer plate of thinly sliced prosciutto, olives, and onions. They ordered drinks, Pete a Chardonnay and Frank a Bloody Mary, and began exchanging stories about the old high-school crowd. After a few minutes, Pete decided to advance to cut to the chase. There were only a few other people in the club that day, and none seated nearby.

"Frankie," he said, "it would be great if you could figure out some way to send me some business. It would really help, you know."

"Yeah, I know, but what can I do? My hands are tied, Pete. Everything's got to go to one of the firms on the list.

They've all cut deals on their rates, and unless a case is really special, we've got no choice." He shrugged, tossed back the last of his Bloody Mary, and signaled their waiter for another.

Pete nodded and bit into a piece of prosciutto. He'd heard this song from Frank many times before, but today he'd detected something new. "What do you mean, Frankie, when you say 'unless a case is really special'?" he asked. "Are you saying there are some kinds of cases that don't have to go to one of your approved firms?"

"Well, sure. If we get a case that's so different that none of our regular firms know quite what to do with it, we can send it to someone else--a specialist. But it's only happened a couple of times in all my years at AU."

Pete sat back and nibbled on another piece of prosciutto as the waiter served Frank's second Bloody Mary. When the waiter left, he leaned forward again. "Maybe that's the way you could do something for us, Frankie. Find a case or two that are...well different. Hell, we have one of the best firms in the city. I'm sure we're experienced in some areas that none of your regulars have dealt with before. Whatcha think?"

"Gee, I donno, Pete," Frank shook his head. "If I got caught doing something funny it would be my ass. Unless I could really justify it, you know what I mean?"

"Yeah, I know. And I wouldn't want to do anything to screw you up." Pete picked up the menu and eyed it idly. "Still, it would be nice if something like that came along." He wasn't going to let it end there; it had ended that way too many times before. He was thinking about what Uncle Ed had said; he had to find the right key to get Frankie to bend the rules. There had to be a way. Suddenly, an idea began crystallizing, slowly at first, then with increasing speed. It was worth a try.

"Frankie," he asked, lowering his menu, "have you ever thought about doing some consulting part-time?"

"Nah, not really." Frank shrugged. "What the hell for? I'm doing okay."

"Well, I was just thinking. If our firm got some really tough case, maybe something with a complicated coverage question, we might want to hire a consultant to help us sort it out. An expert. You know, something like that."

Frank Donatelli looked at his friend, took a healthy sip of his Bloody Mary, and put it back down on the table. He stared at it for a long time before looking again at Pete. "What kind of fee do you suppose someone could get for work like that?" he asked quietly.

"I was thinking of…maybe ten percent of the legal fees?" From Frank's almost imperceptible nod, Pete suspected that the key had opened the door.

Frank was quiet for a moment, then shook his head. "That's tempting…but damned dangerous."

"No reason why the company ever has to learn about it. We hire a consulting firm in a given case, pay them, and list the fee as a disbursement, just like any other disbursement. No one has to know who owns the company except you and me. Call it Acme Insurance Consultants or something like that. You approve the bills on files you send out, don't you?"

Frank nodded, then turned and looked out the window over Michigan Avenue. It was a beautiful clear day, and the traffic below was moving along smoothly, with only the occasional sound of a horn rising to their rooftop lookout.

Pete decided not to press the matter. He wasn't sure just what Frank was thinking. Pete's palms were sweaty and his jaw was clenched shut. He took a sip of water and noticed his hand quivering as he raised the cold glass to his lips. What the hell had he done? He gestured to the waiter for another round of drinks. The silence seemed interminable.

At last, Frank turned back toward him. "Does your firm know anything about directors and officers insurance?" he asked.

Pete nodded. His mouth was dry and he struggled to answer. "We sure do. I've got a fellow who works for me who's one of the best in the city on D&O coverage. That's one of our areas of real specialty." It was a lie, of course; as far as he knew, the firm had never handled a single D&O case.

"Good. I've got three D&O cases on my desk right now. I didn't know where the hell to send them, but now I do. I'll send them over to you this afternoon."

Pete smiled and raised his glass. "I might be needing a consultant on those cases, Frankie," he said quietly. "Do you have any suggestions?"

"As a matter of fact, I do. I'll give you a call in a day or two with the company's name and address." Frank Donatelli popped a black olive into his mouth, returned Pete's smile, then picked up his menu.

Pete Spanos leaned back in his chair and savored the sense of relief, then euphoria, that swept over him. *Damn, that was easy. I should have listened to Uncle Ed years ago!*

—*mm*—

Tony Jeffries lived on the east side of Wilmette, halfway between the Metra railroad station in the Village Center and the Linden Avenue station that marks the northern terminus of Chicago's el system. That gave him two convenient options for commuting to work, but he usually took Metra, not only for the added comfort, but also because he enjoyed the civility of a hot cup of coffee on the way down every morning and a cool drink on the evening ride.

The Jeffries' house was typical of the large stucco homes built in east Wilmette in the first decade of the twentieth century. Two and a half stories, with five bedrooms (one of them now a computer room), it had provided Tony and Karen plenty of space over the years for their once growing, now shrinking, family. Mark and Roger were already away at college; Bill would be leaving for the University of Illinois in the fall; and Debbie, a junior at New Trier, was already thumbing through college brochures and fantasizing about beautiful campuses in exotic places like Santa Clara, Charlottesville, and Vero Beach.

Tony and Karen were home alone that evening, a former phenomenon that had become increasingly common since Debbie had been emancipated by her drivers' license. Sprawled on one of their couches, Tony was emailing a message to the two boys about some family summer vacation ideas that he and Debbie had been debating.

"Tony, here's something that should interest you," Karen said, looking up from her desk across their living room. "Remember last year when the General Assembly passed that bill capping punitive damages in medical malpractice cases at two hundred and fifty thousand?"

"Sure," Tony nodded. "That was a big deal at the time. It was an even bigger deal when the Supreme Court upheld it."

"Well, Dick Vass from Madison County has introduced a bill that would repeal that. Plaintiffs would be able to shoot the moon again, in every med mal case. No limits. What do you think about that?"

"It'll be terrible for both the docs and the insurance industry if it passes," Tony answered after a long sip of Chardonnay. "They'd be getting hammered by punitive damage awards just like they were before. Some of those verdicts were absolutely insane. And it drove a lot of docs out of state." He took another look at his BlackBerry, hit "send," put it down, and began sifting through the stack of legal periodicals and quasi-junk mail that had piled up on his desk at the office during the past week. "What do you think its chances are?" he asked as he picked the top envelope off the pile.

"Zero," Karen laughed. "Your friends in the insurance industry will kill it before it ever gets out of committee. They're organized now."

"I'm not sure I'd underestimate the plaintiffs' bar," Tony said as he glanced at a so-called newsletter and threw it into the waste basket he'd moved to the side of the couch. He had followed this war for years. The medical and insurance industries, reeling from wave after wave of punitive damage awards, finally had engineered a bill into law last year limiting those damages. The lobbying was ferocious; there was obviously heavy money involved on both sides. Tony had always been amazed that the insurance industry, with its almost unlimited resources, rarely out lobbied or outspent the plaintiffs' bar, but they'd somehow been able to last year. The medical profession, of course, was always up in arms over punitive damages, but their lobbying efforts had always been clumsy until last year, when their resources were focused and well organized, and, with the support of all the state's major newspapers, they got their bill passed and signed. And so it stood, unless Dick Vass's bill got through.

Tony's musings were interrupted by the ring of the telephone. "I'll get it," he told Karen as he struggled to his feet and followed the phone's shrill siren call into the kitchen.

"Hello," Tony said as he picked up the receiver. He noticed that the garbage hadn't been taken out yet. Tomorrow's pickup day, he reminded himself. Got to take it out tonight.

"Hey, Tony, it's Cal. How are you?"

Tony was surprised; Cal Cizma never called him at home.

"Fine, Cal. What's up?"

"Chester Melrose had an accident today, Tony. He broke his ankle. He's not going to be able to make his flight to London tomorrow." Cal paused, and Tony tried to sort out the implications of what he'd just been told. He also didn't realize that Chester was going to London that soon. He thought the trip was going to be next week.

Before he could reply, Cal continued. "I spoke to Barton a few minutes ago, and he thinks that one of us should go and make Chester's meetings for him. The medical mal book of business is too important for us to drop the ball right now, and the two of us are the only ones who know enough about our end of the program to answer the Brits' questions, besides Chester, of course."

"Are you asking me if I can fly to London tomorrow?"

"Well, it has to be at least one of us, Tony. My schedule's clear; how does yours look?"

"Impossible. Absolutely impossible." Tony shook his head as he tried to envision his calendar. "I've got a contested hearing tomorrow morning at ten, and a pretrial conference before Judge Dumbrowsky in another case at two. Later in the week, maybe, but not tomorrow."

"We don't want to cancel and reschedule Chester's

meetings, Tony. I've already talked to Chester at the hospital and know his schedule; it's pretty tight."

"It sounds to me, Cal, like you ought to be the one to go. The only question is whether you're going to have enough time to get up to speed on everything."

"No problem. I've got his whole file on the Imperial business here at home right now, including your last summary of all the cases. Believe me, by the time I leave tomorrow I'll know it inside and out. Besides, I'll have seven more hours in the air."

"Well, then, do it. Maybe it's time for the Brits to learn that Wilson & Thompson is something more than a bunch of old men. Good luck, Cal."

"Thanks. I'll give you a call from the Connaught."

Tony hung up the phone and wandered back into the living room. He was concerned about the conversation he'd just had. He wished he'd been able to go to London himself; but Chester Melrose's medical mal book of business was awfully important, both for him and for the firm, and he didn't want anything to screw it up.

"Was that Cal?" Karen asked as he plopped back down onto the couch.

"Yes, it was. He's going to fly to London tomorrow to fill in for Chester Melrose at some meetings. Chester's out of commission for a while; he broke an ankle."

"Oh, that's too bad. I'll drop him a card."

"That would be nice."

"By the way," Karen added, looking back up from her desk, "I was talking to Sandy this morning--we ran across each other at Treasure Island. She's *really* unhappy about the move to Kenilworth. I've never seen her so upset."

"That's funny--just the other day Cal was telling some of us how much Sandy enjoyed their new home and neighbors. He said she was joining the Kenilworth Infant Welfare League or something like that. I wonder if we're talking about the same Sandy Cizma."

"It doesn't sound like it to me."

"Well, that's something for them to work out," Tony said, to grabbing the top brochure from the coffee-table pile. It touted a seminar on improving your communication skills. Tony chuckled as he thought about sending it to the Cizmas, then flipped it into the waste basket.

—*mm*—

Carol James had been working that evening, answering the plaintiff's interrogatories in the *Roosevelt versus Blessed Trinity* case. Plaintiff's counsel had also formally requested copies of Sam Roosevelt's hospital records. Carol wrestled with that for an hour, trying to come up with some legal justification for not producing them. She couldn't, though, and finally stuffed copies of the records into an envelope along with the answers to the interrogatories, and mailed them to plaintiff's counsel, Max Greene She then took a cab to the station and took the train north.

Chef's Station in Evanston was a quiet bistro with just enough light from the small lamps suspended over each table to allow you to make your way to your own, but not enough to allow you discern the shadowy faces of the people (usually couples) you pass. The indistinct, whimsical paintings on the walls and the quiet music suggested a softer, gentler world of some earlier age. After a glass or two of wine at Chef's Station, it was easy to imagine yourself relaxing in a countryside chateau in the south of France rather than under the Davis Street Metra station in Evanston.

Carol walked quickly into the restaurant's entry hall, late for her dinner with Bill Turple. The smiling owner, Peter Mills, sixtyish, with a white beard and hair, greeted her warmly, as he always did, and escorted her to the rear booth where Bill was waiting, finishing a glass of red wine—probably his second. It was a Tuesday evening and the restaurant wasn't too busy.

"I'm sorry I'm late, Bill," she said, putting her hand on his wrist.

"It's all right," he replied curtly. He emptied his glass, then signaled the waiter for wine for both of them. "The usual problem?" he asked, a hint of hardness in his voice.

"Yes, I'm afraid it was." Carol lowered her head. She hated having to justify the time she spent working, having to explain why, at this stage in her career, it was critical that she show just how well she could handle tough cases.

She'd been going with Bill for about four years, and it was a comfortable relationship. He was a partner at one of the major accounting firms and was much more interesting, both intellectually and physically, than any other man she'd been involved with. She enjoyed debating esoteric aspects of economics or foreign policy with him almost as much as she enjoyed snuggling up to him after they'd made love. They talked occasionally about getting married someday, but neither of them pushed it. Bill had been there, done that; and Carol wanted to get her career in order before she embarked on the wife/mother routine. She knew that the two didn't mix well.

And now she was up for full partnership in the firm. She'd been a junior, or nonequity, partner for the past three years, and knew that if she didn't make full partner next year, she probably never would. Being an equity partner in a firm like Wilson & Thompson not only had tremendous financial implications; it also was a recognized benchmark of success in the profession, especially for a woman. Even now, in 2003, relatively few women were equity partners in Chicago's major law firms.

They made small talk over dinner and slowly erased the initial tension. They shared a crab-cake appetizer, then Bill had the seared duck breast while Carol enjoyed the smoked Atlantic salmon, one of Chef Romero's specialties. They were talking about a vacation in the Caribbean--Antigua maybe. Right now their complicated schedules made any specific planning impossible, but it was a delicious fantasy to savor.

After their entrees, Bill pushed his wine aside, took Carol's hands in his own, and leaned forward.

"Carol," he whispered, "I've got a chance to be named managing partner of our Toronto office. It's not set in stone. But if it's offered to me, I don't want to turn it down. How would you feel about living in Toronto?"

She took a deep breath and looked down at their intertwined hands. She didn't want to have to make the choice that Bill was presenting. She took another deep breath and looked up.

"Bill, I love you. You know that. But it would be awfully hard to walk away from ten years of work here. I'm almost a full partner." She shook her head. "I don't know what I would do if I really had to make that decision.... I really don't."

"I was afraid you'd say that," Bill said, nodding his head in resignation. Then he rallied and smiled. "But maybe I won't get the Toronto job, and maybe it won't be an issue at all."

"I hope not." She paused, then squeezed his hand. "I'm sorry," she whispered.

"Me too."

Max Greene took a bite of his corned beef sandwich and leaned forward to examine the latest edition of the *Cook County Jury Verdict Reporter*. He was looking to see if anyone owed him any money. He didn't have to check the notebook in his briefcase to know which plaintiffs' cases he'd referred out, or to whom, or what the fee arrangements were. He never forgot things like that. But he kept the notebook anyway, just to be safe.

Max's office was in the core of the rabbit warren of rooms leased and subleased by solo practitioners and small law firms in the old thirty-five-story building at 188 West Randolph Street. The upper floors had been closed for years, and a wooden canopy covered the sidewalk in front to protect pedestrians from occasional falling hunks of terra cotta. Like most of the other tenants, Max would have preferred to be somewhere else, but at 188 the price was right, he could get a secretary by the hour when he needed one (which wasn't often), and his sublease was month-to-month. He would walk away from this in a minute when one of his big cases came in.

Nobody owed him money this week. Max sighed in disgust as he pushed the *Jury Verdict Reporter* into the pile of disorganized papers on the front of his desk. He took another bite of his sandwich, then reached for the *Sun Times* and flipped to the obituaries. He had written a few wills over the years, usually naming himself as executor, and was always hoping that one of them would "mature." He scanned the names, shaking his head; nothing today.

He turned to the crossword puzzle, folded the page to a manageable size, and began his daily routine of seeing if he could finish it before the mail arrived. He almost made it—who the hell *was* the tenth president anyway?

The mail that morning consisted of ten advertisements, three bills, and one real letter—a bulky one from Wilson &

Thompson. He knew before he opened it that it concerned to the Sam Roosevelt case; that was the only matter he had with Wilson & Thompson. The cover letter was signed by Carol James, the attractive looker who was handling the case on the other side; Max sighed as she took form in his mind's eye. Then he glanced at what she had enclosed. It was the defendant's answers to the plaintiff's standard interrogatories, the names and addresses of anyone who knew anything about the case. She'd also enclosed the hospital's medical records on Sam Roosevelt, per his request.

Max hadn't referred this case out yet. It looked like it might be worth something, and he was hoping for a quick settlement and a fee he wouldn't have to share with anyone else, except for the one percent he owed the fella at the hospital who'd given the woman his card.

This Sam Roosevelt is in terrible shape, Max thought. *But what the hell, guys our age have strokes or broken hips or something else every day--things you never recover from.* Max wasn't going to be able to pin anything on the hospital, he knew that. But he hoped to be able to get a few bucks in settlement.

He finished his sandwich as he read through the hospital records and doctors' notes. Some of the comments were hard to decipher; they'd been scribbled originally and the copying made them even more obscure. But Max had nothing else to do, and decided to give the whole file a once-over. Maybe he'd be able to come up with a phrase or two that would help raise the ante a few bucks in the settlement talks.

Then something jumped out at him: the words "misla-beled CT scan film." Bertha Roosevelt had said something like that when she first came in, and he threw it into the Complaint, but he hadn't taken her seriously. Everybody blames the hospital when something goes wrong. Here it was, though, right in the report of the neurosurgeon, a guy named Michaels. The CT scan film was mislabeled.

Max stood up as he continued reading. *Damn, this is dynamite!* He smiled broadly. He'd been waiting for years for a case like this. The doc admitted in writing that a mistake had been made, and that he'd operated on the wrong side of the patient's head. It looked like he was trying to blame it on the radiologist. This case was worth big bucks: several hundred thousand in lost wages and medical bills for sure, maybe more. Might even get some punitives, up to that damned cap. No, Max wasn't going to let anyone else get their hands on this one. He'd settle it himself if he could and move out of this filthy dump.

—————

"Good talking to you, Lou. I'm looking forward to working with you on this one. Thanks for sending it our way." Tony Jeffries smiled as he hung up the phone. His long-time client Lou Kleppa, Consolidated Steel's gen-eral counsel, had just referred a nice new case to them, an age discrimination complaint filed by a plant manager who'd been canned.

He swiveled back to his desk and picked up the report

he'd been reading. It was late afternoon, and below his window the shadows of the skyscrapers along Michigan Avenue poked eastward into the lake, like long fingers grasping for the scattered sailboats just beyond their reach.

Suddenly, he heard a commotion outside his shut door. Laughing and shouting; it sounded like Curly Morgan. The door burst open and there indeed stood Curly, grinning like a kid, his tie loose, a bottle of Champagne in his hand.

"I won the goddamn Catalano case!" he shouted. "Straight not guilty! The jury was out for three days, and the plaintiffs were already spending their money. Then they come back with a straight NG. God damn, what a nice win!"

He walked into the room, still grinning, slammed the bottle of vintage Mumms down on a corner of Tony's desk, and pulled a handful of plastic cups out of his coat pocket. "You're the only guy around here who really appreciates what that means, Tony," he said, working the cork. "So I decided to celebrate it with you."

"That's beautiful, Curly, congratulations!" Tony answered, rising and grasping his hand. Curly had been on trial for a month, and Tony knew that this was a spectacular victory. That was clear from Curly's face, which glowed with excitement and satisfaction.

"Betty, come on in here," Curly shouted over his shoulder to Tony's secretary. "I've got some for you too." Betty, laughing in the doorway, stepped into the room.

"How much were the plaintiffs looking for?" Tony asked. "At the end, I mean?"

"Five million bucks. It was a bullshit case, and I never offered them a nickel. Not a nickel! Damn," Curly said, shaking his head. "What a beautiful win!" He poured them each a cup, ignoring the liberal spillover onto Tony's desk.

"Betty, it's almost five," Tony said. "I suspect that I'm through for the day," He raised his cup. "To the best damn trial lawyer in this town, Curly, you did it again!"

"Thanks. But one of the *two* best, Tony. You know that as well as I do." They looked at each other for a moment, then downed their Champagne. Tony had never seen Curly Morgan happier.

—*ww*—

The gray BMW eased to a stop on the east side of the 5300 block of Clark Street. The driver got out, pushed the remote to lock the doors, flipped up the collar on his trench coat to ward off the cool night breeze, and walked around the front of his car to the sidewalk. He strode north for a half a block, past several darkened buildings, then stopped by an alley and looked back over his shoulder. No one else was visible.

He walked down the alley, past the garbage cans and scattered boxes, to a solitary wooden door at the base of a brick wall that stretched off into the darkness. A bare light bulb over the door illuminated the word "Mandate" neatly stenciled in white letters. He pushed the small buzzer next to the door and nodded to the small red eye of a television camera looking down from the right. At the sound of a buzz, he pushed the door open and stepped into an inner room not much bigger than a closet, with a wooden door to the right and a small window directly in front of him, through which a young man looked out from behind a sliding glass panel.

The visitor pulled a card out of his inner coat pocket and showed it to the young man, who nodded.

"Good evening, Mr. Brent." The gatekeeper smiled, then pushed an unseen button. The door on the right swung open.

Ron Brent walked through the doorway, down a short corridor, paused briefly to comb back his blond hair, and pushed open another door into Mandate's main lounge. A dozen people were standing or sitting at the plush leather-covered bar; they were difficult to discern in the dim light. He walked past them, as well as others clustered in groups of two or three, some of whom nodded or smiled in recognition, toward the row of small private booths in the back. As he walked through the room he eased off his trench coat and handed it to an attendant. The distinctive sweet aroma of marijuana filled the air. Through an archway to the right surging music from the club's disco, filled with writhing couples dancing under flashing strobes, kept the lounge throbbing to a primal beat.

The clientele was well-dressed and friendly, but the ambience was sensuous and slightly decadent, like that in other very private clubs found in most cities for those with the money and the desire to enjoy their pleasures with impunity. The only difference about this club was that everyone there was male.

Ron Brent walked slowly past the row of private booths until he came to one in particular. He smiled, then slid in beside the well-dressed fortyish black man who was already there. There were two drinks on the table.

"I got your message," Rasheed Collins said, returning the smile, as Ron leaned forward to kiss him.

"Good." Brent put his arm around Rasheed's shoulders. "How's my favorite lawyer?"

"Couldn't be better. In fact, I went to the trouble of getting us a room upstairs. I need a diversion after dealing with mundane Temple business all day. Hope you have some time."

"Of course I do. I'd love to divert you--any way you'd like."

Chapter Five

———*vvvv*———

Cal Cizma felt a tingle of excitement as he sat on
the black leather couch in the Imperial Insurance
Syndicate's reception room. He sensed that this was the
very heart of the British insurance empire, where underwriting decisions were made every day that profoundly
affected millions of people and thousands of careers all
over the world. He glanced at the row of oil portraits on
the paneled wall opposite him: the Ghosts of Underwriters
Past. They seemed to be evaluating him, deciding whether or not he properly belonged in their midst. He quickly
looked away.

It was a large, high-ceilinged room, with clusters of
oversized couches and easy chairs and a half-dozen brass
lamps. The lighting was subdued, or at least that was the
sense created by the darkly paneled walls. At the far end
was the room's only other occupant, a strikingly attractive
brunette in a conservative gray suit, sitting behind a small
desk. Cal sized her up appreciatively. She was reading

something, and Cal glanced at her from time to time to see if she might be looking his way. She never was.

Cal had been fifteen minutes early for his ten o'clock appointment with Gordon Hawke. He wanted to be sure to create a favorable impression; he knew the Brits reputation for being punctual. When the chimes of the grandfather clock struck eleven, he shifted uncomfortably and realized that he needn't have been preoccupied with punctuality.

On his latest look at her, the brunette picked up the brass telephone on her desk, responding to some silent signal. She listened for a moment, then put down the receiver and looked at him. "Mr. Hawke will see you now, Mr. Cizma," she announced with a trace of a smile.

As she spoke, she stood and pushed open a large wooden door adjacent to her desk. Cizma followed her gesture through the doorway and found himself in a carpeted twenty-foot corridor, at the other end of which was a matronly woman with white hair and folded arms.

"This way, Mr. Cizma." She turned and led him through a doorway at the corridor's far end.

The inner office was much larger than Cizma had expected, fully fifty feet long, a huge Oriental rug covering the floor, with a desk and set of chairs near the windows at one end, and, at the other, a collection of overstuffed armchairs grouped around a glowing fireplace. Two well-dressed men sitting at the fireplace rose as Cal entered.

"Mr. Cizma, I presume," the older one said with a

restrained smile as he walked over and extended his hand. "I'm Gordon Hawke."

"My pleasure, Mr. Hawke. I'm very pleased to meet you."

"And this is Ronnie Dasher." Hawke gestured to the younger man standing beside and slightly behind him. "He heads up our claims department."

Hawke was tall and balding, in his early fifties, Cal supposed, with a commanding presence; he spoke and moved with a quiet sense of confidence. As they exchanged pleasantries, he led the three of them back toward the fireplace.

Dasher, maybe a decade and a half younger, was glib and quick and clearly attuned to catering to his chairman's whims. He was as tall as Hawke, but sturdier; he might have been a serious athlete in his younger days.

"We weren't really expecting anyone from your office until next week," Hawke said.

"Yes, I know," Cal replied. "But when Chester was injured, we decided that I should come over here immediately to ensure that there wouldn't be any missed communications between our offices."

"We certainly appreciate that," Dasher replied.

"It's a shame that Chester broke his ankle," Hawke said as he eased back into one of the overstuffed armchairs. He gestured to one of the other chairs; Cal followed his lead and sat down. Dasher took the seat next to Hawke.

"Yes, he may not be able to travel for a while," Cal

answered. "But he specifically asked me to extend his greetings to you," he added with a deferential nod.

"A shame. Still, I understand that you work with him on our hospital program."

"Yes. I really run the administrative side of the program within our firm. And the understanding we have is that I'll gradually be taking over all aspects of the program as Chester eases into retirement."

"Really?" Hawke said, raising his eyebrow. "Well, I take it, then, that you're fully aware of the financial arrangements we've set up."

"Absolutely. And I must say that we're very pleased with the way the program has been running these first few months."

"You don't have any questions about the underwriting aspects of the program? I spelled them out in a letter to Chester at the outset. He concurred in the terms we suggested. It's all quite straightforward, don't you agree?"

"Oh, yes. As I mentioned, we're quite pleased with the arrangements."

Cal knew he hadn't seen any such letter from Hawke in the file. But he didn't want to intimate that there were some aspects of the program that he didn't understand. He knew he had the opportunity for a coup in the palm of his hand, and he wasn't going to blow it.

"In fact," Cal said, opening his briefcase, "I have for you here a full status report on all the cases we're handling under your medical malpractice program. I had my staff put it together last week. I think you'll find it quite complete." He handed Tony Jeffries's report to Hawke and gave a copy to Dasher.

"Good," Hawke said, laying the report unopened on the end table beside his chair. "I'm sure that Ronnie will be in touch with you if he has any questions. But the more important question, Mr. Cizma, is whether your firm is prepared to expand your involvement in the program a bit. We're off to a good start in Philadelphia, Chicago, and Los Angeles, and you seem to be handling the claims and suits in those cities well. Now we're prepared to start offering our policy throughout the States. What I need to know is whether your firm can handle the defense of all our cases nationwide. You may need to open some additional offices. What do you say to that?"

"You give us thirty days' lead time, Mr. Hawke, and we can cover your cases anywhere in the United States. I'll give you my personal guarantee on that."

"Good. Very good indeed." Gordon Hawke leaned back in his chair and narrowed his eyes slightly. "Well, Mr. Cizma, consider this your thirty-day notice. We're off and running."

"In that case, so are we," Cal answered, nodding first to Hawke, then to Dasher. "And to show our firm's commitment to your program, I'll plan on coming here on a regular basis--say, once a month--to keep you fully up to date."

"Excellent. You should make your reports directly to Ronnie here," he gestured to Dasher, "since that's his area of responsibility."

Cal couldn't have been more pleased. He felt he had established a good working relationship with Hawke. He also knew that he'd be picking the lawyers to staff the firm's new offices, and would hire only people personally loyal to him. He was never going to give up this position, not to Chester Melrose or to anyone else.

They chatted a few more minutes; then Hawke rose, signifying that the meeting was over. As he escorted Cal out, Ronnie Dasher turned to him and said, "By the way, Cal, if you don't have any other plans for the evening, I'd love to take you to dinner and perhaps show you around London a bit."

"Why, thank you. I'd be delighted."

"Fine." Dasher replied with a smile. "I understand you're staying at the Connaught. I'll pick you up at eight."

—*mm*—

"The Walbrook CT scan machine is specifically designed, Miss James, to eliminate all possibility of human error." Dr. Rashdani said with an air of accommodating formality. "The patient is placed face-up on this platform here; the machine is turned on; and the platform slowly slides the patient, feet first, through the scanning area. The rate of movement is controlled by the machine's computer, and the images that are created are automatically labeled 'left' and 'right', so that the radiologist can have immediate access to them and know exactly what they show."

"I see," Carol James answered as she stared at the glistening white machine and all its assorted attachments. "But then how do you explain the Sam Roosevelt case, Dr. Rashdani?"

Carol was poking, prodding, trying to figure out what had happened to Sam Roosevelt at Blessed Trinity Hospital. It was a tragic case, and no one seemed to know or admit what had gone wrong. Carol badly needed to understand in order to put together a defense.

"The first CT scan image of Mr. Roosevelt showed the hematoma on the left side of his brain," Carol pressed. "There's no question about that. The film is clearly marked. And Dr. Michaels operated on the left side, based on that film. We know now that that was wrong, and that the injury was always on the right. That's clear from the CT scan taken the next day. But by then it was too late, and the patient had deteriorated to a vegetative state. I just don't understand, Doctor, how that mislabeling could have happened."

"Nor do I, Miss James," Rashdani answered, glancing at his watch. "I've given it a great deal of thought, and all I can come up with is that the computer in the Walbrook machine made an error. Perhaps a speck of dust settled on the wrong chip. I just don't know."

Carol recoiled at the thought that a tiny speck of dust could have wreaked such havoc. Surely the machine's designers had reckoned with that possibility. But if that *is* what happened, any resulting injuries should be responsibility of the manufacturer, not the hospital. *That's something to explore*, Carol thought as she gazed in awe at the huge machine. *Maybe we can force Walbrook to pay the cost of this settlement.*

"Thank you, Doctor," she said. "You've been very helpful. I know you're busy, so I don't want to take any more of your time now. But I would like to spend some more time here on my own, just getting a feel for this equipment, if you don't mind."

"Of course not. I see that you have a copy of the machine's user manual," Rashdani noted, nodding at the spiral-bound document under Carol's left arm. He turned to leave, then added, "If you have any questions about the machinery itself, I'm sure our night technician Stanislaw, or Stan, can help you. He's in back. He's only a temporary employee, but he was the one on duty the night Mr. Roosevelt had his films taken."

Carol sensed that Rashdani wanted to distance himself as far as possible from the Sam Roosevelt disaster. *That might not be so easy, Doctor,* she thought.

She thumbed through the manual. Written in non-medical language, it was easy enough to follow. That surprised her until she recalled that the technicians who operated and maintained these machines weren't doctors. She wandered around the lab, touching the equipment like a used car shopper kicking tires, until she found the maintenance room. Stan, a young blond wearing an unbuttoned hospital jacket, was sitting there reading a newspaper with his feet up on an old desk. A cup of steaming fragrant Starbucks coffee was off to one side--French Vanilla Roast, she guessed accurately.

"Can I help you?" he asked awkwardly as he lifted his feet off the desk. He had a thick Slavic accent, and Carol noticed that the paper he put down was one of the Eastern European weeklies that she occasionally saw around town.

"Yes, I'm Carol James, one of the attorneys for the hospital. I'm just looking around to get a sense of everything that's here. This equipment's very impressive." She nodded over her shoulder as she extended her hand.

"Yes, impressive!" Stan said as he got to his feet and shook her hand. "I run machine at night." He smiled and proudly pointed his left thumb at his chest.

"I wonder if you could show me what you do." Carol said, giving him her most enticing smile.

"Sure. Come. I show you." Stan eased by her, squeezing her arm gently as he walked out into the main lab room and pointed to the bare metal table in front of the cavernous door of the CT scan. It reminded Carol of a giant microwave oven. "Patient lie here," he said, "and I work there." He pointed to a glass-enclosed room at the side. "When doctor say patient ready, I turn on machine." He smiled broadly. "Patient go in machine like train," he said, moving his hand slowly forward.

"Can I see how you do that?" Carol asked, tucking the manual back under her arm.

"Sure." He led her into the glass booth and stood close beside her as she scanned the array of dials and buttons spread before them. The pungent garlic on his breath caused her to lean away, but she kept her eyes on the console.

"I push button to make machine start," he said, pointing to one of two red buttons in the center of the console. Above the button to the right were the words HEAD FIRST in bright red. Above the left button were an equally bright FEET FIRST.

"Do you always push *that* button to make the machine start?" Carol asked, pointing to the one on the right.

"No, either button okay," he replied with a smile. "Machine start the same I push either button. No difference."

"What about those signs over the buttons?"

"Lady, my English not so hot. Not read English very good. But is okay; either button start machine."

Carol knew something was wrong. She edged her way past Stan and out of the cubicle, took a deep breath, and pulled out the Walbrook manual. It didn't take her long; within seconds she found the section she was looking for. One of the benefits of the Walbrook CT scan machine, it explained, was that a patient could be introduced to it either head first or feet first. While the customary method was feet first, if the patient entered head first the computer would automatically reverse the left and right designations on the films to compensate. In other words, the manual proudly stated, there was no chance for human error either way the machine was used. *All the operator had to do was punch the appropriate button, and the machine would do everything else.*

Carol leaned up against the wall and took another deep breath. Now she knew just what had happened to poor Sam Roosevelt. Stan had pushed the "head first" button when Roosevelt went feet first into the machine, or visa versa, and the imaging films had the left and right designations reversed. He didn't know it mattered which button he pushed, and Dr. Rashdani didn't realize that Stan had any discretion to exercise. *Neither one had ever read the manual!*

When those facts came out--and Carol knew they ultimately would--Blessed Trinity Hospital would be hit with a massive judgment.

This case is going to be a catastrophe!

Cal Cizma greeted Ronnie Dasher in the lobby of the Connaught a little after eight and followed him outside to a waiting black Rolls-Royce limo. The uniformed driver opened the rear door as they approached.

"I thought we'd give you a proper tour of London," Dasher said with a grin. "Get in."

Cal was at a loss for words; he really hadn't expected the Rolls. He was even more surprised when he eased into the rear seat and found himself sitting next to the hot brunette from Imperial's reception desk.

"We meet again, Mr. Cizma," she said quietly as he leaned back. She was the image of sensuality, from her enticing smile to the faint scent of perfume that enveloped them both. She was wearing a low-cut beige dress, without a bra. "It's Cal, isn't it?" she asked, putting her hand on his.

"Yes. Yes, it is."

"Cal, I believe you've already met Roxanne," Ronnie Dasher said with a smile as he pulled the door shut behind him. Then, he leaned forward and pulled a bottle from a built-in ice bucket. "Champagne, anyone?"

"Of course," Roxanne laughed.

"Why not?" Cal said as he took a glass.

"Here's a toast," Dasher proposed. "To a long and mutually rewarding relationship."

Cal Cizma took a long draught of the cool Champagne and leaned back with a smile as the limo eased quietly into the London night.

They had dinner with two couples waiting for them in the private dining room of an elegant restaurant overlooking the Thames. The men, both in their forties, were with one of the other insurance syndicates. Their very attractive dates, considerably younger, didn't mention their last names or line of work. Dasher sat on one side of Cal, Roxanne on the other. Her leg was brushing against Cal's all evening. He loved it.

Endless bottles of wine were followed by countless snifters of cognac. After dinner, one of the women, a blonde called Lisa, took a vial of fine white powder out of her purse, carefully spread it into lines on a piece of paper, then tightly rolled up a ten-pound note for sniffing. She took her share, then passed the pleasure on to the others. Cal didn't take any. He was afraid. In truth, until now he'd never even seen anyone use cocaine.

The two couples left about eleven, headed for a flat kept by one of the men. A few minutes later, Dasher scribbled his signature on the bill, grabbed an open bottle of Champagne, and led Cal and Roxanne out to the Rolls, arms around one another for support.

"What a great night!" Cal laughed. He sprawled in the back of the limo, his arms stretched behind his two British friends. Then he had a masterstroke of an idea.

"Why don't the two of you come up to my suite in the Connaught?" He pulled Roxanne a little closer as they turned a corner. She snuggled up under his arm and put her head on his shoulder.

"Great idea!" Dasher answered, raising his glass. "But not at the Connaught. They're a bit prissy about that sort of thing."

"Pity," Roxanne whispered quietly. She snuggled up a bit closer to Cal and laid her hand gently on his thigh.

"You know what you really should do, Cal?" Dasher said, wiping a trickle of Champagne from his left cheek. "You ought to have your firm rent a flat here in London. After all, if you're going to be here every month, it wouldn't cost you more than the couple hundred quid a night you're paying at the Connaught. And it would certainly make things more interesting."

Cal smiled and leaned back. *That's brilliant!. If I can finesse a London flat, my life is gonna change overnight. I could get used to all this very easily—especially her.*

"I'll see what I can do," he said, still smiling. "It's an excellent idea."

"Of course, you realize, old chap," Dasher added, raising his glass again, "that if you have a flat here, the civilized thing to do is to share it with your friends."

"Naturally--as long as my friends share their treasures, too."

"That goes without saying, old boy."

Yes, he decided, he could get used to all this very easily indeed.

※※※

Curly Morgan watched the little white numbers flash on and off as the elevator ascended. 62, 63, 64. It was taking an ungodly long time to go up today. 68, 69, 70. The pounding in his head, an annoyance at ground level, was becoming intolerable. He opened his mouth and swallowed twice. That helped some. 73, 74, 75.

Why the hell did I have to close the Italian Village last night? Damn, that was stupid. But hey, I didn't even get there until ten! My mistake was not eating dinner. Whenever I skip dinner and just drink, it's much worse the next day. Like today. My head is fucking killing me. Tonight I'll have dinner for sure.

And why the hell did their office have to be near the top of the Hancock Building? They were the only major law firm in the building. That was the prize the firm extracted for leasing five full floors. *Damn, would you fucking get there?!* Curly shouted inwardly.

84, 85, 86. The elevator slowed, paused a moment, and opened its doors. Curly took a deep breath, pulled in his gut, and stepped into Wilson & Thompson's parquet reception area. *All right, back into the barrel.* He glanced at his watch; 11:15.

"Good morning, Curly," Julia, the receptionist, said with a smile as he walked past her desk through the inner doorway and down the corridor toward his office on the building's west side. He didn't need any unnecessary chatter right now.

When he got to his office he turned on the computer and began checking his e-mail, his head still pounding. The earliest one, from an address that Curly didn't recognize, had arrived at 8:45 a.m. "Mr. Morgan," it read, "Please call me regarding an antitrust suit filed against our company yesterday. You've been recommended by a mutual friend." It was from Paul Bender, President, American Mining Corp. Morgan stopped and stared at the screen. *A new client. Looks like a good case. Not bad.*

He glanced at the next message, dated 9:30 a.m.. "Morgan, please call re: new suit. Imperative that we discuss immediately. Bender. American Mining." *Shit. Why the hell did this guy have to try to contact me so early? Everybody knows I'm not a morning person.* Irritated, he scribbled the phone number on his note pad and checked the next message. It's time was 10:30 a.m., and it read simply, "Morgan, forget it. I've given case to Cabot and Davis. Bender." *Shit,* Curly said to himself. He picked up the phone to see if he could resurrect the case, while opening the last message on his screen.

"Gotcha!" it read simply. "Tony."

"Asshole," he muttered, slamming down the phone.

He hung up his suit coat, got a cup of black coffee, and began shuffling through the brief he'd been working on the night before. Suddenly, the phone's piercing buzzer drove a spike of pain into his head. He grabbed the receiver quickly to keep it from attacking him again and slowly raised it to his ear.

"Yes?"

"Mr. Morgan, this is Helen Flemming. Mr. Thompson would like to see you in his office."

He took a deep breath. *I don't fucking need this--not right now, anyway.* "What time did he have in mind, Miss Fleming?" he asked, closing his eyes.

"Immediately, Mr. Morgan. He's waiting for you now."

"All right," he whispered. "Tell him I'll be there in a few minutes."

"He's waiting for you *now*, Mr. Morgan." She was unrelenting.

"Right," he nodded. "I'll be right there."

Curly downed the rest of his coffee in two gulps, grabbed his coat from its hanger on the back of the door, and walked down the corridor toward Barton Thompson's corner office. He stopped in the men's room on the way, took a quick but badly needed leak, and splashed some cold water on his face.

Thompson was drumming his fingers on his desk when Curly walked into his office.

"Good morning, Barton," he said quietly as he eased himself into one of the two leather chairs facing the desk. "I understand you wanted to see me."

"Yes, I did." Thompson reached forward to a stapled sheaf of white papers in front of him, thumbed through it in silence for a moment, then flipped it open. "I've been going through the last quarter's figures, Curly," he said. "And I don't like what I see regarding your production." He looked up and continued. "You haven't brought in any new business since the first of the year. That won't do. It won't do at all."

Morgan took a deep breath. *So that's what this is all about.*

"Barton, I may not have brought in any new business, but I've been churning out a lot of work. Most of it on other partners' files, like your Midwest Paperboard antitrust case. And I've been getting some pretty good results, if I must say so myself, including the Catallano case that I won last month for Ralph Stritch."

"That's all well and good, but I don't have the impression that you're making much of an effort to bring in *new* business, Curly. And, as I mentioned to you previously, that's an absolute prerequisite if you expect to remain on the management committee."

"Not making an effort?" Curly fumed. He was getting angry now. "Barton, let me tell you something. My hours may be a little irregular, but I'm one of the hardest-working lawyers here. I may not be here at nine *a.m.* very often, but I'm here at nine *p.m.* almost every night--usually by myself, I might say. Last year I billed twenty-four hundred hours, and if you check your figures there," he gestured at the sheaf of papers on the desk, "you'll see that I'm working at a twenty-five-hundred-hour pace this year. All on profitable matters, I might add."

Thompson waved his hand as if shooing away a gnat. "You're talking like an associate," he said. "As a partner, you're expected to do everything you've just said, *plus* bring in new clients and new business." Thompson leaned forward and began tapping his desk. "And as a member of the management committee, I can assure you, that's required. You're expected to provide leadership to the rest of the firm in terms of marketing. And if you can't handle that, Curly, then maybe I made a mistake in putting you on the committee in the first place." He leaned back in his chair, his eyes fixed on Curly.

Curly felt terribly uncomfortable. Beads of sweat were forming on his forehead. "No, you didn't make a mistake, Barton," he said, shaking his head. He hesitated, then decided that there was nothing to be gained by further argument. Thompson had all the cards. "All right," he said. "I'll make a special effort along those lines, if you feel that it's necessary."

"I do, Curly. And I'm going to be taking a hard look at the figures at the end of this next quarter. If you want to remain on management committee, you're going to have to show some results."

Curly nodded and stood up. The meeting was clearly over, and Curly had an overwhelming urge to get out of Thompson's presence as fast as he could.

"By the way," Thompson said, his tone softening a bit. "I'm going upstairs for lunch in a few minutes. Would you care to join me?"

"I'd like to, Barton, but I've already made other plans." He was lying, of course, but he was *not* going to have lunch with the son-of-a-bitch. "I'm meeting a prospective client," he said.

"Very good, Curly. I hope it's productive. For your sake."

—*mm*—

The Signature Room, soaring a thousand feet over Michigan Avenue, crowns the Hancock Building with one of the world's finest restaurants. Its wine cellar, located far below on the forty-fifth floor in order to minimize the effect of the unsettling sway of the tower, has few equals and no betters. But its greatest attraction to partners of Wilson & Thompson is its proximity: only one hundred feet away, straight up, by elevator.

Tony Jeffries was having lunch with Ralph Stritch, one of the senior members of the management committee. Stritch had a corporate practice, and represented a number of medium-to-large manufacturing companies on Chicago's far South Side. His practice had eased a bit in recent years, as had his own hours, reflecting the business climate in that part of town. Still, he generated substantial enough fees to more than justify his place on the management committee, a position he'd held for over a decade.

Stritch had asked Tony if he was free to join him that day. They did very little business together, and certainly weren't social friends, so Tony wondered just what was up Stritch's sleeve.

They were hardly past the vichyssoise when Stritch got to the point.

"Tony, I take it that you're aware that Barton Thompson's term as chairman of the management committee is about to expire," He put down his spoon as he spoke and casually reached for his glass of water.

Tony was startled. "Why, no," he answered. "I was under the impression that the chairmanship was, well, an open-ended thing that never really expired."

"That's not correct," Stritch said between sips of water. "But I can understand why that's your impression. After all, Barton has been chairman for almost ten years now." He paused to allow the waiter to clear their soup bowls, then turned back to Tony. "The chairmanship has always been a five-year term. That's not written anywhere, but it's been the understanding for as long as I know. And when Barton was re-elected chairman five years ago, it was with the definite agreement that when this term, his second, was over, he'd step down. That'll be coming up in a few months. We'll be electing a new chairman."

"No, I didn't know that at all," Tony said, trying to suppress his surprise. "Now, how exactly is a new chairman chosen?"

"The management committee elects its own chairman. The nine of us. The partnership as a whole is simply told who the new chairman of the committee will be."

"Who do you expect will be elected?" Tony asked. He already knew the answer.

"Six months ago I would have said that Henry Gilcrist was a shoo-in. But now, after Henry's embarrassing departure, I rather suspect it'll be me."

"You'd be a great chairman," Tony answered. He was becoming uneasy about the direction of the conversation.

"Thank you, Tony. I'm glad to hear you say that. That is, of course, what I wanted to talk to you about today. I'd like to be able to count on your support."

"I don't think you have anything to worry about, Ralph. I can't imagine a contest over the chairmanship. You're clearly the best qualified." Tony was trying to avoid making a firm commitment. He didn't know what other office politics were involved, or even if Barton Thompson was really going to step down.

"But can I *count* on you, Tony?" Stritch leaned forward and looked him straight in the eye.

Before Tony could answer, a familiar voice cut through their conversation.

"Good afternoon, gentlemen,"

Tony looked over his shoulder to see Barton Thompson walking up to their table.

"Do you mind if I join you?" Thompson asked as he moved to the chair opposite Jeffries and sat down. "I so hate to eat alone."

"Please do, Barton," Stritch said, a little late. "We were just talking about the outrageous salaries we have to pay to new associates these days. It's just a crime."

It was suddenly clear to Tony that Barton Thompson had no intention of stepping down, and that Ralph Stritch knew that perfectly well. He realized, too, that he was being drawn into a dangerous fight for control of the firm.

Chapter Six

—∿∿—

Tony Jeffries took great pride in his French onion soup. One of his secrets was to use large white onions; they gave the soup a sweeter taste than the smaller onions did. The other secret was to add a liberal dose of good sherry to the pot just before the soup was finished.

Tony was in the kitchen stirring his soup, his bottle of Harvey's poised and ready, when the first of their guests arrived. It was the Cizmas. Tony smiled when he heard Karen in the front hallway greeting them; Cal was always on time to everything, even when he didn't have to be.

They had been planning this dinner party ever since Tony and the others were named to the management committee. It was a celebration of sorts, as well as an opportunity for old friends to get together. The three married couples had taken turns hosting these periodic dinners for years, and it was Karen who realized that they hadn't had the group to Wilmette in some time.

By seven-thirty, with Curly's arrival by cab, everyone

was there. Tony broke open a bottle of Taittinger he had on ice in the living room, served them all, and proposed a toast.

"To old times," he said, raising his glass. "And good friends."

"And better times to come," Pete Spanos added with a smile.

The first part of the evening was spent getting caught up on everyone's family. It was fascinating to Tony just how quickly the little kids playing on their beach in New Buffalo just a few years ago had grown up and were now dating, driving cars, and even applying to colleges. Rasheed insisted that with all the talk about children, he'd report on his cat. Domino was fine, he said, except for being a tad overweight; that was something Domino really had to work on. Sandy Cizma said that she had an excellent book on the subject, which she'd gladly lend to him if he cared to read it to Domino. Rasheed graciously declined.

"By the way, Rasheed," Karen said from the doorway to the dining room, "we keep on hearing rumors about you and Aliza getting engaged. Anything you can report to your old friends?" she asked with a wink.

"No," Rasheed answered, taking a deep breath. "We've talked about it some, but nothing's been decided. Believe me, when it is, you'll be the first people to know. And Aliza extends her regrets for tonight to all of you," he added. "She's chairing a meeting at the temple that she couldn't get out of."

"Well, give her our best," Karen said. "Now, everyone into the dining room."

The onion soup was a success; Tony's culinary skills made him a true renaissance man, the guests agreed. He opted not to advise them that, despite his experiments with other fare over the years, including some of the savory German dishes that his grandmother used to make, onion soup was still the only thing he could prepare with confidence. The soup was followed by a delicious medium-rare tenderloin of beef, served with a tangy béarnaise sauce, one of Karen's specialties.

Over dinner the men congratulated themselves on how well the firm was doing, and they laughed at one another's stories of how they had to scrape to make ends meet when they were young associates. Tony reminded them of the old two-door Chevy he and Karen owned back then, and how proficient he'd become at hiding its rust holes with fiberglass, epoxy, and spray paint. "Yes," he chuckled, "things have changed a lot."

"Aren't these bonuses that the fellas got just great?" Lucy Spanos said to Karen. "Have you and Tony decided how you're going to spend yours?"

Before Karen could respond, Cal, who was sitting next to her, raised his voice. "Tony, I meant to ask you, what kind of cheese do you use in that soup of yours? That cheese is what really makes it."

"Mozzarella," Tony answered. He was proud his soup had made such an impression. "I've tried several different kinds, but mozzarella's the best."

"Wait a minute," Sandy Cizma said quietly. "What was that about bonuses?" She turned to her husband, who was still talking to Tony.

"Mozzarella?" Cal said. "That surprises me. But who am I to question the master?" He laughed. "Where did you get it?"

"Treasure Island," Tony shrugged. "It's just ordinary mozzarella. Nothing special about it."

"Cal," Sandy persisted, raising her voice. "What's this about bonuses ?"

"Fifty thousand dollars," Lucy Spanos answered from across the table. "Didn't Cal tell you? Each of the fellas got a fifty-thousand-dollar bonus last week."

"That was going to be my little surprise," Cal said, turning to Sandy. "The firm's doing so well this year that we gave each of the equity partners an extra distribution, and it came out to fifty thousand for everyone on the management committee. I was going to get you something special for your birthday." Glancing across the table, he added, "Thanks, Lucy, for spoiling my surprise."

"I'm really sorry, Cal. But it's hard to keep good news quiet."

Tony noticed that amid the general good humor, Sandy was staring at her husband in stony silence.

"What I really wanted to talk about," Cal said, looking around the table, "is even more exciting. I think the firm should rent a flat in London. I'm going to have to go there on a regular basis to meet with the underwriters on the medical mal business, and the hotel bills the firm will save if we had a flat there will probably pay for the flat itself. And the great thing is that we could all use it."

"What a wonderful idea!" Karen laughed.

Everyone else seemed enthusiastic too, except Sandy, who remained quiet. They got swept up in a discussion of exactly where it should be, how many bedrooms it should have, and how it should be furnished. It should be roomy enough, they agreed, for at least two couples to stay there at a time, and definitely should have a fully stocked kitchen and bar. And since the five men constituted the majority of the management committee, they could force the motion through. It was a brilliant idea.

Tony sat back, listened, and sipped his wine. He hadn't realized that Cal was planning regular trips to London.

The Cizmas left right after dinner. Sandy wasn't feeling too well, she said. On their way out, Cal promised that the next dinner would be at their new home in Kenilworth.

While Lucy Spanos was helping Karen in the kitchen, Tony and the other three men sat around the dining-room table and talked about their favorite sport, office politics. Tony poured them each a glass of port from the bottle he had brought out, then decided to raise an issue that had been troubling him for some time.

"Guys, let me ask you something," he said, swirling his port in his glass. "Do you think Barton Thompson ever intends to use those letters of resignation we signed when we joined the management committee? I thought about it tonight when someone mentioned that the five of us could force the London flat issue through the committee.

We can't force a damn thing through over Thompson's objection, as long as he holds those letters. If he intends to really use them, that is."

He looked up and saw three incredulous stares.

"You didn't actually sign that letter, did you, Tony?" Curly asked.

"Why, sure," Tony answered. "I had to. We all had to, I thought."

"Jesus Christ, Tony!" Curly leaned back, rolled his eyes and shook his head. He leaned forward, still shaking his head. "That was a goddamn bluff, Tony. He told me the same thing, and I said I wouldn't sign his letter. He seemed a little pissed, but never brought it up again. And you actually signed it?"

"Yes. I thought I had to," Tony answered quietly. He looked at the others. Like Curly, Pete and Rasheed were shaking their heads from side to side.

"There's no way that I would sign an undated resignation letter," Rasheed said. "And I told him so. Even if that meant not being appointed to the management committee."

"So did I," Pete added.

He had been conned. That old son-of-a-bitch had duped him. Tony had never liked the idea of signing that letter, but he drew some comfort from the thought that all five of them were in the same boat. Now it turned out, they weren't at all.

Tony felt ill. He stood up and walked into the living room, anger surging up inside him.

"Damn!" he said aloud.

mm

Curly woke up the next day, Sunday, with a splitting headache and a painful need to take a piss. He wasn't sure which woke him. Or maybe it was the bright midday sunlight pouring in his windows. He usually pulled the curtains shut before he went to bed; apparently last night he didn't. In fact, he didn't remember going to bed at all. He was wearing his underwear and socks; the rest of his clothes were strewn around the floor.

He got to the bathroom barely in time, and as he stood there urinating, realized once again just how satisfying an experience it can really be. Maybe even better than sex. No, not that good, but still very satisfying.

Curly took a couple of aspirin, then shuffled into his living room to look out over the lake. He got only half-way across the room before the blinding sunlight drove him back. He sprawled into the big easy chair in the back corner of the room and put his right hand across his eyes. *Damn, that sun is bright!*

He remembered leaving Tony and Karen's at about eleven. Rasheed gave him a ride, and they stopped at the Pump Room for a drink when they got back downtown.

The broads, yes, the broads. He smiled as he remembered the two women they ran across at the Pump Room. Both blondes; late thirties; not too bad looking. He was deeply involved in discussing an interesting end to the evening with one of them when he realized that Rasheed wasn't there anymore. *What the hell had happened to him? That other chick was all over him.* He ended up just drinking all night with both women; they closed the Pump Room, then the Excalibur on Dearborn, and at dawn they had steak sandwiches at Billie Goat's. There was some kind of a stupid argument with a cabby outside Billy Goat's; he couldn't remember over what.

He had the shorter one's phone number somewhere. What a body! Bald men really turned her on, she'd told him. He wished the hell that Rasheed hadn't vanished; they could have screwed their brains out if he'd stayed around. Still, he chuckled, it was a fun night.

He took a long shower, shaved, got dressed, put on his blue blazer, and went downstairs.

As one of the few permanent residents of the University Club, Curly Morgan treated it like his own baronial mansion. He especially enjoyed the club on days like this, when few other members were around; it took very little imagination to picture himself wandering the corridors of his own medieval castle overlooking the Rhine.

"Good morning, Mr. Morgan," one of the stewards greeted him as he descended the great stone staircase to the second-floor hallway that led to the bar. "May I get you anything?"

"Yes, Jason," Curly muttered without turning. "I'll have a Bloody Mary."

He walked past the suits of armor and tapestries, picked the lone copy of the *Sunday Chicago Tribune* off a small table, and entered the lounge. It was empty except for Willie, one of the staff, standing discretely in a corner, and some red-haired moron at the bar, watching a football game on TV.

Curly went to his usual table next to the windows, eased into one of the old wooden chairs, and began spreading out the sections of the *Times*. Within moments, Jason had brought him his drink and a glass of ice water.

The Bloody Mary tasted very good indeed. Curly shut his eyes and savored the muted tang of the Tabasco as it slowly seeped down his throat. He took another mouthful and realized that all that was left in his glass was ice. He opened his eyes, saw Willie watching from the bar, and nodded for another drink. Then he began poking through the paper, trying to decide what to read first. He decided it would be the sports section; he hadn't heard how the Cubs had done last night in San Francisco. It was early August and they were still in the race.

"Hello, Curly."

He turned to the side and saw Red O'Kieffe walking up to his table. He realized then that it had been O'Kieffe at the bar watching the football game. He shuddered. The absolutely last thing he wanted right now was a serious conversation, even with one of the club's other residents. Curly gave him a polite nod and turned back to his paper.

O'Kieffe was not to be deterred. He pulled up the chair across from Curly and sat down, putting the cup of coffee he had been carrying squarely on top of the *Tribune's* sports section.

"I've been looking for you, Curly," O'Kieffe said. He was a ruddy-faced Irishman, a little overweight, who always seemed to be smiling.

"Is that right," Curly replied, looking down at his trapped paper.

"Yes. It dawned on me that we should be doing business together. It would be good for both our firms."

Curly sighed and looked up.

"Red," he said. "I love you like a brother. Better than that--my brother's an asshole. But I really don't want to talk business first thing on a Sunday morning. If you don't mind."

"Sunday morning?" O'Kieffe laughed. "Curly, it's two o'clock in the afternoon, for Christ sake! You must have had one hell of a night."

Curly shook his head and took a healthy swig of his new drink. *How can it be two o'clock in the afternoon? I just got the hell up.*

"Look, Curly," O'Kieffe said, leaning forward. "You ought to listen to this. I know you're with Wilson & Thompson. Your firm can make a shitload of fees off the deal I have in mind."

That caught Curly's attention. He sat back and looked across the table at the grinning Irishman

"All right," he said, taking a deep breath. "Tell me about it."

————

Karen Jeffries's office in Springfield was standard is-sue for a second-term representative: small, cramped, off a back hallway, a view of the south wall of the post office ten feet away. Still, the old-timers told Karen it was a vast improvement over what they'd had thirty years ago: no private offices at all, with proposed bills as well as mail just stacked up on their desks in the General Assembly.

She was reading through her correspondence that morning. Her secretary had opened the mail, thrown out the junk, and organized the rest by subject matter. Karen was still new enough on the job that she wanted to read all her letters herself. Sometimes she'd run across a par-ticularly well-written note, or recognize a name, and would dictate a personal response. Otherwise, everyone received one of their standard acknowledgments. But it was important to her to see what her constituents had to say, and she was more than a little flattered that so many people would take the trouble to write her.

She had already gone through the stacks of mail on abortion and gun control. Ninety percent of those, she concluded, were form letters distributed by professionals and then copied, signed, and mailed by people in her dis-trict. That was true on both sides of both of those issues; there was very little original thought on display.

She was in the midst of the letters dealing with Dick Vass's bill to revoke the cap on punitive damages in med-ical malpractice cases when her secretary buzzed her. It was Emil Borders, she announced, and he had stopped by to give Karen something.

117

"Send him in, Donna."

Emil Borders was a prominent lobbyist; he'd been a fixture of the Springfield scene long enough that he couldn't be ignored. He had been a state senator from DuPage County for a couple of terms before resigning in the late 1980s while under investigation by the Attorney General's office. The understanding was that charges were dropped in exchange for his withdrawal from the Senate.

"Good morning, darling," Borders called out as he strode into her office. He was wearing a bright plaid sport coat over an open-collared pink shirt, powder-blue slacks, and cream-colored loafers. The contrast between his deeply tanned face and his carefully combed pure-white hair was striking, and his toothy smile was unmistakably that of a professional politician. "Damn, you're looking better and better every time I see you!" He ignored Karen's outstretched hand and gave her a kiss on the cheek. She wondered how many male legislators he greeted that way.

"Good to see you, Emil. Have a seat."

"Thanks. I got something for you, honey," he said with a grin as he sat down. He reached inside his sport coat, pulled out an envelope, and handed it across the desk.

She opened the unsealed envelope and pulled out the piece of paper inside. It was a check for one thousand dollars, payable to Karen's campaign committee. She was sorry that Borders had stopped by; this was bound to become sticky.

"Who's this contribution from?" she asked.

"The Society of Plaintiffs' Lawyers; they're clients of mine, you know. They just hope you vote the right way on Dick Vass's punitive damage bill. It may be assigned to your committee. It's a good bill, Karen."

"A lot of people think it's bad legislation." Karen gestured toward the pile of letters on her right. "These are all letters on that bill, and they run three to one against it. I'd have a hard time ignoring that."

"Well, let me make it a little easier for you," Borders said, flashing another toothy smile. "I'm prepared to make you an offer, just between the two of us, that if Vass's bill gets to your committee, and you help us pass it, my client will make you another campaign contribution. A very substantial campaign contribution."

Karen had heard enough; she stood up and pointed to the door.

"That's it, Emil. I don't like the way this conversation is going. You'd better leave. Now."

"Hold on, sweetheart," Borders said as he slowly rose to his feet. "Let's not be too hasty." He paused, glanced over his shoulder at the shut door, and added, "I'm talking about five thousand bucks, honey. Did you hear that?"

"I heard it, and I don't like it. I'd like you to go."

"Look, the bill's going to be passed anyway," he said with a shrug. "So why not get in on the action? Believe me, there's no harm done. None at all." He looked at her and smiled. "I know what your problem is. It's that husband of yours, isn't it? His law firm's in tight with the insurance industry. He probably won't let you vote for it."

"My husband never tells me how to vote. Nor does his law firm. They wouldn't dare."

"Well, if you've got a problem there, all you've got to do is miss the committee meeting when the bill comes up. Just don't hurt us. Say your car broke down or something. Since we're friends, I can still get you a couple of grand if you do that." Borders eyed Karen up and down in a discomforting way, then continued, lowering his voice slightly. "If you like, I'll get you your dough in cash and strictly off the record. Maybe you can take some special friend on a little junket. You know what I mean?"

"I said get out," Karen said, barely controlling her anger.

"Have it your way, honey." He turned and began walking toward the door.

"You forgot something, Emil," she said, pointing to the envelope and check on her desk.

"Ah, yes, so I did," he said in a feeble W. C. Fields imitation. He returned, picked up the check, and nodded to Karen with a smile. Then he put on his sunglasses, turned, and strolled from the room.

The mood was upbeat in the management committee meeting that week. The firm's billings and revenues were at record levels. The new offices in Los Angeles and Philadelphia appeared to be merging well into the firm and were already generating revenue. To handle the expansion of Imperial's medical malpractice work, Cal Cizma was now negotiating possible mergers with firms in Atlanta, New York, and Denver. Wilson & Thompson had passed five hundred lawyers and was now among the hundred largest law firms in the country. Tony Jeffries learned at the meeting that *The American Lawyer* was preparing a feature story about the firm that described it as the "emerging giant in the Midwest."

One city where Imperial was beginning to generate litigation, though not in sufficient volume to warrant a merger with a local firm, was St. Louis. Four malpractice cases had already been filed there, and more were expected. They needed a reliable St. Louis firm to which and who they could refer the cases. Tony said that an old friend of his from law school, Bill McGruder, was with one of the best litigation firms there, and he'd give him a call.

The decision to rent a flat in London was made without serious objection, although Ralph Stritch questioned it initially. Once he saw that all five of the younger committee members supported the motion, though, he withdrew his objection. They all agreed that Cal would supervise the arrangements, since he'd be returning to London shortly. Cal said he knew a woman on Imperial's staff who'd be able to help locate and furnish the apartment with at least that some rudiments of good taste.

Chester Melrose protested that perhaps he should make the next trip to London; after all, he'd been the one to nail the Imperial account; but Barton Thompson insisted that the difficulty Melrose was still having navigating on crutches would make that impractical. This trip in particular, he noted, demanded a younger man, someone who could traipse about looking for flats and furnishings.

The last item on the agenda was the renewal of the firm's liability insurance policy. Curly Morgan, chairman of the firm's insurance committee, surprised Tony and apparently everyone else by recommending that the firm change carriers and purchase coverage from Acorn Insurance, a newly formed Illinois company. He said that he had looked into the matter and found that they could save forty thousand dollars a year by insuring through Acorn.

When his recommendation was questioned, Curly played his trump card.

"I'll tell you the main reason we should go with Acorn," he said with an impish grin. "I've reached an understanding with the company's president, Red O'Kieffe. They don't insure any major law firm right now. If we go with them, they'll give us all their claims work, at our regular rates, guaranteed for at least the next three years. I figure that'll be worth at least three hundred thousand in fees next year alone, increasing every year after that. They want us as a flagship client, guys," he said, looking around the table.

"What sort of coverage will they provide?" George Lazenby asked. "That's important."

"Yes, I know," Curly answered. "It'll be the same

coverage that we have now: fifty-million-dollar max, with a five-hundred-thousand-dollar deductible. They're a strong, well-financed company and are fully approved by the Illinois Department of Insurance. I think it's a terrific deal."

"It certainly sounds like it," Thompson answered. "And I assume, Curly," he added with a slight smile, "that your group will handle the business they send to us."

"Of course."

"Well, if there's no objection," Thompson said, surveying the room, "consider it approved. Nice work, Curly; that's what I call creative marketing. All right, gentlemen, the meeting is adjourned."

Chapter Seven

The sleek 747 touched down at Heathrow a little after one p.m., under clear skies. Cal Cizma leaned back in his seat and smiled. Things were proceeding perfectly; so well, in fact, that no one had dared object when he had his secretary order him a first-class ticket. This, he decided, was how he was going to travel from now on: first class. He knew that if he created the image of success, even greater success would follow.

He picked up his bag and worked his way through the crowd toward the terminal's outer doors. Ronnie Dasher had left a message that "someone will meet you there."

As Cal stepped out onto the sidewalk and felt the cool, fresh London breeze, he saw a familiar figure leaning up against a black Rolls limo parked at the curb. It was Roxanne. He smiled at Dasher's little joke. *"Someone" indeed!* Roxanne was in a clinging black dress, and Cal felt a surge of excitement as he walked toward her. Her smile was as enticing as he'd remembered. She turned and slid into the car as he approached.

The driver came around, took his suitcase, and shut the door behind Cal. As he sat down, Cal noticed the seductive aroma, the closed window behind the driver's seat, and the head of an opened bottle of Champagne protruding from the ice bucket next to the television set.

"Cal, I'm so glad to see you," Roxanne murmured. She leaned forward with open lips and gave him the most sensuous kiss he'd ever experienced, her tongue dancing with his to a surging, seductive beat. "Welcome back to London," she whispered.

"This is a very pleasant surprise. I was expecting something else. I'm not sure what. But not this; and not you."

She leaned forward, took the Champagne and poured two glasses. "Well," she said, "Ronnie thought that since I'd picked out the flat, I should be the one to show it to you." She handed him a bubbling glass as the limo moved away from the curb, and raised her own to his.

Cal couldn't help grinning as they touched glasses and he took a full mouthful of the cold Champagne. Dasher sure knew how to take care of friends. Cal was already wondering how he could reciprocate if Dasher ever came to Chicago.

"Where am I going to be staying tonight?" he asked. That had been left up in the air.

"At the flat, of course." She smiled. "It's in Sloane Square. Furnished rather nicely, I think. Let's see how you like it."

Cal chuckled. What an arrangement! Of course he'd like it. "And my first meeting?" he asked.

"Is tomorrow at lunch," Roxanne answered. She smiled, leaned back against the tan leather seat, and put her hand on his. "Between now and then, you're free to do whatever you'd like."

"I think we should go to the flat," Cal said quietly. What an exhilarating turn his life had taken! He was never going to give this up.

—*mm*—

"I've gone through the file in the Roosevelt case, Carol, and I agree with you. There's a lot of exposure. We ought to make a real effort to settle."

Tony had spent the past hour reading through Blessed Trinity Hospital's records, the complaint filed on behalf of Sam and Bertha Roosevelt, and Carol's preliminary analysis of the case. Papers covered his desk. It was clear that this was a case that could easily get out of hand.

"I'll tell you another complication," Carol said, leaning back in her chair. "Walbrook, the company that made that CT scan machine, went into receivership last year. There's no way we're going to get even a token contribution from them."

"Beautiful."

"One problem in trying to settle it," Carol said, "is that we don't have any kind of a demand yet from Max

Greene, the Roosevelts' lawyer. I have no idea what he's looking for."

"I've dealt with him a couple of times before," Tony said. "A real scumbag. His license was suspended for a while a dozen or so years ago. He was the bagman for a judge who was on the take."

"Sounds like a real bottom feeder."

"He is. In personal injury cases, he refers out everything that he can't settle for a quick buck." Tony took a sip of his lukewarm coffee and looked up at Carol. "We might be able to use that to our advantage. If we can get some negotiations going before he peddles the file, we might be able to get a good settlement."

"It's probably worth a try," Carol answered. "If we could settle the case now for something in the area of, say, five hundred thousand, we'd be doing the hospital a big favor. If one of the pros, like Hansen or Granaldi, ever got their hands on this, it would cost a fortune before it was over, even with the cap on punitives."

"I know." Tony nodded and looked for Max Greene's phone number on the last page of the complaint. "All right, let's give our distinguished colleague Maximilian J. Greene a call. See if we can get a figure out of him." Tony punched the numbers, and hit the speaker button. The phone rang just once before it was answered.

"Hello."

It was a thick male voice that Tony recognized. *Greene still doesn't have a secretary.* "Hello, Max," he said. "This is Tony Jeffries at Wilson & Thompson. I'm calling about the Roosevelt case. I've got you on the speaker if you don't mind. Carol James is here with me."

"Hello, Max," Carol added, raising her voice.

"Well, this is quite an honor. Being called by two of Chicago's most prominent attorneys at the same time." Greene paused, then added, "What case did you say that you wanted to talk about?"

"The Roosevelt case, Max," Tony answered. He looked at Carol and shook his head. *"Samuel and Bertha Roosevelt versus Blessed Trinity Hospital."*

"Roosevelt. Roosevelt. Which case is that now? Let me think. I've got a lot of cases, you know."

"What a bunch of bullshit," Carol whispered.

"Oh, yes, the CT scan case," Greene said. "Now I remember. Terrible set of facts. You say you want to talk about it?"

"That's right," Tony answered. "I've gone through the file and I think this is a case that we ought to try to resolve. We have some exposure. We know that, and you know that. On the other hand, your clients could probably use the money now, rather than six or seven years from now, after a trial and an appeal or two. So it seems like the kind of case where both sides have something to gain by being reasonable early on."

"I'm glad to hear you say that, Jeffries. What kind of a figure did you have in mind?"

"Well, I don't want to bid against myself, Max. What are you looking for?"

"I don't have authority from my client to accept any

particular sum in settlement," Greene retorted. "But if you give me a number, I'll run it by her and get back to you."

Tony hesitated. He hated to put the first number on the table. It was important, though, to get negotiations started. He decided to lowball Greene, and leave himself plenty of room for movement later. "Two hundred thousand, Max," he said. "I can probably get you two hundred grand on this file."

"Two hundred thousand?" Greene's voice rang with feigned shock. "Jeffries, you've got to be kidding! This case is worth much more than two hundred grand."

"How much more?"

"Hard to tell at this point. We haven't had much discovery yet. I should probably take some depositions before I put a cap on my demand. Maybe that Indian radiologist, Rashdani, or that technician, Stanley what's-his-name. Who knows? I might get some nice admissions from one of them."

"Well, you may or you may not, Max. But I'd like to see if we can settle this case without spinning our wheels on a lot of additional discovery. Why don't you talk to your client and come back to us with a figure. If it's something reasonable, maybe we won't be that far apart. There's a little room for movement on our side."

"I would hope so." Max Greene chuckled, then added, "I'll talk to my lady about it, but I'm going to have to take a couple of deps before I can give you a number, Jeffries. I can tell you this, though; you're not going to get out of this one cheap."

"Okay, Max," Tony sighed. "Work out your deposition schedule with Carol." She nodded as he glanced at her. "But let's try to get this one resolved. We owe it to both our clients."

"I'll be in touch, Jeffries. Always a pleasure doing business with you. You too, Miss James. I'll send you a notice of the depositions I want."

The buzz on the speaker told them that he had hung up. Tony looked across his desk at Carol. "Well," he said, "at least we got the ball rolling."

"Too bad you couldn't get a figure out of him."

"Yeah, but nobody ever accused Max Greene of being stupid. Sleazy, yes, but not stupid." Tony took a sip of his coffee. "Let him take his depositions. He'll come back with a settlement figure before too long. In the meantime, I'm going to reserve the case at five hundred thousand."

Carol stood and began stacking up the papers scattered across Tony's desk. "Let me collect all this stuff," she said, "before you lose it. I'll put it all back in the file."

"Good idea. Wait a minute, though." Tony pulled a piece of blue-edged paper from the stack that Carol had assembled. "This is my Cubs schedule for the playoffs, assuming they hold on and make it. Don't want to lose that!"

Carol laughed, picked up the rest of the pile, and left.

The discussion with Max Greene had reminded Tony of a telephone call he should have made a week or two ago. He flipped through his Rolodex, found the number he was looking for, and punched it up on his phone. It was a direct dial-number, Tony recalled, and should go right through if the area code hadn't changed. It took only two rings.

"Carl McGruder here."

"Carl, this Tony Jeffries. How the hell are you?"

"Tony! I'm doing fine. Good to hear from you. It's been a couple of years, hasn't it?"

"It probably has. Now you're making me feel guilty."

Tony smiled and leaned back in his chair. It was great to hear McGruder's voice. They had become close friends at the University of Chicago Law School years ago, with neighboring rooms in the dorm, and helped each other through the difficult first two years. Both had gotten married between their second and third years, and entertained themselves and their wives during the third year with endless bridge games on Friday and Saturday evenings. That's all they could afford. On the rare occasions when they'd splurge, they'd go to Jimmy's Bar on 55th street for hamburgers and beer. They had kept in touch since then, less regularly in recent years, but remained staunch friends.

"How are Karen and the kids, Tony?" McGruder asked. "Your older boys have got to be in college by now, aren't they?"

"That's right, and Billy's joining them in the fall. I'm

learning how to spell the word 'tuition,' believe me!"
Tony laughed.

They chatted for a few minutes about their families
and old times; then Tony decided to give McGruder the
good news. "Carl, the reason I'm calling, aside from seeing how you're doing," he said, "is to send some business
your way."

"That's terrific. Tell me about it."

"All right." Tony got up and walked over to the window, the phone still in his hand. "Our office administers
a book of medical mal litigation for a British underwriter,
the Imperial Syndicate. You may have heard of them."

"I sure have. They're one of the big boys."

"That's right. They've written a policy that covers
two hospitals down your way, one in St. Louis, the other
in University Heights. Four claims have come in already,
and there are bound to be more. I wonder if your firm
would like to handle them?"

"Absolutely," McGruder answered. "We have some
background in med mal, so we could hit the deck running." He paused a second and continued. "The only
question I've got, Tony, is how does Imperial pay its bills?
Some of those London underwriters are painfully slow."

"That won't be a problem at all with these cases, Carl.
You see, our office pays the bills. An escrow account's
been set up for that purpose, so we can process and pay
any invoices within a couple of days."

"That's great! That's always the main question when
you handle cases for London."

"I know," Tony answered, pleased with the fact that his old friend knew his way around the London insurance market. "But don't worry about it. You'll get our checks before the ink on your bills is even dry. I'll guarantee it."

"Hell, I can't beat that. Send those files down here, and I'll take good care of them for you. And I'll guarantee *that*."

"I know you'll do a good job, Carl. We'll send these first four files this afternoon. And we'll send you all the other new cases that are filed in the St. Louis area. It's going to be fun working together again."

"It sure will!" McGruder laughed. "Say, check your calendar, Tony. The Cubs might be playing the Cards in the playoffs and I've got dibs on four tickets to one home game. You and Karen should come down, and let us put you up and take you out to the ballgame. We'll make a weekend out of it."

"That sounds great. I'll get back to you on that."

Tony Jeffries walked back to his desk, hung up, and couldn't help smiling. Carl McGruder sounded as irrepressible as ever. He was glad that the Imperial business gave them a good excuse to get together again. And it felt good to be able to do a favor for an old friend.

--~~~--

Bertha sat on the weather-beaten bench and watched the two geese paddling around the edge of the lagoon, occasionally dipping down into the water for some hidden snack. She wondered if these were the same two geese that she and Sam had watched and fed last year. They looked the same; and geese, Bertha had heard, mated for life--just like her and Sam. She felt guilty that she didn't have something to offer them, as old friends. But Sam was the one who brought the bread for the geese; he always thought ahead like that. There was a slight chill in the air--a reminder that summer was turning into fall.

She and Sam had walked to Douglas Park on Sunday afternoons for years. And they usually ended up sitting on this same old bench on the north side of the lagoon, watching and feeding the geese. When he was younger, Robert would come with them, but the last couple of years he usually stayed home to practice his trumpet.

This was the kind of day that Sam loved. Bertha sighed. She missed him. She pulled a handkerchief from her pocket and dabbed the tears in her eyes. She knew he'd never be with her in the park again.

~*~

Pete Spanos pulled the white business envelope from his inside pocket, glanced at it for a second, then handed it across the linen-covered table. "Frankie, with this, you've hit forty thousand in consulting fees," he said. "That's not too bad for only half a year."

"No, it's not."

Frank Donatelli took the envelope, opened it, glanced inside, and slipped it into his coat pocket. "Of course, that means that you've gotten four hundred thousand in legal fees. That's not too shabby, either."

"The firm gets the fees, Frankie, not me--at least not directly," Pete corrected him. "But you're right. This arrangement is working out well for both of us." He raised his glass of Chablis to his friend, who touched it with his Bloody Mary. Pete emptied his glass, signaled Luis for another couple of drinks, and leaned back in satisfaction as he contemplated the success of their plan.

They had been meeting here at the Skyline Club monthly ever since Donatelli began sending his directors and officers insurance cases to Pete. It was a perfect location for their quiet discussions. The club was never crowded, and Luis always gave them one of the corner tables, far from curious ears and eyes.

Donatelli's American Union business, coming on the heels of his appointment to the management committee, had caused Pete's stature within the firm to rise sharply the past six months. His total fees collected last year were a little over five hundred thousand dollars. This year they would triple that, and most of the increase was from American Union. Pete knew that he would receive a significant bonus at the end of the year, besides the midyear ones they'd all received, plus an increase in his points. And his position on the management committee would be set in stone.

"Frankie, what've you been up to lately? Beside doing a lot of consulting." They both chuckled.

"I'll tell you, Pete, I've been working my ass off. I

haven't had an easy day since I got back from Vegas two weeks ago. There's a big claim in Pennsylvania that's getting out of hand. A suit's probably going to be filed this week, and we're trying to get ready for it."

"What kind of a case is it?" Pete asked as he sipped his wine.

"Classic environmental fuckup. This company we've insured since the fifties, a plastics manufacturer, has apparently been dumping nine different kinds of chemical shit into the river there for years. No one knows how long. And now the EPA claims our guys have contaminated half the drinking water in the state of Pennsylvania. Negotiations have been impossible. The feds are getting ready to file a suit, and it's going to be a monster."

"Who's going to defend it for you?" Frank's problem was suddenly sounding very interesting.

"DeLong and Rogers in Philadelphia," Frank said as he speared a piece of prosciutto off the appetizer plate. "They handle all our environmental litigation east of the Mississippi. It's right in their backyard."

"You know, Frankie, we have an office in Philadelphia now."

Frank looked at him for a second, then laughed. "No way, Pete. Those guys are experts in that stuff. If I gave the case to you it would stink to high heaven."

"We'd need a consultant if we got that case," Pete added quietly, leaning forward.

"That's for sure, Pete!" Frank laughed. "A *real* consultant. No, Pete; forget it."

"Wait a minute, Frankie, let's talk about this. Let's figure out how you can get that case to us and not raise any eyebrows in the process." The case sounded great - a real fee cow. There had to be some way to get it.

"Can't be done," Frank repeated, shaking his head.

"Who's in charge of environmental litigation at DeLong and Rogers?"

"Lou Rogers. He's been doing that work for at least ten years. Put together a team of solid pros to back him up, too."

"Who are his top lieutenants? The people who really do the work?"

Frank shrugged. "He's got three or four younger partners who work for him. They're all good."

"Who's the best of that bunch, Frankie?"

"Hard to say. Probably Mike Vance." He paused, then nodded. "Yeah, I'd say Vance is his best man."

"How old is this guy Vance?"

"I'd guess about thirty-two, thirty-three. Something like that."

"Is he a full partner yet?"

Pete was putting a wonderful plan together in his mind. He wondered how long it would take Frank to figure out where he was going. He took a drink of wine and leaned back in his chair. *Yes, this could work.*

"No, I don't think so," Frank answered. "The word is that they're slow on promoting people to equity partners, but they make up for it with nice bonuses."

"All right, Frankie, here's the plan." Pete smiled,

leaned forward, and lowered his voice. "Our firm will make this guy Mike Vance an offer he can't refuse. We'll make him a full partner in our Philadelphia office and put him in charge of our environmental litigation there. We'll make sure he gets a big raise; maybe even a signing bonus. You wouldn't have any problem in sending that case to us then, would you?"

"Jesus, Pete, could you do that?"

"Trust me, for a case like this, I can do it." Pete had no idea whether he could pull that off or not. If the case promised enough in fees, maybe he could. But right now he had to get Frank committed; he'd work out the rest later.

"I don't know, Pete." Frank shook his head. "Even with Vance in your shop, it would still look awfully funny. Lou Rogers would bitch like hell. I'd have a tough time explaining it."

"Even with our usual consulting arrangement? It would be a big one in this case."

"I know that, Pete, and the dough *would* be nice, but..." His voice trailed off as he stared down at his drink and swirled it around and around in his glass.

"Let me throw in a sweetener, Frankie." Pete knew that he almost had him. A little more would do it.

Donatelli looked up from his drink without saying a word.

"I told you that our firm's got this beautiful condo in London, didn't I?" Pete asked. "A flat, as the Brits say. What if I arranged for you and your wife to have it all to yourself for two weeks? Fully stocked bar and kitchen; replenished three times a week. Daily maid service. Won't cost you a nickel, except to get there. Could probably arrange for you to have it every year for a couple of weeks. Your own timeshare in the heart of London--on the house. How's that sound to you?"

Frank Donatelli leaned back in his chair, chuckling. "It sounds pretty damn good," he said with a huge grin. "Too damn good to turn down."

"Then let me propose a toast," Pete said, returning the grin. "To my new partner, Mike Vance--whoever the hell he is."

The biggest annual social event at Wilson & Thompson was the late-September dinner-dance welcoming the new class of incoming associates--an obligatory affair not-so-affectionately nicknamed the Prom. This year, like the previous three years, it was being held in the Fairmont Hotel.

Carol James usually dreaded these events. The conversations were often forced or awkward. After dinner, except for the few who were into dancing, the men would gravitate to the bar and leave the women at the tables, where Carol would be forced into dreary discussions of raising children.

But this year was going to be different; Carol was determined to avoid that trap. She'd excuse herself for a drink at the same time that the men did; she certainly felt much more comfortable discussing business with them than she did discussing children with the women. Then, too, from a career standpoint, it was essential that the male partners accept her as an equal and not view her as merely a social contemporary of their wives.

She and Bill Turple arrived at the Fairmont by cab a little after seven and took the escalator up to the second-floor ballroom. Two young women who worked for the firm had a small table covered with nametags outside the ballroom door. Some people complained that nametags were tacky and unnecessary, but Carol was always relieved when she saw that table; she never could remember everyone's name.

The ballroom was jammed when they walked in. It took occasions like this to make them realize just how big the firm had become. Hundreds of people were milling about, trying to carry on little conversations above the din of the crowd and the background music of a cocktail quartet. Servers in black and white moved sinuously through the throng, some taking drink orders and others carrying plates of hors d'oeuvres.

Two of the first people Carol and Bill ran across were Cal and Sandy Cizma. Cal was complaining about the "lazy-ass trolley dollies" on his recent trip back from London. Carol had always liked Sandy, so warm and considerate. But Cal, even though superficially friendly, was way too pushy. He always seemed to be networking. It took him less than a minute to begin pumping Bill for business. *That's a useless exercise*, Carol laughed to herself. She'd already raised the subject with Bill, under much more relaxed circumstances, and knew that he wasn't in a position to influence where his firm sent their work.

While Bill and Cal were talking, Carol saw an opportunity she didn't want to let pass. She quietly excused herself and stepped over to Barton Thompson and Chester Melrose, who were talking just a few feet away.

"Good evening, gentlemen," Carol said with a smile. "Once again you've hosted a magnificent party."

"Thank you, Carol," Thompson nodded. "We're delighted that you and your friend could attend." He turned to Melrose. "It's not like the old days, is it, Chester, when all of us could sit around one big table and take turns toasting each other."

"No, I'm afraid not." Melrose chuckled. "We've grown an awful lot the past twenty, twenty-five years."

"I wanted to tell you, Mr. Melrose, how much I'm enjoying working on your medical malpractice cases," Carol said. "Some of them are really fascinating."

"Well, you're doing a marvelous job, Carol," he answered. "That's been a very profitable book of business so far, and I know that a lot of the credit for that should go to you."

"Thank you. I hope you'll remember that when I'm considered for equity partnership next year," Carol said, struggling to maintain a broad smile.

Chester Melrose laughed, nodded and smiled at her.

"I don't think you have anything to worry about. You've been doing a fine job for years, and not just on these new files. We all know that. Wouldn't you agree, Barton?"

"Absolutely," Thompson replied. "Tony Jeffries has been very complimentary of your work. With him and Chester here backing you, you shouldn't have any problem at all. You certainly have my support."

"Thank you." Carol grinned. That was just what she'd been hoping to hear. A feeling of warm satisfaction welled up inside her. She was going to make equity partner. All the time she'd put in *had* been worthwhile. She decided to excuse herself before she said something stupid. "Well, I should be getting back to Bill," she said, still smiling broadly. "And I really appreciate your comments."

Carol hardly noticed what she was eating for dinner that evening. While everyone else at their table was raving about the food, she was running through her discussion with Barton Thompson and Chester Melrose, over and over again. No, there wasn't any doubt; they had committed themselves. She would be made an equity partner next year unless she really screwed something up. And she wasn't going to let *that* happen.

"Carol, you haven't even touched your roast beef," Bill said to her quietly. "Are you feeling all right?"

"Yes, I feel fine. Wonderful, as a matter of fact." She smiled at him, took her knife and fork, and cut off a small piece of the beef. It *was* good.

The other people at their table included Pete and Lucy Spanos, Jeff Marks and his wife, Gloria, from Los

Angeles, and Charlie and Chris Dickenson. Jeff had recently joined the firm, coming in as a full partner when his office in L.A. merged into Wilson & Thompson a few months back.

"How 'bout those Cubbies?" Pete said. "They've clinched the division, and Kerry Wood is scheduled to start the playoffs next week against the Braves. I'll tell you, they could go all the way this year."

"I agree." Bill responded. "With Wood and Mark Prior pitching back-to-back in every series, I don't see anyone stopping them."

"Well, Pete's big new activity this fall is soccer." Lucy Spanos volunteered to everyone, raising her voice slightly. "He was able to duck it with our older boy, who was never much of an athlete. But our youngest, Billy-- or Bill as he insists we call him now--loves to play. He talked Pete into being their team's assistant coach. And the surprising thing is that Pete loves it. Isn't that right, honey?" She turned to her husband, who was finishing his glass of wine.

"That's right," Pete answered. "But please don't tell Billy or his friends that I was never a jock. As far as they know, I taught David Beckham everything he knows. If the kids knew the truth, my credibility as a coach would be shot forever."

The Markses' son, as it turned out, also played soccer. Gloria Marks remarked, "It's pretty exciting to watch our little boys suddenly becoming little men."

Pete pushed his chair back and stood up. "I'm going

to get us some refills," he said, stretching a bit. "Jeff, you want to join me?"

"Good idea," Jeff replied, rising to his feet. "I'll be back in a few minutes, dear. I'll get you a sherry."

"Thank, Jeff." Gloria Marks smiled at her husband, then turned back to Lucy Spanos.

Carol turned to Bill. "Why don't we get some drinks too?" she said, putting her napkin on the table.

"I've got a better idea: why don't we dance? I like this number."

It was a slow dance; Carol could deal with that, and it would get her away from the table. She took Bill's hand and followed him onto the floor. There were enough people dancing so that Carol didn't feel self-conscious. Tony and Karen Jeffries were dancing too, and Carol gave them a little wave. They always looked so comfortable together.

It felt good having Bill up close to her on the dance floor. She loved the musky masculine aroma of his after-shave. She leaned her head up against him and tried to think how long it had been since they had made love. Too long, she decided.

"I got some news today, Carol," he whispered. "I'm not sure whether it's good or bad, though."

"What's that?" she asked softly.

"I'm being offered the position in Toronto. Managing partner. They want me to go up there next week to meet the staff and to take over on October thirteenth."

Carol felt her shoulders sag as she let out her breath.

She stopped dancing and stepped back a few inches; her arms dropped to her side. She felt terribly empty. She looked at Bill and tried to say something, but couldn't.

"And I want you to come with me, Carol. As my wife. Let's get married here, with our friends, and go up there as a couple."

"And I should resign from the firm?"

"Not necessarily," he answered. "Maybe you can convince them to open an office in Toronto. They're opening offices in other cities."

She turned away from him, shaking her head from side to side. "But not in Toronto. I've already looked into that." She glanced at him for a moment. "None of our major clients do business there. And Imperial Insurance, who I do most of my work for, isn't even licensed in Ontario. It's not going to happen, Bill."

"Well, then, to hell with the firm! There are some things that are more important. Like having a happy personal life, and maybe raising a family. Think about that."

"Maybe *you* should think about that." She turned and looked him straight in the eye. "Why do you have to go to Toronto? Why don't you just stay here? We can get married and live very well here on both our salaries. And if I make equity partner at the end of next year, which I fully expect to do, we can live damn well."

They were standing in the center of the dance floor, oblivious to the stepped-up tempo of the music or the other couples moving around them.

"But I *have* to take the job in Toronto, Carol. My

career's on the line. If I turn this down, I'll never be offered another managerial position."

"And *my* career doesn't count? The ten years I've put in here don't matter?" The more Carol talked about it, the angrier she became. No, she was *not* going to throw all this away.

"I guess, Carol, you're going to have to make a decision," he said quietly, stepping a little closer to her. "I have to take the job in Toronto. I want you to be there with me, as my wife. We can have a nice life there. But you have to decide."

Carol took a deep breath, looked away, then looked back at him.

"I'm sorry, Bill. I'm not leaving Chicago."

They looked into each other's eyes for a moment. Bill nodded, then said quietly, "Well, I guess that's it, isn't it?"

"I guess so." Carol wanted the conversation to end quickly. She wasn't going to change her mind, but she didn't want to start crying right there in the middle of the dance floor.

"Maybe you should leave, Bill. I'll take a cab home."

"Okay." He hesitated. "Are you going to be all right?"

"I'll be fine. Goodbye, Bill."

"Goodbye, Carol." He looked at her for a few seconds, then turned and snaked through the dancers toward the door.

Carol dabbed her eye with her handkerchief, threw back her shoulders, and walked toward the bar and her partners.

Chapter Eight

—*ww*—

"This environmental suit for American Union is going to generate at least a million dollars in fees each year for the next four years, maybe more." Pete Spanos looked up and down the management committee table. "We can't let this opportunity get away."

"And you're saying, Pete, that if we bring in this fellow Mike Vance, American Union will give us the case?" Tony asked. He knew full well the deal that Spanos was proposing; they had discussed it just before the meeting. But there were some aspects of it that bothered Tony, and he wanted the whole proposal put on the table.

"Right. That's the commitment I have from my contact at American Union. But to get Vance, we're going to have to make him a full partner. I've already spoken to him, and there's no other way that he's going to leave DeLong and Rogers."

"One problem that I see, Pete," Tony responded, "is that he's only eight years out of law school. We've got a half-dozen nonequity partners here who are more senior than that, including one who works for me, Carol James. I don't think it would be fair to bring in someone like Vance and leapfrog him over people who've been doing a good job for us for nine or ten years."

"Are you saying, Tony, that you're opposed to this deal, which is probably worth four million bucks, simply because Vance would have to be brought in as a full partner?" Pete asked.

"No, that's not what I'm saying. It sounds like this would be a great case to get. It would make the Philadelphia office a real profit center for the next couple of years. I'm concerned about the question of fairness, as well as the morale of our younger partners. If we're going to make Mike Vance a full partner, then we should make our other people with comparable seniority full partners at the same time; at least the ones who have been doing a good job."

"Now just a minute, Tony," Ralph Stritch said, raising his hand. "You're mixing apples and oranges. If we make this fellow Vance an equity partner it will be strictly a business proposition; and on that basis, I might go along with it. But I certainly don't want us to bring in equity partners wholesale. Everyone else should wait their turn, like we all did."

"I agree." Barton Thompson nodded. "We're going to have to make it clear, though, to Carol James and the others, that our bringing Vance in ahead of them shouldn't be taken as some sort of rejection or disapproval. They're a fine bunch of lawyers, and we wouldn't want to lose any of them. Tony, you explain it to all of them, will you? You can also tell them that if any of them delivers four million dollars in business, we'll make them equity partners ahead of schedule too." Thompson chuckled at his little joke.

"But what if we make this guy Vance, who most of us have never even met, an equity partner, and the business doesn't materialize?" Tony protested. "That could happen. And if it did, we'd look pretty foolish."

"That's a valid concern, Tony," Pete Spanos answered, leaning forward. "I've given that some thought. The whole premise of bringing Vance in as a full partner is that American Union's environmental case will follow him in the door - and, we hope, some more business too. If, for whatever reason, that doesn't happen, we'd also *have* to promote everyone else his age. Otherwise, we'd have a revolt on our hands. Now, I agree with Ralph that we don't want to bring in a whole gang of new capital partners. So we have to protect ourselves. We have to have some insurance that we won't be caught in that trap."

"I think you've stated the problem pretty well, Pete," Cal said. "What's the solution? Or is there one?"

"Yes, I think there is," Pete said, speaking slowly. "It involves playing a little hardball." He shrugged. "But it may solve the potential problem that Tony has pointed out. We bring Vance in, but we don't get around to having him sign the partnership agreement until we actually get the case from American Union. If something happens, and we don't get the file, we'll tell him there was a misunderstanding, and he's going to be a nonequity partner here. I'll have someone with me, probably you, Cal, whenever we discuss partnership issues before he comes over; and if we don't get the business, we'll simply deny that we made a commitment. Vance will be madder than hell; but what's he going to do about it? Quit? Under those circumstances, fine. We don't need him."

"Wait a minute," Tony said, leaning back in his chair. "That's a hell of a thing to do to somebody - especially someone we're calling our partner. I've never met Vance, but if we make a deal, whatever it is, we should be prepared to stick with it. I don't think you've proposed any solution at all."

"I'm just trying to respond to your concerns, Tony," Pete answered across the table. "Holding back the partnership agreement until we know we've got the American Union case is a way of being fair to our junior partners. If Vance can't really deliver those kind of fees, he's no different from the rest of them."

"But you're not going to tell him that up front?"

"Of course not. If we did, he might not come."

"Boy, that *is* playing hardball," Tony said, shaking his head. *Should I continue to object?* he wondered. *Try to block the deal? I probably wouldn't accomplish anything and would just look like an obstructionist! What the hell!* "All right, I'll go along with it," Tony said. "But I am a little uncomfortable."

There was a moment of silence while Barton Thompson looked up and down the table. "Anyone else?"

No one responded. Curly Morgan and Rasheed Collins looked down when Tony glanced their way.

"All right, it's decided," Thompson said. "We'll make Mr. Vance an offer of equity partnership and place him in charge of environmental litigation in our Philadelphia office. Pete, you follow through on this. Promise Mr. Vance the moon, but be a little vague on the details. Give him the partnership agreement to sign only after we receive the environmental case from American Union."

"Fine, I'll take care of it," Pete replied. "And I assume it's understood that Vance will be in my group and that I'll get the origination credit for this business."

"Of course," Thompson answered. "American Union is *your* client."

Tony was still churning the Vance deal over in his mind while Chester Melrose reported on the firm's finances. Billings and collections remained at record levels, and the firm had been able to make its annual contribution to its pension plan much earlier than had been budgeted. The Imperial Insurance fund was still quite healthy; after paying itself $650,000 in fees and expenses, the firm still retained a balance of almost $800,000 in the Imperial account. Tony's attention picked up when he heard that partners' expenses in traveling to London were now being paid directly from the Imperial account. *When was that decided?*

When Melrose finished his report, Curly Morgan

added that the first new files had been received from Acorn Insurance; three, to be exact. He'd been advised just yesterday by Acorn's president, Red O'Kieffe, that a number of other cases were in the pipeline.

They had covered all the items on the agenda, and Tony was folding up his notes and getting ready to leave, when Ralph Stritch spoke up.

"Barton," he said, "there's something else that we should discuss today, I believe." He cleared his throat and glanced across the table at George Lazenby. "Your term as chairman expires next month." He turned in his chair and looked directly at Thompson. "In the past, by this time, there's always been an understanding as to who the new chairman would be. As far as I know, no such under-standing has been reached yet on your successor. Perhaps it's time to set some wheels in motion."

Tony froze. Thompson's jaw was set, and the mus-cles on his neck rippled in anger. He glared at Stritch and seemed about to speak when George Lazenby followed the attack.

"Ralph's right, Barton," he said. "I checked my re-cords, and I'm afraid your term *does* expire next month. You'll recall, I'm sure, that when you were given this ex-tension, it was agreed that it would be your last."

Thompson wheeled and stared at Lazenby. "Well, I'm still chairman today," he hissed through clenched teeth. "And I will be for the next month, perhaps longer. Until then, any discussions of a successor are out of order. This meeting is adjourned!" He pushed his chair back, shot a searing glance at Ralph Stritch, then stood and strode from the room. Tony and the other younger members of the committee sat in stunned silence.

Before Tony could say anything, Lazenby, Stritch, and Melrose rose and left, speaking quietly to one another.

"Jesus Christ," Curly muttered after they'd left. "How the hell is *this* going to be resolved?"

"I don't know," Cal answered. "But I've got a hunch we're going to have to vote on something before long. And if we vote wrong, it'll be a real career buster."

—uun—

Pete Spanos had never been so proud. The groundbreaking for the addition to Saints Peter and Paul was being conducted that afternoon. The patriarch had asked Pete and his family to sit at the head table at the dedication dinner, in recognition of the generous gift that he gave to the church.

Pete's mother, sitting at his right, reached over and squeezed his hand when the patriarch mentioned the special gift that Pete had given. It wasn't clear to the audience that the donation came from Wilson & Thompson rather than from Pete Spanos personally, but that didn't matter. What mattered was that Maria Spanos was basking in her son's success; she was smiling and giving little waves to all her old friends in the congregation. Pete loved it.

Things had been going extraordinarily well for Pete the past few months. It all began when he decided to take

Uncle Ed's advice and become more aggressive in making sure things went his way. The agreement he'd reached with Barton Thompson was a good example. He had figured out what Thompson really wanted, reelection as chairman, agreed to help him get it, and in return got the donation for his church. It was so simple. Uncle Ed was right, everyone *does* have his price, and if you keep that in mind there's no limit on how well you can do.

———

"What do you mean, you didn't even try out for the basketball team?" Cal snapped. He crumpled the newspaper down on the couch beside him and stared at his son, who was slowly hanging his jacket up in the front hall closet.

"There wasn't any point, Dad."

"What? I can't hear you. Don't look away when you're talking to me."

"I said there wasn't any point," Lenny said, turning toward his father. "I mean, I talked to the coach, and he… well, you know, he had his team already picked. They won the conference last year, and all the starters are back."

"But you didn't even try out?" Cal couldn't believe that his son had given up so easily. He stood and walked over to Lenny. Out of the corner of his eye he saw Sandy come in from the kitchen

"That's right, Dad," the lanky teenager muttered. He turned sideways to his father, looked down, and added,

"You can't walk on as a senior and expect to make the basketball team at a school like New Trier."

"You probably had that all figured out before you even talked to the coach, didn't you?" Cal said. Lenny was never going to succeed at anything with an attitude like that. "You just gave up, didn't you!"

Lenny turned to walk away. "Bullshit," he muttered under his breath.

"What did you say?" Cal snapped. None of his children had ever used that kind of language with him before, and he wasn't going to let it start now. He grabbed Lenny by the arm and spun him around.

"I said 'bullshit'!" Tears began filling Lenny's eyes. "I love basketball. I would have started if we'd stayed in Broadview. Why the hell did we have to move up here?"

Cal's hand snapped up and slapped Lenny hard across the face. Lenny's glasses flew off and he staggered back, tripped over a footstool, and fell to the floor.

"Don't ever use that language with me again, young man!" Cal said, pointing at Lenny. He looked at Sandy, who was watching him with her hands at her face. "And you," he said, pointing at her, "you've been poisoning the kids against the North Shore. You started it even before we moved here. You weren't going to let it succeed, were you?"

He glared at her for a moment, turned, and walked into the den for a drink.

—*mm*—

Bertha Roosevelt got off the subway at the Randolph Street stop, worked her way through the panhandlers and street musicians on the platform, and headed toward the escalator. She kept a tight hand on her purse as one person after another jostled her in the crowd. She'd been robbed there twice before, and she wasn't going to let it happen again.

On Randolph Street she got her bearings and headed west toward 188. A big clock in front of one of the stores read 3:30; she wouldn't have any trouble making her appointment with attorney Greene.

She called him that morning at the insistence of her sister, Carolla. She had been complaining to Carolla about her financial difficulties, and Carolla told her to talk to the lawyer. Their case against the hospital was good, she'd said, and the lawyer should be able to advance Bertha some money from the settlement. Bertha was nervous about calling attorney Greene, and probably wouldn't have, except that the landlord showed up later that morning and gave her something called a Landlord's Five-Day Notice. Bertha hadn't paid her rent in three months and knew that sooner or later this would happen. So she called attorney Greene and told him that she wanted to see him about money. He seemed understanding and asked her to stop by around four.

It was a longer walk to 188 West Randolph than Bertha remembered, and she had to stop twice along the way to catch her breath.

When she reached the building she went inside, dug

an envelope out of her purse and held it up close to look at the numbers in the corner. They were written in a fancy script that was hard to read, especially in the dim lobby lighting. And she hadn't replaced her glasses since her purse was stolen a couple of weeks ago.

1567. She could make out the numbers now. Attorney Greene's office was in room 1567.

She found the elevators that went to floors 14 through 29, got in an empty one, and pushed the button for 15. After a few seconds the doors slowly shut and she could feel the elevator ascending. It had a funny smell: the same smell Bertha remembered from the washrooms in the old Greyhound station.

On the fifteenth floor Bertha got out and turned to her right. She remembered that the lawyer's office was down at the end of the hallway. The door to 1567 was frosted glass, with Maximilian J. Greene, Attorney-at-Law painted on it in fading letters. She stopped in front of it and looked at her watch. The light here was even dimmer than downstairs, and she held the watch close to her eyes to read it. It was ten minutes to four. She was on time.

Bertha opened the office door and walked into a small reception area. It had the old wooden desk she remembered from before, and two straight-back chairs against one wall. Through the doorway on the opposite side of the room she saw attorney Greene working at his desk. He glanced up, smiled when he saw her, and stood up.

"Come on in, Mrs. Washington," he said, coming around his desk. He stopped, shook his head and corrected himself, "I'm sorry, it's Roosevelt, isn't it. Mrs. Roosevelt." He met her at the inner doorway and took her hand. His palm was sweaty, and she discretely wiped her hand on the side of her dress when he let it go.

"I let my secretary go home early today," he said as he gestured toward the empty reception room. "So I can't offer you a cup of coffee. But come on in and have a seat."

His secretary hadn't been there the last time she was there, either. Bertha wondered where she sat when she *was* there, since there wasn't any chair behind the old desk.

Attorney Greene's desk was covered with papers. He must be a terribly busy man, Bertha thought. On the wall behind his desk was a collection of framed certificates. Bertha couldn't make them out, but she did notice that most of them were hanging crooked. *That's something a good secretary should take care of,* she thought. In the corner, next to the window, was a wastebasket overflowing with crumpled papers. Lying next to it was a small stack of newspapers.

"Well, Mrs. Roosevelt, you're looking good," attorney Greene said as he sat down behind his desk. Bertha had taken the wooden armchair in front of it. "Now, what was it that you wanted to see me about today?" he asked, leaning forward on both elbows.

"It's about money," Bertha answered. She felt terribly uncomfortable. She took a deep breath, then went on. "I'm flat broke, attorney Greene," she said. "My landlord is going to throw us out if I don't pay the rent. I'm supposed to be getting welfare checks, but for some reason they never come. I just don't know what to do. I make a little bit cleaning two houses in Kenwood, but that just barely pays for our groceries." She hesitated, then said what she had to say. "I was wondering if there was some way I could get an advance on the settlement we're going to get from the hospital."

Greene leaned back in his chair, shaking his head from side to side, his eyes still on Bertha. "You know, Mrs. Roosevelt," he answered. "This is going to be a very tough case. They haven't offered anything in settlement yet."

"Nothing?"

"Not a dime."

Bertha let out her breath. She felt a hollow feeling in her stomach. *Nothing?* Her mind was swimming; what was she going to do? "But I thought you said we had a good case," she ventured after a moment. "You said we'd get some money."

"I know I did, and I still believe we will," he answered. "But they're not going to make it easy for us. Their attorneys are probably trying to generate some fees on this case. The big firms often do that; it's terrible. It looks like we're going to have to go through a lot of discovery before they'll make us any kind of a serious offer. In fact, I'm taking the depositions of some of the hospital personnel next week."

"Do you think they'll offer us some money after that?"

"Mrs. Roosevelt, with the approach they're taking, it

could be several years before we see any money in your case. Several years."

"Oh my God." Bertha leaned back in the hard chair and shut her eyes. Her head began to hurt terribly.

"But I would like to help you somehow." Greene's words were like cool, fresh water washing over Bertha. She opened her eyes and looked at him. He was smiling. "I know you're in an awkward position," he said. "So let me suggest this. I'm not a wealthy man. But I could scrape together some money, maybe as much as two thousand dollars, if that would help you. And in exchange, we would modify the fee agreement between us."

"Two thousand dollars!" Bertha blurted. "That would be wonderful. I could pay most of my bills. Oh, attorney Greene, thank you, thank you!"

He smiled and held up his hand. "I'm just glad that I *can* help." He opened his right-hand desk drawer and pulled out an envelope. It contained a stack of money bound by a rubber band. He thumbed through the bills, quietly counting.

"There's two thousand dollars here," he said when he had finished. He laid the bills halfway between them on his desk. Then he picked up a piece of white paper that had been lying to his left, looked at it for a moment, and handed it to her.

"This is an amendment to our fee agreement," he said. "It changes my fee from one-third to one-half of whatever we recover, plus our expenses, of course. If you'll just sign this, you can take your money with you today." He smiled again as he handed Bertha a ballpoint pen.

"Half the money? That doesn't sound quite fair, attorney Greene." Bertha wasn't very good at numbers, but that seemed like an awful lot. "I think maybe I should talk it over with my sister."

"Well, you do whatever you think you should do," attorney Greene said, reaching forward and pulling the stack of bills slightly away from her. "But I'm leaving town tomorrow and won't be back for two weeks."

Bertha had to get some money *now*. In two weeks she and Robert might be out on the street. She took a deep breath, scribbled across the bottom of the paper and handed it back to him. He signed it too, added his notary's stamp, then folded the paper and put it in his desk drawer.

"And here's your money," he said, smiling again as he pushed the pile of bills toward her. "I want you to count it, to make sure it's all there."

Bertha took the money and cradled it in her hands for a moment, just looking at it. She had never held two thousand dollars before. There was a crisp hundred-dollar bill on top. She flipped it back and saw another crisp hundred-dollar bill beneath it….and another beneath that. She thumbed through them, pretending to count. She knew that the number was right; she had seen attorney Greene count them, and he wasn't likely to make a mistake. She put the bills back into the envelope, carefully placed the envelope in the inner pocket of her purse, and snapped the purse shut.

"Attorney Greene, you're a good man," she said, looking up at him.

"Thank you, Bertha. I hope you don't mind if I call you Bertha."

She smiled and shook her head.

"Fine. Now, Bertha, I don't want you telling anyone else about our little deal here. Lawyers aren't supposed to give money to their clients, and I might get into trouble if the wrong people found out. So, this is just between the two of us, all right?"

"Oh, yes sir, attorney Greene. I certainly wouldn't want you to get into any kind of trouble. Not after what you've done for me."

They both stood up and he walked around the desk to take her hand. His palm felt even wetter than before. She turned, and as she walked into the reception room, once more wiped her hand on her dress.

In the elevator on the way down Bertha decided she'd go straight to the landlord's and pay up her rent; then she'd find Mr. Rees and arrange for Robert to start taking his trumpet lessons again. Things were working out just fine!

—⁓⁓—

"Mr. Cizma, there's a gentlemen here in the reception room who has something for you. His name is Jones, and he says he was instructed to deliver it to you personally."

Cal put down the phone, buzzed his secretary, and

told her to head for the reception room and bring back Mr. Jones. It sounded like he was someone's courier. The Brits were always doing things like that.

As Cal waited, he leaned back and admired his collection of British naval paintings hanging on the opposite wall. He had insisted on, and finally received, a larger office, and he'd filled the added wall space with reminders to everyone of his connection to London.

After a few moments, Mr. Jones was escorted into Cal's office. He was in his fifties, wearing a rumpled gray suit, a clipboard holding a number of documents in his left hand. He didn't look like much of a courier.

"I'm Cal Cizma, Mr. Jones." Cal rose to greet him. "What can I do for you?"

"Mr. Cizma, I'm Wallace Jones from the Sheriff's Office. I have some papers for you." Jones loosened a bundle from his clipboard and handed it to him.

"What's this?" Cal asked. He didn't have any business with the Sheriff's Office. He scribbled his signature on the receipt that Jones put in front of him on the clipboard, and unfolded the papers he'd been handed.

"Son-of-a-bitch!"

It was a Complaint for Divorce. *Sandra Cizma versus Calvin Cizma.*

"There's also a Temporary Restraining Order there, Mr. Cizma," Jones told him. "Until further order of the court you're restrained from entering your house in Kenilworth, or having any contact with your wife or children except through their attorney. Pleasure meeting you," he said with a slight smile, then turned and left.

"Son-of-a-bitch!" Cal said again. He felt as though he'd just been stabbed in the back. Then he looked up and saw his secretary staring at him.

"Get out!" he snapped. "And close the door behind you."

As the door shut, he knew that it hadn't been accidental that they'd served him at his office. That was calculated to embarrass and discredit him in the firm; it would be a big item of office scandal before the day was over. *Damn!* He looked down at the papers he was still holding in his hand. *That bitch!* How could she do this to him? Well, he'd show her. She wasn't going to humiliate him like this and get away with it. *All right, you bitch! You want a fight? You've got one!*

Chapter Nine

~~~

"The hospital is willing to throw in its hundred thousand deductible?" Tony Jeffries looked up from the letter he had just finished reading. Sister Mary Ann Currier, Blessed Trinity Hospital's General Counsel, sitting across from him at his desk, returned his look and nodded.

"This is a bad case, Mr. Jeffries," she said. "If it goes to trial, the Roosevelts are going to recover a substantial verdict. Possibly several million dollars. We're terribly embarrassed by what happened. But we're also realists, and we don't want our deductible to stand in the way of any settlement. If you have any possibility of settling the Roosevelt case, take it. We'll pay our deductible without any argument."

Tony liked Sister Mary Ann. This was the third medical malpractice case they had worked on together. The hospital's insurer was Imperial, so Wilson & Thompson was handling the defense. Because of the potential magnitude of the damages, Sister Mary Ann had asked to meet with Tony and to be able to sit in on his next conference with Max Greene.

She was in her early fifties, and maintained a certain formality that Tony was comfortable dealing with. She had closely cropped gray hair, wore no makeup that Tony could discern, and was always well dressed in tailored dark-blue or charcoal suits. Her only jewelry was a small silver cross that hung from a thin chain around her neck. She also had one of the quickest minds Tony had ever encountered. She was the ideal person, Tony had decided, to protect her order's interests in the dangerous waters of Cook County litigation.

Tony turned to Carol James, sitting to his right on the leather couch. "That'll make our job a little easier," he said, "if Max Greene makes any kind of a reasonable settlement demand."

Carol nodded her assent. "I'm not sure, though, how reasonable he's going to be. Dr. Rashdani was terrible when Greene took his deposition last week. He started out arrogant, but collapsed when Greene leaned on him a little. Admitted that he should have known that the CT scan didn't look right. Turns out, another hospital only ten minutes away had a functioning CT scan machine that night. They could have transported Sam Roosevelt there and had another set of films within an hour. Nobody thought of that. Greene looked pretty pleased at the end of that session."

"Well, he's waiting in the conference room down the

hall," Tony said, turning back to Sister Mary Ann. "Shall we go and see what our worthy opponent thinks his case is worth, now that he's had the discovery he wanted?"

"Why not, Mr. Jeffries," she answered with a tight-lipped smile as she stood. Tony grabbed the stack of pleadings and yellow pads on his desk, gestured to the two women, and followed them out the door.

Max Greene was deeply engrossed in the *Sun-Times* crossword puzzle when they walked into conference room B. When he saw them he quickly slid the folded newspaper under a yellow pad, then rose and took Tony's outstretched hand.

"Good morning, Max. It's been a couple of years, hasn't it?"

"Yes, I believe it has been," Greene responded. "And I see that you still have the good judgment to surround yourself with beautiful women."

Tony chuckled to himself. Max Greene hadn't changed a bit. He had put on a few pounds, perhaps, and had more gray in his hair and mustache than Tony remembered. Otherwise, he looked the same as he did way back when the newspapers printed his picture and the story about his suspended law license.

"Max, I understand you've already met my partner, Carol James." Tony gestured to Carol, who smiled and offered Greene her hand.

"Indeed I have." Greene replied with a smarmy smile as he took Carol's hand in both of his.

"And this is Sister Mary Ann Currier," Tony said, turning to his left. "She's the hospital's General Counsel."

"A nun? Surely you jest!" Max let Carol's hand slide out of his and turned all his attention to Sister Mary Ann. "What a pleasant surprise! Why, I thought all nuns were supposed to be bundled up in black shrouds, or whatever, not sporting Bloomingdale's finest." He took Sister Mary Ann's hand and stepped up a little closer than the situation warranted. "A very pleasant surprise indeed."

The guy's a regular Casanova, Tony thought, feeling a little protective of his two colleagues.

"Thank you, Mr. Greene. You're too kind." Sister Mary Ann smiled politely, extracted her hand from his, and walked over to one of the chairs at the conference table. "I understand that you're interested in discussing settlement of the Roosevelts' suit against the hospital. Is that correct?"

"Ah, yes, the Roosevelt case," Greene said. He looked at her for a moment, then turned back to the chair he had vacated.

Tony took the seat directly across from Greene, with Sister Mary Ann to his right and Carol to his left. Greene was still the smarmy sleazebag, Tony thought. His tactics can't have been too successful, Tony deduced, noting the frayed shirt cuffs and a suit that looked like he'd slept in it.

They talked about the case in general terms for a

while. Greene wrung his hands as he described the horrible situation the Roosevelts were now in as a result of the hospital's negligence; every time he visited Bertha and her son in their home, their situation seemed more desperate. Tony responded by reminding him that Sam Roosevelt had suffered his blood clot *before* he arrived at the hospital, and there was no assurance he would have come out any better even if things had been handled perfectly.

Greene was shocked, he said, by what he'd uncovered in the depositions. It was appalling that the hospital's nighttime CT scan technician couldn't even read the machine's instruction manual. He obviously had pushed the "feet first" button in total ignorance that it would cause Sam Roosevelt's CT scan image to be reversed. Greene was even more shocked that Dr. Rashdani hadn't realized what had happened. Apparently, Rashdani was preoccupied with something far removed from Sam Roosevelt that night - his investments maybe, or some young nurse on staff. Greene suggested that any jury would punish the hospital badly for setting up a situation where such compounded negligence could befall an unsuspecting patient.

The requisite foreplay over, Tony laid his pencil on his yellow pad, folded his hands, and looked across the table. "Max," he said, "we all agree that it's unfortunate what happened to Sam Roosevelt. But the question before us is whether we settle this case now, and get some money to Bertha Roosevelt and her family, or screw around for another five years and then roll the dice with some jury.

And at that point," Tony paused for effect, "who knows? Sam Roosevelt may have passed away and you won't even have a claim for long-term hospitalization costs." He waited a moment, looking in vain for some reaction in Greene's eyes, then went on. "We've already put a couple hundred thousand on the table. You say that won't do it. All right. Give us a number, Max. A realistic number that we can live with. What'll it take to settle this case now?"

Greene looked at Tony long and hard before responding. Tony could see sweat forming on Greene's forehead and in his thinning gray hair. It occurred to him that Max Greene had probably never had a case this big before, and wasn't sure how to respond. Maybe it just now occurred to him that he was in over his head.

"Three million bucks," Greene finally said, sitting back in his chair and squaring his shoulders. "That's what it'll take. We'll settle this case for three million dollars."

Damn, Tony thought. *Greene knows what the case is worth.* They weren't going to get out of this cheaply after all. Still, Tony had to do everything he could to hammer Greene down. He had to find out what his bottom line really was. From the corner of his eye he saw Sister Mary Ann lean back in her chair and fold her arms.

"Three million bucks! Come on, Max. I asked for a *realistic* figure, not some pie-in-the-sky fantasy. For that kind of money, we might just as well let a jury take a shot at us. We might do better than that in a trial."

"I don't think so, Jeffries," Greene answered, wiping his forehead with a soiled handkerchief, then sticking it back in a side pocket. "And I don't think you do, either. You've got a lot of exposure in this case. A *lot* of exposure."

"I know we have some risk, Max. That's why we're talking right now. But it's not unlimited. Our people say that there's a seventy-percent chance that with that clot in his brain Sam Roosevelt would have ended up comatose no matter what happened on the operating table." That was only a slight exaggeration of what their medical consultant had told Tony.

"Right," Greene answered with a smirk. "And we're going to show up at trial with three experts who will swear that Sam Roosevelt would have won the decathlon at the next Olympics if your guys hadn't screwed him up." He shrugged. "So that'll be a wash. And on top of that we'll have the sympathy factor going for us, big time!"

Tony looked across the table at Greene and caught a twinkle in his eye. Max had a winner, and he knew it.

"Max, I'll be honest with you," Tony said after a moment. "We've got the case reserved for five hundred thousand bucks. That's the full amount, isn't it, Carol?" He turned to his left.

"That's right," Carol affirmed. "Five hundred thousand." She thumbed through some papers in front of her, circled a figure on one of them, and shoved it across the table at Greene. "You can see for yourself," she offered.

Max Greene glanced at the paper and shrugged.

"I'll tell you what I'll do," Tony said, leaning forward. "I'll recommend that we give you the full five hundred grand. In addition, the hospital's willing to throw in their full deductible. That's another hundred thousand. That's six hundred thousand we're putting on the table. We won't hold anything back. I don't like to do that, but I will in this case, because I think this is one that ought to be settled. That's as far as I can go, believe me. Take it or leave it, Max."

"Two and a half," Greene said.

"What?"

"Two and a half," Max Greene repeated. "I'll settle the case for two and a half million. Nothing less." He pulled a cigar out of his coat pocket, unwrapped it, and lit it with an old Zippo lighter. He puffed on his cigar three or four times to make sure it was lit, then looked at Tony.

"This is a no-smoking building, Max," Tony said, instinctively leaning back from the acrid smoke.

"That's your problem, not mine," Greene replied with a shrug. "But if you want to settle this case it's going to cost you two and a half million bucks." He glanced at Sister Mary Ann, then at his cigar. "Pardon me, Sister, but this is a habit that I just can't break. Tried, but can't." He took a slow drag, looking at Tony, and added, "And if you think you can sit on this file for five years and wait us out, you're wrong. I've talked to Mike Granaldi. If we don't settle this case in the next thirty days, I'm bringing him in as co-counsel. And he'll file a motion to have the case advanced for an early trial based on the Roosevelts' financial situation. He thinks it'll be granted. If it is, it'll be before a jury within six months, with Granaldi trying it. That's something for you to think about." He took another deep drag on his cigar, flicked the ashes into his half-full coffee cup, and leaned back in his chair.

Sister Mary Ann turned to Tony. "Perhaps this would be an appropriate time for us to caucus," she said.

"All right." Tony pushed his chair back and stood up. "We'll be back in a few minutes, Max. And throw your ashes in the waste basket there, if you don't mind."

"Take your time," Greene said with a nod. He pulled the folded *Sun-Times* out from under his legal pad and laid it in front of him. "By the way," he asked as they turned to leave, "do any of you know who wrote *The Power and the Glory?*"

Tony stepped into his office, paused at the doorway to let Carol and Sister Mary Ann walk in, then shut the door and took the seat behind the desk. Mary Ann Currier reclined in one of the armchairs across from Tony, and Carol took a seat on the couch.

"Well, you heard it," Tony said, looking from one to the other. "He wants two and a half million. He'd probably settle for a little less. But there's no way I could recommend that kind of money."

"Oh, I think there is, Mr. Jeffries," Sister Mary Ann answered, her hands and her fingers forming a chapel.

"I'm sorry, Sister. I don't understand."

"The hospital's position, Mr. Jeffries, is that you

173

should accept the plaintiffs' demand." Mary Ann Currier gave him a soft smile and leaned back in her chair. "The insurance coverage we have through your client is five million dollars. You know the law. If a case can be settled within the policy limits, and the insured wants to settle, the insurance carrier must settle. If the insurer refuses, it's responsible for the full amount of any judgment, even if that exceeds the policy limits. It appears that that's where we are in this case. The hospital can't risk having a judgment entered against it in excess of our insurance. The case has terrible exposure. It can be settled now within our policy limits, and we want it settled. I'm sorry, but that's our position."

"Sister, isn't it a bit early to take a stance like that?" Tony was uncomfortable with this turn of the conversation. He glanced over at Carol and saw that she had picked up her pad and was taking notes. "Why don't you just wait and see whether Mike Granaldi gets into the case, and whether it's in fact advanced for an early trial?" He was trying to sound as conciliatory as possible. "I don't think this is a good time for us to start giving each other ultimatums."

"I understand, Mr. Jeffries." She nodded. "But if we wait, as you suggest, then perhaps we won't be able to settle the case for the sum we can today. Mr. Granaldi is very good. Once he gets involved, the stakes will undoubtedly be raised. The demand on the table today is within our policy limits, and we believe it's reasonable, all things considered. I'm afraid that from our standpoint, we can't let this opportunity pass. We want the case settled. Do you understand that, Mr. Jeffries?"

"Yes, Sister, I guess I do." Tony took a deep breath. He always knew she was tough, but he never realized just how tough. "Of course," he continued, "we only have settlement authority for one million. Anything in excess of that has to be approved in London. There's a reinsurer involved."

"Well, I suggest that you contact the reinsurer in London, Mr. Jeffries, and spell it out for them. And to make sure there's no misunderstanding, I'll e-mail you a letter this afternoon reconfirming our insistence that the case be settled within our policy limits." She lowered her chin and looked at Tony over her glasses. It was the same stern look that Tony recalled getting from Sister Eva back in grammar school, when she warned him not to be late to class one more time or he'd get his knuckles rapped. He'd never doubted then that those good sisters were quite serious, and there was no doubt now that Sister Mary Ann was deadly serious, too. And the damn thing was, Tony knew she was right.

"Well, we've got thirty days to work with," Carol interrupted. "At least that's what Greene indicated. Maybe we ought to tell him today that we're considering his demand and will get back to him in a week or two. By then, we'll have our response from London. Do you have any problem with that, Sister?"

"No, not at all." Mary Ann Currier stood, and added, "But I *will* e-mail you that letter this afternoon."

Tony stood up. "I understand," he said. He knew the flap that her letter would be causing in London before the week was out.

———〜〜〜———

"So, you think we ought to request settlement authority of two million, four hundred thousand in the Roosevelt case, Tony."

"That's right, Cal," Tony answered, taking a sip of his coffee, then putting his cup down on the small marble-topped conference table in Cal Cizma's office. "It's a bad case. We may even have to admit liability at trial. Max Greene's at two and a half now, and I'm not sure he's going to lower it before he brings in trial counsel. And then all bets are off. That's a lot of dough, but the hospital's insisting that we settle within their limits, and they're willing to throw in their hundred grand deductible. We've got to do it."

"I'm not going to second-guess you, Tony. You're the litigator. Why don't you put a memo together spelling it all out. I'll e-mail it to London with a note that I concur in your recommendation."

"Do you think we should run this by Chester Melrose?" The Imperial Syndicate was, after all, Melrose's baby and this was a major settlement. Tony knew that Melrose wasn't likely to disagree with them, but the token deference seemed appropriate.

"Hell, no!" Cal said, shaking his head. "What does he

know about this case? Nothing! Besides, Chester's a real pain in the ass to reach right now, with him and his wife on their cruise ship somewhere between Miami and Rio. I know - I tried yesterday on another matter and wasted the whole morning." He shook his head again. "No, we'll handle this ourselves."

"Well, you may be right." Tony would have preferred to bring Melrose into the loop, but there wasn't a lot of time to screw around with formalities. With the pressure Blessed Trinity was putting on them, they had to have the case settled and put to bed within thirty days. "By the way," he added, "how much do we have in our Imperial account right now?"

"Good question." Cal stood up, walked over to his desk, and sat down facing his computer. He punched a series of keys and the screen flickered from one green menu to another. Cal looked at the last screen for a moment and turned to Tony. "A little over six hundred thousand," he said. "It's been drifting down the past few weeks."

"You'd better mention that in your cover note to London," Tony said. "The reinsurance kicks in at a million, so Imperial's going to have to make up the four hundred thousand difference. They're probably not going to like that, any more than the reinsurer's going to like paying a million four on top of that. But it's the only way to handle this case right now. You've got to make that clear to them."

"Oh, I think I can." Cal smiled and leaned back in his swivel chair. "I know those folks pretty well by now. They'll take my advice."

"Hope you're right." Tony stood and turned to leave, then recalled something and turned back. "Say, are you still on for this evening?" he asked.

"I sure am. I don't know what it's all about, but Rasheed made it clear it's important. Six at Ditka's."

"Right." Tony chuckled. "Leave it to Rasheed to make it sound mysterious. It's probably some oddball tax issue for the Temple of Islam."

"God, I hope not." Cal grimaced. "Give me a buzz when you're ready to head out. I'll meet you in the reception room on eighty-eight."

Rasheed Collins finished his Coors Lite and signaled Lillian for another. *Am I doing the right thing?* he fretted, nervously picking the label off his bottle. He had been thinking about this for months and had gone back and forth on what he should do. Maybe this was a gigantic mistake. He had just about peeled off the last of the label when Lillian brought him his next beer. He filled his glass and took a deep swig. As he was putting his glass down he saw Tony and Cal walk through the door. *Well, this is it.*

"Evening, gentlemen," he said as they approached the table. "You'll have to do some fast drinking. I'm already two ahead of you."

"Hey, if that's a challenge, you're on," Tony said as he sat down. He picked up the glass of Chardonnay Lillian put in front of him and raised it to Rasheed. Cal did the same with his Dewars and water. The ever-vigilant Lillian had ordered their drinks from the bartender as soon as she saw them walk through the door.

"Can you believe those Cubs?" Cal said, shaking his head as he put his glass down. "They beat the Braves in the first round of the playoffs and were leading the Marlins three games to one in the league championship series, and they blew it! Unbelievable!"

"Right," Tony answered. "But if that guy Bartman hadn't interfered with Alou catching that ball in the fifth game, I don't have any doubt they'd be going to the series." He took a deep breath. "Oh well, there's always next year." Tony took another sip of his wine and turned to Rasheed. "Now, what's the big secret?" he asked, leaning forward and smiling

"Well, there's something that I wanted to talk to the two of you about," Rasheed said. "It's very personal. It's something that I've been living with, and wrestling with, for a long time." He looked first at Tony, then at Cal, and took a deep breath. "You guys are my two closest friends, but there's a side of me that you don't know at all." He paused for a sip of beer, but put his glass down quickly when he saw that his hand was shaking.

"Don't tell me that all these years you've been a closet Democrat," Tony interjected with a smile. "Oh my God!"

That's kind, Rasheed thought. *He's trying to make it easier.*

"No, but some people would say it's the next worst

179

thing." He hesitated, looked at the two of them, then went on. "I'm gay." *There, I've said it.*

Tony looked at him for a moment, then said softly, "Rasheed, I've known that for a long time. When you're around someone as much as we've been around each other, you pick up little things. So, to be honest, I'm not surprised. And I'll tell you something else. It doesn't make a damn bit of difference to me."

Rasheed felt a wave of relief. Not a hint of hostility or shock in Tony's voice. Tony leaned across the table and put his hand on Rasheed's arm.

"And I appreciate your sharing this with us," Tony said. "It must have been tough."

"Tough? You can't believe how tough." Rasheed felt tears welling up in his eyes. He picked up his cocktail napkin and wiped them away. Yes, he had done the right thing. He knew that now.

"It's not going to change a thing," Cal said, smiling.

"Thank you, guys," Rasheed said, looking from one to the other. "I'm going through a difficult period right now, trying to sort things out. And I just wanted the two of you to know this part of my life, and to understand it."

"What about Aliza?" Tony asked. "How does she fit into all this?"

"That's part of what I'm trying to sort out, Tony," Rasheed answered, leaning forward. "Reverend Lund sure is putting pressure on me to give Aliza a ring, and I just don't know what to do. Aliza's a fine person. If I'm ever going to have any kids, Aliza's as good a woman as

I'm going to find to be their mother. Besides," he paused, searching for the right way to put his thought, "she's a little on the innocent side. If we got married, she might not think anything of it if I maintained some of my old bachelor friendships."

"So you're not going to tell her?" Tony asked.

"How could I, Tony? She wouldn't understand."

"But she'll find out pretty fast when you're in bed together, won't she?"

"Oh, not really," Rasheed answered with a little smile. "I can rise to the occasion when necessary, especially if the lights are out. I think I could perform often enough so that she wouldn't know. And her father…Jesus, if he knew, he'd go absolutely crazy! He's a classic homophobe, just like my father. Who *also* doesn't know, by the way." Rasheed emptied his glass and then looked up at Tony and Cal. "But that's what I'm wrestling with right now. And I need some friends who know the whole picture. People I can lean on for a little support if I need it. You guys know what I mean?"

"I sure do," Tony replied. "And you've got it."

"Right," Cal echoed.

"Thanks, guys. I can't tell you how much this means to me."

They all leaned back while Lillian served another round of drinks and a full bowl of cashews. Rasheed took a couple of deep breaths. "I'd like to take you guys somewhere tonight," he said. They both looked at him quizzically. "It's a place called Mandate. A private gay club on the north side. I'd like the two of you to meet some of my other friends, and get some sense of what the other half of my life is all about. Are you willing?"

Cal looked at his watch. Before he could say anything, Tony responded. "Of course we would. Cal and I have blocked out the evening. We'd like to meet your other friends."

"That's great. It would really mean a lot to me."

This couldn't have gone any better, Rasheed's anxiety was all gone. He pulled his cash out of his pocket and laid three twenties on the table - more than enough to cover the tab and a nice tip for Lillian. "All right, then - drink up," he said. "You guys are going to have an interesting evening, believe me."

Chapter Ten

〰

Cal strode into the elevator, turned around, and slammed his fist on the button for the eighty-eighth floor. The button shattered and fell to the floor in pieces as the doors closed. *Cheap damn plastic.* It already had been a rough morning and it wasn't even nine o'clock. He hadn't gotten to bed until twelve-thirty, after leaving Rasheed and Tony, and he had to be back up at six for a breakfast meeting at the Mid-America Club.

He had just left his wife's attorney, an avaricious jerk named Bernie Fontayne, and his stomach was still churning. Cal had made a very reasonable settlement proposal: three thousand a month to Sandy until she remarried or got a job, with a max of five years, and he'd be responsible for the kids' college education. Cal would keep the house in Kenilworth, of course, and Sandy could move back to the western suburbs with the kids, which is what she wanted anyway. But Fontayne wouldn't even negotiate – a real asshole. He kept demanding copies of Cal's tax returns and the firm's financial statements. There was no way in hell that Cal was going to give him that kind of information.

By the time the doors opened on eighty-eight, Cal had buttoned his coat and composed himself. He was determined not to let his personal problems interfere with his work. He had seen too many other men screw themselves up that way, and it wasn't going to happen to him.

He walked through the reception room, nodded to Julia, and headed down the hall toward his office. He was surprised how many of the other attorneys weren't in yet; especially some of the younger ones. *This is a law firm, god damn it, not a country club!* He made a mental note of the nameplates alongside the darkened offices he passed; Mark Watson, William Lee, Carol James. Those folks were going to get a real surprise the next time raises came up; he'd see to that!

When he got to his office Cal found a multiple-page fax lying in the middle of his desk. He couldn't miss it; it was the only thing there. He made a point of keeping his desk perfectly clean at all times, and it was certainly that way when he left last night.

The fax was from Ronnie Dasher in London. It was a six-page response to Cal's message requesting settlement authority of two million, four hundred thousand in the Roosevelt case. He was troubled as he sat down and began reading. What could be so complicated about settling the Roosevelt case?

There appeared to be a bit of a misunderstanding,

Dasher's letter began. The escrow fund that had been established in the firm's name was designed to cover the first million dollars of any settlement, along with their fees and expenses, he explained. If there was a shortfall between the amount of money in that fund and the million-dollar mark where the reinsurance came into play, that was the law firm's responsibility, not Imperial's.

Cal froze as he read that. Was Dasher saying that the firm had to come up with four hundred thousand dollars if they were going to settle the Roosevelt case? *That's insane! That can't be right.* He reread that paragraph. Yes, that's exactly what he was saying. Dasher went on to say that before this proposal was presented to the reinsurer, perhaps they should make sure that Wilson & Thompson understood its obligations and was still recommending the settlement.

Cal feverishly read the rest of Dasher's fax. It kept referring to the terms of their March 15th letter agreement. *What letter agreement is he talking about?* He had never seen any such agreement. He had gone through the entire file several times, and there was nothing like that there. He suddenly recalled that Gordon Hawke had referred cryptically to some letter agreement during their initial meeting in London. *Damn! What's this all about?*

Dasher's letter ended on page three of the fax, but there were three more sheets attached. Cal quickly flipped the page. There it was. A copy of a letter from Gordon Hawke to Chester Melrose dated March 15th, 2003. On the last page, just above Hawke's signature, was the closing remark. "Please indicate your firm's concurrence in these terms by signing and returning this letter, keeping the enclosed copy for your records." At the bottom he recognized Chester Melrose's scribbled signature.

Damn, Cal muttered, as he stared at that signature. What the hell did the old fool agree to?

He went back and carefully read through the text of Hawke's letter to Melrose. Its terms were chillingly clear. One-half of all net premiums received by the Imperial Syndicate for their medical malpractice line of insurance would he deposited in an escrow fund with Wilson Thompson & Gilcrist. He used the firm's old name, but that didn't make any difference. Wilson Thompson & Gilcrist was fully responsible for all losses, settlements, and defense costs related to claims made under those policies, and had full authority to use the money in that fund to pay them. The letter went on to provide that Imperial would obtain reinsurance for all losses exceeding one million dollars in any given case. Any expenses incurred and settlements made prior to the reinsurance coming into effect would be the law firm's responsibility, to be paid out of the escrow fund.

Cal laid the fax on his desk, pushed it away, and just stared at it. The agreement made the law firm the insurer for the first million dollars of any loss! Nobody ever anticipated that. He turned to the last page again. He recognized both Hawke's and Melrose's signatures, and the letter was certainly on Imperial's letterhead. But why wasn't a copy in their file? And why didn't Melrose ever mention it? *Why the hell didn't I ask him about the letter after Hawke referred to it in London?* Cal sat back and shut his eyes. Where would Melrose have put something like that if he didn't put it in the file?

Cal pushed his chair back, got up, strode out of his office and down the corridor on the north side of the eighty-eighth floor, ignoring the four or five people who greeted him, and stormed into Chester Melrose's corner office. Melrose's secretary tried to stop him, saying he wasn't in, but Cal just brushed her aside. He walked behind the desk and yanked open the top drawer. *The idiot never locks up anything!* But Cal was glad of that right now.

"Mr. Cizma, what are you doing?" Melrose's secretary, Alice, pleaded. "You shouldn't be doing that! Mr. Melrose will be very upset!"

"Shut up!" Cal snapped, as he dug through the old junk in the drawer, grabbing handfuls of papers and pencils and strewing them across the desk.

Within seconds he found it: their copy of the letter agreement. It was the same letter, no doubt about it.. Melrose had signed it and just stuffed his copy in his drawer.

"The goddamned old fool probably didn't even understand it!" Cal said aloud. He looked up and saw Alice staring at him, her hands in front of her mouth. "Clean this up," he ordered, gesturing at the debris scattered across the desktop. "And I'm taking this." He held up the letter, and walked past her out the door. He was going straight to Barton Thompson.

———

Tony Jeffries was surprised when he saw the e-mail calling a special meeting of the management committee in thirty minutes. It was almost noon, and he had just begun a conference call with four people, including Carol James, who was in New York, to discuss the strategy that Carol should use in defending one of their witnesses in a deposition the next day. Tony watched his desk clock and excused himself at the last minute. Carol had a good command of the subject matter and could handle the rest of the meeting herself.

When Tony got to conference room A, Barton Thompson told him to shut the door and have a seat; they'd begin immediately. Tony glanced around the table and saw that everyone else was already there except Chester Melrose, still on his cruise.

"A serious matter has come up," Thompson announced from the head of the table. "It appears that we've had a misunderstanding with the Imperial Insurance Syndicate regarding the scope of our obligations in their medical malpractice book of business."

That caught Tony's attention. What sort of a misunderstanding?

"As you know," Thompson continued, looking up one side of the table and down the other, "An escrow fund has been established, in our firm's name, that's been used to pay claims as well as our fees and expenses in handling

Imperial's cases. Up until now, that's been a lucrative account. What we didn't know, and what we just found out, is that our firm is in essence the insurer for the first million dollars of any loss. If there's a deficiency in the fund, up to one million dollars per claim, it's our obligation to make it up."

"What?" George Lazenby exploded. Everyone else looked at one another in shock.

Tony knew immediately that they were talking about the settlement of the Roosevelt case and the four-hundred-thousand-dollar shortfall. *Jesus,* he said to himself. *That's our responsibility? How could that have happened?* Everyone was talking at once, asking the same questions. Thompson let them go on for a minute, then raised his hand.

"It appears that our absent partner, Chester Melrose, acquiesced to such an agreement last March but didn't bother to tell the rest of us." Thompson raised some papers in his right hand. "Here's the agreement. We just obtained a copy from the client. Cal here" - he nodded to Cizma - "found our copy in Chester's desk. Until today, no one but Chester had any inkling that such an agreement existed. As a partner, he certainly had the authority to bind the firm, but frankly, I doubt he understood its impact. But we're bound by it, and it might cost us four-hundred-thousand-dollars."

The room erupted with animated questions, even shouts. When those had subsided, Thompson asked Cal to explain the proposed settlement of the Roosevelt case and how the issue had arisen. Cal gave a straightforward explanation and asked Tony to confirm the gravity of the case. Cal then read the message he had sent to London requesting settlement authority of $2.4 million, and Ronnie Dasher's response. He also explained how he'd had found their copy of the letter agreement. By the time he had finished, everyone was shaking his head and muttering.

"Chester should have retired years ago," Pete Spanos said, looking across the table at Tony. "This is outrageous."

Tony certainly agreed. Melrose had put both him and Cal, as well as the whole firm, in a terrible position.

"The first question, Tony," Thompson said, looking down the table at him, "is whether you firmly believe that the Roosevelt case should be settled for two and a half million. If you do, then let's bite the bullet and get that over with."

Everyone turned to look at him. Tony took a deep breath. "Yes, I'm afraid so. We're dealing with terrible injuries and clear liability. It's a very bad case. The hospital's insisting that we settle within their policy limits, and right now we can. They're also willing to throw in their hundred-thousand deductible. The plaintiffs' current demand is two and a half million, and they might take a little less. But, frankly, two and a half million would be a bargain in this case, all things considered."

"Do we have the four hundred thousand that we'd have to contribute?" Rasheed asked.

"Of course we do!" Thompson snapped. "It may eliminate next month's bonuses for equity partners, but that's not a serious problem." He looked around the room, seeking out each of his partners' eyes. "I take it, then, that it's agreed to proceed with the settlement of that case?" he asked.

After a moment he went on. "All right, Cal, contact London. Tell them we understand our obligations, and will contribute our one million, including the balance in the escrow fund. Tell them that we want them to obtain authority from the reinsurer to settle for up to two and a half million if necessary, with the balance, less the hospital's deductible, to come from them. Let's get rid of this case, and then get that book of business cleaned up."

"Right," Cal responded. "I'll go over there and renegotiate our arrangement with Imperial. On a prospective basis, of course."

"Good," Thompson said. Then, glancing down the table, he continued, "Pete, did you want to add something?"

Pete Spanos leaned forward, his hands folded on the table, his brow furrowed. "Yes," he answered. "This incident has brought up an issue that's been troubling me a lot. It's sensitive, and very personal to several of the men here, but it's something that I don't think we can ignore any longer."

Where in the hell is he going? Tony wondered.

"What I'm talking about," Pete continued, "is that we have too many very senior men serving on the management committee of this firm. Many people lose their sharpness and slow down as they get older. No one likes to admit that, but it's true, and lawyers certainly aren't an exception. And when you have senior men with a lot of authority and discretion, but who can't understand a simple contract, you're inviting disaster."

"You're referring to Chester," Ralph Stritch said, nodding. "And it does look like he made a serious mistake. But let's not rush to judgment. After all, Chester isn't even here to defend himself. There might be a purely rational explanation for what he did."

"Ralph," Pete answered, "I'm not just talking about Chester. I'm also talking about you. And George too." He gestured across the table at George Lazenby. "You fellows are like Chiang Kai-shek's army. You've grown old together. In fact, to be candid, you can't even recognize how old and slow you've all become."

"Now just a minute!" Stritch shouted. "I'm not going to take that kind of talk from you! I've brought more business into this firm over the years then you'll ever dream of producing!"

Tony glanced at Barton Thompson. Thompson was leaning back, just watching. He didn't seem at all surprised by what was happening. At that moment, Tony understood.

George Lazenby's face was red with rage. He slammed his fist on the table and stood up. "I've had enough of this," he said, turning toward the door. Ralph Stritch, sitting next to him, pushed his chair back in accord.

"The meeting's not over yet, George," Thompson said quietly.

Lazenby stopped and turned back. He glared at

Thompson for a moment, then followed Thompson's eyes to Pete Spanos.

"Mr. Chairman, I have a motion," Pete said.

"Go ahead."

"I move that we recommend to the firm that, except for the current chairman, no one over seventy years of age be permitted to serve as a member of the management committee, effective immediately. I also move that the size of the committee be reduced from nine to six."

"I'll second both motions," Cal quickly added.

"What the hell?" Stritch blurted. "That's outrageous!" He turned to Thompson. "This is all your doing, isn't it? You're trying to institutionalize yourself."

"Let's not personalize this, Ralph," Thompson said. "Pete's raised a good issue. This firm has a problem with the age of its management. It cost us a lot of money today. Next time could be worse - much worse. It's only good business for us to address the problem."

"Business my ass!" Stritch snapped, sitting back down "Well, your resolutions will never pass, either here or before the firm." George Lazenby slowly sat back down beside him, his face flushed with anger.

"Let's just see about that." Thompson looked down the table at Tony. "How do you vote on the two resolutions, Tony? We can presume that Pete and Cal support them, since they made and seconded the motions."

"Well, to be honest," Tony answered, "I think it's a fairly drastic response to the problem that Chester created. This committee *is* getting old, but I'm not sure we have to go as far as Pete's resolution suggests." Ralph Stritch leaned forward, staring hard at Tony and nodding.

"Are you sure about that, Tony?" Thompson opened a leather folder that had been sitting at his side on the table. He took out a piece of letter paper, unfolded it, and looked over it at Tony. "I received your letter this morning," he said. "Would you like me to read it to the committee?"

Damn. The undated letter of resignation. Tony felt his throat tighten. Thompson was playing his ace. He and Thompson looked at each other down the long length of the polished table. A chilling smile slowly crossed the chairman's face. Thompson had him by the balls; they both knew it.

Tony looked down. "No," he said quietly. "That's not necessary. I support the two resolutions."

"Son-of-a-bitch!" Stritch exclaimed, leaning back and throwing his hands in the air.

"Fine. I thought you'd see the light," Thompson said, carefully folding the paper and placing it back in its folder. "That's three votes. I believe I'll vote for the resolutions; that makes four. And I may have another vote right here." He reached inside his coat pocket and pulled out another piece of paper. "Yes," he said. "This is Chester Melrose's proxy. He gave it to me some time ago in case he ever missed a meeting. I think this would be an appropriate time to use it. Chester votes for the two resolutions also." There was an unmistakable glow of triumph on his face as Barton Thompson placed Melrose's proxy on the table.

"That's despicable!" Lazenby shouted. "Using Chester's proxy against him!"

Ignoring him, Thompson looked down the table at Rasheed Collins and Curly Morgan. Neither had said a word. "Well, gentlemen," he asked. "We already have a majority. Would you two care to add your support?"

Curly cleared his throat. "Yes, of course," he replied nervously. "I'll support the resolutions."

"So will I," Rasheed said in a whisper, looking straight ahead.

"All right. That does it." Thompson turned to Stritch. "You see, Ralph, you were wrong."

"What a sleazy demonstration, Barton," Stritch answered, shaking his head. "Well, I suspect that the rest of the firm isn't going to be quite as docile. I'm going to spell this all out in a memo that every partner will have on their desk first thing tomorrow morning. You're not going to get away with this." He stood and looked at Lazenby. "Care to help me draft something up, George?"

"I'd be delighted. Let's go to the Union League Club. The stench here makes it hard to concentrate." He followed Stritch out the door.

No one else moved. Everyone seemed to sense that the last card hadn't been played yet.

"Well, gentlemen," Thompson said finally, looking at the five of them. "I appreciate your support. I know we're going to be able to work well together. By the way" - he glanced at his watch - "we're going to be holding a special partnership meeting in one hour to consider Pete's two resolutions. This matter's going to be over by the time they distribute their little memo tomorrow morning. I already have proxies from many of the partners in our other offices."

As they stood to leave, Tony realized that he was soaking with perspiration. He felt dirty and used, like he'd been forced to take part in a mugging. He wanted to wash his hands - and, if he could, his soul.

Barton Thompson couldn't help chuckling as he walked down Chestnut Street toward Michigan Avenue, the late-afternoon pedestrian traffic of tourists and shoppers swirling around him like the cool fall breeze off the lake. The emergency partnership meeting had gone as smoothly as he had expected. With Melrose, Lazenby and Stritch otherwise engaged, no one had dared to challenge the two resolutions recommended by the rest of the management committee, knocking the three absentees off the committee and reducing its size to six. *What a bunch of sheep!*

He chuckled again as he thought of Tony Jeffries squirming when he'd pulled out the letter of resignation. Jeffries was the key. Thompson knew that once he caved in, Morgan and Collins would follow suit. And to be able to use Chester Melrose's proxy as the deciding vote was exhilarating. Thompson laughed out loud, ignoring the busy shoppers around him and the heavy traffic moving past him on Chestnut.

He wouldn't have to worry about anything for the next five years. Then, maybe, he'd do the same thing all over again - throw out this bunch and lock down another five years. He was smarter than all of them put together.

Barton Thompson savored the sweetness of his victory as he began crossing Michigan Avenue. He was totally oblivious to the CTA bus speeding to clear the intersection before the light changed. Other pedestrians jumped back, but the bus hit Thompson broadside and shattered his brittle bones in a hundred places. He was dead before his body hit the pavement.

—*mm*—

The shock of Barton Thompson's death was still reverberating through the firm the next day when they decided by consensus to close at noon in his memory. Funeral arrangements were still uncertain.

Tony came back to the office after lunch. He shuffled through papers for a half hour, then concluded that he wasn't going to get any work done and might just as well leave. He couldn't keep his mind off the irony of Thompson being struck down just a few minutes after he'd pulled off his unsavory coup. Every time he thought about it he shook his head in disbelief.

He threw a couple of files into his briefcase; it was Friday, and he might do a little work over the weekend. He turned out his office light and headed out to the reception room and the elevators. There were only a few people around; most had taken advantage of the early close.

He was out of the building and heading toward Michigan Avenue when suddenly he stopped. This *was* Friday. Were they there?

He continued walking and crossed Michigan Avenue. They wouldn't be there - not today. Not now, at two in the afternoon. But on the west side of Michigan Tony found his pace quickening. He turned right into Ditka's and saw that it was almost empty, except for Lillian by the bar and a familiar group of men at a table in the far left corner.

"It's about time you got here! Tony," Lillian said with a smile. "The usual?"

He hesitated for a moment. "Of course," he answered, then hurried toward the table.

They were all there waiting for him: Rasheed Collins, Pete Spanos, Curly Morgan, Cal Cizma. And one empty chair.

"We thought you'd never get here!" Curly said as Tony sat down.

He sat looking at them for a few seconds without saying a word. Cal had an odd smile on his face. Lillian brought Tony his glass of Grgich Hills Chardonnay. No one said anything until she left.

Cal raised his glass first, followed by all the others. "It's ours, gentlemen," he said quietly. "Wilson & Thompson is all ours."

Part 2

FEEDING FRENZY

Chapter Eleven

~~~

It was odd, the five of them sitting around the large table in conference room A, meeting to conduct the firm's business. It seemed to Tony that others should be there - the *real* members of the management committee.

But there wasn't anyone else. The five of them *were* the management committee of Wilson & Thompson. The chair at the head of the table was empty. They had all carefully avoided it when they came in.

Tony had something on his mind. "Fellas, I want to say a couple of words before we begin discussing business," he said. His friends looked at him, some with surprise, others with relief that they hadn't had to speak first.

"An amazing thing has happened to us. Through a series of flukes, or accidents, or whatever, the five of us happen to be running one of the largest and most powerful law firms in the country." He didn't really know what he was going to say next, but he wanted to keep talking because he knew that what he had bottled up inside him was important.

"Now, we can handle this in one of two different ways. One way would be to squeeze this firm for every dollar it's worth. Give the associates and staff only token raises. Maybe even pull up the ladder, no new equity partners. Force out any partner who's had two bad years in a row. Maximize bottom-line profits - to those who survive, that is - and keep the management of the firm tightly controlled, just the five of us. If we do those things, chances are we'll make a hell of a lot of dough - for a couple of years, anyway. But eventually something will happen, a coup or a mass exodus, and all of us will find ourselves out in the cold, like Melrose, Stritch, and Lazenby found themselves last week, just so someone *else* can make a few more bucks."

"Sorry to interrupt," Pete said "but Stritch and Lazenby resigned from the firm today. They're both retiring. Ralph's secretary handed me a note just before I walked in."

"What about Melrose?" Cal asked. "I understand he's in the hospital."

"He had a stroke when he got word he'd been dumped," Pete answered with a smirk. "He won't be coming back, either."

They all looked at each other for a moment. "That's what I mean," Tony said. "Those men were giants in this firm. They spent their entire lives building it into what it is today. And they ended up leaving unexpectedly and madder than hell, because they were outmaneuvered at the end. Things shouldn't work that way. But that's the way this firm has always operated, up to now. We can run it differently. We have that chance; it's in the palms of our hands. We can decide right now, the five of us, not to play games with each other or with our other partners. No secret agendas. We can also make a commitment to deal with everyone – *everyone* - fairly and aboveboard."

Tony looked around the room. He had their attention. He still wasn't sure where he was going, but he knew he had to get there.

"For one thing," he continued, "why not decide that everyone on the management committee, the five of us, will all get the same draw? Eliminate the *need* for secret agendas. Is that so nutty? It would sure as hell encourage cooperation, *real* cooperation, between us."

"I don't know," Pete responded, shaking his head. "We've always compensated everyone on the basis of their productivity and collections. If someone brings in a major new book of business, he *should* be paid more."

"Well, maybe at the lower or mid ranges in the firm," Tony answered, "but not among us - we're all making damn good money. Now, I guess we could always give someone a bonus if he did something extraordinary or brought in a major new client, but keep the draws the same. I really think that would be healthier for the firm."

He could see that Pete had reservations; the proposal had obviously caught him by surprise. "I'm not suggesting that we should make any decision like that today," Tony said. "But think about it. It's just one example of what I'm talking about."

"I'll think about it," Pete answered, leaning back and folding his arms.

"Let me give you fellas something else to think about," Tony continued with a smile. "Can you imagine the lift in the morale around here if we announced, for example, that vacancies on the management committee will be filled by election? A *real* election. Hell, I'll go further than that. Let's make it a *secret-ballot* election."

Cal smiled and looked around the table at the others. "I'm afraid our Mr. Jeffries has gone quite mad."

"No, I'm serious, Cal," Tony said. "Listen to what I'm saying. With Barton Thompson's death we have a vacancy on this committee right now. What would be so terrible about announcing that the position will be filled by a secret-ballot election of the equity partners? The five of us would still run the firm, but it would give everyone else a real sense of participation in management. And in the long run, if we kept that tradition alive, I'm convinced that it would be very healthy for the firm. It would force us, or whoever else is in these seats, to be accountable to the rest of the equity partners. And, after all, it's the equity partners who own the firm."

"If that's a motion, I'll second it," Rasheed said. "That might be the single most rational statement made in a management committee meeting since we've all been attending."

"I agree," Curly added.

Tony looked around the table. He felt that the moment was his. "Does anyone have any objection?" he asked.

"Well, not really an objection," Cal answered. "But I'd rather let the five of us get a handle on things before we bring in someone else. I think that just makes sense. But I'd be happy to give your idea some thought down the road."

"I'd prefer that," Pete added. Rasheed and Curly nodded affirmatively.

"I'll accept that as a compromise," Tony said. "Frankly, I'd love to send a memo out to all the partners announcing that *all* future vacancies on the management committee will be filled by secret-ballot elections - including *our* seats when they come up. Hell, if the rest of the partners don't think we're doing a good job, we *shouldn't* be reelected. If they do, we *will* be. What could be more fair?"

"Interesting concept," Cal answered, rubbing his chin and glancing at Pete. "But I don't think we need to resolve all of that right now. Let's kick it around a bit among ourselves before we announce anything."

"Fair enough," Tony said. "That would be a great start. Guys, there's really no limit to what we can accomplish with an aboveboard approach." *God,* he thought, *this is going to be exciting!*

The next order of business, they all agreed, was to select a chairman. They agreed, too, that the chairmanship should not be permanent; rather, it should rotate among them. One-year terms seemed reasonable, since there were five of them, and they all had been selected to serve for five years.

They discussed various methods of setting the order of their chairmanships. Alphabetical? Pete Spanos wasn't too excited about that. The amount of business each controlled? The argument over that method quickly ruled it out. Who "controlled," for example, Imperial Insurance's substantial book of business, Tony or Cal? They finally decided that the simplest criterion would be the best: seniority with the firm. Under that approach, Cal would be the first chairman, followed next year by Tony, who'd joined the firm just a couple of days later, then by Pete, Rasheed, and Curly, in that order. Curly groused a bit, but finally agreed that this approach was as reasonable as any.

Cal got up, walked slowly to the head of the table, and took the chair. He looked out of place there, Tony thought, like a little kid who crawled up on the king's throne when nobody was watching.

"Thank you, gentlemen," Cal said, looking at each of them in turn. "Let's deal with the chairmanships of the other committees next. Pete, why don't you take over finance."

Tony was startled by the finality of Cal's pronouncement. Then he recalled that the chairman of the management committee had always appointed the other committee chairmen, a prerogative that Cal Cizma clearly wasn't about to relinquish. *Well, what's the difference?* Tony thought. *Next year it'll be my turn.*

Cal completed his appointments by asking Tony to stay on as head of the hiring committee, Curly to continue to chair insurance, and Rasheed to replace Ralph Stritch as chairman of the secretarial/personnel committee. Cal would assume responsibility for the associates' evaluation and compensation committee. They agreed they'd collectively set the partners' compensation.

They discussed the clients of their recently retired senior partners and assigned someone to contact each of them to ensure the continuity of the business. In recent years most of those clients had been dealing primarily with younger, mid-range partners, rather than the senior men who had first brought in the business, so the retirements needn't make any serious financial waves.

The five men reviewed the firm's finances and the year-to-date figures. Tony was pleased that the firm was still in good shape, even with the million-dollar reserve earmarked to settle the Roosevelt case. With six hundred attorneys in nine cities, Curly proudly pointed out, Wilson & Thompson was now one of the fifty largest law firms in the country.

"Anything else for the good of the order," Cal asked, "before we adjourn?"

"Yes, there is," Pete answered. "I've got some good news. My friend Frank Donatelli at American Union called this morning." He paused and looked around. "We're getting the environmental case in Pennsylvania. The big one."

"Beautiful!" Cal exclaimed, pumping his fist in the air. Pete basked in a round of congratulations.

"This means that I can give Mike Vance the partnership agreement to sign," Pete added with a laugh. "He's been bugging me for it ever since he joined the firm. I've been ducking his calls the last couple of weeks." He looked across the table at Tony. "You see, pal, there was nothing to worry about."

Tony shook his head. He knew just how sticky it would have been if they'd brought Vance in and *hadn't* gotten that case, but he didn't want to argue about it anymore.

"Well, if that's all the business we have, let's go out and make some money, boys."

Cal stood as he finished speaking. The meeting was adjourned.

———

Bertha Roosevelt laid her Bible in her lap and looked at her husband lying motionless in his bed. He hadn't moved all afternoon except for the slight, almost imperceptible heaving of his chest as he breathed. Sam had lost a lot of weight, she could tell. His face was gaunt, and the skin on his arms hung loose. Bertha sighed sadly. It was a good thing that Sam couldn't see himself; he always took such pride in staying in shape.

The room was simple; concrete-block walls painted off-white, linoleum flooring with a brown pattern, and an acoustical-tile ceiling missing the occasional piece. There weren't any curtains on the window, but Bertha noted the metal brackets that probably once held a curtain rod.

Outside, a block away, on the other side of a vacant lot littered with trash, was the brick back wall of the old

McKenzie factory. Bertha's father lost his right hand there in a punch-press accident back in the seventies. Bertha thought about him from time to time as she sat next to Sam and gazed out the window. Poppa had always wanted to buy the family a house in one of the suburbs; some place like Maywood or Robbins that was already integrated, so there wouldn't be any problems. But all that ended with his accident. Bertha took a deep breath and looked at the McKenzie plant again. It seemed to be closed now. There was graffiti on the back wall, and weeds were growing in the empty parking lot. The rear windows were boarded up, and she hadn't seen any sign of life there in all the months since they'd moved Sam from Blessed Trinity.

She wondered what ever happened to old man McKenzie. He probably ended up in a place just like this. Maybe it had curtains on the windows and a picture on the wall, but otherwise it likely was pretty much the same.

Sam's roommate was an old white-haired man named Belkins. Nobody ever came to see him. They moved him in about a month ago when Mr. Goldberg died. Like Sam, neither could speak and hardly ever moved.

Bertha put her Bible into the side pocket of her purse and pulled out a white envelope. She opened it, read the card inside, took out her pen, and carefully signed it. *Sam would like this; sentimental, but not too mushy.* Bertha opened the card and stood it on the little table next to Sam's bed. Then she leaned over and kissed him.

"Happy anniversary, sweetie," she whispered as one tear slid down her cheek.

She looked at her watch. If she left now, there'd be plenty of time to make it to Attorney Greene's office by four. He told her he'd have some money for her this afternoon.

Three times now he'd advanced her money when she needed it; five thousand dollars in all, counting the money he promised her today. She didn't know how she and Robert would have survived without his help, especially since the hospital's attorneys hadn't yet offered anything in settlement. Attorney Greene had her sign a paper each time, changing the fee agreement. She knew she'd have to sign another paper today to get her money. She didn't like the fact that he was taking advantage of her, but she desperately needed the money.

—*uuu*—

"I haven't felt this good about the firm in a long time." Tony Jeffries lounged back on the couch, swirled his Chardonnay in his glass, and smiled at his wife. "I tell you, Karen, the spirit of cooperation we had at our management committee meeting the other day was exciting. No – exhilarating! That's the best word to describe the feeling I had at the end of the meeting; exhilaration."

"My, you're getting easier and easier to satisfy!" Karen said, leaning forward and lightly rubbing her finger up her husband's leg.

Tony chuckled and looked at her admiringly. He was proud of Karen: she had kept her figure and could still be a very sensuous woman when she wanted to be - like tonight, with her blouse unbuttoned just enough to capture his interest. *Hmm…it's a good evening for us to head to bed early, before Debbie gets home. Or has Karen already decided that?* Tony chuckled again.

He took another sip of his wine and pulled her close to him on the couch. She snuggled up and put her arm across his chest. It felt good to have her there.

"This next couple of years should be great," Tony said, his voice softer now, "both for the firm and for the two of us. I've got a hunch that years from now, we'll be looking back on this as the best, most exciting time of our lives."

"I hope you're right," Karen said, her voice even softer than his. She ran her hand down his chest and started unbuttoning his shirt. "And speaking of excitement," she whispered, "I've got a suggestion."

─────ⁿⁿⁿ─────

"Hey, Curly! How's my man?"

Red O'Kieffe slid onto the barstool, slapped Curly on the back and gestured to the bartender. Duncan, who'd been tending that bar at the University Club for twenty years, had a glass of ice and a double Cutty Sark in front of O'Kieffe even before he'd lit his cigar.

Curly ignored him and took another sip of his own regular club drink, twenty-five-year-old Macallan single-malt scotch. Despite their business arrangement, Curly still didn't like O'Kieffe. First of all, he was an asshole. And secondly, anybody who pretended to be a high roller and still drank cheap scotch was a double asshole.

"I said, how are you doin', pal?" Curly flinched at a second slap on the back.

"Just so-so, Red. I don't feel much like talking tonight, if you don't mind." He focused on his Macallan.

"How do you like all those cases I'm sending your way?" O'Kieffe asked, draping his arm around Curly's shoulder. His cigar breath smelled like sour garbage. "My claims manager told me we sent over six more cases yesterday. That makes thirty or so." He patted Curly's shoulder and added. "Yeah, Acorn's keeping up our end of the bargain, all right."

"Pay your fuckin' bills, Red," Curly said firmly, without even looking at O'Kieffe. He'd been drinking for a couple of hours and didn't feel like socializing with anybody, much less this idiot.

"What's that?"

"I said pay your fuckin' bills, Red." Curly emptied his glass in one swallow, then laid it down heavily on the bar. Duncan immediately refilled it. "You've had our first set of bills over a month, Red. They're overdue. Pay 'em!"

Curly could see in the bar's mirror that he'd put O'Kieffe on the defensive. *Good.* He really didn't give a damn about the bills.

"Jesus Christ, Curly! What's thirty days? We pay everything once a month. You'll probably get a check in the next few days."

Curly chuckled to himself. He loved to do that to people: put them on the defensive and insult the shit out of them. And this guy really deserved it: he was an asshole to the core. It was time to really twist the knife. He turned to O'Kieffe. "We paid your bill for the firm's insurance the day we got it, didn't we?"

"I don't know. I don't keep track of that kind of stuff."

"Bullshit! You know we did. I had the check sent to your attention. By messenger. We didn't wait any fuckin' thirty days!"

Curly turned back to the bar and fired down his glass of Macallan. He felt a momentary shiver that eased into a delicious tingle. "Pay your fuckin' bills, Red," he repeated after a moment, looking down at the bar.

"Hey, I don't need this shit," O'Kieffe said, sliding off his barstool. "I was going to ask you if you wanted to have dinner, but forget it." He initialed his bar tab and started to leave, then turned back. "You know, Curly, you can be a real jerk when you've had a few too many."

"A jerk? You're calling *me* a jerk?" Curly slammed down his empty glass and sat upright.

But O'Kieffe was gone. He had scurried off somewhere, like a rat. Curly laughed out loud. *Damn, that was fun!*

The House Insurance Committee had been meeting all day, and Karen Jeffries was exhausted. She could see that everyone else was too. She had hoped that they'd adjourn in time for her to catch the six o'clock plane back to Chicago. She and Tony had planned on having a late dinner, but that was looking less and less likely. The six o'clock flight was the last one out, and if Karen missed it she'd be stuck in Springfield one more night. She could always rent a car, of course, and drive back, but she was too tired, and with the light snow that was falling the roads could be unpredictable. She was mulling over her alternatives while she checked off the bills the committee had dealt with.

The only reason she was staying was to vote against Dick Vass's bill to remove the cap on punitive damages in medical malpractice lawsuits. Several other members of the committee had already slipped out, and it was a safe bet they wouldn't be returning. Karen strongly opposed Vass's bill, and with the trial lawyers pushing it and lobbyists like Emil Borders working hard to move it onto the House floor, she knew that every vote counted.

The Vass bill was last on the agenda. She knew that that wasn't a coincidence. Nothing that happens in Springfield when the legislature is in session is a coincidence.

By the time they called the bill it was five-thirty. Karen had already given up any hope of making the last plane out. Dick Vass appeared before the committee and made an impassioned plea for its passage. Badly injured patients, he said, should have the right to every bit of compensation that juries of their peers feel they're entitled to, and that includes punitive damages to send messages to careless physicians. The so-called medical malpractice crisis that had frightened the legislature into capping those non-economic damages last year was a hoax perpetrated by the insurance industry and the medical profession, and it's time to correct that wrong. As he went on, Karen noticed several of the state's most prominent plaintiffs' lawyers sitting in the back of the room, nodding in agreement.

The president of the Illinois State Medical Society, Dr. George Baumrucker, a urologist from Hinsdale, followed Vass and challenged all of his assertions. Before the cap was imposed, he argued, outrageous punitive damage awards had been destroying the medical profession and driving up the cost of medical insurance for everyone. More and more employers were being forced to turn to managed-care providers of questionable quality. Without a cap, every medical malpractice case filed, no matter how minor, carried the potential of massive punitive damages: ten million, twenty million, even more - awards that bore no real relationship to the damages suffered. Physicians felt compelled to give every patient an endless number of tests, some very expensive, to protect themselves from malpractice claims and possibly career-ending punitive damage judgments. Malpractice insurance premiums skyrocketed, causing many physicians to move to states with a friendlier environment. The main beneficiaries of that system, Dr. Baumrucker said, gesturing over his shoulder, were the plaintiffs' personal-injury attorneys. The current system, he pointed out, still enabled injured patients to recover substantial damages when medical malpractice occurred, including the cost of all future medical care, compensation for lost earnings and punitive damages of up to a quarter of a million dollars. And since the cap had been in effect, insurance premiums had dropped steadily, doctors were returning to Illinois, and the cost of medical care had not only leveled off but was actually beginning to decline.

When Dr. Baumrucker was finished, Karen, as a member of the committee, remarked that her mail ran over three-to-one against Vass's bill. Under the old system, she said, punitive damages had gotten totally out of hand--a fact virtually everyone recognized.

She was surprised that no one besides Dick Vass spoke up in support of the bill--not a single representative; or anyone else. She leaned back in her chair with a sense of relief and satisfaction. The bill would go down in flames; she had overestimated the strength of the plaintiffs' trial bar.

And then the vote was taken. The bill passed, twelve to one. Karen was shocked; she was the only member of the committee who voted against it.

Immediately after the vote was announced, the chairman gaveled the meeting to a close. Karen's mind was still swimming with the decisiveness of the vote as she collected her papers and watched her colleagues file out. Dick Vass looked at her from the back of the room, nodded with a slight smile, and walked out too.

Outside the door on her own way out, Karen saw Emil

Borders off to one side, grinning broadly. One by one, many of the representatives were stopping by to shake his hand and say a few words. Several also stopped for hushed exchanges with the plaintiffs' lawyers who were standing nearby.

Karen tried to avoid Borders, but he caught up with her as she walked down the hallway. He was still grinning. It was surprisingly chilly in the corridor, and Karen shuddered.

"You see, honey," he said, "there was no stopping it. Not here, and not on the House floor. Same thing's gonna happen in the Senate. And I have every reason to believe," he paused and gave her a knowing smile, "that the governor will sign the bill the day it reaches his desk. I just have that feeling. You blew your chance for an easy couple of grand." He shook his head, still smiling. "You'll learn. Everyone does."

⁓*mm*⁓

"I will *not* pay for psychological counseling for the kids!" Cal shouted into the phone. "That's bullshit, and you know it!"

"Mr. Cizma, believe me, it would be advisable for you to be reasonable about this. If you don't pay these bills voluntarily, I'm sure I can get a court order compelling you to do so."

"Well, then, you just do that!" Cal slammed down the phone and sat shaking at his desk for several minutes.

How had Sandy found such a slimeball for a lawyer? This guy Fontayne was trying to escalate everything into an irresolvable confrontation. Cal knew his kids better than Fontayne did, and probably better than Sandy did, too. They were perfectly fine. If they needed counseling, it was because Sandy had drawn them into the divorce and filled them with animosity toward him. She was using the kids as weapons, and he deeply resented it. He certainly wasn't going to pay exorbitant counseling bills just to fuel the fire she had lit. It was obvious what Sandy was doing, and, if she insisted on taking the issue to court, no judge was going to let her get away with it.

A knock at the door interrupted his fuming.

"Come in!" he shouted.

His secretary pushed the door open timidly, waited for Cal to nod to her, then walked in and handed him a fax. She said it had just come in. After waiting a moment for any further instructions, she turned and quickly left, shutting the door behind her.

The fax was from Ronnie Dasher; Cal immediately recognized the crown on the letterhead. It was short, only three sentences: "The reinsurer declines recommendation to authorize settlement of the Roosevelt case for 2.4 million dollars. The reinsurer believes exposure is overestimated. Proceed with trial preparation and keep us advised." It was signed "R. Dasher".

Cal was stunned. He had never heard of a reinsurer declining the settlement recommendation of trial counsel. This was crazy. Had they actually read the report? Did they understand how American juries can work, especially in cases with very serious injuries?

Cal shook his head, then grabbed the phone and punched in a number. It rang once before a familiar voice answered. "Tony Jeffries."

"Tony, this is Cal. We've got a problem. The reinsurer has declined to give us settlement authority in the Roosevelt case, even after we offered to put up our dough. They want you to try it."

"What?"

"That's right. You'd better come take a look at the fax yourself. If we can't get them to reverse themselves, this thing could unravel pretty quickly, especially since the hospital's insisted that we settle if we can. Imperial and its reinsurer might be rolling the dice for a lot on this one."

"I'll be right up."

You'd better be worried, Tony, Cal thought. *If this case turns into a can of worms, it sure as hell isn't going to be my responsibility. I'm going to make damn certain of that.*

Chapter Twelve

~~~~

Cal Cizma was surprised he wasn't able to see either Gordon Hawke or Ronnie Dasher--surprised and disappointed. He thought it had all been arranged. He had taken the late-night American flight to Heathrow in order to be at Imperial's office for a two o'clock meeting on Monday. It was important to resolve whatever misunderstandings there were regarding the settlement of the Roosevelt case, as well as to reach a broader agreement on the whole medical malpractice book of business. There were a lot of open issues on the table right now, issues that really couldn't be put off.

But Hawke had an emergency meeting in Geneva, and Dasher was hospitalized with a severe case of bronchitis, Roxanne told him when he arrived at Imperial's offices. They knew the meeting was important, though, and both men wanted him to stay until they could reschedule.

Roxanne stood up behind her desk and moved close to Cal, her breasts under her blouse brushing up against him. As ever, the smell of her perfume was intoxicating. "I'd like you to stay, too," she whispered. "It's been much too long. And as long as both the big cats are away, who's to care if this little mouse comes out to play?" She smiled and rested a hand gently on his chest. "I've got something to share with you," she continued, her voice alluringly low. "Something special. You've come at just the right time."

"Well, I guess I could endure a few days' wait," he said, returning her smile. He wanted to put his arms around her and pull her close. It had been weeks since they'd been together, and he realized how little of that time she'd been absent from his mind.

There was a click of a door behind Roxanne and she quickly stepped back. Over her shoulder Cal could see Hawke's matronly secretary staring their way.

"Well, I'm sorry that Mr. Hawke isn't in today," he said to Roxanne, raising his voice slightly. "I'll be in town the rest of the week, at our firm's flat. Please give me call if either he or Mr. Dasher is available before the week's end."

"I certainly will, Mr. Cizma," Roxanne answered in a crisp, businesslike tone. "And I'll see you there about six," she whispered with a wink and a smile.

Cal couldn't help returning her smile, even with the older woman looking on. He nodded to her politely, then turned and walked toward the door. He could feel his pulse racing.

God, how he loved being with Roxanne!

—*mm*—

"Brothers and sisters, I'm pleased to present the newest member of the board of trustees of the Grand Temple of Islam, our general counsel and my good friend, Rasheed Collins."

Rasheed stood and acknowledged the enthusiastic applause from the crowd in the Temple's ornate Hall of the East, then shook Minister Lund's hand while two photographers took the publicity shots. He was pleased to have been named to the Temple's board, but embarrassed by the excessive attention given the event. He glanced over at Aliza. She had a proud smile and was clapping furiously.

"I can't tell you how pleased I am that you were elected to the board, Rasheed," Minister Lund said quietly as they shook hands, the photographers swirling and flashing around them. "I've never told you this, but my dream is to someday step down as chairman of the board and devote all my energies to the Temple's ministries. I could never do that, though, until I had a successor as chairman in whom I had total confidence. That's you, Rasheed. We seem to think the same about everything. I'm just sorry that you don't have a degree in ministry," he added with a smile. "But maybe I can talk you into that as a second career."

"Thank you, Minister, I'm deeply touched." Rasheed *was* moved, and he returned the minister's firm handshake while the two of them exchanged a long, friendly smile. This was more than he had expected. Minister Lund was treating him like the son he'd never had. Rasheed appreciated that. He made a commitment to himself, standing there in the Hall of the East surrounded by flashing lights, that he would *never* do anything to embarrass or disappoint the old man.

—*mm*—

The late-afternoon sun played across the paisley wallpaper in a way that seemed to bring it to life. The yellow flowers were all bobbing and weaving together, as though dancing to some distant music. Then it was the reds, the powerful reds, asserting their dominance, while dancing to the same faint rhythm. From time to time a dark shadow would sweep across the field of flowers, jumbling the yellows and the reds, along with the greens and the browns, but before long they returned to their familiar swaying patterns.

"Care for some Champagne, love?" Roxanne whispered sensuously in his ear.

"Wonderful idea."

She leaned over and kissed him from above, her hair softly falling down both sides of his face. He responded to her tongue and opened his mouth to find it suddenly filled with bubbling Champagne. He let it trickle down his throat and out the corner of his mouth as he put his hand around her smooth shoulders and held her close to him. Roxanne laid her head on his shoulder and began running a hand through the hair in his groin. Cal let out a quiet moan; he loved what she did to him.

"I thought the Champagne was all gone," he said after a few minutes.

"I called down to Bellie's for another case while you were sleeping, love," she said softly. "Like we did on Tuesday. Told them to put it on the account."

"Good girl," Cal chuckled, his eyes closed. "You're definitely trainable."

Her hand traced soft circles, tickling the hair on his groin. *She understands me perfectly*, Cal thought, his excitement rising. *Why didn't I meet her years ago? All those wasted years with Sandy...*

"Talked to my friend Rudy, too," she whispered. "He's going to drop off enough coke to take good care of us. The pure stuff, like we had last night."

"That's great."

"Rudy is going to need some money when he gets here, love. I promised him. Is that okay?"

"Sure. How much will he need?"

"Three thousand," she said softly.

"Three thousand? Pounds or dollars?" Either way, that seemed like a lot to Cal. It brought him back a little from the euphoria in which he had been drifting. *But what the hell. The firm's going to pay for it anyway.*

"Dollars, love."

"I'll have to give him a check. I don't have that kind of cash with me right now. I'll make it payable to his company. What's it's name, again?"

"Cooper Enterprises, I think. I'm sure he'll take it. He knows it won't bounce," she giggled as she slid her hand down and gently held him. Cal arched his back; it was wonderful.

Then he remembered something Roxanne had said a few minutes ago--something about Tuesday. "What day is this?" he asked, opening his eyes and looking at the darkening shadows on the wall.

"Friday, love."

"Friday? Damn! I was hoping to see Hawke or Ronnie before the week was over." He sat up in bed and shook his head. Roxanne pulled her hand back a bit but kept it resting gently on his thigh. *Where in hell has the week gone?*

"I checked for you, love," she answered quietly. "Neither one was in today. Gordon hasn't returned from Switzerland, and poor Ronnie's in Intensive Care; his bronchitis has turned into some kind of pneumonia. You're going to have to come back some other time to see them. And me, too."

Cal lay back down and stared at the ceiling. Had he been here all week? Was that possible? Memories began tumbling back: turning off his BlackBerry and the flat's phone so there wouldn't be any interruptions, making love more times than he could count, endless lines of coke, late-night meals at Bellingham's Tavern downstairs, Champagne, more sex and more coke. It had been unbelievable. But had it been a whole week? Cal chuckled out loud. Yes, it had been, and it had been wonderful. The Imperial Insurance Syndicate and its problems seemed very insignificant. Whatever they were, they could wait.

And Roxanne was right: what a wonderful excuse to come back to London!

—*mm*—

"I like this case, Max. I think it can be a real bell ringer if we get the right jury. Yeah, I'll take it on." Mike Granaldi leaned back in his black leather swivel chair, with the green of Grant Park and the dark blue of the lake behind him accentuated by the late-afternoon sun, and gave Max the nod he was waiting for.

"Good. And you think you can get it advanced for an early trial? Not wait the usual two or three years? That's important."

"I know, I know." Granaldi dismissed Max's concern with a wave. "It always is. But in this case, that shouldn't be a problem. Our plaintiff's comatose in a public-aid nursing home. His wife and kid are starving and not even getting welfare checks for some ungodly reason. It's the kind of case that *should* be advanced. I'll bring our motion before Judge Flannagan. He owes me. I chaired his goddamn reelection committee last year. Yeah, it'll be advanced."

Max Greene couldn't have been more pleased. Mike Granaldi was the best plaintiffs' lawyer in town, and with him trying it, Max knew they'd collect big. This was going to be the payday he'd always hoped for. The hospital's attorneys hadn't responded to his settlement demand. The thirty days he gave them ran out today, and he wasn't going to wait any longer, not with Mike Granaldi interested in taking the case.

"What kind of fee arrangement do you have?" As he spoke, Granaldi stood up and walked over to the bookcases that lined one wall of his office. He touched it and a section slid back, revealing a fully stocked bar glistening with brass fixtures. Granaldi turned back to him. "I asked what kind of fee arrangement you have, Max."

"Oh, I'm sorry. A third straight one-third," Max stammered, his eyes still fixed on Granaldi's elaborate bar.

"Plus expenses, I take it." Granaldi had his back to him and was pouring a drink. He'd taken off his suit coat, and a lean, athletic body was evident under his tailored shirt. Max had heard that Grinaldi had a private gym adjacent to his office and that he worked out every morning.

"Right. Plus expenses."

"So… what'll you have?" Granaldi turned with a gesture toward the bar.

"Bourbon and water, if you don't mind."

"No trouble at all." Granaldi turned back, grabbed a bottle, and within seconds was handing Greene his drink. "To our good fortune," he said, raising his own glass.

"Yes, our good fortune," Max responded nervously. He felt awkward sitting there, with Granaldi hovering over him.

"I'll want twenty-five percent of the recovery, Max," Granaldi said, still looking down at him. "That'll leave you with only eight and a third. Can you live with that? If you can't, there's nothing more for us to talk about."

"Yes, that's fine with me," Max answered quickly. "I heard that was your usual deal, and I can live with it." He added, "Hell, eight-and-a third-percent of what you'll recover is a hell of a lot more dough than I'll get if I try the case myself. I know that. It's a deal."

"I want to see your original fee agreement. Just to make sure there's no misunderstanding."

"No problem." Max reached inside his coat pocket and pulled out a folded piece of white paper. He had taken it out of his briefcase and put it in his pocket during the elevator ride up to Granaldi's office. It was a little damp from his perspiration. He wished he didn't sweat so much. "Here it is," he said, handing it up to Granaldi, who was still standing disconcertingly close. "You can see it's straight one-third, plus expenses," he added.

Granaldi opened the paper gingerly, using only the tips of his fingers. He looked at it for a moment, nodded, and walked back to his desk.

"I'll keep this, if you don't mind, Max." He pushed a button on his desk, and a moment later a tall blonde in a tight white skirt walked in. "Gloria, type up a co-counsel agreement between our office and Mr. Greene. The usual twenty-five percent for us. And attach a copy of this to Mr. Greene's copy, if you would. We'll keep the original."

"Certainly, Mr. Granaldi." She flashed him a smile, then turned and walked from the room. Max's eyes followed her white skirt all the way out.

"Yes, Max, this could be a nice one." Granaldi raised his glass to him and smiled. "I think we're both going to make some money."

Ten minutes later, the elevator doors slid shut and began descending from Mike Granaldi's penthouse office. Max waited until the elevator had gone down three or four floors, then dropped his briefcase and raised both his hands and his eyes. *Yes! I did it!* He had pulled off the greatest financial coup of his life!

If Granaldi had known that Max's *current* fee agreement with Bertha Roosevelt gave him *eighty percent* of any recovery, plus expenses, he'd have insisted on much more. Even in his state of elation, Max was able to make the calculations. With Mike Granaldi agreeing to handle the case for twenty-five percent, he stood to recover over half of any judgment. *That might be a couple of million bucks!* He'd let Granaldi present the original fee agreement to the court for approval after the trial, then he'd spring his amendments. Granaldi would be royally pissed, as might be the judge, but he'd have to approve them; they were signed and notarized; consideration had changed hands; they were enforceable. He shut his eyes and grinned, pumping his hands in front of him. He wanted to shout out. He was finally going to score, and score big!

As the elevator slowed down, Max began composing himself. He picked up his briefcase, suppressed his smile, and walked out into the lobby as calm as ever when the doors opened. The first thing he would do, he decided, was to send Bertha Roosevelt two dozen roses. No, that was a bit much; one dozen. It was the least he could do.

~~~

Carol James hung her coat on the back of her office door, sat down on the couch, and changed from her Nikes to her office mid-heels. It was December, and there had been a distinct chill in the air as she walked to work that morning from her condo in Streeterville. She enjoyed these brisk early-morning walks.

She picked the pot up from her coffee maker and carried it to her floor's kitchen to be filled with water. There weren't many other people around yet in her area, just a couple of secretaries and a paralegal. Carol liked being at work early. She could get a lot done before the phone started ringing and people started dropping by.

Her plan that morning was to get caught up on her time sheets. Throughout the week she made notes on her desk calendar as she worked on client matters, and about once a week she entered them onto the firm's official time records through her computer. It was tedious, but a necessary evil of legal work. By the time her coffee had brewed, she'd made it through Wednesday, and she took a short break to fill her mug. She'd already had a cup at home, but it always took this second round to really get her going.

When she was done, Carol made some quick calculations and saw that, through the end of November, she was on a pace to record twenty-two hundred billable hours for the year. That was good. It was well ahead of the required two thousand, and should put her in good stead when she was considered for equity partnership next year.

The mail arrived about eight-thirty, her packet bound by a rubberband. Freddie from the mailroom, who dropped it off, had been with the firm at least as long as she had. She remembered meeting him on her first day there, ten years ago last September.

As Carol began sorting her mail into stacks of varying priorities, a routine she followed every morning, one envelope in particular caught her attention. It was hand-addressed, looked like a personal letter, and she decided to open it first. It was from a law-school friend of hers, Maria Southern, who now practiced in the Toronto office of one of the big New York firms. Maria wrote that she had run across Bill Turple a few days ago. He was engaged to a woman who lived in Maria's building and they planned to get married soon. Maria recalled that Carol and Bill used to know each other and thought Carol might be interested.

Carol put Maria's letter down and stared out the window. *No, I hadn't heard about Bill. How long has it been since he moved to Toronto? Two months, maybe a little more. That sure happened fast.*

She looked down at Lincoln Park to the north and thought of their many picnic lunches there as they watched the boats moving in and out of the lagoon. After a moment, she forced herself to look away, up into the sky. There was a plane far overhead, flying southeast from O'Hare. They never had taken that romantic trip to the Caribbean they'd always talked about. Tears began to cloud her focus on the plane. Carol wiped them away, took a deep breath, and turned back to her desk.

There was an awful lot of junk in the mail today, she thought, picking up that stack on her desk, thumbing through it and throwing it all into the waste basket. She tore open the remaining envelopes, scanned their contents without really reading them, and pushed them to the side. *So Bill's getting married.* She wondered what kind of a woman his fiancée was, and if she'd be good for him. Was she a good lover? Bill needed that; he needed to know that he was both loved and desired.

No, Carol said to herself, *I've got to put that out of my mind. I made my decision, and I've got my own career to pursue, right here.*

She looked at the papers scattered across her desk and picked up the first one she was able to focus on. It was a Notice of Motion in the Roosevelt case, addressed to her and Tony Jeffries. It said that Michael Granaldi would be appearing before the Honorable Judge Edward Flannagan next Thursday, December 18, at 9:30 a.m., asking for leave to file his additional appearance as counsel for the plaintiffs. He would also be moving to file an Amended Complaint and to have the case advanced for an early trial.

Michael Granaldi! Max Greene had done it; he hadn't even waited for their response. Of course, they were a little late, she knew that, but they hadn't been able to reach Cal Cizma for over a week, and they didn't know whether or not they had settlement authority from Imperial's reinsurer. Well, it didn't matter anymore, she thought. The fat's really in the fire now.

She flipped to the Amended Complaint attached to Granaldi's motion. She could tell immediately that it was tighter and better written than Greene's original pleading. And she noticed something else.

Mike Granaldi was suing for punitive damages in excess of ten million dollars!

—*mm*—

"We can't be sentimental about these things, Pete. We're running a business with a budget of close to two hundred million dollars, and I think that you and I are the only two men in the firm who appreciate the enormity of that task." Cal tapped the table as he made his point, then paused and added, "And the opportunity."

Pete Spanos was glad that Cal had suggested that they have dinner at the Signature Room that evening. For some time he had sensed that he and Cal had one vision of the firm's future while Tony and the others had quite another. It was time for the two of them to have a candid discussion of their long-range plans and objectives.

"I agree," Pete answered. "And one of the first things

we've got to do is to stop giving away money like it was candy. I'm talking about the associates' salaries now." He was pleased to see Cal nod his concurrence. "These raises we've been giving everyone the past few years are crazy. Fifteen, twenty thousand bucks a year; those kinds of increases should only go to people who earn them, not to everybody."

"In other words, establish a meritocracy," Cal replied. "Give good raises to the people who merit them, and hold everyone else flat. And get rid of people who don't cut the mustard."

"Exactly. That would make raises mean something, and at the same time bring more money to the bottom line."

"Of course, if we do that," Cal said, "we'll have to make sure that the people who work for the two of us-- who, as far as I'm concerned, are the best young attorneys in the firm - get decent raises. I can't afford to lose anyone, and I assume you can't, either."

"That's right," Pete responded. "But that's something we have some control over, you and I. All the associates will be getting their annual evaluations next June, with the July raises in mind. You're chairman of the associates' compensation committee. Make sure *our* people are covered."

"They will be." Cal nodded. "The rest of the troops around here, though, are going to find that raises aren't going to come easily--not easily at all. And if that drives some of the weak sisters out, all the better." He nodded at their waiter, who was standing at a discreet distance. The waiter approached, took their drink orders, and left the menus and wine list.

The restaurant was quiet that evening. Only a few tables were taken, and Pete noticed that the maitre d' had seated the groups far enough apart from each other to avoid any prying ears. *Very thoughtful of him.* He peered at the other tables through the subdued light. He recognized a local talk-show host at one, speaking with a slight, dark-skinned man who was very well dressed and looked like he could have been an Arab prince. At another table, two of the senior partners from another law firm were dining with a white-haired gentleman who looked vaguely familiar to Pete. After a minute or two it hit him: Senator Rowland Carlson of Nevada. Pete smiled to himself. Mama would be proud if she could see him dining there. The quiet energy that Pete could feel pulsing around them; the twinkling lights of the city far below: he felt like one of the gods atop Mount Olympus. This was what success was all about.

Thinking about Mama brought a pang of guilt. He'd always wanted to take her to dinner up here, but never did. It would have embarrassed him to introduce her to his friends or partners and hear her stumble through a greeting, sounding like a refugee just off the boat. He wished that she'd learned English better.

"Oh, I almost forgot to tell you," Cal said. "I got some great news from Imperial today."

"What's that?"

"They're going to start using us for their transactional work. We're going to be their principal corporate attorneys in the United States." Cal's grin was contagious.

"That's fantastic!" Pete put his glass of wine down. This was exciting.

"Yeah. The first deal involves their purchase and consolidation of three small insurance companies in the Caribbean. On each acquisition, they're going to wire us the funds to hold in escrow until the closing. When we get the word, we'll wire the money to the sellers' bank. Not much to it, as far as our end goes, but we're getting twenty grand for each deal. The main thing, though, is that they're going to be using us in matters beyond just litigation."

"That's great, Cal. Congratulations!"

"Thanks." He raised his Dewars and water and took a sip.

The waiter returned and asked if they were ready to order; he recommended the rack of lamb. Pete took his advice, asked for it medium rare, and said he'd begin with a Caesar salad. Cal ordered veal and a cup of lobster bisque, a house specialty

"There's something else I've been thinking about," Cal said as the waiter walked away. "We should be doing more for our partners in terms of providing better fringe benefits. Tax-free benefits."

"That's not a bad idea. What do you have in mind?"

"Well, for starters," Cal said, taking a sip of his drink, "we ought to expand our medical package. It's really pretty primitive. Do you realize, for example, that it doesn't provide anything for mental health care?"

"No, I didn't. But, frankly, I haven't really looked at our coverage closely."

"Well, I think it's a scandal that a firm like this doesn't provide mental health coverage for its employees, or at least its partners and their families," Cal continued. "You and I will probably never have the need for it, but somebody will, and our policy should provide that kind of coverage."

"That sounds reasonable to me. Our medical coverage is written through American Union. It would be easy for me to get a quote."

"Why don't you just go ahead and have them add that coverage, Pete. One hundred percent reimbursement for all mental health expenses for partners and their dependents. Probably can't get it retroactive, but let's get that coverage as soon as we can."

"That might be expensive, Cal."

"Well, it's the right thing to do, damn it! Our firm can afford it, whatever the additional premium is."

Pete nodded. *So,* he mused, *the Cizma kids are having psychiatric problems. Or Sandy, maybe.* Neither would surprise him. Cal was so transparent. Everyone knew he'd been thrown out of the house in Kenilworth and that he and Sandy were at war on a dozen fronts. This was probably one of them. Then Pete had an idea; he might just as well get something out of this, too.

"How does our medical policy define dependents?"

he asked. "Does it include dependent parents?" He was thinking of Mama's shrill remarks last Sunday about the skyrocketing cost of their supplemental medical insurance.

"No, I'm sure it doesn't," Cal answered. "That would be pretty unusual coverage, Pete. And as long as we're talking about expense, that would be *damn* expensive."

"Well, as you said a minute ago, Cal, our firm can afford it. And it *would* provide a nice additional benefit for some of our partners."

Cal looked at him for a moment and smiled. "You know," he said, "the more I think about it, the more sense it makes. Why don't you call American Union tomorrow and add *both* coverages to our medical plan; mental health care for dependents, and 'dependents' redefined to include dependent parents. We'll just announce it to the firm without mentioning the additional cost, whatever the hell that is."

"What about the insurance committee?" Pete asked. "Curly's chairman. Won't he be pissed off if he's cut out of the loop?"

"Screw him. We'll tell him that the management committee approved it at a meeting that he missed. He'll be too embarrassed to check with anyone else. And if Tony or Rasheed asks, we'll tell them that the insurance committee made the decision. Nobody will be sure, and in the meantime we'll just go ahead and do it."

"I'll make the call tomorrow." Pete leaned back as the waiter served their soup and salad. What a great Christmas present to give Mama and Papa, he thought. It never had occurred to him to try to add them to the office's medical policy, but the opportunity Cal presented was too golden to ignore.

The Caesar salad was good; it had enough anchovies to give it some bite. Like good Greek salad, Pete thought. Whoever invented it probably stole it from the Greeks in the first place.

"Another thing we've got to do," Cal said, leaning forward. "is reduce the number of equity partners. I've mentioned this before in general terms. I've run the figures out now, and the results are incredible, Pete. We've got one hundred and ten equity partners in the firm right now. At least a third of them aren't carrying their weight and ought to go, or at least be de-equitized. If we can arrange that, push them out one way or another, and hold off naming any new equity partners for a couple of years, we can make a hell of a lot of dough; a hell of a lot!"

Pete could tell from the intensity of Cal's voice and of his tight-lipped smile that he was very excited about this. Pete couldn't have had a better ally. Cal's goals were obvious; they always had been. If Pete helped him get them, he knew that he could exact a tremendous price in return.

"I agree, Cal. The only reservation I have is that I've got someone who's up for equity partner this coming year. Larry O'Neal. I've pretty much promised him that he's going to make it. If he's passed over, he's going to be really pissed. I might even lose him."

"How important is he to you, Pete?"

"Very."

"All right, that's easy." Cal leaned back with a smile. "O'Neal makes it, but nobody else does. For the next couple of years. We'll have to figure out some way to justify it. How's that sound to you?"

"Excellent." Pete raised his glass. "Cal, I think we understand each other. This should work out very well for us. And as you said earlier, the opportunities we have," he touched his glass to Cal's across the table, "are unlimited."

—*mm*—

There was tension in the management committee meeting that week--the kind of tension that Tony hadn't noticed since the five of them took over. Of course, there were only four today. Curly was ill and hadn't come to the office. Tony suspected he knew what that was all about.

Maybe the tension came from fact that the settlement negotiations in the *Roosevelt versus Blessed Trinity Hospital* case had broken down. Since they hadn't settled within the policy limits, as the hospital demanded, the insurer was liable now for the full amount of any judgment. Cal said that he had tried to explain that to the underwriters at Imperial, but he wasn't sure they understood. There was a lot at risk now, including a relationship with a key client. Tony wasn't looking forward to trying that case.

Or perhaps the tension that Tony felt came from the fact that for the first time this fiscal year, the firm's cash flow had become soft. Accounts payable were way up, partly because the firm wasn't paying any routine bills on the Imperial book of business. Court reporters and expert witnesses could wait. The $600,000 in the Imperial account had all been earmarked to cover the firm's exposure in the Roosevelt case, and until that fund got back up to over a million, it couldn't be used for anything else; except to pay the fees of law firms in other cities that they'd hired, and the expenses for the London trips, of course. But receivables were slow, too, and Pete Spanos, as chairman of the finance committee, said he'd look into the matter.

Perhaps the tension that pervaded the meeting came from something else. The sense of civility and cooperation that Tony had noticed in their earlier meetings just wasn't there anymore. Tony couldn't put his finger on it, but as Cal ran quickly through the items on the agenda, things seemed ....well, different.

The last item on their agenda was consideration of new equity partners. It was January, and if new equity partners were going to be brought in at the end of the year, it was time to start discussing names.

"I'd like to put this matter off for a while, fellas, if you don't mind," Cal announced. "Now that we have new management, I'd like us to draw up some specific criteria to follow in admitting new partners, and not just rely on the old who-knows-who routine."

"I agree with that, Cal," Pete added. "And I'll be happy to work with you in drawing up some criteria. We shouldn't be in any rush to bring in new equity partners, anyway. That just diffuses the profits more. There's no harm in delaying the process a bit."

"What do you mean by 'a bit'?" Tony asked. "I've got someone who's up for consideration this coming year--Carol James. She, and the others who are in the same spot, will be expecting an announcement by fall. If it's not made, they'll all assume they were passed over. And I can tell you, the impact on their morale will be crushing. We owe it to those people to begin making decisions now, or at least over the next couple of months. We can begin deciding who's definitely in, who's definitely out, and who needs further review."

"We'll tell them the truth," Cal answered. "We'll tell them that we're developing new criteria for admission of equity partners, and as soon as they're developed, we'll advise everyone. They'll all be treated the same, so there's no prejudice. And frankly, I think it's just good business to approach this subject in an orderly way. We've made too many people equity partners in the past just because they'd hung around for ten years and avoided getting fired. It's time for us to develop some standards, and take the time to do it properly."

"I don't like it," Tony said. "For those people, like Carol, who've done a good job and who've earned full partnership, it'll be profoundly disappointing to have this put over. I don't like what you're proposing, and I won't vote for it."

"I was hoping we could reach a consensus on this, Tony," Cal responded, "and not have to actually vote.

That might tend to be divisive."

"Well, I'm sorry, Cal, but I feel very strongly about this. I'm not going to concur in any plan that will defer a decision on Carol and the others who should be up for consideration this year."

"I agree with Tony," Rasheed added. "I've got *two* people who are up this year, and in a month or so they're going to be asking me what's going on. It's just not fair to string them on."

Cal looked at both Tony and Rasheed, then turned to Pete Spanos. "I take it, Pete, that you agree with me on this issue."

"Yes, I do," Pete answered.

"Well, in that case it looks like we have a two-to-two vote," Cal said. "A tie. And as chairman, I'll cast the deciding vote. We're not going to make any decisions on new equity partners for the time being. Pete and I will comprise a special committee to draft up some criteria for admission of new partners, and we'll announce it to the entire firm when we're ready. It might not be for some time."

"I don't like this, Cal," Tony said.

"Sorry, Tony, but that's the way it's going to be."

Chapter Thirteen

"Carol, we just had a meeting of the management committee." Tony eased into one of the upholstered armchairs across from Carol James' desk as he spoke. He was uncomfortable, but knew that he had to tell her right away what the committee had done. He didn't want her to hear it from anyone else first. "The committee decided," he said, "over my objection, to defer any decisions on new equity partners for the time being."

"What?" Carol snapped forward as if she'd been poked with a tasar. The shock in her eyes and her open mouth were exactly what Tony had feared.

"Now, don't overreact," Tony said, raising his hand. "Cal wants to develop some criteria that'll be applied to everyone, so that equity partnership isn't automatic, but given fairly. There's nothing to worry about. No matter what standards they come up with, you'll do fine. You've been the most productive person in your class since the day you walked in the door. So it's not going to be a problem for you. Irritating, yes, but not a real problem."

"Yes, I'd say it's irritating. I don't like this idea of changing the rules in the middle of the game." She looked at him for a second, then asked, "When's this all supposed to happen?"

"Well, not necessarily right away. Cal and Pete Spanos are going to draft some criteria, but they might not get them finished and circulated until some time later this year."

"Damn!" she sat back, looked down at her desk, and shook her head. After a moment she looked up at Tony. "They're playing games with us. I know it. Just watch--the criteria will be that you have to work for a senior partner who's either Greek or who owns a house in Kenilworth. They're going to figure some way of squeezing some of us out. I just know it."

"Now, come on, Carol," Tony said, leaning forward with one hand on the edge of her desk. "I'm not going to let something like that happen to you, and no one else is, either."

"Well, at the very least, we're going to lose a year. I'll bet anything on that. They won't come out with their criteria till August or September, the firm will kick it around for six months, and we'll be made equity partners two year from now, if then. We will have lost a year. If that happens, it'll cost me, and everyone else in my class, thirty or forty thousand dollars. That's money that we'll never make up." She stared down at her desk and shook her head. "Damn!" she repeated.

Tony's stomach was churning with frustration; he didn't know what else to say.

She turned and looked out the window at the blue expanse of the lake far below them. "I hope I haven't made a mistake," she said quietly.

—*uun*—

"Curly, do you have a second?" Pete stood in Curly Morgan's office doorway, holding the computer printout he'd received from accounting that morning. Curly held up his left hand as he furiously scribbled away on a yellow pad. Open case books and pleadings surrounded him at his desk. Pete waited…and waited. Finally, Curly put down his pen and looked up.

"Sorry. I wanted to finish that thought before I forgot it," he said. "We're going to kill these guys with our reply brief. What can I do for you, Pete?"

"I'm running down some of our bigger accounts receivable," Pete said, stepping into the office. "You know the cash flow problem we're having at the moment. And I see that your Acorn Insurance account is really getting stale." He glanced down at his printout, then up at Curly. "They owe us over three hundred thousand bucks and haven't paid a thing in over two months. Can you do anything to get that brought current?"

"Damned if I know," Curly answered with a shrug. "I used to see Acorn's president at the club a lot, but he moved out a couple of weeks ago. I don't run into him anymore."

"Well, what do you suggest, Curly? We're handling something like forty files of theirs and running up time and disbursements every day. Do we have a problem with these guys?"

"I'm sure it's nothing to worry about," Curly said, waving him off. "Listen, this brief has to be filed by five o'clock and it's going to be close. But I'll give Red O'Kieffe a call at his office first thing tomorrow."

"Thanks. Let me know what he says so I can make a note for my file. And maybe follow up with a letter, too, to put a little more pressure on him. It's just too big a receivable to carry like this."

"Don't worry, I'll take care of it," Curly said, already back to his yellow pad.

Pete stepped out into the hall and jotted a note on his printout. He'd give Acorn thirty more days, then he'd cut them off cold. No more work on credit until their account was paid in full. As chairman of the finance committee, Pete would make sure of that.

Curly might be a good lawyer, but he's a rotten businessman. In fact, there are a lot of rotten businessmen among the partners, and they're wasting money every day. Now that he had access to all the firm's financial records, Pete could see that clearly. *Cal's right,* he thought. *If we impose some tough business standards, and cut out the partners who aren't really producing, we can dramatically improve the bottom line. And isn't that, after all, the whole idea?*

"All right, here's my order," Judge Flannagan announced briskly. "Plaintiffs' counsel has raised some compelling points regarding the impoverished condition of his clients. The Roosevelt case will be advanced for an early trial. Discovery is to be completed by June first, that's a little over three months. All pre-trial and dispositive motions must be filed by August first; responses due fifteen days thereafter, and the case will appear on the trial call on September seventh. I want both sides to be ready. It will be assigned out that day to the first available judge. Any questions, gentlemen?"

"Not a question, Your Honor," Mike Granaldi said with a polite smile. "We appreciate the court's ruling. As I recall, though, we also have a pending motion for the production of the hospital's insurance policies and all correspondence and documents, including e-mail messages, that relate to its insurance. The hospital's indicated that they'd produce the insurance policies, but are resisting the production of the related documents and correspondence."

"Yes, of course," the judge nodded. "That should all be produced, Mr. Jeffries, within ten days. Make that part of the order. Mr. Clerk, call the next case."

Tony stepped back as another pair of lawyers approached Judge Flannagan's bench. Granaldi had gotten everything he'd asked for. The brief that Carol had written, opposing the Motion to Advance, was good, but it didn't look like the judge had even read it. *That was a wasted effort,* Tony thought, dumping his notes into his briefcase. At the other table Mike Granaldi was writing the order. Flannagan's courtroom was crowded that day. This was his regular motion call, and there were dozens of lawyers milling around awaiting their turn. Granaldi showed Tony the order reflecting the judge's rulings, asked Tony to initial it, then handed it to the clerk to be signed and stamped. Tony stuffed his copy into his briefcase and walked out into the hall. Granaldi was a few steps behind him.

"Congratulations," Tony said, turning slightly as the courtroom door shut behind them.

"Didn't surprise me," Granaldi shrugged. "You can congratulate me when we bring in the verdict."

They were both walking toward the elevator corridor, taking their time. Other attorneys, most of them young, were scurrying by, trying to get from one courtroom to another, juggling impossible docket schedules. It was a clear day, and the sun was pouring in the floor-to-ceiling windows in the Daley Center, the monolithic building that was the home of the Circuit Court of Cook County.

"This'll be an interesting case to try," Tony commented. He wanted to draw Granaldi into discussing it.

"Interesting for me," Granaldi replied with a smile, looking straight ahead. "Maybe not so interesting for you."

Tony didn't particularly care for Granaldi. He had met him a few times before, but they had never tried a case against each other. Granaldi's reputation for arrogance appeared to be well earned.

"We had some settlement discussions with Max Greene before you got involved, Mike. I'm not sure they were ever completed. Are you interested in pursuing them?"

"Not particularly," Granaldi said, still looking straight ahead.

Tony stopped and let Granaldi walk on. *If this guy is going to be a complete asshole, let him. I'm not going to chase him around the courthouse.* He sighed. *Well, it looks like the Roosevelt case is going to be tried after all.*

———*mm*———

"Mr. Cizma, I have had it with these dilatory, obstructionist tactics of yours." Judge Juanita Hernandez leaned forward from behind her bench and pointed her gavel at Cal. "This may not be the United States District Court, or the Seventh Circuit Court of Appeals, but I can assure you that the Divorce Division of the Circuit Court of Cook County takes itself quite seriously. And we take our orders quite seriously. Am I making myself clear?"

"Yes. Quite clear, Your Honor." Cal shifted his feet and shook his head. "But perhaps I didn't explain my position very well," he said. "My income-tax returns contain confidential information about my law firm. From the schedules that are attached, anyone can calculate exactly how much each capital partner in our firm made last year. There's no way that my wife, or her attorney, should be allowed to see those figures. I don't want that information showing up next week in the *National Enquirer* or some other scandal sheet, and I'm afraid that's exactly what will happen if I turn over my tax returns."

Bernie Fontayne, standing to his left in front of the judge's bench, raised his hands in mock despair and smiled. "Your Honor," he said. "We've been through this before. My client and her children are entitled to reasonable support payments while this case is pending. There's no way that we, or the court, can determine what's reasonable without knowing Mr. Cizma's income. And he's totally stonewalled us on that."

"I understand completely, Mr. Fontayne." Judge Hernandez turned again to Cal. "First of all, Mr. Cizma," she said in quiet, measured tones, looking him hard in the eye, "I doubt very much if anyone outside this room gives a damn what you or your fellow partners at Wilson & Thompson made last year. Secondly, I've already entered an order that all financial records produced in this case will be confidential and may not be divulged to any other party without leave of court. Third, I assume that those are joint returns that you filed with your wife. She has every right to have copies. And finally," she picked up her gavel and pointed it at him, "we had a very similar discussion the last time you were both before me, over a month ago. I ordered you then to produce those returns, Mr. Cizma, and now I'm ordering you again. I want all your federal and state tax returns for the past three years, together with all their schedules and attachments, delivered to your wife's counsel, Mr. Fontayne, by five o'clock today."

"Your Honor," Cal laughed, "that's impossible. They're with my accountant."

"Where's his office?" The anger in Judge Hernandez's voice was rising.

"Evanston, Your Honor."

"That's less than a thirty-minute cab ride from here, Mr. Cizma," she said. She glanced at the clock on the wall of her courtroom, then looked back at him. "It's ten-thirty now. There's no reason in the world why you shouldn't be able to get those returns to Mr. Fontayne by noon, much less five o'clock. And that, Mr. Cizma, is exactly what I'm ordering you to do. Five o'clock today. Not one minute later!"

Cal took a deep breath. She sounded serious. He couldn't figure out how someone like this could become a judge. It was unbelievable. She was probably nominated to satisfy some minority quota--or, more likely, she was sleeping with the right alderman. She looked like that sort. And what was she doing sitting in divorce court, of all places? Her bias against men was blatant. But he was trapped; he had to deal with her. Besides, he had an important meeting to get to. This stupid hearing was taking way too long.

"All right," he said, looking down and shaking his head again. "I'll produce our returns, today."

"Fine."

"Your Honor." Bernie Fontayne stepped back up to the bench. "We'd like an award of our fees in having to go to the trouble of bringing this motion to compel today.

It shouldn't have been necessary, in view of the court's prior orders."

"Now, just a minute...." Cal began. This was going too far.

"I agree, Mr. Fontayne," the judge interrupted. "I'm going to impose sanctions. How much do you request?"

"I'd say three thousand dollars, Your Honor, when you consider all the time we spent preparing our motion, conferring with our client, and attending the hearing today."

"That sounds quite reasonable," Judge Hernandez answered. "Mr. Cizma, you will attach your personal check for three thousand dollars, payable to Mr. Fontayne, to the tax returns you're going to be delivering to him this afternoon. That's an order."

"Your Honor," Cal protested, "its going to take me a couple of days to get that kind of money into my checking account."

"I doubt that very much," the judge answered. "If your income, and that of your partners, is so high that it would create a national scandal if it became public, you shouldn't have any trouble at all raising three thousand dollars. Borrow it from petty cash, if you must." Several people in the back of the courtroom, waiting for their cases to be called, tittered and smiled. They were enjoying the entertainment this one was providing. A well-dressed man in his fifties, sitting alone in the back row, seemed particularly interested in the scene.

Cal was outraged, but he struggled to keep his cool;

losing it would only get him into more serious trouble with Hernandez. He turned and stared at the back of the courtroom, clenching his fists to control his anger.

"There is one more matter, Your Honor." Bernie Fontayne leaned forward and handed the judge another set of papers. "These are the bills for the Cizma children's psychological counseling. They add up to $3,600, and are accruing at the rate of $600 per week. Mr. Cizma refuses to pay them, even though you've directed him to do so. We've discussed this several times, and I'm afraid that it's not going to be resolved without the court's intervention."

You son of a bitch, Cal said to himself. *Twisting the knife every chance you get. I'll get even with you for all this bullshit.*

Judge Hernandez shuffled through the bills, shaking her head. Her jaw tightened as she put the last of them down.

"These bills, Your Honor..." Cal's voice rose as he spoke. He pointed to them, piled in front of the Judge, his hand shaking in anger. "These bills are not only un-necessary but are outrageous. There's absolutely no way that I'm..."

The shattering impact of the judge's gavel slamming down on her bench froze Cal's words in his mouth.

"Mr. Cizma," she said, her voice tense. "I see that I've underestimated you. And that I've underestimated the depth of your contempt for this court and for the judicial process. But that's over! I'm ordering you to pay these bills immediately--immediately! And I'm sentencing you to thirty days' confinement in the Cook County Jail for direct contempt of this court. I'm going to suspend that sentence, but only for so long as you are in full and absolute compliance with every word of every order that this court enters. If you appear before me again, with even a hint of disrespect for this court, or your family's welfare, or your wife's counsel, I assure you, you will spend the next thirty days in the Cook County Jail!" She punctuated her pronouncement with another resounding bang of her gavel.

Cal was in shock. *What in the hell is going on here?*

"And, Mr. Cizma," Judge Hernandez said with an unfriendly smile as she leaned forward, "a bit of advice."

"What's that?"

"Get yourself a lawyer."

Chapter Fourteen

—*www*—

Curly Morgan popped a couple of vitamins and an Extra Strength Tylenol into his mouth. He grimaced as he drank them down with a swig of black coffee. *The damn coffee's cold!* He'd grabbed yesterday's cup rather than this morning's. He dumped the rest of it into the sink to be sure that he wouldn't make that mistake again, then found the hot coffee and drank it all down.

He put on his tie and walked over to the window to look out. It was a clear day, and the sun was already high. The last snow had melted and Grant Park looked as cold and foreboding as the gray, choppy lake beyond it. Curly glanced at his watch: almost eleven. Well, hell, he'd worked until midnight finishing that damn Motion to Dismiss, then went out for dinner and a couple of drinks. He was entitled. He just hoped that Jackie could read all his handwriting. Even if she couldn't, there was plenty of time to make corrections and still get it filed this afternoon.

He locked his room, walked down the marble stair-case to the University Club's lobby, picked up a copy of the *Tribune* from the tobacco stand, and tucked it under his arm.

"Morning, Mr. Morgan," the doorman said. "It's a beautiful day today. Can I get you a taxi?"

"Yes, Eddie. Thank you very much."

Curly preceded Eddie through the revolving door, then stepped aside to let him hail a cab. It *was* a nice day, with a cool breeze coming off the lake. Within seconds Eddie had a taxi, told the driver to go to the Hancock Building, and held the door open while Curly got in. As he did, Curly gave him his customary dollar tip.

The cab was new; he could tell from the smell. There was something refreshing about the aroma of new cars. He leaned back and opened his *Tribune*.

The headline hit him like a baseball bat right between the eyes. INSURANCE EXEC ARRESTED IN FRAUD SCHEME. Under it was a photo of Red O'Kieffe, try-ing to hide his face behind a raised arm. Curly quickly scanned the article; his stomach muscles tightened. After the close of business yesterday, the *Tribune* reported, the Illinois Department of Insurance seized the records and bank accounts of the Acorn Insurance Company. Apparently, Acorn had invested virtually all its assets in now-worthless junk bonds and was completely insolvent. Later in the evening, the article continued, the compa-ny's president, Walter "Red" O'Kieffe, was arrested by the FBI at O'Hare just before he was scheduled to board a plane to Mexico City. He was charged with fraud for splitting two million dollars in commissions with the broker who had sold the junk bond portfolio to Acorn.

"Here ya are, pal," the cabby announced as they eased to a stop. "Hancock Building. That'll be eight bucks."

Curly pulled a ten out of his pocket, quickly handed it to the cabby, pushed open the door, and stepped out. *That son of a bitch.* O'Kieffe had been dodging his calls for the past two weeks, and now Curly understood why.

On the elevator ride up to the eighty-sixth floor, he tried to calculate how much money Acorn owed the firm. It was over three hundred thousand when Pete Spanos last mentioned the account to him, a couple of weeks ago. It had to be close to four hundred thousand now. They had just started work on four new files that Acorn sent over. *Damn, this is going to cause all kinds of problems!*

The flak began to hit as soon as he walked into the reception room.

"Mr. Morgan, several people have been looking for you this morning, including Mr. Spanos," Julia said from her desk. "And I know that Jackie has a bunch of messages for you. You're a popular man this morning."

"Right." he growled as he walked past her and down the corridor to his office. He knew that most of the calls and messages would be from people involved in lawsuits that Curly was defending under Acorn's insurance policies. Everyone would want to know whether their insurance was still good. And some of the calls were bound to be from plaintiffs' attorneys wanting to know if they could settle their cases "fast and cheap".

"Curly, I'm glad you're here," Jackie said as he approached his office, and she handed him a small stack of paper. "You've got a lot of phone messages and faxes, all about this Acorn mess. You've heard about that, haven't you?"

"Yes, I just read about it." He took off his suit coat and hung it on the back of his door. "Jackie, could you get me a cup of coffee?"

Curly sat down and began going through the pile of messages and faxes that she had handed him. He turned on his computer and saw that he had dozens of new e-mails, almost all referencing litigation involving Acorn in the subject line. These people will probably be covered by the Illinois Guaranty Fund, he thought, since they were sued before Acorn's collapse. The poor bastards who are going to be left out in the cold are the ones who get sued *after* the company's gone south. *Their insurance is going to be worthless.* The thought sent a sudden chill through him.

"Well, your goddamn client Acorn really did a job on us, didn't it?"

Pete Spanos was standing in his doorway. He was angry - angrier that Curly had ever seen him. His face was red as he pointed a shaky finger at Curly.

"I told you to get that money collected - I told you that weeks ago! And what did you do? Nothing!" He paused, still shaking, then went on. "Do you know how much money Acorn owes us this morning? Do you know, Curly?"

Curly took a deep breath. "Not exactly, but I have a fair idea."

"Four hundred and ten thousand dollars; that's how much. That money's gone, Curly - gone!" Pete looked at him accusingly, his jaw clenched, his head slowly shaking.

"It's worse than that, Pete." Curly leaned back and shut his eyes. He had to tell him.

"What do you mean, worse?" Pete shouted. "What could be worse than losing four hundred and ten thousand dollars in a single stroke?"

"Losing our insurance," Curly said quietly, opening his eyes and looking straight at Pete. "We had all our insurance written through Acorn, including our professional liability coverage. That was the deal. It's all worthless now."

"Rasheed, I just don't see how you can do it. You're not going to be happy with her. It's bound to end in divorce and cost you nothing but grief and a lot of money. Don't do it." Ron Brent leaned forward in their booth and put his hand on Rasheed Collins's arm.

Rasheed knew he was sincere. That's what made this so difficult. He loved Rod; they had become close. He had agreed to meet him here at Mandate to talk about it again, rather than at either of their condos, but now that was beginning to seem like a mistake. It was becoming too emotional.

"Ron, I really don't know what I'm going to do. But I've told you, if I marry her we'll still be able to see each other. I wouldn't leave you, or the community. I just wouldn't be around quite as much, that's all."

"But why are you even thinking about it? Just to appease His Eminence, Minister Lund? That's one hell of an appeasement."

"I know," Rasheed answered, looking down and shaking his head. "But maybe there's more to it than that. Maybe I'd like to have a couple of kids. That's not so nutty, is it? Hell, I'm forty-three years old. It's something that I've given a lot of thought to, Ron, and I really would like to have a family - my own family." He looked up at his friend. "To be honest, that's one of the things that's been bothering me lately in" he paused a moment, "in our relationship. As great as its been otherwise."

"If you want a family, you and I can adopt a couple of beautiful little kids. That's being done these days, in case you hadn't noticed."

"Right," Rasheed laughed. "And stay in the closet? I don't think so. That's not a viable option."

Ron leaned back in the booth and folded his arms across his chest. "Why don't you be honest with me for one second. The only reason you're thinking of marrying this woman is because her homophobe father runs the great Temple of Islam. You know damn well that he's never going to fire his own son-in-law as general counsel. That's what this is all about, isn't it? Be honest! All you're thinking about is your damn career!"

Ron's voice had been rising, and the two men in the booth across the aisle were staring at them. Rasheed nodded and raised his glass to them. "No, that's *not* what this is all about," he said quietly, turning back to Rod. "Having Minister Lund as my father-in-law would be a mixed blessing, as we say in the religion business. You're right, it certainly wouldn't hurt my career. But if he ever found out that I'm gay, or bi, there'd be all hell to pay. It's a risk I'm weighing, though, and one of the coins on the scale is whether I really want to have a family, Ron. Do you understand?"

"What a crock of shit!" Ron shook his head and looked down at the table. "If you believe that," he said, looking up at Rasheed, "then you've conned everybody, including yourself."

This wasn't the way that Rasheed wanted the conversation to go. He needed Ron to understand. Even more, he wanted his blessing. "Let's get another drink," Rasheed suggested as the waiter approached their table. "I'm buying tonight."

Ron gave him an icy stare. "Is our big successful attorney going to buy his little faggot friend a drink?" he asked. "How generous of him! He must be doing very well. Perhaps he sees a good career move just down the road. A strategic marriage, perhaps?" His eyes were moist as he slid out of the booth and stood up.

"Ron, please don't leave right now," Rasheed pleaded. "Not like this."

"Why shouldn't I? All you're trying to do is justify

yourself. Well, it doesn't wash--it doesn't wash at all." Ron turned and walked toward the door, leaving Rasheed with a gnawing ache in the pit of his stomach.

~mm~

"We've got to get this problem solved immediately," Cal Cizma said from the head of the table. "We can't run a business like this without liability or malpractice insurance. It's absolutely essential. Where do we stand on getting new coverage, Curly?"

Tony glanced across the table at Curly. He looked hung over again; his eyes were bloodshot, and he seemed to have trouble focusing. *Damn it, Curly, pull yourself together and don't screw around on this. It's too important.*

"I've got our broker working on it," Curly answered, clearing his throat. "But he hasn't had any luck so far--says the market's gotten tight. I call him every day."

"Pete, what about American Union?" Tony asked. "You're close to some of those people. Can't we get coverage through them?"

"I've already checked into that." Pete replied. "They're not writing law firms right now. They've been burned badly a couple of times. Our broker's right - the market has gotten very tight the past month or two."

"Well, keep working on it, Curly," Cal said. "We've got to get that coverage replaced. I'm going to London next week to try to straighten out our situation with Imperial. If you haven't found coverage for us by then,

I'll raise the issue with them. In fact, I'll send them an e-mail this afternoon and ask them to get some quotes together. I'm sure we can get coverage in London, if nowhere else."

"That could be damn expensive, especially if they know we can't get coverage here," Rasheed said.

"I know," Cal replied. "But it may be our only alternative. We can't run bare like this for long." He glanced down at some notes on his yellow pad, then looked back up. "Curly, what's the status of the Acorn cases we're handling? I understand we have forty-seven of them."

"Actually, no," Curly said, leaning over and pouring himself a cup of coffee. He took a sip and looked down the table at Cal. "We sent them all over to Drepler and Levin yesterday afternoon," he said. "They're going to be the attorneys for the liquidator."

That surprised Tony. "Why couldn't we handle that?" he asked. "Those fees are going to be paid by the Guaranty Fund. Might not be our regular rates, but at least it would be something."

"I know," Curly shrugged. "It was a matter of politics. Jack Drepler is the director's brother-in-law. Nobody was going to overcome that. We tried."

Tony was about to raise another point when Pete spoke up.

"Curly," he asked, "how many attorneys have you had working on the Acorn book of business?"

"Three, full-time, besides myself," he answered. "I've been spending about twenty percent of my time on the Acorn files. In addition, I've had a paralegal assigned to the Acorn account. Julie Goldstein. She's good." He looked around the table, ending with Pete. "I know where you're going, Pete. I have overcapacity in my group now. Those people are available to be reassigned."

"That's not where I was going at all," Pete answered. "I think those people should be let go. Today. With their secretaries. Unless someone here has any particular use for them."

"Well, that seems a bit extreme," Tony said. "Some of those attorneys have been with the firm five or six years. They had nothing to do with our losing that business. I don't think it's fair to just summarily fire them - or their secretaries."

"That's right," Curly said. "I assigned Acorn's files to those people. I could have assigned them to other attorneys. Why penalize some good people because we have some bad luck? After all," he raised his hands and glanced around the room, "this is a two-hundred-million-dollar-a-year business. I can't believe that we don't have at least enough compassion among us to carry those people until we can find new work for them."

"Curly," Cal cut in "you're talking like this is some kind of a charity rather than a business". "You can't run a law firm on sentimentality. I agree with Pete entirely - all of those people should be given their notices today. Give the attorneys a month's severance pay, if that'll make you feel better. Two weeks' for the others. We simply can't afford to carry folks who aren't producing. Those people are adults--they'll understand."

"Isn't Mark Dragos one of them?" Tony asked.

"Yes." Curly answered. "He's a good lawyer. I'd hate for us to lose him."

"We won't," Tony replied. "I'll take him and Julie Goldstein, the paralegal. I can use both of them." Tony was stretching a bit when he said that, but he'd find work for them somewhere, probably on the Consolidated Steel cases. Maybe he could use Julie on the Roosevelt case too.

"Can anyone else use any more help?" Cal asked, looking down both sides of the table.

Rasheed cleared his throat. "Curly," he asked, "who else are we talking about? Who are the other two attorneys?"

"Sarah Wexler and Lew Manitella. They've both been with us for about five years."

"I don't really know Wexler very well," Rasheed said, "but I know Manitella. He's too good to be just thrown out. Maybe I could use him in the Temple's litigation."

"Well," Cal said, "I think that's a pretty good compromise. Tony will take two of the people who were working on the Acorn files, Rasheed will take a third, and we'll let the other one go. The secretaries will follow the lawyers."

"Wait a minute!" Curly interjected, shaking his head. "I don't agree that Sarah Wexler should be fired at all. She's a graduate of the U of M Law School and is one of the hardest-working..."

"Curly," Cal said sharply, "I'm not sure you catch my drift. The Acorn account was a disaster from the beginning. We brought it in to accommodate you, and we ended up losing over four hundred thousand bucks as well as our liability insurance. Some people would say that should be your responsibility. Other people might say that you should incur some sort of a penalty--perhaps even a significant penalty." He looked at Curly intensely. "But nobody *is* suggesting that, Curly. Not now, anyway. What's being suggested instead is that one of your superfluous associates and her secretary be let go. All things considered, that sounds pretty reasonable to me." There was a cold, threatening tone to Cal's voice.

Curly leaned back and looked at Cal without responding.

"Be a team player, Curly," Cal said, staring hard at him. "Sarah Wexler's husband is a commodity trader at the Merc. They don't need the money. Besides, she's already had one baby, and I'm sure she plans to have more. She can't raise a family and be a lawyer here too. She might not understand that, but we do. Believe me, we'll be doing her a favor."

"All right," Curly said, head bowed. "I'm not sure I agree with all that, but I guess I'll go along with it. I'll tell Sarah myself."

"Thanks, Curly," Cal replied with a smile.

"On a more positive note," Pete said, "accounting received two nice checks in the mail this morning--one hundred thousand each from the Temple of Islam and from American Union. Those will definitely help with the cash flow situation."

"Good," Cal remarked, closing the leather folder in front of him. "Well, I think that's about it."

"One question before we leave, Cal," Tony said. "How are you and Pete coming along on your criteria for promotion to equity partner? I don't want that to drag on too long."

"We're working on it," Cal answered. "It's not an easy issue to address." He glanced at Pete and added, "We're trying to put some formulas together that really measure an attorney's worth to this firm." He picked up his folder and announced briskly, "The meeting's adjourned, gentlemen."

Cal Cizma was enjoying a quiet Saturday evening in the den of the coach house he was renting in northeast Evanston. It was a sublease from a Northwestern professor on sabbatical in England. The furniture was comfortable, if a bit dog-eared, and while the place wasn't everything he wanted, it would tide him over until he found something better. And it was on the North Shore, which was important to him.

He'd stoked a cheerful fire in the fireplace, opened a bottle of Stag's Leap Cask 23 Cabernet, turned his favorite Eric Clapton album, and settled back into an overstuffed chair with printouts of the firm's latest production records. Now, *this* was the way to spend a pleasant evening.

The firm's productivity for the past month and the first quarter of 2004 was good, even factoring in the increased number of attorneys, but receipts were behind budget and their accounts receivable continued to grow. While Pete Spanos's fees from American Union were up dramatically, that was balanced off by the slowdown in receipts from the Imperial Syndicate and the necessary write-off of the Acorn receivables. Tony Jeffries's client Consolidated Steel was a solid contributor, producing fifty to a hundred thousand a month. But the one set of numbers that Cal kept coming back to was the fee receipts from the Temple of Islam: three hundred thousand last month alone--might hit three million for the year! Ten lawyers were working on their matters right now, everything from litigation to copyrights to overseas construction projects. The Temple had become one of the firm's largest clients, and certainly the most profitable.

Cal put the reports down, leaned back, and stared at the crackling flames in the fireplace, shaking his head. *How the hell did Rasheed ever get a client like this? He inherited it, that's all. Didn't establish the relationship. Didn't develop it. Just sat there, shuffling papers and having tea with Lund, until his uncle croaked--then it was his. Absolutely unbelievable! And now he's among the highest-paid partners in the firm. Makes more than I do, for Christ's sake!*

Cal laughed as he refilled his glass, contemplating the

irony of Rasheed Collins, a closeted gay, building a lucrative law practice around a fundamentalist Islamic church. Lund and his board would die if they knew the truth.

The hypocrisy of the situation struck Cal. The Temple was a client of the firm's, not of Rasheed's personally. Didn't the firm have an obligation, as the Temple's attorneys, to provide a general counsel who shared their most basic beliefs? Didn't he, as the firm's managing partner, have a duty to level with such a valued client? And wouldn't *he,* if he were the Temple's general counsel, be more forthright and effective than Rasheed? He wasn't black, of course, but he was sure that issue could be overcome if the situation arose...maybe by hiring a young black associate as his liaison to the Temple.

Something to think about.

———*mm*———

Pete put the report down and shook his head. This was going too far; something had to be done immediately. He'd called Luke Smith, head of the firm's accounting department, up to his office and was thumbing through Luke's report one more time while he waited for him to arrive.

"Hi, Pete. You wanted to see me?"

Pete looked up and saw Smith standing in his doorway. He waved him in. "Come on in, Luke. Oh, and shut the door, if you don't mind."

Smith closed the door, then sat down across the desk

from Pete. He was balding, in his middle fifties, and seemed ill at ease without his hands on a computer keyboard. A CPA, he'd been hired fifteen years ago when the firm realized that they needed a real professional to handle its finances. He organized the accounting department, hired most of the staff, and had just supervised the installation of a new computer system.

Pete had never had much contact with Smith until he was named chairman of the finance committee. Now Smith reported directly to him. He could tell that Smith regarded this as a serious meeting; he'd put on his suit coat before coming up.

"We completed those four acquisitions for the Imperial Syndicate this morning," Smith began. "I just wired the last ten million to a bank in Barbados."

"That's great, Luke. But that's not what I wanted to talk to you about. I read your report on the London expenses" He lifted the stapled packet of white paper a few inches off the desk. "It looks pretty serious."

"I'm glad you agree, Pete." Smith looked relieved. "I typed it up myself since it was so sensitive, then deleted it from my system. You have the only copy. I wasn't sure how you wanted to handle this."

"I appreciate that, Luke," Pete responded. "You were correct in coming to me first. Now, as I understand it, your overall conclusion," he paused and looked at Smith.

"Is that Cal Cizma is spending outrageous sums of money on his London trips." Smith answered quickly. "Sums that can't possibly have any relationship to the firm's business." He sat forward in his chair. "Look at some of them," he said, pointing at the report. "Under tab A, two thousand dollars in one week at a place called Bellingham's Tavern! Four thousand for a limo and a driver! Three thousand to an outfit named Cooper Enterprises for miscellaneous entertainment expenses! It goes on and on. That last week he spent in London cost the firm twenty-four thousand dollars!"

"Now, these expenses are all paid out of our Imperial escrow account, aren't they?" Pete asked, flipping through the receipts under tab A. *These are pretty outrageous*, he thought.

"Sure. We're trying to build the account back up to a million to cover the firm's obligation in the Roosevelt case, and these expenses keep draining it back down. Pete, do you realize that Cal has spent over a hundred thousand bucks on his London trips in the last six months? And I'm not including the rent and maintenance costs for the flat itself, which run another five grand a month."

"Luke, are you questioning Cal Cizma's authority to incur these expenses on behalf of the firm?"

Smith sat back and blinked. He seemed surprised by the question.

"Am I questioning his *authority?*" he asked. "Why, no. Not his authority. He's a full partner. He's chairman of the management committee. He can commit the firm to any kind of expense he wants. But I thought you should know."

"And what makes you think I didn't know about all

these expenses?" Pete asked. "How can you presume that all of these items weren't discussed at length and agreed on by the management committee?" He stood up. "The only thing that surprises me about this whole matter, Luke, is that you have such distrust of the management of this firm. Frankly, I'm a bit shocked. I thought you understood what we're trying to do here. We're trying to build one of the world's greatest law firms. And Cal Cizma, as chairman of the management committee, has the primary responsibility to make that happen, to fit the pieces together, and to bring in the business we need to sustain our growth. It takes money to do that, Luke." Pete's hands gripped the back of his chair as he fixed his eyes on Smith, who shifted uncomfortably.

"And you know what else it takes to build a great law firm, Luke? It takes a supportive staff. Not one filled with people who question and doubt the intentions of the firm's leaders. Most importantly, it takes a supportive chief financial officer." Pete raised his hands and shook his head. "Luke, you've put me in a very awkward position."

"Pete, I had no intention to question the management of the firm. But some of these expenses looked a little… well, you know… a little funny. And I thought it was my responsibility as the firm's CFO to say something."

"No, you thought you'd use this opportunity to cause dissension between two of the top partners in the firm, didn't you?" Pete shot back. "You thought that if Cal Cizma and I got into a pissing contest over this issue, and you held all the cards, you'd somehow come out the winner, didn't you? Well, it's not going to work that way, Luke. I'm not going to let you provoke Cal and me into a fight that would only be destructive to the firm. And I'll tell you something else, Luke," Pete spat out, pointing a finger at Smith. "There's no place here for someone with that kind of negative, destructive attitude. You'd poison the whole accounting department against the firm's management if you stayed. No, I'm sorry, Luke, you're gone."

"Wait a minute, Pete. You can't mean that. I've been here fifteen years. I'm just doing my job." Smith groped for words, his face contorted in disbelief.

"You should have thought of that before you decided to launch this attack on the firm's management, Luke. We'll give you a month's severance pay, plus whatever vacation time you've got. We'll send it to your home tomorrow, along with all your personal things from your office."

"Do you mean that I can't even . . ."

Pete quieted him with a raised hand, then reached down and pushed a button on his phone. "Lois, send Kevin in, please." Smith was silently wringing his hands, his eyes avoiding Pete's.

"One last thing, Luke. We'll give you a letter of recommendation, but only on the condition that all the firm's business remains confidential--all of it. Do you understand?"

Smith nodded, then looked away, out the window, shaking his head.

Within seconds the door opened and Kevin, the firm's messenger, stepped in. He was a big Irishman from the southwest side and was wearing his usual Levis and Bears sweatshirt. Pete knew that he always followed orders, which is why he had him waiting outside.

"Kevin, I'd like you to escort Mr. Smith out of the office," Pete directed him. "He's leaving the firm, and he's not to stop in his office or anywhere else, or pick up any papers of any kind on the way out. Only his wallet and his topcoat, if he wore one today. Do you understand?"

"Yes, sir, Mr. Spanos," Kevin answered, his back stiffening as he turned to Smith.

Smith slowly stood up, his shoulders sagging. He looked up at Pete and opened his mouth to speak.

Pete cut him off. "Sorry, Luke. You overplayed your hand and didn't leave me any alternative. Goodbye." Kevin took Smith by the arm and led him from the office, shutting the door behind him on the way out.

Pete exhaled and sat down in his chair. That was easier than he'd thought it would be. He knew as soon as he'd read Smith's report that he'd have to act decisively. If that report had ever gotten to the partners, or even to the other members of the management committee, Cal would have been badly wounded. And without Cal's help, for the time being, there was no way that he was going to be able to complete his takeover of the firm.

He pushed the intercom button again. "Lois, call Wanda in accounting and have her come up to my office."

"Right away," she answered.

Then he picked up the phone and punched another number.

"Cizma here."

"Cal, this is Pete. I just took care of that problem with Luke Smith. I canned him, and I've got the only copy of his report. I'll shred it. Luke's being escorted out of the office as we speak."

"That's great, Pete. I really appreciate it."

"As I said, Cal, we can accomplish a lot by working together. I'll handle the finance committee, and you cover the rest of the firm."

"You got it," Cal answered. "I've got to run now for an important meeting this evening. And in the morning I'm catching a plane for San Francisco. Giving a talk on law-firm management. I'll talk to you next week."

"Right. Have a good trip."

Pete put the phone down and put Smith's report in his top right-hand desk drawer - the one he locked every night. He sure as hell wasn't going to shred it. *So far, so good.*

Within a few seconds there was a soft knock on his door.

"Come in," he said, raising his voice.

Wanda from accounting stuck her head in. "Did you want to see me, Mr. Spanos?" she asked.

"Yes, Wanda. Come on in. Have a seat."

"Thank you." She took one of the chairs across from him and folded her hands in her lap. She was in her early thirties, Pete imagined. Straight hair, not much makeup, a little on the plain side. He probably hadn't spoken ten words to her prior to today.

"Wanda, how long have you been with our firm?" Spanos asked, trying to sound as friendly as possible.

"A little over five years," she answered nervously. "March first was my anniversary date."

"That's fine. And you've been Mr. Smith's assistant all that time?"

"Yes. Yes, I have been."

"And you know how all the accounting systems in the office work?"

"Sure. I'm not a CPA, but I know how all the systems work. In fact, I designed some of them."

"Excellent. Well, Wanda, I have a little surprise for you," Pete said, smiling at her. "You're going to be promoted. Mr. Smith had to leave the firm; something rather sudden came up. And we'd like you to take his place."

"Me? The whole department?"

"Yes, Wanda, the whole department. You'll be working directly for me, and I'll help you with the reports. We're going to be changing them a bit. You've been doing a fine job, and I know you can handle it."

"Gee, that's great. Thanks, Mr. Spanos."

"Now, I want you to understand, Wanda, that you'll be on probation as the head of the department the first few months. Just so we can both see if you're comfortable with the job. There'll be a raise, of course. Five thousand dollars a year now, and another five thousand if I decide that you can handle the job on a permanent basis."

"That's wonderful, Mr. Spanos," she replied with a smile.

She looked eager enough, Spanos decided. He had read her personnel file and knew that she'd been working as a bookkeeper since graduating from high school. No college; some computer work the past few years. Dedicated, but not too bright. He doubted he'd have any trouble getting her to make the changes he had in mind.

—*mm*—

Cal paused in front of a seedy-looking bar on North Clark Street, hesitated for a moment, took a deep breath, pushed the door open, and walked into the stench of stale beer and old tobacco. He hadn't been in a place like this in years, probably not since his college days--not until last week, when he stopped in for a few minutes to check it out. There was a brown mutt curled up on the wooden floor in front of the bar. In the dim light he could see that the place was almost empty, just as he'd hoped. The only ones there were a pot-bellied old bartender cleaning glasses, two guys who looked like construction workers nursing beers at the bar and watching a flickering television set, and a well-dressed man with blond hair sitting by himself at a table in the rear, eyeing him.

Cal walked past the bar, turned to order a Bud, and continued to the table in the rear.

"Hello, Ron," he said as he sat down. "I'm Cal Cizma. As I recall, we met when Rasheed took Tony Jeffries and me to your club a few months ago."

"Yes, I recall," he replied quietly, his eyes still on Cal while he took a sip of his beer.

"Thanks for agreeing to meet with me. And in this neutral environment." Cal smiled a bit as he gestured around them.

"You're welcome. You said you wanted to talk about Rasheed." He paused. "I'm not sure you've heard, but he and I are no longer, as they say, an item."

"Yes, I've heard. He's getting married to Aliza Lund. That has to be very painful for you." He leaned back as the bartender set a bottle of Bud and a glass in front of Cal. He poured himself half a glass and took a sip. It was too cold, but he wasn't paying attention to its taste.

"Painful isn't the half of it," Ron said, staring off into the darkness. "On the one hand, I want to hurt him for what he's done to me--really hurt him. And on the other hand, I want to do something, maybe something dramatic, to show him how much he means to me, and to make him come back..." His voice trailed off as he shook his head.

"I understand exactly how you feel. And that's why I wanted to talk to you. I have something in mind that may do just what you want to do. I think it may help you ac-complish both your objectives."

"Really?" Ron replied, eagerly. "Tell me about it."

"I think you should out him. Send a letter to Minister Lund, Aliza, the Temple's Board, Rasheed's parents--anyone else you can think of who's close to him; tell them that he's gay and he's been hiding it for years. Go into detail, so they'll know it's true. And send a copy to Rasheed. He may be hurt initially, but I bet it'll shock him into accepting who he is. He'll also realize that he'd be a fool to walk away from the love that the two of you have found. You'll have him back within a week, believe me."

"Are you nuts?" Ron exclaimed, pushing back his chair. "If Rasheed wants to come out of the closet, that's his call, no one else's. He's the best judge of who to tell, and how to handle it. No, I wouldn't do that to anybody. No way!"

"Well, the end justifies the means, no?" Cal answered. "Think about it." He was surprised by Ron's reaction.

"No, I'm not going to think about it. I'd love to have Rasheed back, but not that way." Ron stood, slapped a five on the table, turned and walked out.

Cal stared at him as Ron disappeared out the door. *Well, son-of-a bitch. Maybe I'll have to do it all by myself.*

Chapter Fifteen

~~~~~~

Tony Jeffries eased his Lincoln Town Car into the left-hand lane, flicked on the turn signal, then swung off Lake Shore Drive to the south entrance of the Field Museum. Ahead, he could see a steady stream of cars dropping off well-dressed couples and a half-dozen spotlights sweeping back and forth across the sky.

"Is this all for the firm?" Karen asked, leaning forward as their car approached the entrance.

"I'm afraid so," Tony answered, shaking his head. "Cal was insistent that we have a big PR bash to celebrate the firm's centennial. Told everyone he'd handle all the details himself, and it looks like he went all out."

"But, as I said the other evening, I thought the firm's centennial was two years ago. I remember the dinner party that the Thompsons had."

"Surely, my dear, you must be mistaken," Tony replied with a smile. "If Cal Cizma says that this is the one-hundredth anniversary of our firm's founding, then, by God, it must be."

"But I remember. . ."

"Yes, I know," Tony sighed. "That event wasn't given any publicity, however. So Cal recalculated a few things and proclaimed *this* year our centennial. It's supposed to be a golden marketing opportunity." He tapped on the brake to allow a gray Cadillac to ease in front of them. "By the way, is my bow tie on straight?"

"Yes, it looks fine. You always look good in your tux."

"Thanks. You look great yourself."

Tony slowed to a stop in front of the museum's entrance. Uniformed attendants opened both their doors, and the one on Tony's side handed him a numbered parking stub. The elegantly attired guests in the two cars ahead of them were being greeted at the same time. There had to be at least thirty young people parking cars.

A chilling early spring breeze was coming off the lake as he walked around the car, took Karen's arm, and led her up the steps. A dozen or so other couples were walking up at the same time. Most of the men, like Tony, were in tuxes. The women displayed a dazzling variety of light furs. Karen was wearing the long white cashmere coat that Tony had given her last Christmas.

"I didn't know you could rent the Field Museum for a private party," Karen said quietly.

"I guess you can, if the price is right."

At the top of the steps a fifty-foot banner over the

doors proclaimed: WILSON & THOMPSON – 100 YEARS OF GREATNESS. Tony shook his head. *Nothing pretentious about this affair!*

They left Karen's coat with an attendant in the reception area, and walked into the museum's Great Hall. Tony stopped in disbelief inside the entrance. Thousands of people milled around the two iron mastodons and Sue, the Tyrannosaurus Rex, in the middle of the room. Four musical groups, one in each corner, sent their music into the absorbing din of the center. Massive tables of hors d'oeuvres, overflowing with delicacies, were scattered throughout the room, as were the bars.

"Wow," Karen whispered. "Are you sure we're at the right party?"

"We sure are. And do you want to know something terrifying?"

"What's that?"

"You and I are paying for part of all this."

"Oh my god. And yesterday I was upset because they raised the price of milk twenty cents!"

They'd begun working their way into the room when a young woman with a tray intercepted them and handed them each a flute of Champagne. Tony glanced around as he sipped his. There had to be five thousand people there. Some he recognize--people from the firm, clients, local politicians--but most he didn't. He saw Minister Habib Lund and his wife talking to Rasheed Collins. Next to them, Aliza Lund and Carol James were engrossed in discussion.

"Hello, Tony." A voice behind them caught his attention, and Tony turned to see a grinning Cal Cizma. "Isn't this something?" Cal gushed. "The greatest thing that's ever happened to our firm--absolutely the greatest!"

"Great party, yes. But Cal, what the hell is this costing us?"

"Don't worry about that. You can't put a price tag on this kind of publicity. All the society reporters are here. So are two of the TV stations. By tomorrow night we'll be the most prominent law firm in the state."

"But I thought we were already having a cash flow problem," Tony whispered, turning his back to Karen. "How the devil are we going to pay for all this?"

"No problem." Cal smiled and waved to someone in the crowd. "The bank extended our line of credit."

"Jesus Christ!" Tony shook his head. He was about to add something when he saw a familiar face off to their left. "Isn't that Senator Langford from California?" he asked under his breath.

"Sure is," Cal answered, grinning again. "Impressed?"

"I guess so. But how'd you get him here?"

"All we had to do is pay his usual fee--twenty grand for an hour's appearance. Plus expenses, a suite at the Four Seasons, and a little nookie."

"What?"

"See that tall brunette standing a little behind him?" Cal nodded in the direction of the senator and the group he was regaling. The strikingly attractive woman in the low-cut white dress was hard to miss. "She's the nookie,"

Cal said with a smile. "Cost us an extra two grand."

"Do you mean the firm's bought a hooker for him?"

"Now don't get sanctimonious on me," Cal answered, keeping his voice low. "This is strictly business--and if you ask me, it's damn good business. All the news media will report the fact that Senator Roscoe Langford, chairman of the Senate Judiciary Committee, was at our centennial party tonight. That kind of publicity is priceless. Besides, that's what it took to get him here."

"Mr. Cizma, excuse me." A young man with a red carnation in his tux lapel interrupted them. "It's time to introduce you. Your children are ready."

"Good," Cal answered, glancing at his watch. "I thought a few comments from the firm's chairman would be appropriate tonight. Don't you agree, Tony?"

"I guess so." Tony shrugged. It was obvious that Cal was going to make some remarks, whatever Tony thought of the idea idea. Behind the young man stood Cal's son and daughter. They looked grim, and the girl's eyes were red.

Tony walked over to them; they looked like they were overwhelmed. "How are you, Lenny? Stephanie? This is some party your dad has put together, isn't it?" he said, forcing a smile. They nodded: then Stephanie turned to Cal.

"Daddy, I really don't want to do this," she said quietly.

"Of course you do," Cal answered firmly but with a smile. "You look lovely, honey. You look great too,

Lenny," he added, patting his son on the shoulder. The thin teenager glowered at him.

Tony watched Cal follow the young man with the red carnation through the crowd, shepherding his two children ahead of him, smiling at everyone and stopping occasionally to shake hands. *Just like a presidential candidate at an Iowa caucus,* he thought.

"What a sweetheart," Karen said sarcastically, moving to Tony's side.

"That's not the word that comes to my mind."

In a few moments Cal had reached the center of the Great Hall and ascended some steps to a small platform surrounded by flowers. With Lenny on one side and Stephanie on the other, he raised his right hand, and the three were immediately bathed in the iridescent glow of floodlights converging from the four upper corners of the room. The music stopped.

"May I have your attention, please!" Cal's voice filled the room. *He's got a body mike*, Tony concluded. Within seconds the crowd quieted. "I'm Cal Cizma," he announced, smiling and turning to look around the sea of uplifted faces. "I have the privilege of being chairman of Wilson & Thompson. On behalf of our firm and my family here, I'd like to welcome you to this, our firm's centennial celebration." He paused, playing the silence to milk a wave of applause.

He made a few comments about the firm's long history of leadership in Chicago's civic affairs and mentioned the names of some of the firm's better-known partners from the past, each evoking scattered applause. With every new name, Lenny and Stephanie looked more uncomfortable.

"When do you suppose he's going to mention Henry Gilcrist?" Tony heard someone behind him ask in a stage whisper. He turned and saw a smirking Curly Morgan.

"You mean our esteemed partner in the slammer?"

"*Former* partner, if you please," Curly replied with a slight bow.

"I have an important announcement to make now," Cal said, raising his hand, his voice bouncing from the domed ceiling of the hall. Tony wondered what Cal had up his sleeve. The only announcement that would have made him happy would be that the bars were closing in ten minutes.

"We're honored this evening to be able to add a new giant to the firm's pantheon of great attorneys." Cal trumpeted. "I'm proud to announce that Wallace Covington, the attorney general of the state of Illinois, has agreed to join our firm as a partner and to serve as chairman of our litigation department!"

A smiling Wally Covington took the dais next to Cal, stepping in front of Stephanie, as four more spotlights beamed down on him and enthusiastic applause swept the room. With carefully coiffed, flowing gray hair and a politician's toothy smile, he waved to the crowd, acknowledging friends, real and imagined.

Tony felt numb. *What in the hell is this all about?* This was the first he'd heard of Covington joining the firm.

As the applause subsided, Cal and Covington stepped down into the crowd and the music resumed.

"I didn't know the firm had a litigation *department*," Karen said.

Tony turned to her and Curly, who was standing beside her. "We don't," he answered. "Half the firm does litigation. We have six litigation groups. They're all equal. Curly heads up one; I head up another." He looked at Curly. "Did you know about this?"

"No," Curly answered, downing the last of his Champagne. "But it doesn't take me long to learn. I think we've just witnessed the creation of a litigation department. Somehow, old boy, I have the feeling that you and I are being left out in the cold."

"But why? What's the point?" Tony tried to keep his voice down as the crowd milled around them. He could feel his anger rising. "We're the firm's senior litigators..."

Curly held up his hand and smiled. "Ah, yes," he said. "But we're not *Cal's* litigators. Covington is. To Cal, that makes a world of difference. Just watch. New litigation will be directed to Covington, not us. Besides, Covington's a little younger than we are. Cal won't have to worry about him, the way he probably worries about us."

"Son-of-a-bitch," Tony muttered, half to himself. "You're probably right." Why else would Cal pull a stunt like this without even discussing it with him? *The bastard!*

"Let's get out of here, folks." Tony said, turning toward the door. "This party's nothing more than a coronation - Cal's coronation. I don't want any more of it. Let's go over to Morton's and watch the ballgame. Zambrano's pitching the season opener tonight against Houston. That's bound to be more entertaining than this."

"That's fine with me," Karen answered. "I'd prefer someplace quieter. Curly, you joining us?"

"I'd be delighted." Curly grabbed another flute of Champagne from a passing tray and raised it slightly to them. "To our partners," he said with a wry smile. "Even the double-dealing, back-stabbing, egomaniacs among them. They are, after all, *our* partners."

———

Bertha Roosevelt sat in the first row of folding chairs in the Abraham Lincoln School gym, her eyes riveted on the young man on the stage. Beautiful music from his golden trumpet filled the room. She had never realized before how really talented Robert was. He was a wonderful musician. The rest of the members of the school band stood back, listening in awe as Robert completed his solo, the finale of the band's concert that evening.

The audience burst into applause when Robert finished. Bertha jumped to her feet, clapping frantically while tears of joy ran down both cheeks. All that practicing, all those lessons, all that money was justified in this moment.

When he came down from the stage Bertha threw her arms around her son and squeezed him to her. "I'm so proud of you!" she said, her eyes gleaming with tears.

Other parents, standing in nearby clusters, smiled at her and nodded approvingly.

"Thank you, Mom," he answered, trying to free his arms to return her hug.

Their exit from the gym was a slow one; so many people - parents, teachers, other students - came up to congratulate Robert or pat him on the back. Robert, initially taken aback by all the attention, began grinning widely.

"You have a very talented son, Mrs. Roosevelt," the assistant principal, Mr. Amos, said with a smile as they reached the rear of the gym.

"Thank you. I think so too."

"Would you care for a ride?" he asked. "I'd be happy to drop you and Robert off."

"Yes. Thank you. We'd appreciate that." They only lived three blocks away, but Bertha knew that a ride was a good idea.

When they walked through the door onto Forty-fifth street, the cool night air sent a shiver through Bertha. She buttoned her sweater up and followed Mr. Amos to his car in the faculty parking lot next to the school, Robert tagging behind.

"Zip your jacket up, Robert," she said, turning toward him. "You're going to catch your death of cold."

"Oh, I'm okay, Mom," he said, one hand stuffed in the pocket of his open Bulls jacket and the other carrying his brown leather trumpet case. She decided not to bug him any more tonight. After all, this was *his* night. He could do what he wanted.

As she turned back, Bertha noticed a group of young men standing in the shadows at the far end of the lot next to the school. She knew who they were; they were the Lords, and they began walking toward them as they approached Mr. Amos's Chevrolet.

"I think you'd better get in quickly," Mr. Amos said, holding the door for Bertha and keeping his eyes on the rapidly approaching group of men. Bertha slid in the front seat, pulling the door shut behind her and locking it while Robert did the same in back. By the time Mr. Amos was in the driver's seat with the door shut and locked, the gang had surrounded the car. There were eight or ten of them, several carrying baseball bats or tire irons.

"Give us your wallets," one of them shouted.

Mr. Amos didn't answer; he started the car and began slowly moving through them. As he did, there were shouts and loud thumps on both sides; suddenly the left rear window exploded inwards, spraying glass across Robert and the backseat. Mr. Amos gunned the engine and the car leaped forward, tires spinning on the damp asphalt.

When they reached the street he turned right, glanced over his shoulder, and slowed down a bit. Bertha could see beads of sweat on his forehead.

"Damn punks!" he shouted. "They just won't leave decent people alone."

"Too bad about your window," Bertha replied. "But I sure do appreciate the ride now." She turned toward the backseat. "You alright, Robert?"

"I guess so," he whispered, clutching his trumpet case

to his chest. Shards of shattered glass surrounded him on the seat.

Bertha sat back and tried to compose herself. This was the last straw. *I've got to do something,* she swore to herself. *Anything! But I've got to get us out of here.*

—*mm*—

Tony Jeffries leaned back, let out a deep sigh, and stared at the mass of papers covering his desk. Pleadings from the Roosevelt case were covered by statements from witnesses, interminable medical records, yellow pads filled with scribbled notes, and open case books that only confirmed the defense's desperate situation.

There's nothing here. Nothing to build on.

He had spent the entire day going through the Roosevelt file one more time, searching for some straw - something he could use to convince a jury that Blessed Trinity Hospital hadn't committed an atrocity against Sam Roosevelt; an atrocity justly punishable by a judgment of massive proportions, and limitless potential now that the governor had signed the bill removing the cap on punitive damages. And once again Tony could find nothing.

His line of thought was broken by the sudden ring of the telephone. *Damn! I thought I'd told Betty to hold my calls.* He reached over and grabbed the phone.

"Yes?"

"Sorry to interrupt, but Bill McGruder is on the other line. You told me to always let you know when he called."

"Right. Thanks a lot." He looked at his phone console and pushed the blinking button. "Hey, Bill! How the hell are things in St. Louis?"

"Not bad," the familiar voice answered. "Except for our accounts receivable. Anything you can do for us?"

"What are you talking about?" Tony sat up and put his pencil down. He didn't like the tone in his old friend's voice.

"Well, you guys owe us about eighty grand," McGruder answered. "We haven't been paid for any of the cases we're handling for you in a couple of months. The medical mal files. I assume you've seen the letters I've written to your accounting department."

"Why, no, Carl, as a matter of fact, I haven't," Tony answered, embarrassed. "Did you say that we're a couple of *months* behind?"

There was a pause at the other end of the line. "Yes, I did," McGruder said. "And frankly, it's causing me some problems with my partners. When we took on this line of work last fall, I assured them that there wouldn't be any problem getting paid. Told them that we were friends from way back, and that your firm would be cutting the checks. You remember telling me that?"

"I sure do," Tony answered. "And I've got to admit that I wasn't keeping close tabs on things. I'm really sorry about that. I'm sure it's just some screw-up in our accounting department. I'll call down there and get a check issued to you right now."

"Thanks, Tony. I'd really appreciate that," McGruder

said. "I'm sorry to call like this, but I've been getting some shit from my partners."

"I understand. Don't worry about it anymore. I'm on the goddamn management committee here. I'll get that check issued today. What did you say your bills total?"

"Eighty-two thousand, five hundred."

Tony flipped to a blank page in his yellow pad and scribbled the figure. "Consider it done," he said as he tore the page off, folded it, and stuffed it into his back pocket. "You'll have the money by the end of the week."

"Thanks a lot. That'll help."

Tony hung up the phone, glanced at his list of interoffice numbers, and punched one in. He held the phone to his ear and waited.

"Wanda Pencowitz," a cheerful voice answered.

"Wanda, this is Tony Jeffries. I was embarrassed to just learn that we haven't paid Jackson, Wyman and McGruder, our local counsel in St. Louis, in a couple of months. I sent a memo down some time ago that their bills were to be paid as soon as they were received. But I've been told that we owe them something over eighty-two thousand bucks. If that figure's accurate, Wanda, we should issue a check to them immediately. I'll be happy to sign it myself."

"I'm sorry, Mr. Jeffries, but I can't do that."

"What?" Tony stood up. "The firm has made a commitment to these people. I want that check issued today."

"Mr. Jeffries, I can't. I've been given instructions not to issue any checks for the time being to that firm or any other law firm."

"Instructions? By who?"

"By Mr. Spanos. He's my boss. I'm sorry, but those are my orders."

Tony stared at the phone for a moment. He couldn't believe what he'd just heard.

"First of all, Wanda," he snapped abruptly, "you work for the law firm, not Mr. Spanos personally. Don't you forget that! Secondly, either Mr. Spanos or I will be getting back to you on this shortly. *Very* shortly!" He slammed the phone back into its receiver.

Son-of-a-bitch! This should never have happened. He'd made a promise to Carl McGruder and he damn well was going to keep it.

Tony strode out of his office and headed toward the far end of the eighty-fifth floor. When he reached Pete's office, the door was closed and three young associates were standing expectantly outside. "Excuse me," he said as he stepped between them, knocked once, and pushed open the door.

Inside, Pete was on the phone. When he saw Tony he smiled and waved him in. Tony took a seat on the couch and waited for Pete to finish his call. It took an ungodly long time; Pete kept laughing and lapsing into Greek. Finally, he hung up and turned to Tony, still chuckling.

"What's up?"

"Pete, there's been some sort of a misunderstanding," Tony began. "We're not paying our bills from Jackson, Wyman and McGruder in St. Louis. They're handling our Imperial med mal cases there. I made a commitment to

Carl McGruder that we'd stay current with them, which I just reaffirmed. We need to have that check issued today."

"Sorry," Pete answered, shaking his head. "Can't do it. The Imperial account was depleted down to just about zero when we paid our last round of London expenses. So McGruder's bills have to get in line with all the rest we've got. We've instituted a new cash-management policy in accounting. As long as we're having a bit of a cash-flow problem, bills like those just aren't going to be paid - not right now, anyway. They don't charge interest. That's just good business."

"Good business? Bullshit! I promised McGruder that we'd pay his bills as soon as we received them. I made a commitment, goddamn it! He's a friend of mine, and I want those bills paid."

"No way. If we paid every bill we've got right now, we'd have to dip even further into our line of credit at the bank. I'd rather not do that right now. We're already two million bucks into the bank, after paying for the centennial party. We have a big medical insurance premium coming due in a couple of weeks, our biggest ever, and we'll need our full remaining line of credit to cover that." He shook his head again. "I ran all this by Cal, Tony, and he concurs."

"Well, in that case I want a special meeting of the management committee," Tony said, rising from the couch. "I'm not going to let this lie, Pete."

Pete shrugged. "You can't do anything right now. The only person who can convene a meeting of the management committee is the chairman, and Cal's in the Cayman Islands. No Blackberry service there. He won't be back until next week; you can talk to him then."

Pete turned to his right and pushed a button on his desk. "Send them in, Maria."

"Look," he said, turning back to Tony. "I'm awfully busy right now. I know you're not happy with what we're doing, but believe me, it's just good fiscal management."

Before Tony could answer, the door opened and the three young associates walked in with their pads of paper and the expectant look of suckling calves and took seats around Pete's desk. Tony looked at them for a second, glanced at Pete, then turned and stormed out, furious.

Rasheed Collins walked down the corridor toward his office humming a melody from Bellini's *I Puritani.* He and Aliza had been to the Lyric Opera last night and then stopped for a late dinner at the Chicago Chop House. Several cast members showed up too, and there was singing around the piano bar till closing time. *What voices!* It had been a wonderful evening.

"Good morning, Rasheed," Wendy greeted him as he passed her desk. She looked particularly fresh and perky.

"Morning," he answered, downshifting from exhilarating opera to mundane working world. "Mail in yet?"

"Yes, it's on your desk. I'll get your coffee."

Rasheed hung his suitcoat on the back of the door. If it

hadn't been office protocol, he wouldn't even have worn his suit today. Warming weather had arrived in Chicago, and even in mid-morning the temperature outside was in the high seventies.

He sat down and began thumbing through the pile of mail on his desk. There were a half-dozen notices enclosing pleadings. He glanced at them, scribbled in their upper-right corners the initials of the associate who was handling each case, and tossed them into his Out box. A couple of ads for books and seminars went straight into the waste basket. He was left with four or five letters. They'd all been slit open, except for one in a plain envelope marked "Personal."

Rasheed picked that one up and noted that it didn't have a return address, on either the front or the back. He opened it and pulled out the letter inside. It was typed on several pages of beige bond paper.

"Dear Minister and Mrs. Lund," it began. Rasheed was puzzled and flipped to the last page. The typed signature simply read, "A Friend." Copies were shown going to Aliza Lund, all the trustees of the Temple of Islam, all the members of the firm's management committee, his parents, and to him.

What the hell in this?

"In view of the possible marriage of your daughter Aliza to Mr. Rasheed Collins," the letter began, "I feel an obligation to advise you of certain aspects of Mr. Collins' private life that, I am confident, he has not disclosed to you or your daughter. As someone who knows him rather well, indeed intimately, I am quite sure he has hidden his real nature from you. In short, Mr. Collins has been an active practicing homosexual for the past twenty years."

Oh my God! Rasheed leaned back in his chair and shut his eyes. His arms dropped to his side and he began shaking. *The Lunds! My parents! Who could have done this? Ron?*

Rasheed picked up the letter and looked at it again, trying to focus through his tears. He wiped his eyes and turned to page two. It was describing Mandate, the "secret" gay club on the North Side, Rasheed's regular attendance there, and the cozy little rooms upstairs. Rasheed's participation in a variety of sexual acts, some with multiple partners and all with men, was described in vivid detail.

He stood up. The letter dropped to the floor as he walked over to his open office door, shut it, and turned to stare out the window at the lake. He was shaking with spasms of tears. He was destroyed! His client, his family, his career, his plans, Aliza; they were all gone now. Everything!

He staggered over to the window and looked out at the cold blue-gray of Lake Michigan. Below, taxis moved like toys along Delaware Street on the north side of the building.

Wendy Brown walked up to Rasheed's office with his cup of black coffee and stopped. The door was closed.

Rasheed never shut his office door, except when he was in conference with Minister Lund, and she knew that he wasn't scheduled to be there that morning. She hesitated, then raised her hand to knock.

Suddenly, the door burst open and Rasheed stepped out, his hands hiding his face, tears streaming between his fingers. He pushed his way past her. "I'm sorry, Wendy," he cried, "I'm out of here." Then he turned and ran down the corridor toward the elevators. Wendy stood there, stunned. The other nearby secretaries watched Rasheed dash around the corner, then turned to her, their mouths open in shock.

"What a shocking development," she heard someone say, very close to her. She looked back and saw Cal Cizma. "A terrible tragedy," he repeated, glancing down at the beige sheets of bond paper he was holding. She nodded and tried to walk away. She didn't know what to say, but Cizma grasped her arm to stop her.

"Just a minute, Wendy, I wonder if you could get me Minister Lund's private phone number. I should give him a call."

She blinked and looked at him. "What did you say?"

"I said, I'd like to call Minister Habib Lund," he repeated, this time more firmly. "And I'd like you to give me his private number. *Now*, if you don't mind."

Chapter Sixteen

—*⁗⁗⁗⁗*—

"I've talked to Minister Lund and convinced him to leave the Temple's business with us," Cal Cizma said to Tony and Pete across the Skyline Club's linen-covered table. "But it was touch-and-go for a while. He was in such a state of shock after the revelation about Rasheed that I couldn't tell what he was going to do."

"How's Aliza taking it?" Tony asked, leaning forward and pushing his coffee cup to the side. "Karen tried to call her last night, but couldn't reach her. Just left a message."

"Apparently, pretty badly. I couldn't see her last night when I stopped at their home. They told me that she was in her room under sedation." Cal answered. "I guess she was just devastated. Oh, and I assume you both received copies of Rasheed's resignation letter this morning."

"Yes," Tony replied, shaking his head. "I don't know why he felt he needed to do that. I called his condo this morning, couldn't get him, then called his building's management office to see if they knew anything about

Rasheed. All they could tell me was that he took a cab to O'Hare early this morning and told the doorman he might not be back for a long time. I just wish Rasheed had talked to me after he received that letter. Maybe there's something I could have said or done to soften the blow." He leaned back and stared at the far wall of the club. He hadn't slept all night.

"I assured Lund," Cal continued, "that we'd put this scandal behind us and that I'd personally supervise the Temple's work and would vouch for every attorney who worked on their matters. That's important. I also told him I was assigning one of our best young associates, Leon Walker, to serve as the liaison between our firm and the Temple, and to make that his full-time commitment."

"Walker. He's our new black associate, isn't he?" Pete asked.

"Yes. I think he'll be perfect."

"I'm not sure I'd call Rasheed's being gay exactly a scandal, Cal". Tony said. "After all, you and I have known about it since last fall, and I don't recall you ever coming into my office wringing your hands in righteous despair over how we're going to solve our *scandal*."

"I didn't know that you guys knew about Rasheed," Pete interjected. "Thanks for keeping me in the loop. But that's beside the point. Cal's right, Tony--the key thing now is keeping the Temple as a client. That's why we called this emergency meeting of the management com-mittee this morning. With Curly on trial in California, it's just the three of us. We need a clear game plan. Cal, you met with Lund last night and you think we can hold the business?"

"Yes, I think so," Cal answered, sipping his coffee. "But if there's even a hint of scandal about anyone else from this firm who does work for the Temple of Islam, that business will be gone in a second. I'm sure of that."

"Well, you'd better watch that carefully," Pete said. "With almost three million in billings a year, the Temple is one of our biggest clients. Who are you going to assign their work to, besides Walker?"

"I'll let Rasheed's associates keep the Temple's files they've been working on, and just have them report to me now," Cal answered, reaching for the basket of bread. After a bite and another sip of coffee he continued. "The only change I'll make will be to assign the Temple's litigation to Wally Covington. He needs some work, and Lund will love him."

"You know," Tony said, trying to clear his head, "my group and I could handle the litigation."

"I know you could," Cal nodded. "But I'm trying to get this Litigation Department off the ground, so I'm going to ask Covington to do that work."

"Do you want to explain to me, Cal, why in the hell Wally Covington is even here?" Tony stared across the table at him.

"Oh, Jesus, don't get your nose out of joint! I felt we needed a high-profile litigator like Covington to attract the big national cases. We'll say he's head of our Litigation Department just to give him some credibility, but it's not going to affect you. Don't worry about it."

"Well, for one thing, I'm concerned about the cost. What are we paying Covington?"

"Four hundred, as a base."

"Four hundred thousand bucks for a guy who doesn't have any business?" Tony shook his head. "I sure would have liked to have discussed that before you made a commitment. That's ridiculous." He looked at Pete for support, but Pete was preoccupied with stirring his coffee.

"If that bothers you, I apologize," Cal said, shrugging. "But now that he's with us, I want to get him some associates and a couple of good cases. He *is* the former Illinois Attorney General, and I want to build on his reputation while his name recognition still has a lot of punch."

"You want Covington to have a few more cases?" Tony asked. "Fine. I'll give him a couple of the medical mal cases to handle. In fact, I'll give him the Roosevelt case to try. You think he can handle it?"

"With his hands tied behind his back," Cal laughed. "Those cases aren't tough. It just takes someone with the balls to try them. Sounds like you're losing yours."

"Bullshit! All right, Covington's got the Roosevelt case! It's going to trial in September. I'll give him the file as soon as I get back to the office. And I'm going to enjoy watching the so-called head of our Litigation Department make a goddamn fool out of himself on that one."

"He won't, believe me," Cal added before taking a sip of his coffee. "Don't be a prima donna. You're not the only trial lawyer in this firm."

Tony leaned back and glanced around while the bus-boy cleared their dishes. Cal had become an insufferable boor. It was difficult to discuss anything with him without becoming angry. Fortunately, the club was almost empty that morning, and there wasn't the usual need to keep their voices subdued.

Tony did feel some perverse relief, though, in knowing that he wouldn't have to try the Roosevelt case after all. He chuckled to himself. It was going to be interesting to watch Covington try to deal with that nightmare.

"That whole issue aside," he said, "I'll tell you something else that bothers me. The McGruder firm in St. Louis should be paid for the work they've done for us. I made a personal commitment to Carl McGruder that he wouldn't have any problems getting his bills processed. And now I find that we haven't paid them in months. I understand that was your decision, Cal, and frankly it pisses me off."

"As I recall," Cal said, turning to Pete, "that was tied in with our cash-flow problem, wasn't it?"

"Absolutely," Pete answered, looking at Tony. "We've already discussed this. Don't beat a dead horse. Firms that don't charge us interest get paid last. That's all there is to it. If we make an exception for your pal, then we'll have to make a hundred exceptions. Besides, we just don't have the cash right now."

"Well, that's rotten management if you ask me," Tony's voice rose. "We can borrow a million bucks or so to stage an extravaganza at the Field Museum, but we can't even pay our own bills? That's bullshit!"

"Now don't start criticizing the centennial party," Cal answered testily, and pointing his finger. "That was the most successful public-relations event in our firm's history. All the trials you've won were forgotten six months later. But that party got us national publicity. You should see the mail I've received. No, you're barking up the wrong tree on this one."

Cal's face was flushed. He stared at Tony for a moment, then looked down at his watch. "I've got to run," he said. "I've got a flight to London tomorrow, and I've got a ton of things that I have to get ready."

"Wait a minute," Tony protested. "We haven't resolved some of these matters yet." He glanced at his own watch. "It's not even nine yet. You've got plenty of time."

"I'm afraid not," Cal said as he rose. "Besides, I think we've discussed everything we need to. Oh yes,…" He paused. "There is one more thing. It has to do with Curly. I've really got to go. Pete, you fill Tony in."

Tony's eyes followed Cal out of the Skyline Club. *God damn it, the son-of-a-bitch is stonewalling me on everything!* When Cal had walked down the stairs, he turned to Pete.

"Now, what's this about Curly?"

"Well," Pete said, looking down and adjusting his silverware slightly. "Cal and I have decided that Curly is really overpaid and that an adjustment is in order. He lost his biggest client, Acorn Insurance, you know, and it's awfully hard to justify his draw based on his current productivity."

"That may be, but why bring it up now? Everyone's draws will be reevaluated at the end of the year when all the numbers are in."

"No, we think an adjustment in Curly's draw is in order *now*. Curly has to be given a message that if he doesn't get his production up by the end of the year, he may not have a future here."

Tony slowly sat back and stared across the table in disbelief. Pete avoided his eyes.

"What are you saying, Pete? That you and Cal are all ready to dump Curly just because he lost a client? For Christ's sake, the guy's been here for twenty years! With all his faults, he still one of the best trial lawyers around. Usually bills over two thousand hours a year. Besides, he's a friend – a *close* friend. Not just mine, but yours and Cal's too."

"This is business, Tony," Pete said, looking at him now. "And Curly isn't cutting it. If he was thirty or thirty-five and making two hundred, or something like that, I'd say he'd look pretty good. But he's in his mid-forties..."

"Forty-three."

"Whatever. He's a senior partner making over three hundred thousand bucks and his own business doesn't amount to a damn now. Barely covers his draw. I don't care if you're the best soldier in the world, that just doesn't cut it."

They've already decided that Curly is going. Tony

shivered from a sudden chill that ran up his spine. *If they're doing it to him, they can do it to me.* He thought he knew these men, Pete and Cal. But perhaps he didn't know them very well at all.

"How much were you and Cal thinking of cutting Curly?"

"Fifty percent." Pete put some marmalade on a piece of toast, took a bite, and looked up. "And he'll lose the rest at the end of the year if he doesn't pull off some kind of a miracle. If he goes, we'll give him a good severance package. Something like six months' draw. At the reduced level, of course."

"I don't recall this being discussed at a management committee meeting. Did the two of you guys just decide this?"

"Yes, as a matter of fact we did," Pete answered, taking another sip of coffee. "As I said, it's all business. Someone around here has to be able to make the tough decisions, and Cal and I have decided to start doing that." He put his cup down, scribbled his signature on the tab, and stood up. "I think we're about done, Tony. Don't you?"

"Son-of-a-bitch!" Tony slammed his napkin onto the table, rattling the silver, and pushed his chair back. He watched Pete turn and walk out, seeing him through eyes that had never really seen Pete Spanos before.

Curly Morgan stepped out of the cab and handed the driver a ten through the window. "Here, keep the change."

"Thanks," the cabby mumbled. He waited for Vic Novacek to get out of the other side, then gunned it and pulled away.

Novacek stepped up onto the curb and put down the two trial bags he was carrying. Curly could see that he was already sweating under the warm California sun.

"We had a pretty good day today, Vic," he said, pausing to look past the palm trees at the rolling surf.

"I'll say we did," the young man agreed. "The way you took their expert apart on cross was something else. I've never seen a witness turn like he did. You were great!"

"Yeah, we did alright," he said, turning back to Novacek. "But you've got to keep things in perspective. As big a trial as this is, it's not likely to be a career buster for anyone."

"You're talking about Mr. Collins's resignation yesterday."

"Right." Curly shook his head. "That really hit me. I tried to call him last night, but couldn't reach him. Didn't even have his answering machine on. Frankly, I had trouble concentrating today. We're lucky we did as well as we did."

Curly turned and walked through the open doorway of the Hotel Del Coronado. Novacek followed him, shoulders drooping from the weight of the two oversized briefcases. As soon as they were inside, Curly could feel the refreshing coolness of the air conditioning. He stopped and turned back to his associate.

"Let me have the transcript of the Harris deposition. They're going to put him on tomorrow, and I want to work on his cross tonight. Gotta keep focused."

"Sure." Novacek dropped the bags, knelt down, and opened one. He thumbed through the contents for a moment, then pulled out a thick blue-bound volume and handed it up. "How do you want to handle dinner tonight?" he asked as he snapped the bag shut.

"I'm going to stay in my room. Probably just have something sent up. This," he nodded toward the transcript, "is going to take a little time." "Why don't you work on the jury instructions. We've got to change them after the admissions their guy made this afternoon. I'll meet you for breakfast about seven."

"In the restaurant off the lobby?"

"Right."

Novacek nodded, picked up his two leather bags, and walked toward the lobby's lone elevator, while Curly turned and stepped over to the front desk.

The lobby was fairly crowded for the Del Coronado; a dozen or so couples were milling around; some checking in, others apparently waiting to meet someone. Most were tanned and all were well dressed. He loved the old Del Coronado; it was *his* hotel in San Diego--a bit far to the courthouse, but its charm more than made up for the inconvenience. It was one of the Grand Dames, like the Plaza in New York used to be and the Drake in Chicago still was: hotels where the staff takes exquisite care of you, and caviar and Champagne are available at two in the morning if you're so inclined.

At the desk there were two items for him; a message to call Tony Jeffries and a sealed hotel envelope. He stuffed them both into his inside coat pocket and headed over to the elevator.

On the way up to the third floor he thought again about Rasheed's sudden resignation and his shock when Tony called him last night to tell him. "Damn…damn!" he muttered. Two older women with blue-white hair turned and stared at him. Before he could decide whether to try to explain, the elevator door opened at three; he stepped out and walked down to his room.

It was a nice suite, newly redecorated, with a balcony overlooking the ocean. There was a Victorian desk by one of the windows, where he could get some work done at night. The sunsets over the Pacific had been spectacular the last two evenings.

He hung up his suit coat, took the envelope out of his pocket and his BlackBerry out of his briefcase, then unbuttoned his collar and pulled off his tie. The envelope opened easily; only the tip of the flap had been sealed. Inside was a fax from the office.

Curly sat down at the desk and unfolded the paper. It was a memo addressed to him. "Due to your reduced client responsibility and other matters related to productivity your monthly draw will be reduced by fifty percent, effective immediately." *What the hell?* The memo was simply signed "Wilson & Thompson," but the handwriting was unmistakably Cal Cizma's. His stomach muscles tightened as he stared at the memo and read it again.

"God damn it!" he swore as he grabbed his BlackBerry. He punched in a series of numbers. He wondered if Cal would still be in the office. After three rings, Wilson & Thompson's night operator answered.

"Maggie. This is Curly Morgan. I'm in San Diego. Is Cal Cizma still there?" He was seething with anger.

"Yes, I believe he is, Mr. Morgan. Just a minute."

He waited an interminable moment, then heard her come back on the line.

"I'm sorry, Mr. Morgan. Mr. Cizma's in a conference with Mr. Spanos, and can't take any calls right now."

"Well, this is one call he's going to take," Curly stood up. "Tell him it's from me and that it's damn important. And if he's with Pete Spanos, that's fine. I want to talk to both of them."

"Yes, sir, Mr. Morgan."

He stood by the window as he waited, gripping the phone to his ear. *The arrogance of those bastards! Pulling a stunt like this when I'm out of town. Who in the hell do they think they are?*

"Mr. Morgan?"

"Yes."

"I'm afraid that I can't put you through. Mr. Cizma said they can't be interrupted, but if you leave your number, he'll call you back as soon as his meeting is over."

"Son-of-a-bitch!"

"Pardon me?"

"No, Maggie, not you." He apologized, then left his number and said he'd wait for Cal's call. Just as he was about to hang up, he remembered the other message he'd received. "Maggie," he asked. "Is Tony Jeffries still in?"

"Yes, I believe he is. I'll ring his office for you."

A moment later, Tony's voice came on the line. "Curly, I'm glad you called back. Things are going from bad to worse here. First, Rasheed's resignation. Now, it looks like Cal and Pete. . .".

"I know all about that. Cal sent me a fax. Says my draw is being cut in half. And the bastard won't even take my call. I just tried to reach him, the son-of-a-bitch!"

"I just walked by his office," Tony said, sounding puzzled. "He and Pete are sitting there having coffee. Just shooting the breeze. He won't take your call?"

"No, he's supposedly in conference. What a sack of shit!"

"I agree. They sprung it on me this morning as a done deal. That's when I put my call in to you. Apparently, you'd already left your room. Tried to reach you on your phone, but couldn't get a response."

"Yeah, I got up real early to meet a witness, then went directly to the courthouse. Had my Blackberry turned off so I could concentrate on the trial. Damn, I wish I was back there." Curly's mind raced through the trial schedule. "There's no way I can leave here though until this case is over, and that's going to be at least another week. Fifteen million bucks is on the line."

"Curly, we've got to do something about those guys. They're absolutely out of control."

"Well, I sure as hell can't survive on half my draw. If they think I'm overpaid, let's at least talk about it. Those two just stabbed me in the back."

"They sure did," Tony agreed. There was a pause before he went on. "Do you think Cal's going to call you back tonight?"

"He told Maggie that he would. He and Pete are probably trying to figure out what they're going to say. They'll probably call me together. I'm going to wait right here. This is one call I don't want to miss."

"Good luck. Let me know what happens. And when you get back, we've got to figure out how to deal with those guys."

"Right. Talk to you later, Tony."

Six hours later Curly closed the transcript of the Harris deposition and rubbed his eyes. The pad on his desk was filled with notes and questions for the cross-exam tomorrow. The scraps from his dinner were on the room-service cart near the door and his bottle of MaCallan was half empty. But his phone hadn't rung all night. He knew then that the bridges had been burned. They had taken away all his options.

He picked up his BlackBerry, opened up his address book, scrolled down to "Cal Cizma," and pushed the e-mail button. He paused for a moment to collect his thoughts, then began typing.

"Dear Cal, you contemptible bastard," he wrote. *Damn, that felt good.* "If controlling the firm means that much to you, you can have it. I hereby resign, effective July first. That will be about two weeks after my trial in California is over. Go to hell. Curly." He looked at it for a few seconds, then nodded to himself and hit the send button.

He leaned back and settled into the hotel's armchair. Yes, he concluded, that felt very good. Hell, he didn't need them. With the files and clients he had, he'd have no trouble at all finding another firm. He was one of the best goddamn trial lawyers around. Everybody knew that. Everybody, that is, except Cal Cizma. *That asshole!* Curly was sorry he'd be leaving Tony, but maybe Tony would be joining him at his new firm someday.

He shut his eyes, thought about what he had just done, and chuckled. He hadn't felt that good in a long time.

A few minutes later, Curly placed his wake-up call and went to bed. He fell asleep immediately and slept more soundly that night than he had in years.

mm

"Bertha, I've given it a lot of thought since you called the other day," Max Greene said, leaning back in his chair and exhaling a cloud of cigar smoke. "A lot of thought." He paused, flicking his ashes into the overflowing wastebasket next to his desk, then continued, "And there *is* one more thing I can do for you."

"Oh, thank you, Attorney Greene. I was praying to God that you could help me again, somehow." Bertha sat forward on the edge of her chair, kneading her scarf in both hands. "We've just got to get us out of that neighborhood."

Max Greene nodded. She looked and sounded desperate - desperate enough to take the offer that he'd decided to make. It entailed some risk on his part, but held the possibility of being a financial masterstroke. Her lawsuit was worth a fortune, and with the trial scheduled to begin in less than three months, this might be his last opportunity to improve his share of the take.

"As you know," he said, "my resources are rather limited, but I do have a few dollars put aside in an IRA. It's my retirement account, and has about fifty thousand dollars in it." He paused to make sure he had her undivided attention. She was leaning forward and had blinked when he mentioned the figure of fifty thousand. He knew she'd take his offer.

"I'm willing to withdraw that money and give it to you. All of it. In exchange for your agreement that I'll receive all your remaining interest in Sam's lawsuit."

"Oh, Attorney Greene," she grinned. "I just..." She shook her head and wiped the corner of her eye with her scarf. "Thank you. Thank you so much."

"But I have to have some assurance that you'll attend the trial and will testify like you did in your deposition. Some protection; you can appreciate that." He watched as she nodded her agreement. "So what I'm willing to do is this," he continued. "I'll give you ten thousand dollars now, so that you and Roland..."

"Robert," she corrected him, still smiling.

"Right...Robert. So that you and Robert can move out of that neighborhood now and rent a nice place somewhere. I know that's important to you. And the rest I'll give you right after you've testified in the trial, even before the verdict comes in. I'll take all the risk. Maybe we can even get you a little bonus if things go very well in the trial. That sounds pretty fair, don't you think?"

"Oh, yes, Attorney Greene," she gushed. "Couldn't be fairer. No, it couldn't be fairer. Especially if we might get something more if the trail goes well--a bonus, like you said." She was grinning, and touched her scarf up to the corner of her eye again. "Maywood," she said. "We're going to move to Maywood."

"That's a nice town," Max Greene replied, nodding approvingly. He didn't have the remotest idea where Maywood was or what it was like. Nor did he care. "Now, you understand, Bertha," he said, "that in exchange, my co-counsel and I will receive whatever judgment we get from the jury in Sam's case. You understand that?"

"Yes, I do," she nodded. "And that's fair, since I'm getting all this money now." She glanced around his desk. "Do you want me to sign something again, to make it legal?"

"Oh, I think so. As you say, just to make it legal." Max was barely able to suppress a chuckle as he pulled an envelope and two pieces of paper out of his desk drawer. He took the check for ten thousand out of the envelope, laid it on the desk just out of Bertha's reach, and put the revised fee agreement and the General Power of Attorney in front of her.

"If you'll just sign these, the check is yours."

She took his pen and carefully signed one document, then the other. He could tell that she didn't read a word on either page; she could just as well have signed a couple of suicide notes for all she knew.

"And here's your check," he said with a smile, pushing it across the desk. "You'll get the other forty thousand right after you've testified in the trial."

She picked up the small rectangular piece of paper, looked at it a long time and shook her head. "Thank you," she whispered.

"You're welcome, Bertha. I'm just glad that I was in a position to be able to do the right thing." As he spoke, Max affixed his notary seal on both documents.

As soon as Bertha left, Max opened his desk drawer, took out his pillbox, and popped two of the little white pellets into his mouth. He could feel his heart racing with the excitement of what he had just pulled off. He took the two pieces of paper she had just signed, along with the ones she had signed earlier, and folded them in half. He looked around his office for somewhere secure to put them. Certainly not in his desk or his office safe; both had been broken into during the past year.

Then he had an idea. He smiled as he pulled a thin

book off one of his shelves. It was the American Bar Association's Canons of Ethics. *No one will ever look here.* He folded the papers again, stuck them inside the front cover, and put it back on the shelf.

—*mm*—

Gordon Hawke raised his glass of brandy, marveled at the colors of the fire reflected through it, and looked at Ronnie Dasher, sitting in one of the other overstuffed chairs in front of the hearth. The flickering light from the fireplace was the only illumination in the room.

"So, Ronnie, our friend Mr. Cizma is coming to visit us tomorrow."

"Yes. He'll be here at two. Always punctual. Wants to adjust the arrangement on the medical malpractice book of business." Dasher took a sip of his brandy.

"I'm sure he does," Hawke chuckled. "Well, I rather don't think he's going to be very successful."

Dasher smiled quietly, saying nothing.

"Let's see him at about half past three," Hawke continued. "I want him to cool his heels properly."

"Right."

They both sat and watched the fire for a few minutes. Hawke enjoyed these moments, savoring the day's kills and planning tomorrow's.

"He also wants to talk to us about liability insurance for his law firm," Dasher added. "Seems as though their prior carrier went belly-up and they're running bare."

"Poor devils." Hawke finished his brandy, leaned over for the bottle on the brass table between their chairs, and refilled his glass. "I don't think they're a very good risk right now, do you, Ronnie?"

"No, I don't think they're a very good risk at all."

"You might pass that word to our friends on the street. Hate to see someone get burned, you know."

"I'll do that."

Dasher got up and put a small log on the fire, then sat back down. Flames, crackling in anticipation, licked around the edges of the new log and within a minute or two had enveloped it.

"Does Cizma have any idea what's going on?" Hawke asked.

"Not a clue."

"You're sure of that?"

"Positive," Dasher answered with a smile. "Our source couldn't be closer to him."

"Good. Well, let's placate him tomorrow, without really giving him anything." He took another sip of brandy and rolled it around his mouth for a moment, savoring its delicate flavor, before letting it ease down his throat. Then he looked over at Dasher. "Oh, Ronnie," he said. "One more thing."

"Yes?"

"Be sure to give him plenty of 'old boys' and 'old chaps' tomorrow. The Yanks do so enjoy that."

Chapter Seventeen

London was colder than Cal had expected for early June. He could feel the chill through the windows as the limo slowly edged through the traffic. The steady rain, pouring out of a dark, low sky, drummed unendingly on the car's roof, drowning out the sounds of the city around them.

He looked down at his watch. It was too dark to read and he flicked on the overhead light for a moment. One-thirty. Early afternoon, but every car had its lights on, and every office window was lit.

"Here you are, Mr. Cizma," his driver said through the opened glass partition. "The Imperial Insurance Syndicate."

"I expect to be an hour or so, Charles. Wait for me here."

"Yes, sir, Mr. Cizma. I'll get the door for you, sir."

Cal buttoned his coat while the chauffeur stepped out into the rain and opened his door for him. He flipped up the collar on his raincoat and walked quickly to the building's front door. This was one of those days, he thought, when he could have used a hat. He had never found one, though, that looked good on him. He stopped in the lobby to wipe off his face and recomb his hair, and took the elevator--the lift, as the Brits called it--up to the third floor.

It would be good to see Roxanne. He had tried to call her several times to let her know he was coming, but never caught her in. He hoped she didn't have a busy schedule this week. Cal pushed open the heavy wooden door to Imperial's executive offices and walked into the reception room. His eyes immediately shot to Roxanne's desk. She wasn't there. In her place was an older woman with gray hair and a pinched face.

"Can I help you?" she asked, raising her voice and looking at him over her glasses.

He glanced around the room as he approached her. No one else was there.

"Yes. My name's Cizma. Calvin Cizma. I have an appointment with Mr. Hawke and Mr. Dasher." He pulled a business card out of his suitcoat pocket and laid it on the desk in front of the receptionist.

She picked it up without looking at him and lifted the black phone to her left.

"Mr. Cizma to see Messrs. Hawke and Dasher," she said briskly. She listened for a moment, nodded, and put the phone down.

"Have a seat, please," she directed. "They'll be with you in due course."

He started to turn toward the group of overstuffed chairs where he usually waited, then stopped. "Excuse me," he said, turning back. "Where's the usual receptionist? Roxanne, I believe is her name. I hope she's not ill."

"No, she's on holiday this week," she answered, looking down at a paper on the desk in front of her. "Now, if you'll have a seat, Mr. Cosmo, I'll tell you when they're ready to see you."

"It's Cizma. Calvin Cizma."

"Yes, so it is," she said, looking at his card off to one side. "Still, if you'll have a seat, please," she gestured toward the chairs.

He hung his raincoat on the mahogany rack, then took a seat and picked up a copy of *The Economist* from the marble-topped end table next to his chair. He flipped through the pages without focusing on anything in particular. Now he understood why he hadn't been able to reach Roxanne. *She's out of town. Damn.* He had really been looking forward to being with her. He felt a twinge of anger, she should know when he's coming over. It was inconsiderate of her to be away.

Cal glanced down at the magazine in his lap. It was opened to an article entitled "London Insurers Reel Under Continuing Losses." He began reading to pass time. It was a long article, discussing in grim terms the fact that Lloyds was in the process of experiencing its third successive year of heavy losses. The Imperial Syndicate, he read with some satisfaction, was one of the few that seemed to have evaded the disasters that had swept the London market the past several years.

When Cal finished, he lay the magazine on the table beside him and stretched in his chair. He looked up at the grandfather clock across the room and saw that it was two forty-five. This was one thing that really irritated him: being kept waiting interminably. He *did* have an appointment. He leaned over, opened his briefcase, pulled out the section of the *New York Times* that he had been saving, and began thumbing through it without focusing on anything in particular.

It was almost an hour later when the pinched-faced woman at the desk picked up her phone, nodded, and looked at Cal "Mr. Hawke will see you now," she said as she replaced the receiver. She gestured toward the heavy wooden door to her right. "That way, please."

"Yes, I know," Cal answered as he tossed the newspaper onto the end table. *It's about time*. He picked up his briefcase, walked across the room ignoring. the receptionist, and pulled open the door that lead to the inner offices. He was met by Mrs. Walters, Gordon Hawke's private secretary, who gave him a polite nod and escorted him back to the chairman's office.

"Good to see you, old boy," Hawke called out as he entered. He was seated behind his desk at the far end of the room, while Ronnie Dasher was in one of the armchairs off to the side. They rose as Cal approached. Both seemed more restrained than they'd been on prior occasions. Through the windows behind them, sheets of rain were still falling on the city.

"Sorry to keep you waiting, Cal," Dasher said as he stepped forward and shook his hand. "We've had a bit of a bad day. A plane we insure appears to have gone down in India. It's thrown our schedule all to bloody hell. Hope you don't mind."

"Oh no, of course not. I understand." Cal turned to Hawke who had come around his desk. "Good to see you, Gordon," he said, shaking his hand. "I'm sorry about this loss of yours."

"All in a day's work, I'm afraid," Hawke answered. "Now, have a seat and tell us how our medical business is going in the States. I hope you have better news for us than we've heard so far today."

Cal took one of the overstuffed leather chairs as Hawke and Dasher returned to their seats. They don't seem to want to waste time on amenities, he thought. Might as well get right to it.

"I'm afraid not," he began. "There's a problem we're going to have to resolve."

"Oh, what's that?" Hawke asked.

"There's been a misunderstanding, a serious misunderstanding, on our firm's overall obligations under the medical malpractice book of business." The other two leaned back in their chairs, their eyes on him. Cal felt uncomfortable, but knew he had to go ahead.

"Our firm never contemplated having a million-dollar

potential liability in every suit we handled for you. In fact, if I can be candid, we were surprised, to say the least, when we saw that we were responsible for the first million dollars of exposure in the Roosevelt case. The funds in the reserve account are virtually depleted at the present time. Now, we're willing to accept our responsibility in that case, and bite the bullet for the shortfall, but we can't have that situation arise again. We're defending a hundred and fifty-seven suits for you right now, and our potential exposure is, in a word, staggering. We must have the language in our agreement clarified."

There was an uncomfortable silence when Cal finished. After a moment, Dasher turned and looked at Hawke. "Clarified?" Hawke asked with a quizzical smile. "I think the language in our agreement is quite clear."

"Then modified."

"But, old boy, you chaps agreed to that arrangement. Our underwriting projections were based on the fact that our exposure didn't begin until after the first million dollars in each case. Our arrangement with the reinsurer was based on the same premise."

Cal took a deep breath. "I understand. But, frankly, Chester Melrose didn't appreciate that nuance of the agreement. And it's a significant misunderstanding. I'm sure you'll agree. We simply must have some modification in the agreement."

"You're asking too much, old boy," Hawke said, his eyes narrowing. "A deal is a deal."

"In that case we may be forced to abrogate the agreement and let the courts sort it all out. And in the meantime, your medical malpractice book of business will be in shambles. I don't think that approach would serve either of us very well, but you may not leave us any other alternative."

"Let me suggest something," Dasher said. "A deal, as Gordon says, is a deal. But let me throw it back in our underwriters' laps, and see if they can come up with something that we all can live with. Perhaps some limitation on your firm's exposure in exchange for an adjustment of the fees you receive. We certainly don't want you chaps unhappy with the arrangement. After all, we expect to have a relationship with you for many years to come. Let me see what our underwriters can come up with."

"I'd greatly appreciate that, Ronnie," Cal said. He glanced at Hawke and was relieved to him nodding his assent.

"Of course," Dasher added, "We'll need to get the re-insurer's concurrence before we can actually change the agreement. You understand that."

"Of course," Cal answered, troubled a bit. "Essen Reinsurance has been difficult to deal with at times, though. I'm thinking of the Roosevelt case in particular, when they refused to authorize a settlement. Do you think they'll cooperate with us on a modification of the agreement?"

"I certainly hope so," Dasher said. "I understand how you feel about the Roosevelt case, but I'm afraid they felt that you folks just overstated the risk. I know them rather well. I expect them to cooperate with us on this."

"Good. By the way, I wonder if you could give me a short letter of introduction to Essen Re. I thought I might stop in Munich on this trip and introduce myself. That might minimize misunderstandings in the future, you know."

"Just a minute, Cal," Dasher answered, sitting forward in his chair. "Our relationship with them is rather delicate. We'd rather that you not contact them directly."

"I agree," Hawke added. "That isn't the proper protocol. You should deal with them only through us. We'll be happy to pass on to them any of your concerns."

"I'm sure you will," Cal said. "But I would like to meet those folks. For one thing, I want to make sure they understand the exposure they've created for themselves by refusing to let us settle the Roosevelt case. They're responsible now for the full amount of any judgment against the hospital; after our firm's initial layer of responsibility, of course. Besides, if our relationship with them is going to be long term, as you suggest, it would be very helpful for us to get to know each other."

"Absolutely not," Hawke said, raising his voice. "I won't have it. We pay ten million pounds a year to Essen to have them reinsure all our business. I don't want anyone interfering with that relationship. You may *not* contact them directly. That is *not* the way things are done in this business. Do you understand?"

Cal was startled by the harshness of Hawke's reaction. He'd apparently overstepped some bounds of propriety.

"I'm sorry, Gordon. Of course, I won't contact them if that's your wish. I certainly didn't intend to breach protocol."

"Fine," Hawke said as he sat back. Then he turned to Dasher. "Ronnie, be sure that our underwriters look at the medical malpractice book of business without any delay. It's clearly something Cal and his firm are concerned about, and we owe it to them to see if some accommodation can be made."

"Right."

"I'll look forward to their report," Cal said. "Oh, yes. There is one additional matter. As I mentioned in my e-mail, Gordon, I'd like to discuss the possibility of our firm obtaining our liability insurance from you folks. I've always preferred to do business with people who do business with me, and...."

"Sorry, old boy," Hawke interrupted, holding up his hand. "We're just not underwriting American law firms these days. No one, not even our dearest friends. Can't help you on that." Cal began to respond, then stopped when he saw Hawke vigorously shaking his head from side to side. It was clear that pursuing the issue wouldn't be productive.

They chatted for a few more minutes, then Hawke said that he and Dasher really had to return to their airplane crash problem. Cal rose, thanked them for their time and their sensitivity to the issues he had raised, and left.

In the elevator on the way down, Cal kept thinking about their reaction when he told them that he wanted to meet with the reinsurer directly. That was surprising. *Well, to hell with their protocol.* He was going to get a good night's rest at the flat, as long as Roxanne wasn't in town, would fly to Munich in the morning and would meet the officers of Essen Reinsurance. *Fuck Hawke. Fuck Dasher. Shit,* he thought, *I'd rather be fucking Roxanne.*

—*mm*—

Curly took a sip of his black coffee while he listened to the buzz of the phone ringing back in Chicago. He disliked using the hotel phone which was cumbersome as well as expensive, but he didn't have any choice this morning; for some reason his BlackBerry wasn't working.

The sun was just rising and early morning shadows shrouded the beach area below his window in the Del Coronado. It was difficult to do business with people two thousand miles away, especially when you were in a trial that ran from nine until five or six every day and demanded every waking moment of your time. He hoped this conversation would be more worthwhile than the first one he'd had that morning.

"Hello."

"Fred, how are you?" he said, leaning forward and putting his cup down. "This is Curly Morgan."

"Curly, good to hear from you. What's up?"

"Well, Fred, to be honest, I'm fed up with my firm.

Not at all happy with our current leadership. I've been out here in California on trial for the past couple of weeks, but when I get back, I want to look around to see what my options are. I've always liked the way you folks practice law, and I wonder if there's anything we can talk about?"

"Hey, that's flattering as hell. And very exciting. We'd love to have you and your clients over here. Sure, we'd be very interested in talking to you about making a move."

Curly strained to pick up any nuance in the other voice that would give some hint as to what he really meant. It was hard. People like Fred Kulof were successful because they could mask their true feeling so well. He couldn't pick up a clue.

"I'll be back in town next week," Curly answered. "Maybe we could tentatively set up a date to get together."

"Great idea. Let me get my calendar here." There was a brief pause. Curly took another sip of his coffee; he noticed that his hand was shaking. "Here it is," Kulof continued. "Let's see. How about June twenty-eighth or twenty-ninth for lunch?"

"The twenty-eighth looks good." He scribbled Kulof's name opposite 12:00 on his calendar.

"By the way, Curly, it might speed this whole process up if, in the meantime, you could send me a list of your clients and last year's collections from each. You know, just to give us something to think about."

"Well, I have my clients, of course. But frankly, I'd hoped that a senior litigator like me would have some value to your firm apart from the billings I might bring along with me. I'd prefer that to be the focus; what I can do for you and your clients."

"You're damn good, Curly. But, to be honest, litigators are a dime a dozen - even good ones. I've got litigators here who could use some more work. What we'd be most interested in is the amount of business you could bring with you - pretty much guaranteed." Curly didn't like the distance he could hear creeping into Kulof's voice.

"Oh, last year I billed my current clients about four hundred thousand, Fred, and generated about an equal amount on work that my group did for other partners' clients. I'm sure that all of that first four hundred would come with me, and probably some of the second four hundred as well. We won't know for sure until I make my move because I can't contact the clients in advance. You know, the Canons of Ethics."

"Yeah, I know." Kulof sounded even more distant now. "That's a little thin, Curly. If you could guarantee five hundred thousand in collections the first year, we might be able to work something out. Anything less than that, and I'm afraid that I've got a couple of partners who probably wouldn't support it. I would, of course. But some of these guys are real bottom-liners."

"I understand, and I'm comfortable guaranteeing five hundred. My clients will all come with me--I don't have any doubt about that. I'm confident some other business will too. Sending you a list would be a little awkward while I'm out here, though. My secretary wouldn't know where to look for that kind of data. But I'll put it together when I get back in town and bring it with me on the twenty-eighth."

"Fine. Give me a call that morning, and we'll confirm the time and place. Looking forward to seeing you."

Curly's hand shook as he hung up the phone. This was tougher then he had expected. His first call hadn't even gone as well as this last one; he had been questioned about the Acorn business, which he hadn't included in his projections. He realized suddenly that he was sweating profusely. He took a deep breath and walked into the bathroom for another shower.

A light rain was falling outside. It gave the green grass in the Jeffries' yard a sheen that looked oddly surreal.

Tony stood there in his dining room gazing out the window, both hands in his pockets, watching two squirrels darting around the trunks of the trees next to the house. Were they like kids, excited with the arrival of the rain, Tony wondered, or were they desperately trying to find seeds and other sustenance buried in the dirt and leaves? Probably the latter, he concluded.

"I'm surprised you're still here," he heard Karen say from the kitchen. "Aren't you going to work today?"

Going to work? Tony chuckled to himself, still staring out the window. *Why the hell should I go to work? Another confrontation? Another fight that I can't win?* He hated going to the office these days.

"I said, aren't you going to the office today?" Karen's voice was nearer now, just behind him.

"I guess so." He sighed, turned around and looked at her. She was in her bathrobe--the white one with a hood that he got her at the Fairmont. He noticed the lines in her face. It surprised him that he had never noticed them before.

"What's the matter?" she asked, putting her hand on his arm. "Aren't you feeling well?"

He took a deep breath. "Oh, I'm fine," he answered. "I'm just depressed about the way things are going at the office. First Rasheed, and now all this." He shook his head. It was hard to put his finger on exactly what troubled him most. He knew, though, that he was deeply upset about the firm and hadn't slept well in days.

"It's the way Cal and Pete are treating Curly, isn't it?"

"They're treating him like a stranger," Tony said, looking past her. "Not a partner. Not a friend. An enemy! They've pushed him into resigning. Damn, I wish he wasn't leaving." He shook his head again and turned away. He stared out the window in silence for a moment. The squirrels were gone.

"I've known these men all my adult life," he said, half to himself. "I've grown up with them. I thought I knew them inside and out. And it turns out that I didn't know them at all - not at all." He paused a moment, then went on. "Power and control... Cal and Pete are consumed with it now. It's like the way blood in the water drives sharks crazy. Once they've tasted it, they're insatiable.

Cal and Pete have tasted that blood, that power, and now they can't get enough. It's becoming really intolerable."

"If you're that unhappy, you can always leave."

"I can't leave," Tony laughed. "This is my firm. I've spent my whole adult life building it. Hired probably a third of the lawyers there now - at least the ones here in Chicago. No, I can't leave. Somehow, I've got to straighten it out. But I don't know how. I just don't know how."

Karen came in close to put her arms around his waist and laid her head on his shoulder. What a wonderful feeling, he thought, as he put his arm around and held her. He wished it could last forever just like this. But then he thought about the two Consolidated Steel cases he was scheduled to try in the fall, roaring down on him like locomotives, and the stack of unanswered messages on his desk. He took a deep breath and squeezed Karen once.

"I've got to get going. Already missed one train. I shouldn't miss another."

"I know." She kissed him hard, then stepped back and smiled. "It'll work out. I know it will. But if Cal and Pete won't listen to you, talk to other people in the firm. You can't be the only one who's upset about the way things are being run. Don't just give up. You're a litigator. A fighter. Remember?"

"Thanks," he whispered. Tony looked into her eyes for a second, smiled, and turned to get his suit coat from the closet. He thought of the quarterly capital partners' meeting coming up in August. *Yes, I'm going to fight this. And if there has to be a floor fight to turn things around, that'll be the perfect occasion. By God, I'm going to make this work out!*

—〰〰〰—

Cal looked at the number on the building, glanced down at the piece of paper in his hand, then looked back up at the number.

This is it. Not much of an office, though. It was a two-story brick building in an older section of Munich. Warehouses and garages filled the rest of the block, and the only vehicles on the street were trucks and vans making their mid-morning deliveries under an overcast sky. The surprise cold front that had dumped rain on London yesterday had reached the continent, and there was a thin, cool mist in the air. The taxi that had dropped him off was long gone, and Cal wondered if he hadn't made a mistake in not having it wait.

He pushed open the front door and walked into a small, dimly lit lobby. Straight ahead, an open doorway led to a hall with a series of doors on the left side, running back to the rear of the building. To the right, a wooden set of stairs ascended to the shadows of the second floor. From somewhere in back, behind one of those closed doors on the first floor, he could hear the clickety-clack of an old typewriter. There was a musty smell in the air and it was chilly.

He looked around for a directory of some sort. All he could find was a typed list taped to the left side of the far wall next to the numbered metal mailboxes. He walked over and peered at it. His eyes took a few seconds to focus on the faded print and the German spelling. Several of the tenants' names were crossed out and replaced with handwritten entries. Finally, he found it. The Essen Reinsurance Company was in room 208.

This wasn't what Cal had expected--not at all. What the hell was Essen Re doing in a building like this? He walked over to the stairs, glanced up into the shadows of an even more dimly lit second floor, and slowly ascended. Every stair creaked as he stepped on it.

There was only one small bulb lighting the second-floor corridor. Like the floor below, the hall ran the full length of the building, with a row of doors on the left side. Faded, cracked linoleum covered the floor, with wood showing through scattered holes. The doors were wooden, with translucent panels of glass in the upper half. Most were dark, but at the far end of the narrow hall one was bright. Someone was there.

Cal walked toward the lit office, glancing at the others as he passed. Some of the doors had company names stenciled on them: others bore only taped business cards. A mouse scurried down the hall ahead of him and disappeared into the shadows.

When he reached the end of the hallway he looked at the name printed on the illuminated glass panel, then blinked and stepped back. Essen Reinsurance. The number 208 was over the door. He hesitated, then reached up and knocked. Three time, lightly. He had no idea what to expect.

"Come in," a voice called out. It sounded vaguely familiar.

He turned the knob and pushed the door open.

"Hello, old boy."

It was Ronnie Dasher, sitting behind an old wooden desk, bundled up in a cardigan sweater. He gave Cal an odd smile. "Well, do come in," he said. "And please shut the door. What little heat we have here we don't want to escape."

Cal was dumbfounded. *What the hell is going on?*

"I said, come in and shut the door," Dasher repeated, waving him forward.

He stepped into the room, shut the door and looked around. All the room contained was the desk where Dasher was sitting, four folding chairs, a space heater, and an old television set on a two-drawer file cabinet. Next to the desk was a door to another room. The walls were a dirty gray, and the one soot-covered window faced a brick wall across a narrow alley.

"This is Essen Reinsurance?" Cal asked, looking back at Dasher.

"Why no, not really," the Englishman responded, still sitting and smiling at him. "There *is* no Essen Re. Never was. But this *is* a convenient place to stash ten million pounds or so a year. That reinsurance," he said, shaking his head, "costs a bloody arm and a leg."

"Are you saying that Essen Re is just a sham?"

"Well, not entirely," Dasher replied, his smile hardening a bit. "After all, it does perform a very important function. It cashes Imperial's checks every month."

"So there isn't any reinsurance? Either on our medical malpractice book of business or anything else?"

"You Yanks can be slow learners."

Cal slowly sat down in the folding chair across from Dasher. He was having trouble sorting out all the thoughts swimming through his mind.

"You look like you could use a bit of brandy," Dasher said, pulling open a drawer. He took out a bottle and two glasses and laid them on the desk. Without waiting for a reply, he filled both halfway, and pushed one toward him.

"Thank you," Cal whispered. He reached forward and took the glass. He didn't know what was going on, but he knew he'd been lied to. And he was getting angry.

"To surprises," Dasher said, raising his glass. He took a sip, then leaned forward. "Actually, Cal, I rather expected you a couple of hours ago."

"You did?"

"Certainly. The moment you left our shop yesterday I turned to Gordon and said, 'I believe our friend Mr. Cizma is going to Munich to meet the folks at Essen Re, regardless of your instructions.' You had that look about you, Cal. And Gordon said, 'Well, if he does, you'd better be there first.' And so, here I am. Had to take the bloody red-eye."

"So Hawke knows all about this?" Cal gestured around them.

"Knows about it?" Dasher laughed. "He set it up. The man's an absolute genius."

"And when you told us that the reinsurer wouldn't approve the settlement of the Roosevelt case, it was you, you and Hawke, who made that decision, wasn't it?"

"Well, of course, old boy. We weren't going to let you waste a million-and-a-half dollars of our money."

"You sons-of-bitches." Cal put his glass down and shook his head. "You've got us out there bare, don't you? There's no reinsurance on top of our million-dollar exposure."

"But there is Imperial. We're still on the risk. And the last time I looked at our balance sheet, our net assets were something over two hundred million - pounds, not dollars. We'd just rather not have our funds tied up in unproductive reserves."

"And you're skimming the reinsurance premiums. You and Hawke." Cal looked at him across the old wooden desk and suddenly had a very interesting idea. He reached forward for his glass, took a sip of brandy, and put it back down.

"Well, Ronnie," he said, "I've got some news for you. You and Hawke have a new partner. Me. You cut me in on the skim, or I'll tell every insurance regulator in England and in the States what you're up to. They'll put you out of business and throw you in the brig so fast, you won't know what hit you. And I won't be greedy. I'm a humble man. I only want ten percent." He sat back to watch Dasher's reaction. It wasn't what he expected. Dasher's smile broadened into a grin. He laughed, then sat forward with both arms on the desk.

"Cal, Cal, Cal," he chuckled. "What a simple ass you are. Do you think we'd go to all this trouble, and not protect ourselves from this sort of blackmail? Let me show you something. I think you'll find it rather interesting." Dasher took something out of his right-hand sweater pocket. It was a small black object. He held it up and pointed it at the television set behind Cal. In an instant, the screen crackled into life.

Cal turned to look. *What the hell is this all about?* The picture was fuzzy at first, then slowly came into focus. It was a couple, both naked, having sex in a big bed. Suddenly it hit him. It was Roxanne and him in the flat. He spun and looked at Dasher. The Englishman smiled and winked.

"You're going to love this next part, Cal," he said, fingering the remote control.

Cal glanced back at the screen. Now they were engaged in oral sex with each other. The sound rose, and their moans filled the room. He remembered that day. Roxanne could never get enough, it seemed. Now he understood. "God damn you," he said through clenched teeth.

"Oh, it gets better, much better," Dasher chuckled as he fast-forwarded the DVD. When the picture refocused, they were still lying naked in bed, sniffing lines of cocaine from the back of a book that Roxanne had placed between them. Line after line, then laughing and falling back into the pillows. Finally, the picture went black.

Cal was shaking with anger. "What are you going to do with that disc?" he hissed. He wanted at that moment to kill Ronnie Dasher. He also wanted to get his hands on that disc. He had to destroy it.

"Oh, it's not just *this* tape," Dasher answered. "This is only a copy. There are several others. All in proper places that you'll never find. What are we going to do with them? Why, nothing at all. Nothing, that is, unless you do something stupid - like reporting our business dealings to anyone who has no business knowing about them."

"Well, if you're threatening to send one to my wife, I really don't give a damn. Our marriage is already on the rocks. It would be a little awkward, but wouldn't really change anything."

"No, old boy, not your wife. Your wife's *lawyer*, Mr. Fontayne. I understand that you're behind in your support payments again. Bad form--very bad form. I rather suspect that if Mr. Fontayne is armed with a copy of this tape the next time he has you before Judge Hernandez, she's going to throw you in the bloody Cook County slammer. That's what I suspect. Can't pay your child support, but can afford to frolic in a London flat with a beautiful tart, sniffing coke at the same time. I don't think Judge Hernandez would take kindly to that at all." Dasher leaned back, his eyes on Cizma, and downed his brandy.

"You son-of-a-bitch!"

"I've been called worse," Dasher replied, smiling again. "Oh, yes, I almost forgot. There's someone else who might be interested in a copy of this little disc. Your friend and client Minister Habib Lund. Think it might have a little impact on your firm's business with the Temple of Islam?"

Cal let his breath out. His shoulders sagged. They had him. He suddenly had a compelling need to get out of there; he felt trapped. He stood up, turned, and walked uncertainly toward the door. When he reached it, he put his hand on the knob, then turned back to Dasher.

"One thing I don't understand," he said quietly, "is how the hell you convinced Roxanne to do all those things if it was just a setup. And on camera! I don't understand that at all. Why would she do all that?"

"Why don't you ask her yourself?" With that, Dasher leaned over to the adjacent door which was ajar, and pushed it open. "Roxie," he said, "would you care to join us?"

He was stunned as Roxanne, wearing a long brown coat, emerged from the shadows, put her hand on Dasher's shoulder, and looked at Cal. "Hello, love," she said softly with a smile. "All in a day's work."

"Oh, I'm sorry," Dasher said. "I don't believe I've properly introduced the two of you. How careless of me. Cal, I'd like you to meet my *wife*, Roxanne. And in answer to your question, I didn't have to convince her of anything, old boy. We planned it out together. Every bloody detail."

That hit Cal like a kick in the groin. He pulled open the door, stepped out into the dim corridor, and pulled it shut behind him. He leaned up against the wall and shut his eyes. Cal could taste the bile rising in his throat. From behind the closed door, he could hear them laughing—the Dashers, husband and wife.

Chapter Eighteen

⁓⁓

Curly Morgan stepped out of the elevator and walked into the firm's reception room. "Good morning, Julia," he said as he passed her desk.

"Good morning, Mr. Morgan," she answered without looking up.

Not much of a reception, he thought as he turned and walked down the corridor toward his office. Especially after his nice win in California. She must have heard that he was going to leave. Cal and Pete probably told everyone about his resignation. In fact, knowing them, they probably said he'd been fired. He wouldn't put that past them

He was especially irritated because he'd just learned that morning why his BlackBerry hadn't been working the past ten days and why he hadn't been able to receive or send any messages or calls on it. T-Mobile told him, when he finally reached a live person at their service desk, that his BlackBerry was part of the law firm's system, and that it had been disconnected by the firm. *What a bunch of assholes,* he thought, *I'm glad I'm going to be getting out of here.* The problem had been compounded by the fact that he hadn't been able to reach his secretary, Ruth, during that period; when he called in on the hotel phone he was told that she was sick and that there weren't any messages for him. Nor were there any voice messages on his phone when he checked.

When he got to his office there was a strange woman sitting at Ruth's desk. Ruth's things were gone.

"Pardon me," he said. "I'm Curly Morgan. Are you filling in for Ruth today?"

"No, Mr. Morgan. Ruth doesn't work here anymore. I'm Mr. Spanos's backup secretary." She looked down and resumed typing.

"Ruth doesn't work here anymore? When did that happen?"

"At least ten days ago," she answered without looking up. "That's when I was hired. She was gone when I got here."

What the hell? He pushed open the door to his office and was hit with another shock. It was bare, except for the furniture. His plaques were gone from the wall, the books were gone from the shelves in his bookcase, and his desk was bare except for one white envelope in the center. Even the computer was gone. He stepped in and looked around. None of his things were there.

He walked over to his credenza and pulled open the top drawer. It was empty. *Damn.* Then it hit him. All his files were gone. He looked for his Rolodex. It was gone too. They'd taken everything.

He stared at the envelope addressed to him, carefully centered on his desk. He knew what it was. The bastards didn't even have the guts to face him when they did it. He picked it up and pulled out the single sheet of paper inside. "We accept your letter of resignation," it said, "effective immediately." It was dated June 16th--the day he'd sent his e-mail. The typed signature on the bottom simply read "Wilson & Thompson."

"Mr. Morgan, I'm supposed to escort you out of the office, if you don't mind."

Curly looked up and saw Kevin, the big kid from the mailroom, standing in the doorway.

"What did you say?"

"I said, I'm supposed to escort you out of the office," Kevin repeated, taking a half-step into the room. "I'm sorry, but that's what I've been told."

"Just a minute," Curly said, holding up one hand. "I want to get a few things straight. First of all, where the hell is all my stuff?"

"I was told it's not your property, Mr. Morgan. Everything that was here is the firm's property. It's been given to other attorneys or put in storage."

"Well, damn it, it's not that simple. Even if those bastards are throwing me out today, I need my files, my client list, my billing records, my. . ."

"Sorry, Mr. Morgan, that all belongs to the firm. That's what I was told." Kevin walked over and took him firmly by the arm. Curly thought for a second about slamming his fist into the big Irishman, but immediately realized that that would be a serious mistake.

"God damn it!" Curly hissed through clenched teeth as Kevin pushed him across the office and out the door. The bastards had taken everything.

By the end of the day Curly realized that they'd taken even more: his clients. Everyone he called told him essentially the same story: a week or ten days ago they'd been contacted by Cal Cizma, who'd said that Curly was leaving the firm and probably even the practice of law. He said that Curly had resigned, then just dropped out of sight. Probably the old drinking problem. That theory seemed to be confirmed when they couldn't reach him. When several clients said they'd left voice messages for him that were never returned, Curly realized that the firm had either intercepted or deleted them. Wally Covington, head of the firm's Litigation Department, would handle their files from now on, Cal had said. And from what Curly could gather, Covington had been very busy since then. Each of his major clients had spent long days with Covington and his associates, going over all their cases and working out strategies. In many cases depositions had been scheduled and motions filed. Everyone seemed impressed with Covington, and while they were glad to hear from Curly, almost all said that under the circumstances, they'd leave their work with Wilson & Thompson.

He hung up the phone after the last call, laid back on his bed in his room at the University Club, and stared at the ceiling for a long time. He was numb. They had gutted him - taken away any possibility that he could negotiate a deal with another firm. There was nothing to negotiate with anymore. He was ruined.

—*mm*—

"This package just came in by FedEx, Tony."

He looked up as Betty dropped an opened foot-square box on his desk. It was from Jackson, Wyman and McGruder in St. Louis. *Damn*. He was afraid what this might be.

"Thanks, Betty. I'll take care of this." Tony had a sinking feeling in his stomach as he stood up to look in the box. Inside was a letter addressed to him, on top of a stack of files.

"Dear Tony," it began. He took a deep breath and sat down. "Enclosed are our complete files on the fifteen medical malpractice cases we have been defending for you and your client, the Imperial Insurance Syndicate. You will note that each file contains a recent court order authorizing our firm to withdraw as counsel, and leaving your firm as defense counsel of record. Since all these cases have scheduled motions and depositions, and three are set for trial this fall, I suggest that you make alternate local arrangements immediately."

Son of a bitch! He slammed his fist on the corner of his desk and looked out over the city. It wasn't just the return of the files that disturbed him. He knew he had lost a friend forever. *Damn*, he said to himself again, and looked back to the letter.

"Your firm currently owes us $102,600," it continued. "Copies of all those bills are enclosed. I have been instructed to advise you that unless we receive full payment within thirty days we will file suit against your firm for collection. Sincerely, Carl McGruder."

Tony crumpled the letter in his right hand, stood up, and stormed out of his office.

"Don't forget your management committee meeting," Betty reminded him as he walked past her.

"I won't. That's where I'm going right now."

He walked down the carpeted hall, ignoring greetings from several people, trying to control his anger, and took the stairs up to the eighty-sixth floor. *This didn't have to happen. It was completely unnecessary.* When he reached the conference room and pushed open the door, Cal and Pete were already there, along with two younger partners who worked for them, Irv Gold and Chris Chamberlin.

"I hope you guys are satisfied," Tony said, looking from Cal to Pete. "Wyman, Jackson and McGruder have returned all our files from St. Louis, and unless we pay them in full within thirty days they're going to file a goddamn lawsuit against us. And I've probably lost a friends in the process. Beautiful; fucking beautiful."

Pete, who had a deep tan, looked at him for a second,

then spoke up. "Well," he said, "it sounds like there's only one thing to do."

"What's that?" Tony snapped.

"Wait another twenty-nine days, then offer to pay them eighty percent," Pete laughed.

"You can't treat people that way, Pete--either McGruder or me. That's bullshit!"

"Sit down, Tony," Cal said. "When McGruder gets our offer, he'll be pissed, but he'll take it. And don't take everything so personally. It's just good business to hold creditors off as long as you can. Everyone does it."

"No. *Everyone* doesn't do it. *I* don't do business that way!"

"Tony," Cal said, his voice rising. "It's over. Now sit down."

"Well, I don't like it. Especially when we've made promises. I like to keep my word, Cal." He slowly sat down at the end of the table directly opposite Cal.

Cal shrugged. "I think you'd better find another law firm down there to handle those cases," he said. "And this time don't make any promises about when they'll be paid. Our cash flow hasn't improved at all."

Tony started to respond when Cal cut him off.

"Look; stop bitching! We've got more important things to talk about. For one thing, I've appointed Irv and Chris to the management committee." He nodded to them as he went on. "We had two vacancies before, Barton Thompson's and Rasheed Collins's seats, and now we have Curly's spot. That's just too many vacancies, so I exercised my prerogative as chairman to fill them on an interim basis."

"We've never done that before," Tony answered. "The firm has always left vacant seats open until the next quarterly partnership meeting."

"Not really," Cal answered. "I've gone through our records and found precedent. Not recently, maybe, but precedent all the same."

"When were those other appointments, Cal?"

"Several years ago," Cal replied, looking down and shuffling through the papers in front of him.

"When?"

"Most recently in 1988," he answered, looking up at Tony.

"Shit!" Tony leaned back and shook his head.

"Still, it's precedent And that's the way it's going to be. Now, if you don't mind, I'd like to cover the firm's finances. Why don't you bring us up to date, Pete."

"I'll be happy to," Pete answered, opening a folder and passing out stapled sets of financial statements to the others. "As Cal mentioned, our cash flow is still negative. Receipts are down from our projections, and our costs are up substantially. As of this morning," he glanced down at some notes in front of him, "we're into the bank for five and a half million."

"Five and a half million!" Tony exclaimed. "How in the hell did we get so far in the hole?"

"Everything's going up," Pete replied. "Rent, salaries, the firm's medical insurance, payments into the pension plan, travel, marketing expenses, entertainment. . ."

"Let's talk about those last items," Tony said, leaning forward. "I think it's insane what we're spending on entertainment these days. Especially if we're short. The museum party, the London trips - I'm telling you guys, if we're that far in debt, we can't afford all those things right now."

"I think Tony's just jealous because he doesn't get to go to London," Pete said, smiling at Cal.

"No, that's not it at all. It's just that we can't keep borrowing all the time. Where's the money going to come from to pay it all back? Don't tell me the Imperial Syndicate. They're falling farther and farther behind in their payments as it is. I'm getting nervous about that whole situation."

"There's nothing to worry about, Tony," Cal answered, waving his hand at him. "I had a good meeting with the top people at Imperial last week, and we're in the process of restructuring our deal with them. Believe me, it's going to be much more profitable for us next year. Besides, I've got a couple of deals cooking with some other overseas syndicates. Essen Reinsurance, for one. They're big in Germany, very big. There's nothing to report now, but long-range prospects look awfully good. The key thing, though," Cal pointed his finger at Tony, "is to maintain our image as an expanding, dynamic firm. If we lose that, we lose everything. And if we cut back on the programs that you're complaining about, we'll lose our image in an instant."

"What kind of European deals are you talking about, Cal?" Tony asked.

"It would be premature to go into any detail right now. But believe me, it's going to generate a lot of revenue for our firm down the road."

"In the meantime, though," Pete continued, "We have this cash-flow problem that we're just going to have to live with. I'm studying our expense records to see where we can cut costs internally, and expect to have some recommendations at our next meeting. I'm looking for savings that won't be apparent to the outside, like cutting out year-end bonuses to associates and nonequity partners. Things like that."

"Well, that would sure knock the hell out of morale," Tony responded.

"Just a thought," Pete shrugged. "As I mentioned, nothing's been decided yet."

"Thanks for your report, Pete," Cal said, opening his folder. "One of the other things that I wanted to talk about this morning is the question of making new equity partners."

"It's about time we got around to that," Tony said.

"Pete and I met a number of times," Cal continued, "trying to draw up some criteria that we could fairly apply in evaluating our junior partners. We're trying to depersonalize the process. And we finally asked Wanda Pencowitz in accounting to put together a formula that would take into account everyone's hours, billing rates, profitability, and some other factors that I've forgotten right now, to see how all our nonequity partners compare. And I think, Pete, you've got her final report, don't you?"

"Yes, it's right here," he answered, passing out copies of a single typed sheet. "And, as you can see, one person stands out from all the others rather dramatically. That's Larry O'Neal. No one else is even close to him."

Tony looked down at the sheet of paper he'd been handed. It contained nothing except for a column of names followed by numbers. O'Neal's name had 908 next to it. The next highest person was Carol James, with 531. Several others had scores around 500; the rest had scores in the 400s. *What the hell do those numbers mean? And how in the devil did they arrive at them?*

"What was the formula, Pete?" Tony asked. "I don't understand how Carol James could score lower than Larry O'Neal. It doesn't make sense to me at all. I'd like to see the formula that Wanda used."

"I don't have it right here," Pete answered, "It's rather involved, though, I know that. But if this is how the numbers come out, I'm prepared to accept it."

"Well, sure, because O'Neal is one of your guys. Would you say the same thing if Carol had come out higher?"

"Absolutely."

"I think the numbers are pretty clear," Cal said. "My suggestion is that we recommend to the firm that Larry O'Neal be made an equity partner at the end of the year, with the others being deferred."

"Wait a minute," Tony protested. "I want to see how

those numbers were arrived at. Carol always has better hours than O'Neal, and she's worked on some very profitable matters. I just don't understand how he could score higher. And I certainly don't want to make any decision until we get that clarified."

"Look," Cal said with a smile. "What's the big deal? Larry O'Neal is with us for the long haul. A woman like Carol will be gone in a couple of years. She'll find some guy to marry and start having babies and she'll be gone. All the studies show that women don't stay in law firms. So why use up a valuable equity partners' slot on someone who won't appreciate it and who very likely isn't going to be with us for her whole career?"

"But Carol *has* decided to make this her career. She's turned down opportunities to do the family thing, and I think we owe it to her to give her a fair shot. Jesus, I can't believe you're even arguing about this, Cal!"

"I'm not arguing. You are. You're the one who won't accept the way the numbers come out. And I'm just telling you not to get so wrapped up in the subject. If Carol James doesn't become an equity partner, it's no big deal. I'm sure, Tony, in her heart, she knows she'll never be a full partner in this firm."

"Is that what you're saying, Cal? That Carol will *never* become an equity partner here? If you are, I want to know that right now!"

Cal shrugged and looked at Pete.

"Tony," Pete said, "we've got too many equity partners in the firm. One of the ways we can all make more money," he pointed around the table as he spoke, "a *lot* more money, is to gradually reduce the number of equity partners. And tightening up the entry standards is one of the ways to do that. Carol just might not shape up, that's all."

"What about all the people who've been working hard here nine or ten years, people like Carol, who've had the understanding that if they do good, profitable work, they'll become equity partners eventually?" That's what we told them - or rather that's what *I* told them - when we hired them. Are we throwing all those assurances out the window just so we can make a few extra bucks now?" Tony's stomach was churning with anger. He looked at Cal. "Or is this another case, Cal, where a promise doesn't mean a damn?"

"Things change, Tony," Cal said. He paused a moment and glanced around the table. "All right, I've heard enough discussion," he said. "Let's take a vote. All those in favor of recommending to the firm that only Larry O'Neal be made an equity partner at the end of this year say aye."

"Aye," Pete said, followed by Gold and Chamberlin.

"And, of course, I vote aye too," Cal added. He looked at Tony. "Any nay votes?"

"Yes, I vote nay."

"Looks like a clear majority, gentlemen," Cal said, sitting back with a smile. "That'll be our recommendation to the firm, that only O'Neal is invited in."

"This is bullshit, Cal," Tony fumed. "And I intend to make a floor fight out of it at the firm meeting. As well as the whole goddamn way this firm is being run these days!" He stood up and looked at Cal and Pete. "This law firm isn't your personal fiefdom," he said. "You've got to run it for everyone's benefit, not just your own."

They looked back at him impassively, without responding.

"Before you leave, Tony," Chris Chamberlin said after a moment, "there's something else I'd like to bring up."

Tony remained standing behind his chair. *What in the hell can Chamberlin have in mind? He just got on the Committee.* Tony had never liked Chamberlin. He was tall, with an incongruous cherubic baby face, and had followed Cal Cizma around like a lap dog ever since he was hired a dozen or so years ago.

"I understand," Chamberlin said, folding his hands in front of him, "that Cal was elected to a one-year term as chairman of the management committee last winter with the idea that it might be rotated after that."

"That's right," Tony answered. "That was the deal."

"Well, I know that I'm one of the new kids on the block," Chamberlin said, smiling as he looked across the table at Spanos and Gold, "but it seems to me that continuity is something of value in management. And with all the changes we've gone through this past year, I just think it would be a mistake to change managing partners every year. I'd like to move that Cal Cizma's term as chairman be extended at the end of this year - let's say, for one more year, at this point."

"Wait a minute!" Tony shook his head and raised his hand in protest. "Cal was elected with the clear understanding that the chairmanship would be rotated. And, as I recall, I'm next to succeed. . ."

"I'll second Chris's motion," Irv Gold said, ignoring Tony.

"Well, then, let's vote on it," Cal said, trying to suppress a smile. "All those in favor, say aye."

A chorus of "ayes" swept the room. Tony stood silent, staring at Cal.

"Nay," he said quietly.

"Well, I'm afraid the ayes have it," Cal said, unable to hide his smile any longer. He looked supremely pleased. "Gentlemen, I appreciate your support."

Tony looked at the cold unsupporting eyes around the table. He knew he couldn't win. "I've got work to do, he said quietly. "Excuse me."

Chapter Nineteen

—〜〜—

Antigua would be wonderful in the fall, Frank Donatelli thought as he flipped through the brochure from the Caribbean Beach Club. One picture in particular caught his attention. It showed a sensuous blond in a bikini lying on a white sand beach, frosty drink in her hand, gazing dreamily at the clear blue water that ran off to the horizon.

Yes, Frank thought, that looks pretty interesting. He and Pete Spanos had decided it was time for them to take a trip somewhere in the fall--without their wives. Semi-business, as Pete called it. *What the hell, with all the money we're making, no reason why we shouldn't really enjoy ourselves.* Since fall was only a couple of months away it was time to start making plans.

He picked up another brochure, leaned back in his swivel chair, and put his feet up on his desk. Frank glanced at the blinking lights on his phone and chuckled. He'd diverted all his calls to his secretary; none of the assholes could reach him.

This brochure was from Tahiti. A stunningly attractive young woman smiled at him from its pages. Her skin was a soft cocoa color. As far as he could tell, she was clad only in a towel loosely tucked around her waist and a garland of flowers around her neck. He shut his eyes and imagined himself pulling her close and reaching up under the flowers. Her smile broadened and she put her arms around him.

"Hey, Donatelli, wake up!"

Frank blinked, took his feet off the desk and instinctively leaned forward. He glanced around the room and saw Jake Muscat, his group vice-president, standing in the doorway.

"Hope we're not interrupting you, Frank."

"Why no, not at all," he answered quickly, rearranging the papers on his desk to cover the travel brochures. "I was just thinking through the settlement strategy in one of my environmental cases. Lots of loose ends I'm trying to tie together."

"Well, don't worry about it," Muscat said as he walked into the room. He was followed by an attractive, thirtyish woman whom Frank didn't recognize. "I'd like to introduce you to Marge Davenport," Muscat continued, motioning the woman forward. "She's been with the Liberty Group that we just acquired. Does the same kind of work that you do." The woman, who was dressed in a conservative gray suit with a white blouse, stepped forward and extended her hand.

"Well, my pleasure," Frank said, standing and coming

around his desk to greet her. "If there's anything I can do for you, Marge, just stop by or give me a call. I've been around here long enough to know where all the skeletons are and which closet doors you probably don't want to open," he said chuckling. "Where's your office going to be, by the way?"

"Well, actually, right here," Muscat answered, glancing around them. "I tried to reach you this morning, but couldn't get through. We're doing some reorganizing, and are going to combine your job and Marge's. We've got a new spot for you in personnel."

"But, I . . ." Frank was stunned. "I really don't want . . ." He shook his head and groped for words. "Jake, I'm quite happy right here."

"I know you are. But we all have to make these moves from time to time for the good of the company. Actually, you should take it as a compliment. I figured that a veteran like you could make the move to personnel easier than Marge could." Muscat glanced her way and gave her a smile.

"Well, but still …"

"I know it's a little sudden," Muscat said, cutting him off. "And to sweeten the move for you, we're going to give you a raise. An extra two thousand bucks a year. How's that?"

"Two thousand bucks?" Frank laughed. That was nothing. He made that in a couple of weeks on the cases he sent to Pete Spanos.

"I knew that would make you happy," Muscat replied,

smiling broadly. "And I knew I could count on you to make this transition smooth."

Frank caught his breath and stepped back slightly. *They're serious about this!*. "When is all this supposed to happen?" he asked. He clearly wasn't going to be able to change Muscat's mind; he just needed some time. "There are a lot of things I've got to take care of first." He knew that the monthly bills from Wilson & Thompson would be arriving any day. He had to be sure they were approved and paid before he moved. He also had to clean up some records.

"No rush at all," Marge Davenport answered, looking around the office. "There's plenty of time. Why don't I meet a few of the other folks in the department, maybe have a cup of coffee with some of them, and come back in, say, an hour. That should give you enough time, don't you think? In the meantime, I'll just leave my bag here." She laid her thin paisley briefcase on Frank's coffee table and gave him a polite smile.

"That's great," Muscat said. "I knew the two of you would get along well. Stop by my office later, Frank. I'll bring you up to speed on your new job in personnel. You're going to like it." He nodded, turned, and led Marge Davenport from the office. At the door, she glanced back, looked at him for a moment, and pulled it shut behind her.

Frank stared at the closed door. He had broken out in a cold sweat; a bead of it was running down his back. He walked slowly over to his desk, sat down, and stared at the enticing travel brochures sticking out from under the papers he'd shuffled a few minutes earlier. They didn't have to decide which trip to take after all; there wouldn't be any more trips, with or without the wives.

Frank picked up the phone, punched in a couple of numbers, and leaned back. His mind was still swimming. The phone rang twice before it was answered.

"Hello, Spanos here."

"Pete," he said, shutting his eyes, "this is Frank. We've got problems."

***

"That's the recommendation of the management committee," Cal Cizma said, standing at the head of the long, polished table, looking around the crowded room. "That Larry O'Neal be made an equity partner, effective the first of next year, a little more than four months from now, and that everyone else on the eligibility list be deferred. Can I have a motion to that effect?"

"I'll so move," Pete Spanos answered, seated at Cal's right. The two men's eyes scanned the room, challenging any potential dissidents.

"Second," Irv Gold added flatly.

Tony Jeffries was seated halfway down the table, flanked by Chris Chamberlin and Mike Vance. He, too, looked around, trying to measure the reaction of the other partners. He had spoken to a few of them in advance and knew that there was growing uneasiness with the course the firm was pursuing, but it was unclear how many would openly oppose Cal and Pete. Fear of retaliation had become a reality in the halls of Wilson & Thompson. Several of the partners shifted uncomfortably and looked down at their coffee cups. Others, Tony noticed, were looking at him.

He didn't feel well that morning. A pain in his stomach had kept him up all night. He'd had it before, but never this bad. More likely, though, as he thought about it in the morning, it had been his concern about the meeting that kept Tony awake. This would be his last-ditch chance to turn the firm around.

There were about sixty men and a few scattered women there, most of the Chicago equity partners. Those not seated at the large table were in rows of chairs around three sides of the room. Speaker phones on the table and a large-screen television set in the corner of the room behind Cal connected the partners in the branch offices. As Tony looked around, he was conscious of the many changes that had occurred. The old-timers who had run the firm for years were gone, of course; but then so were Curly and Rasheed. In their places, though fewer in number, were men whom Cal had brought in as partners either to staff the branch offices or to support himself and Pete.

"Any further discussion?" Cal asked.

"Yes," Tony said, standing and pushing back his chair. "I'm opposed to the motion. I'm opposed to the idea of pulling up the partnership ladder, which is what the motion suggests, because in the long run that'll drive good people out and destroy this firm. And I'm opposed to the secret process that was utilized in this instance to anoint Larry O'Neal and exclude everyone else." He paused and looked around the room. It was deadly quiet. Every eye was on him.

"I don't believe it's a coincidence that O'Neal is Pete Spanos's lieutenant," he continued. He knew that it was now or never. "And I don't believe it's in the best interests of this firm to have the consolidation of power and control in one or two men, as we're seeing happen right now."

He turned and looked at Cal, who still stood at the far end of the table. Cal's arms were crossed in front of him; his eyes were narrowed and his jaw was clenched.

"This firm is being managed right now for the exclusive benefit of a couple of men," Tony continued. "And the firm is being managed right down the tube. We're millions of dollars in debt to the bank and can't pay our creditors. At the same time the chairman of the firm is living like a goddamn baron. He spends weeks at a time traveling around the world or living in a lavish London flat that few people in this room have even seen, much less had the opportunity to use. For what? To cultivate business? The London business has been a disaster for us. We're going to have to pay a million bucks in the Roosevelt case, and we've got similar potential exposure in dozens of other cases. Are we making that up in fees from our dear friends at the Imperial Syndicate? We are not! In fact, they're falling farther and farther behind and currently owe us something like two million bucks. We carry that on our books as an asset, but are we ever going to see it? I doubt it. They're using us, and the chairman of this firm either doesn't see that, or is so enamored with his lifestyle in England that he doesn't give a damn."

Tony paused to catch his breath. He noticed several heads nodding in agreement, and he knew he'd struck a responsive chord.

"Let me ask you all something," he said, looking around the room. "Why in hell would a major London insurance syndicate choose a medium-sized firm from the Midwest to handle multi-million-dollar transactions in the Caribbean for them? I'm not just talking about the medical malpractice book of business, I'm also talking about all their other international banking deals we've been handling this past year. Why us?" He paused to let them think about that for a second.

"Let's not kid ourselves," he continued. "We've been successful and we've grown. But there are still a dozen firms in New York that could swallow us in a day. Firms that have been international players for a hundred years. Why have we been blessed with all this London business? Let me tell you what I fear in my gut. I think we're being used. The leadership of this firm is so blinded that they can't see it--but we can, if we look closely. We're handling pieces of large international transactions that we don't fully understand, and our bills for that work are stacking up, unpaid. We're slipping deeper and deeper into debt at the same time that our expenses are skyrocketing. Our financial sheet is an embarrassment, and if we discount some of our questionable accounts receivable, our financial statement is an absolute disaster."

"That's right," he heard someone say to his left.

"I'm worried about this firm," Tony continued. "Worried to death. We've got to get the management back under control, and the first place to start is to tell Cal Cizma and Pete Spanos"--he flashed his eyes at them-- "that this firm isn't their personal property. It belongs to all of us, and it has to be managed for all our benefit, not just theirs. I *oppose* their motion to only make Spanos's bagman Larry O'Neal an equity partner at the end of this year. I propose instead that the top four eligible candidates be made equity partners. They've *all* earned it." Tony surveyed the eyes around the room; they were supportive. Many heads were nodding. He had made his point; they were going to be able to turn this around. The firm was theirs again. He slowly sat down.

"Are you quite finished, Mr. Jeffries?"

Tony looked up at Cal. There was an odd smile on his face.

"Yes, I am. For the time being."

"I don't think I've ever heard a bigger bunch of bullshit in all my life." Cal shook his head. "Here's a guy who starts out being pissed off because Carol James isn't nominated for equity partnership, and we can only guess his motivation on that"--he paused long enough to give a wink to a couple of the other men--"and he ends up launching an attack on the whole firm management. Talk about getting carried away!"

"Absolutely ridiculous," Pete echoed.

"Here's a guy who's opposed every innovative thing we've tried to do this year," Cal went on, pointing at Tony while his eyes swept the room. "He was opposed to the firm's centennial celebration, which was a public relations bonanza. He was opposed to our putting this firm on a businesslike footing by cutting out some of the deadwood. He was opposed to our bringing in Wally Covington here, one of the best-known trial lawyers in town." His nod of acknowledgment was returned by Covington. "A little jealousy there, maybe, Tony?" Cal shot him a glance and went on. "And he's been opposed to our cultivating the European insurance industry, which is going to be the long-range salvation of this firm."

"Yes, I've spent some time overseas," Cal continued. "Time that I would have preferred to spend with my family, I might add. But that time's been well spent. We have a presence and a credibility now in London and in Munich that we never had before. And it's starting to pay off, gentlemen. Yes, it's starting to really pay off."

"I'll believe that," Tony said, raising his voice, "when I see some money come in the door. Not bullshit - *money*."

"You want to see some money?" Cal leaned forward with both hands on the table. "You want to see some money come in to prove that my time in Europe has been worthwhile? Is that what you want?"

Tony sat back in his chair and didn't respond. Cal had something up his sleeve.

"How's twelve million bucks, Tony? Is that enough

money to make you shut your mouth?" Cal stood up straight, reached into his coat pocket, and pulled out a rectangular piece of paper. He looked hard at Tony for a moment, then raised his eyes to the other partners around the room.

"Here's a check from Essen Reinsurance, payable to our firm in the amount of twelve million bucks," he said, holding the piece of paper high. "The largest fee this firm has ever earned. I received it by courier this morning. It's in payment of my services, as managing partner of this firm, in putting together a massive reinsurance program for them over the past three months. Services that aren't even reflected by a bill yet. Here," he said, putting the check on the table and pushing it toward Tony. "Let our doubting partner, Mr. Jeffries, see it. Let him put his hand in the wound. And please note, Mr. Jeffries, that the check is certified."

Tony felt his mouth go dry. He watched as the check was passed from one partner to another down the table. When it reached him, he took a deep breath. It was in fact a certified check issued by Citibank in the amount of twelve million dollars payable to Wilson & Thompson. In the lower left corner was typed "Remitter: Essen Re." He nodded, felt his body go limp, and handed the check to his left.

"Do you have anything you'd like to say, Mr. Jeffries?" Cal asked, raising his voice.

"Congratulations," Tony replied softly, looking straight ahead. Cal had made a complete fool out of him.

"Is that all? No apology? No acknowledgment that maybe I know something about how to run this firm after all?"

He sat there, every eye on him, at a complete loss for words. *How in the hell did Cal raise a fee like that?*

"Well, Mr. Jeffries made a mistake. He made a mistake because he doesn't understand what we've been doing overseas this past year. It's been time consuming, and expensive, and very draining on me personally, but as I said a few minutes ago, it's finally starting to pay off. This money," he said, pointing to the check which was being passed up the other side of the table toward him, "will be used, first, to fund a million-dollar reserve to cover our exposure in the Roosevelt case, and a two-million-dollar reserve to cover our accounts receivable from the Imperial Syndicate. That latter part is really unnecessary, because I know as a fact that we're going to be paid in full by Imperial. But if it concerns some people"--he glanced again toward Tony--"we'll cover that receivable with a reserve."

"Secondly," he continued, "we'll pay off our bank line of credit and all our other obligations in full. Third, we'll put aside a half-million bucks for our staff's, associates' and nonequity partners' year-end bonuses. There's been talk about cutting out bonuses, but I for one won't stand for that. These people have worked hard and are entitled to share in our good fortune." Many heads around the table were nodding in agreement.

"That'll leave almost four million bucks," he continued

"which I propose be distributed by the management committee immediately to all the capital partners as special bonuses."

From the smiles and nods that Tony saw around the room he knew that Cal had totally carried the day. He was a hero.

"And frankly, I take this motion on the floor to be a vote of confidence in the present management of this firm," Cal said. "If you like what we've done today--and believe me, we can do it again if our hands aren't tied--then vote in favor of the motion proposed by the management committee. Larry O'Neal will be made an equity partner next January, and the others will be deferred. We've given this a lot of thought, folks, and believe me, this is the right thing to do this year."

He looked around for a moment, then asked, "All those in favor?" A chorus of "ayes" swept the room and was echoed from the speakers from the other offices.

"Any opposed?" Cal asked, turning toward Tony with a smile.

"Nay," Tony answered, shaking his head. He was alone.

"The motion carries," Cal said. "Thank you. We stand adjourned. This has been a very productive meeting."

—*uuu*—

Carol James walked slowly south on Michigan Avenue, oblivious to the shoppers rushing around her. Her walk had been aimless ever since Tony told her that she'd been passed over for equity partnership. She knew what that meant; her life was in a complete shambles. Tony had been kind, and tried to convince her that next year would be a cinch, but she knew better. She could see the direction the firm was taking, and knew there wouldn't be a next year for her.

She paused and looked to the west, waiting for the light to change before crossing Ohio Street, where she could see a beautiful sunset between the buildings. It was a warm evening and most people would have savored the cool breeze coming in from the lake, but Carol paid no attention to that. The twinkling lights along north Michigan Avenue seemed to be mocking her; they were reminders of the joy and pleasure with which everyone else' life seemed to be filled, but not hers.

She was thirty-five and had given the firm ten years, maybe her best ten years, only to be squeezed out. At her age it would be hard to find a comparable job in another firm, maybe impossible. She had turned down Bill's offer to get married and settle down in Toronto. For what? To have a couple of jerks screw up her life?

After another block she stopped and turned toward a display window, partly to see her reflection as she wiped her eyes, and partly to turn her back to the passing crowd.

Why hadn't Tony been able to do more for her? Had he really tried? Had she made a mistake years ago in aligning herself with him? Perhaps. She took a deep breath, turned, and continued walking south, toward the Tribune

Tower. *No, it isn't Tony's fault. He probably did everything he could. And he's under attack too.* She wished there were something she could do to get back at them--Cizma and Spanos and the rest of the firm. Something that would hurt them as much as they had hurt her.

"It's just not fair," she said aloud. "Not fair."

"What's not fair, Carol?"

She stopped, startled at the voice beside her, then turned to see a familiar-looking man with a pleasant smile. He was fairly tall, in his early forties, in a well-dressed in a dark blue suit. Unlike the package-laden shoppers around them, he was carrying only a leather briefcase. Carol's mind had trouble focusing. *Where do I know him from?*

"Brandon Keyes," he volunteered, still smiling. "Remember me? The Consolidated Steel case a couple of years ago? I certainly remember you. You and your partner really beat us up."

"Yes," she nodded, managing a smile. It was coming back now - the case that she and Tony tried in Cleveland. "Yes, sure I do. You were a real gentleman, even though your client was . . ," she hesitated.

"A son-of-a-bitch. And a dumb one at that!" Keyes laughed. "He turned down your settlement offer in order to have his day in court, as he called it, and then you killed him. Remember? I warned him that's how the trial would come out. Haven't seen him since. Got stiffed on our fees, too."

"What are you doing in Chicago?" she asked, brushing

her hair back from her face. She realized that she must look awful.

"We're thinking of opening an office here. It would be a natural for us. Chicago's a major business center, and some of our clients have plants in the area. In fact, I just met with a broker. I've got a ton of information on space and rates to digest." He raised his briefcase and patted it with his other hand. "I've been delegated our point man on putting it all together, including the lawyers."

"Really."

"Well, the right lawyers, you know. Headed up by someone who knows their way around the Chicago legal scene and who has an established book of business. I'm meeting with a head hunter tomorrow to get our search going."

"Brandon," Carol said, moving a little closer and taking him by the arm. "We should talk. Let me buy you a drink."

Pete Spanos thumbed quickly through his pile of incoming mail. Nothing from American Union Insurance. *Damn.*

It had been two weeks since he mailed last month's bills, and he was anxious about getting them paid. Even one check would be a good sign. If he had known that someone besides Frank Donatelli would be reviewing the bills, he'd have been more careful in putting them together. He had spoken with Frank almost daily since he'd been sent down to American Union's personnel department, but neither of them had a hint how this Davenport woman would handle bills from outside law firms. One thing was clear, however: the days of their splitting "consulting fees" were over. They both knew it would be too dangerous to continue that game.

But the firm still had the files. Pete drew some comfort from knowing that even if they never received another case from American Union, the suits they were already defending would last for years. He had a dozen attorneys working on American Union cases. He would bill it straight from now on, and American Union would still be one of the firm's biggest clients for the next three or four years, second only to Essen Re, the giant client that Cal Cizma had just brought in.

He went back through his mail, this time actually reading the letters and pleadings. It was the usual junk: threatening letters from other lawyers, requests for the production of documents, interrogatories, and a couple of court orders setting status hearings. He was about finished when his secretary stuck her head in his door.

"Phone call for you, Mr. Spanos. It's Marge Davenport from American Union."

"Thanks, Maria." He nodded, hesitated a moment, then picked up the phone and waved her out.

"Hello, Marge?" he answered as the door shut. "This is Pete Spanos."

"Hello, Mr. Spanos," a woman's cold voice answered.

"I've replaced Frank Donatelli in claims at American Union. I assume you received my letter."

"Yes, I did. And I'm glad we're finally having the opportunity to talk. I'd planned on stopping by and introducing myself after you've had a chance to get organized. We do a lot of work for American Union, as I'm sure you know, and I think it's important for us to get to know each other."

"Perhaps." There was a distance in her voice that Pete didn't like. "What I'm calling about right now," she went on, "are your bills. I've gone over them in some detail and I'd like to discuss them with you."

"Of course," Pete replied, sitting forward in his chair. "I'd be happy to answer any question you have."

"First of all," she said, "it's only fair to tell you that I've never seen such heavy billing by a law firm in my life--and I've been doing this work for eight years now. Two or three people attending every motion, even routine status calls. Three or four people at every deposition, including out-of-town deps where there are significant travel costs involved. Research projects that never end. Every case seems to be loaded up the same way. I've got to tell you, Mr. Spanos, that these bills are outrageous."

Pete instinctively stood up. He had to do something to defuse the situation.

"I'm sorry to hear you say that. And if it's true, I'm very embarrassed. That last set of bills went out without my personal review. Frankly, I'm very sensitive to associates loading up on files, and when I see that happening, I write off the excess time and tell the attorney involved that if it happens again he or she will lose their job. Our integrity is our greatest asset. And if one or two of our people have abused it, and caused you to be overbilled, we'll certainly make an adjustment. Why don't you just send that whole stack of bills back to us, Marge, and let me take a hard look at them. Mark it to my personal attention." He had copies, of course, but had to get those bills out of her hands.

"Your comments are interesting, because I've gone back through our files and reviewed a number of your prior bills. They all follow the same pattern, Mr. Spanos. Everything appears to be double or triple-billed."

Pete sat back down, unbuttoned his collar and loosened his tie. He was in trouble. "There must have been some sort of mistake," he said after a moment. "Or else the time wasn't recorded accurately. That happens sometimes, you know."

"Oh, I'm aware of that," she replied evenly. "So I decided to cross-check by taking one of your attorneys and adding up all his recorded time on all our files in one month, just to see how it looked. I checked *your* time, Mr. Spanos, since I assume that your time entries should most accurately reflect your firm's billing policies. Does that sound reasonable to you?"

"Well, I don't know," Pete said, standing again. Sweat was running down his forehead and neck. "I work harder than a lot of other people around here."

"Yes, I would say you do, Mr. Spanos. In fact, it's amazing how hard you work. Do you know how many hours you billed us for your personal work in the month of July, Mr. Spanos? Just July?"

"No, I don't, not really," Pete muttered. "Except that I recall that it was a busy month--very busy month."

"It must have been." There was a steely-hard tone to her voice. "You billed us for seven hundred and fifty-five hours of your time in July. That's quite remarkable in view of the fact that July doesn't even have that many hours in it - not in the whole month." She paused. "Do you have any explanation for that, Mr. Spanos?"

"Well, all I can think of is that someone else's time and mine were combined by mistake. You know, we have a new associate whose initials are the same as mine. I'll bet that's what happened. Our accounting department must have lumped all our time together." Pete pulled out his handkerchief and wiped his face.

"And billed us at your rate, rather than his," she added.

"Yes, I guess so. I'm glad you caught that, Marge, because that's another adjustment we'll make when you send those bills back. And I'll tell you something else. There are going to be some heads rolling down in accounting for all these screw-ups. There's no excuse for it and again, I apologize."

"There's another thing about these bills that troubles me, Mr. Spanos."

"Oh? What's that?"

"The consulting fees. Every bill includes a disbursement for fees paid to West Suburban Insurance Consultants. Why is that?"

God, she's got me! He sat back down and shut his eyes. He had to get out of this somehow. "Those are folks we use as coverage consultants," he answered, his eyes still closed. "They're really very good."

"But in *every* case, Mr. Spanos? Why is that necessary? Especially since so many of our cases fall into the same categories. Surely you don't need a coverage consultant for the fifth or tenth cases involving the same issues. And isn't that what your firm is supposed to provide--coverage expertise? I just don't understand."

"Well, perhaps we got into a bad habit there," Pete replied, groping for a reply. "You're right. We've probably overused them. Tell you what. We won't use them anymore without discussing it with you first, how's that?"

"It's not that simple. Not that simple at all."

"Why? What do you mean?" He didn't like the tone in her voice. What was coming down?

"I've noticed that the consulting fees always equal twenty percent of the bill for legal services, Mr. Spanos. Isn't that odd? Every case, every bill. No, that's not quite right. In the beginning, it was ten percent. But it went up to twenty percent with last March's bills. In every file."

Pete held the phone at his ear but couldn't respond. She had him by the balls, and they both knew it. There was nothing he could say.

"Are you still there, Mr. Spanos?" she asked after a moment.

"Yes," he whispered.

"Well, Mr. Spanos, we'd like all our files back. Now.

Please have them delivered to our offices by five o'clock this Friday afternoon. Everything. Depositions, documents, correspondence, everything. We'll have people at this end sort it out. Do you understand?"

"Is that really necessary, Miss Davenport?" Pete said, again almost whispering. "Isn't there something we can work out on this?"

"No, I don't think so. But there is one bit of information I can give you."

"What's that?"

"You won't be able to reach your friend Frank Donatelli here anymore. He's no longer with our company."

Pete heard her hang up, and slowly did the same. He took a deep breath, then looked out over the gray lake. It could not have gone worse. One thing he knew for sure, though. Cal must never learn of this. At least not now. Cal would throw him out of the firm in an instant if he knew that American Union had been lost.

Chapter Twenty

~~~

Tony Jeffries was nervous as he walked across the Hilton's lobby toward the small group seated under one of the large windows overlooking Michigan Avenue. Was his tie straight? Were his shoes shined? He glanced down; yes they were. He felt like a high-school kid on his first date.

Carol James rose as he neared them, as did the two men. "Tony, you remember Brandon Keyes," she said with a smile, gesturing toward the taller man.

"Of course I do," he replied, taking Keyes's hand. "I never forget a good trial lawyer."

"I don't think I was very good in that case at all," Keyes replied, returning his smile. "As I recall, the two of you made us look pretty foolish."

"Oh, we got a little lucky," Tony said laughing. "But it's good to see you again."

"Likewise. Tony, I'd like you to meet my partner, Miles Coogan," Keyes said, nodding to the stocky bald man standing beside him. "Miles is our managing partner, and I thought it might be worthwhile for the two of you to continue the discussions that Carol and I have begun at a very informal level."

"Fine, I'd like that," he answered, shaking Coogan's hand. The older man's firm grip and steady eyes were the sort that engendered confidence. Tony had heard of Coogan: first as the trial lawyer who beat the government in the copper antitrust case twenty years ago, and more recently as the man who built Catlin & Coogan into one of the major law firms on the national scene. He had a reputation as a no-nonsense businessman who also just happened to be a pretty damn good lawyer.

"The first question I have, Mr. Jeffries," Coogan began as they sat down, "is why in the world you would want to leave a fine firm like Wilson & Thompson. Many lawyers would give a lot to be a member of a firm like that, and I'm, shall we say, curious as to why you're even considering leaving."

Tony smiled and leaned back in the couch, looking at the ornate wall high above Coogan's head for a moment. How could he capsulize in a few words the frustration and anger that he'd been experiencing the past eight months?

"You're right." Tony paused to focus his response. "It's a very difficult decision to even consider. I've spent most my adult life there, and I've poured my soul into that firm. To leave it now would be like cutting off my right arm. But..." he hesitated, "law firms change. They have personalities, as you know, and over a period of time those personalities can change dramatically. That's what happened at Wilson & Thompson. It's not the same firm that it was when I joined it twenty years ago, or even the same firm it was two or three years ago. It's personality now is - what's the right word..." He groped for a moment. "Carnivorous. Yes, that describes it. The personality of the firm has become carnivorous."

"Interesting way to put it, Mr. Jeffries."

"Don't misunderstand me," Tony replied, looking first at Coogan, then Keyes. "We're in a competitive business. And I'm a very competitive person - Carol here knows that."

"So do I!" Brandon Keyes added.

"That's right." Tony returned his smile, then looked back at Coogan. "But there's something fundamentally wrong when you have to watch your partners more carefully than you do your opponents. Especially when they'll cause you more serious damage, if you turn your back, than any opponent would ever dream of causing you." Tony shook his head. He was having difficulty remaining unemotional. The others were all watching him. He wondered if he was making a fool of himself.

"And finally it occurs to you," he said, "that some of your partners are terrible people - real bastards. It also occurs to you, after a point, that you're not married to them. You really don't have to spend the rest of your life worrying about what dirty little plots they're hatching. You might have other alternatives. And I guess that's why we're talking now." He opened his hands, palms up, and asked, "Does that make any sense at all?"

"Yes, Mr. Jeffries, it does," Coogan answered with a smile. "Although you could also be an expert con man. There are a few of those in our business. There could be other reasons why you're looking for another firm. However, since I've checked you out a bit, and know your reputation, I'll give you the benefit of the doubt. For the time being, that is."

They spent the next hour talking about the possibility of Tony and Carol joining their firm, without any commitments being made. Catlin & Coogan had already leased space in the IBM Building, and hoped to open their local office in four to six weeks. One of their junior partners and two associates had been assigned to Chicago on an interim basis, and Brandon Keyes planned to be there three days a week until the office got off the ground. Their long-range plan was to find a relatively senior Chicago attorney with an established practice to step in and run the office. Tony might very well fit that bill, they agreed.

Tony, for his part, made it clear that if he joined them he'd want to bring Carol James and an associate, Charlie Dickenson, with him. He also made it clear that Carol would have to come in as a full partner and that they'd all expect to be paid about the same as their contemporaries were being paid in Catlin & Coogan. They discussed the numbers in general terms and Coogan said that none of those issues should pose serious problems, although he repeated the caveat that they were only at a preliminary stage in their discussions.

They spoke of Tony's client base for some time, and Coogan probed the billings each of his clients generated. Tony didn't even mention the Imperial Syndicate's medical malpractice book of business. Cal Cizma could keep it.

His clients, as a group, had produced over a million dollars in fees in each of the past several years, half of which came from Consolidated Steel. Coogan said that, based on those billings, they were interested in pursuing the deal, but Tony had to guarantee that his clients would follow him, particularly Consolidated Steel. Without that business, Coogan said candidly, they simply weren't interested.

Coogan said that he appreciated the delicacy of Tony's position. Under the Canons of Ethics, Tony couldn't solicit any of his clients to change law firms while he was still at Wilson & Thompson. He had to resign *first*, then ask them to follow. Catlin & Coogan would be at some risk; and if the major clients didn't follow Tony, his career at the new firm would be very short-lived. Still, both men agreed that the Canon of Ethics must be followed.

"My goodness," Coogan said suddenly, glancing at his watch. "We've been talking a long time. We've got to run to catch our plane. It's been a pleasure, Mr. Jeffries," he said rising. Keyes followed his lead. "I'm very interested in pursuing these discussions. If you and Miss James are too, why don't you fly out to Cleveland next week some time and meet a few more of our partners," He squeezed Tony's hand, then Carol's. Brandon Keyes followed suit, then both men turned and left.

"Very interesting man," Carol said, watching them exit through the hotel door. "I like him."

"So do I. I like them both." He turned and looked at Carol. "Well, what do you think?" he asked.

"Hey, I'm ready to go right now," she answered with a grin. "But you're the one with the deep roots. What do you think?"

"It looks like a great opportunity for us," Tony said, nodding. "But I have to talk it over with Karen. It's a big move, and she's got to be on board before I make any decision." He looked up at the large clock at the north end of the lobby. "I can just make the train if I leave now. Do you want to share a cab and drop me off at the station?"

"Sure." Carol grabbed her purse as they started for the door. "Be careful who you discuss this with, though. If Cizma or Spanos have any inkling what you're up to, they'll slit your throat. You saw what they did to Curly. They got to his clients first and kept all the business. He was ruined. Still doesn't have a job."

"I hear you." Tony made a mental note of Carol's admonition as he followed her out the hotel door to the cab stand. Still, he had a sense of elation that he hadn't felt in months. At last, there was a way out of this quagmire.

—◠◠◠—

Karen, predictably, was completely supportive. As much as she had loved Wilson & Thompson – the *old*

Wilson & Thompson - she hated what it had become and what it had been doing to her husband. She'd never seen him so depressed and despondent.

They had dinner alone that night. That was becoming the norm now, with Billy away at college and Debbie wrapped up in the adventure of being a high school senior. Tony opened a bottle of Scheid Pinot Noir, and they talked about the excitement of joining a new firm. He'd have to prove himself all over again. But that didn't bother him; in fact, he was looking forward to building Catlin & Coogan's Chicago office, with all the hiring, planning, and marketing that would go with it.

"Have you scheduled your physical yet?" Karen asked as she made herself a cup of coffee. "That's something that you really should do before you change firms. You're going to be swamped afterwards."

"I know, I know. I just haven't had the time."

"I'm concerned, Tony, about those stomach pains you've been having. Don't put it off."

"I'll try to get it taken care of," he answered. He *knew*, though, that wasting a whole day on a physical wasn't at the top of his list of priorities.

They moved into the den when it was time for the ten o'clock news, Tony with a glass of wine, Karen with her coffee. He hadn't felt this relaxed and at ease in a long time. The first couple of news items were of no interest, the usual body-bag reporting. Then something came on that caught Tony's attention like a strobe light. He turned and stared at the screen.

"...One of the largest frauds in the history of the British insurance industry," the announcer was saying. "The Imperial Insurance Syndicate is licensed in forty-seven states in this country, with outstanding policies estimated to be in the billions of dollars."

"Isn't that your client?" Karen asked, turning to Tony, wide-eyed.

"The firm's client, yes," he whispered, as the announcer continued.

"British sources report that the principals of the Imperial Syndicate, Gordon Hawke and Ronald Dasher, cannot be located. Rumors persist that they have fled the country to the Caribbean, where more than three hundred million dollars in assets were allegedly transferred earlier. The British Ministry of the Interior issued a statement that it has taken over the operations of the Imperial Syndicate and that the company is solvent and will remain in business, notwithstanding the massive loss. The FBI confirms that it is actively cooperating with British authorities in the investigation, and that anyone found to have been part of this conspiracy will be subject to criminal prosecution."

"Damn, I knew it!" Tony clenched his teeth. "They were using us all the time!"

"What do you mean?"

"Those assets transferred to the Caribbean were all moved through our firm. We were the conduit. We're going to be in this up to our ears. Damn!"

"All the more reason to get out of there as fast as you can, Tony."

"You're right," he said, half to himself. "Unless it's too late. Remember, I was on the management committee when all that happened, and still am."

—*mm*—

"Pete, did you want to see me?" Larry O'Neal asked, standing in the doorway.

"Yes--come on in," Pete answered, looking up from some papers on his desk. He had been worrying about this conversation for the past two days. There was no putting it off now; American Union wanted all their files back.

"If you don't mind, Pete," O'Neal asked as he sat down, "I'd like to ask a question first. What's the story on the Imperial Syndicate? How is this loss they suffered going to affect us? Everyone in the office has been talking about it."

"How? Not at all." Pete sat back and put his hands behind his head. "Worst-case scenario is that they don't pay what they owe us. Remember, we have a two million dollar reserve to cover their accounts receivable. So we're not going to lose a nickel there. They'll certainly stay in business, even with new management, and chances are we'll continue to get all their North American work. But even if we don't get any new files from them, the runoff on the cases we already have could last for two or three years. We'll be okay," he finished with a smile.

"Thanks for the background on that. As I said, there's

been a lot of talk, and I'm glad I can tell people there's nothing to worry about."

"Right--you do that, Larry." Pete's cheeks hurt from maintaining his stupid smile, and his body ached from exhaustion. *What a bunch of bullshit!* He knew that one way or another they'd probably lose Imperial as a client, but he didn't want to convey any sense of concern. He had to talk to Cal about that. Pete was the only one who knew, though, that the firm would be losing not one major client, but two. There was no question that losing Imperial would be a disaster; but with American Union gone too, only Pete knew its full extent.

"Larry, let me tell you what I wanted to talk to you about," he continued. "American Union has instituted a new policy of maintaining scanned copies of all their outside claims files, and they'd like us to send all our files over for copying."

"Okay," O'Neal shrugged. "What do they want us to include?"

"They asked for everything, so let's send them everything - pleadings, correspondence, discovery, *everything*. It's not worth our time in sorting it out, and they're not going to pay us extra for doing that, so let's just send them the whole damn file in all their cases."

"Fine. When do they want us to begin? Some of their cases are pretty active, and it'll be awkward to have those files out of the office right now. I'd like to be able to send over one or two at a time, as things slow down in particular cases."

"I know, so would I," Pete agreed. "But they've got some new vice-president over there who wants this all done in the next couple of weeks. Obviously, the gal doesn't know a thing about litigation. The upshot is that they want everything this week, so that all the files can be copied and returned to us by the first of the month."

"That's crazy," O'Neal replied, leaning forward in his chair. "We've got motions set, depositions scheduled, pretrial orders due--a hundred things set in the next two weeks. You're talking about sixty or seventy active cases, you know."

"Believe me, I know," Pete said, raising his hands. "I made all the same arguments over the phone this morning. But I guess they've hired this copying service--got a special rate--and those guys are only there until the end of the month. So we've got to do it, that's all there is to it. And you and I have to work it out so that the least disruption is caused."

"Damn, that's going to be tough," O'Neal said, sitting back.

"Well, I'd like your help on this. I'll send out a memo today to everyone working on the American Union cases that everything that's scheduled during the next three weeks - every motion, deposition, hearing and trial is to be put over for at least thirty days. There's going to be a lot of bitching about that, and in some cases it's going to be harder than hell to pull off. But we've just got to do it, even if cases are set for hearings or trials. And I want you to work with everyone to make sure it's done, and to explain to everyone what's going on. If we have to come up with some bullshit affidavit about a key witness being out of town or in the hospital, or something else like that, then just make something up. But do it! When each file is cleared, get it up here to my office, and I'll have it sent over to the client. And remember, they've all got to be there by the end of the week."

"Okay," O'Neal said, shaking his head as he stood up. "If we gotta do it, we gotta do it. But I hope you can convince those idiots over there that we need to get the files back here as fast as we can. There's a lot of stuff cooking in those cases."

"I will, Larry - and I really appreciate your help with this."

The story held up pretty well, Pete thought. The next problem would be to explain why the files weren't coming back. But at least he'd have some time to think about that. He had to delay as long as possible having the firm--and Cal in particular--learn that he had lost America Union.

—*mmm*—

Tony Jeffries picked the stack of papers out of the Xerox tray and handed them to Betty. "Okay, these are the last ones," he said. "Put the original file back where it was, and put these copies in the trial bag next to my desk. They should just fit. Label this stack 'Consolidated Steel, 2004 correspondence.' "

"Right." She turned and walked off, following a path

she'd traveled a hundred times that weekend.

Tony left the Xerox room and headed around to the north side of the floor. It was still dark outside. He glanced at his watch, it was 4:15 a.m. When he reached Carol's office, she was taping shut the last of four boxes on her desk. She glanced up but didn't stop working and didn't say a word.

They were exhausted, all of them. They'd worked all night Friday; copying, boxing, and moving their records and personal belongings. When dawn came Saturday, they had left, each carrying out two stuffed trial bags. They got some rest during the day Saturday, while others were doing their usual weekend work around the office, then returned Saturday night to pick up where they'd left off.

"Got your client and prospect data?" he asked Carol.

"Box three." She nodded toward the box next to the one she was taping. "It's with our billing records, and copies of all our marketing proposals. Both hard copies and disks."

"Good. I may have copies of some of that too. But between us, I'm sure we'll have everything we need."

"Good morning, folks." Tony turned to see Charlie Dickenson standing in the doorway, a steaming cup of coffee in his hand.

"I just took down two more full briefcases," Charlie said. "Transferred the contents into cartons in the trunk of my car, and brought the bags back up. It's amazing how building security will inspect any box you try to take out of here, but anything a lawyer hauls out in a briefcase is okay, even if you walk past them twenty times a day."

Tony had a pretty good idea how Cal and Pete would react when they received their resignations Monday morning. He assumed they'd seize all their files and records, and do all they could to keep Tony and his group from contacting or servicing their existing clients. They'd send partners out to all those clients, assuring them that the firm and was ready and willing to continue taking care of their legal needs. The firm would have all the leverage. To obviate that problem, he was having copies made of everything that he could. No original client files were being taken from Wilson & Thompson, but Tony and his crew would have copies of anything they needed to maintain continuity and hold on to what Tony had developed and felt was rightfully theirs.

By six a.m. they were finished: the last records had been copied and taken downstairs to their cars; the letters of resignation had been typed and signed; their office doors had been closed. They hoped no curious member of the firm would stick his nose into one of their offices on Sunday and discover their plot. Their secretaries intentionally left a few personal trinkets in their work areas to defuse suspicion.

The plan was for the six of them--Tony, Carol, Charlie and their secretaries--to drive their cars, loaded with the copied records, down on Monday morning and park them in the Marina City garage, across the street from the IBM Building. They'd meet upstairs at Catlin & Coogan and take cabs together over to the Hancock Building to submit their letters of resignation. Right after that, the three lawyers would hit the road, visiting all their clients, explaining the move, and asking them to sign letters transferring their business to the new firm. At the same time, their secretaries and others from Catlin & Coogan would begin moving their boxes of documents upstairs and setting up their offices. Tony insisted that they not deliver anything to the new firm until they first submitted their resignations to Wilson & Thompson. Speed in contacting the clients was essential. Carol and Charlie were assigned to contact the ones in the Chicago area. Tony had the biggest assignment: Consolidated Steel in Pittsburgh, the one client they *had* to deliver.

The three attorneys and their secretaries walked into Wilson & Thompson together at 9:30 Monday morning. The secretaries proceeded to the administrative manager's office to deliver their letters of resignation, while Tony and the two other attorneys walked back to Cal Cizma's office. As they had calculated, he had just arrived.

"Good morning, Cal," Tony said as they walked into his office. "We have something for you."

"I'm sorry," Cal answered, holding up his hand. "But I'm really busy this morning. Why don't you check with my secretary to see when I'll be free, if you don't mind."

"No, Cal, you're going to talk to us now."

Cal looked up, clearly irritated.

"We're leaving the firm, effective immediately. Here's my letter of resignation." Tony pulled his letter out of his inside coat pocket and handed it to Cal, at the same time Carol and Charlie handed him theirs.

"What the hell?" Cal scowled. "You can't do that! You've got to give us reasonable notice - at least two weeks. This is bullshit!"

"And give you time to contact our clients first? No way." Tony answered with a smile. "Cal, I've had it with the way things are being run around here. You know the fights we've had. We're leaving today and going to Catlin & Coogan." He paused a moment, then added, "I'm sorry it turned out this way, Cal, but you really didn't leave us any alternative. Goodbye."

Carol started speaking, but Cal stood up and cut her off. "Don't think you're taking any clients or files out of this office," he shouted at Tony, "because you're not! Not one piece of paper - nothing! And if I find that you've violated the Canons of Ethics in pulling this stunt, God damn, I'll have you disbarred! All of you!" He shot glances at Carol and Charlie.

"Let's go," Tony said, turning his back on Cal. He knew the situation would deteriorate if they stayed any longer. They walked briskly down the hall to the reception room, where their secretaries were already waiting for them. Behind them they could hear Cal shouting to someone. Within seconds, while they were waiting for the elevator, Kevin ran up the stairs from the mail room and confronted them.

"Hold it, Mr. Jeffries," he said, breathing heavily. "You're not taking anything out of here, you understand?"

"You're right, Kevin," Tony answered as pleasantly as he could. He unbuttoned his suitcoat and spread his arms wide. "We're *not* taking anything out of here."

Kevin looked quickly from one of them to the other. Charlie had unbuttoned his coat like Tony, and Carol, wearing a blouse and skirt, just shrugged and smiled. The three secretaries did the same.

"Well, all right," Kevin said after a few seconds. He looked confused. "Just... just don't do it again."

"I'm sure we won't, Kevin," Tony answered as they stepped into the elevator. "You can count on that."

When the elevator doors shut, they just looked at each other for a moment, then all let out a shout. They had done it! They had pulled it off! They were out! They laughed and hugged each other all the way down. Tony felt giddy, he was so exhilarated. Tears rolled down his cheeks, he was laughing so hard. As the elevator slowed, they started to pull themselves together. Tony wiped off his cheeks and put his tie back inside his coat where it belonged. He still couldn't help chuckling. Cal had looked absolutely dumbstruck. *Beautiful!*

Tony felt a little discomfort in his stomach. Indigestion? He'd probably just been laughing too hard.

"Well, are you ready to capture Consolidated Steel?" Carol asked as the elevator slowed to a stop.

"I sure am. Got my ticket right here," Tony patted his inside coat pocket. "Plane leaves O'Hare in two hours, and I've got an appointment with the general counsel at three this afternoon, their time. He doesn't know why I'm coming, but he knows it's important."

"I'd say it is," Betty said. "All our jobs are riding on it."

The doors opened and Tony stepped back to let the women out first, then walked out into the Hancock Building's elevator lobby. He was about to say goodbye to the others when he suddenly felt an excruciating pain in his abdomen. He tried to remain standing, but couldn't, and toppled over onto his side.

"Oh my God," he heard Carol say. The pain was getting worse, and Tony doubled up in agony. It was throbbing now, deep in his gut. Someone shouted, "I'm calling 911!" and then he blacked out.

Tony was groggy when he woke up; it took him a few minutes to realize that he also had a terrible headache. His stomach still hurt, but it was a different kind of pain. He looked around and realized that he was in a hospital. A bag of fluid was hanging alongside his bed, attached to his left arm. There was an antiseptic smell in the air and a man in a white gown was standing over him, watching him closely

"How are you feeling?" he asked.

"I don't know." Tony's mouth was dry and tasted foul. "What happened?"

"You've had emergency surgery," the man answered. "It was a badly bleeding ulcer. You're lucky you were near a hospital - otherwise, you might not have made it. I'm Dr. Cruthers, by the way. Bill Cruthers."

"Doctor," Tony was trying to clear his mind. "How long am I going to have to stay here? There's something very important I've got to do."

"Not today you don't," the doctor laughed. "And not this week. You're going to be laid up for a while. You'll be able to go home in about three or four days, and you'll have to take it easy for another week or so after that unless you want to pop all those stitches we just put in you." He pointed toward Tony's groin.

Tony shut his eyes and moaned. It wasn't the pain in his gut--it was the pain of knowing that everything was going to fail.

—*mm*—

"You say that Tony is in a hospital? He didn't even get out of the city?" Cal couldn't believe what he had just heard.

"That's right," Chris Chamberlin said over the phone. "I was waiting for the elevator in the lobby. . ."

"Wait a minute, Chris," Cal interrupted. "Pete is right here. I'm going to put you on speaker. I want him to hear this too." He pushed a button on the phone console. "Go ahead." A grin began creeping across Pete Spanos's face as he leaned forward in his chair.

"As I said," Chamberlin continued, "I was in the lobby when his whole crew came out of the elevator. They must have just left you. They were all laughing and slapping each other on the back. Then all of a sudden, Jeffries keels over. Like he was shot. I stayed around long enough to learn that they were taking him to Northwestern Memorial. While I was standing there I figured out what had just happened. They were all talking about quitting and the new firm. They must not have noticed me; there were a lot of people milling around. Carol James was real upset about Jeffries missing some flight out of O'Hare. Anyway, I had to get over here to court. But when my hearing was over - it was only a status call - I took a cab to Northwestern. I told them I was from the firm and wanted to confirm Jeffries' situation for medical-coverage purposes. They wouldn't tell me much because of HIPAA, but I learned enough to know that Jeffries is in bad shape and won't get out of there for at least a couple of days, maybe longer."

"That's great," Pete said quietly, stretching luxuriantly in his chair.

"Good work, Chris--damn good work!" Cal added. "I'll talk to you when you get back here. We might have a special project or two for you." He leaned over and pushed the button terminating the call.

"If I know Jeffries," Pete said, still grinning "he's played it straight. He hasn't talked to his clients yet.

That's why he was on his way to the airport."

"Right. To fly to Pittsburgh. Consolidated Steel's his biggest client. Of course he'd go there first. He'd let James and Dickenson contact the locals, but he'd handle Consolidated himself." Cal leaned forward, pointing a finger at Pete. "That's the one client he can't afford to lose."

"We can't either, Cal. We can't take another hit right now."

"Well, we're not going to. We're going to do a preemptive strike on Consolidated Steel. I'll set up a meeting with their general counsel tomorrow. I'll take Wally Covington with me, and have Mike Vance fly in from Philly. By the time Jeffries gets off his back, we'll have Consolidated nailed down so tight he won't even be able to get a toe in the door."

Chapter Twenty-One

—um—

Tony carefully eased himself down into the airplane seat, holding his breath until he had settled in. *So far, so good.* The pain in his groin was constant but flat; he could live with that. If it didn't get worse, he'd be all right.

He had dressed and slipped out of the hospital as soon as he'd booked a plane reservation to Pittsburgh. He'd hoped to be able to put this ordeal off a couple of days; but after he called Lou Kleppa, Consolidated Steel's general counsel, and learned that Cal and several of the senior partners would like to meet with Kleppa as soon as possible he knew he couldn't wait. "What the hell's going on, Tony" Kleppa had asked him. "I haven't gotten this much attention from Wilson & Thompson since we started doing business together."

Tony knew he had to tell Kleppa what was up. He said that he'd accepted a position as a partner in the Chicago office of Catlin & Coogan, had brought his team with him, and in fact wanted to talk to him about the possibility of keeping Consolidated's work. Kleppa said that he understood, but warned him that they generally didn't move files from one firm to another, even when the lawyers working on their cases changed jobs. Still, he said, he'd always liked Tony's work and would be happy to consider both sides' positions before making a final decision. When Tony learned that Cal and his team were scheduled to be there at four, he said he'd be there too. He knew he had to be there in person; a phone call wouldn't do.

The cab ride to the airport had been rough. A couple of times they hit potholes that sent ice picks of pain into his gut. The driver spoke no English, and every time Tony asked him to take it easy, he stepped on the gas.

Tony was glad he'd been able to get into first class. He was uncomfortable already and wanted all the room he could get. The wait on the ground at O'Hare was interminable. After twenty minutes or so, the combination of a throbbing headache and the pain from his surgery began getting to him. He asked for some water and took a couple of pain-killing Tramals. It seemed like only an hour or two since he took the last couple.

Once the plane was in the air Tony eased his seat all the way back and tried to relax. That seemed to take some of the strain off his stomach. He felt very tired and shut his eyes. That felt better, much better.

Tony opened his eyes to see one of the flight attendants staring down at him. She looked worried.

"Mr. Jeffries, are you alright?"

"Of course I'm all right. Why do you ask?"

"Well, your shirt..." she said, pointing down. "It's, ah...."

Tony quickly looked down and saw a large red spot over his surgery. *Damn, I've broken a couple of stitches*!

"It's nothing." He feigned a laugh. "Old wound. Nothing to worry about. I probably could use a couple of napkins, though, if you don't mind."

She looked at him like he was a madman, then scurried up to the galley and returned with a big handful of napkins. "If you need anything else," she said, "please tell me."

"I will," Tony answered with a little laugh. *She just doesn't want me to die on her watch. How the hell would she report that - bad coffee service?* He chuckled a little, but stopped quickly at the pain that it caused.

He tucked the napkins under his shirt, then folded the airplane blanket and pulled it over his chest. He didn't need any more reminders about the insanity he was engaged in. He shut his eyes again and forced himself to think about the status of all the Consolidated Steel cases they were handling.

A little over an hour later, they set down in Pittsburgh. The jolt as the plane hit the runway was the hardest part of the flight. He had to grit his teeth to keep from shouting out in pain.

Before they got off, the flight attendant asked him again if he was okay. Tony assured her that he was, and buttoned his coat to hide the growing bloodstain. He walked slowly up the jetway and through the concourse. He wasn't concerned about the others hurriedly rushing past; his slow, measured steps were the best he could do.

In the airport Tony spotted a Brooks Brothers shop and bought and put on a new shirt, throwing away the old blood-soaked one. He also bought a dozen handkerchiefs, which he wadded up into a bandage over his wound. He had to look presentable for at least a few minutes.

The cab ride to Consolidated Steel's headquarters took about thirty minutes. Tony glanced at his watch as they arrived. It was 4:10--*not too bad under the circumstances.* Five minutes later he was escorted into Lou Kleppa's large carpeted office. Cal Cizma, Wally Covington, and Mike Vance, who were already there, turned as he entered. Cal in particular looked shocked. None of them said a word.

"Good afternoon, gentlemen," Tony said cheerily. "Sorry, I'm late. Lou, it's good to see you again," he shook Kleppa's hand for a moment and looked him in the eye.

"Good to see you too." Kleppa answered with a smile. From the twinkle in his eye, it looked like he was enjoying this moment. "I was under the impression," he added, nodding toward the other three, "that you were laid up and wouldn't be on your feet for several weeks."

"Really?" Tony chuckled, glancing at Cal, who was staring straight ahead. "What a bunch of jokers. Always good for a laugh. I had a little bug yesterday, but it's nothing to worry about."

"Good," Kleppa said, leading him to the seat next to his desk. "Well, let's get to the business at hand. I understand, Tony, that you've changed law firms."

"Yes," Tony replied as he slowly sat down. "I've gone to Catlin & Coogan, Lou. They're one of the finest firms in the country and are just opening an office in Chicago." As he sat back, he instinctively began to unbutton his suitcoat, then thought better of it.

"I know the firm," Kleppa answered, nodding. "Very good reputation, especially in litigation."

"That's right. And I've brought all the senior people on my team with me. Carol James, who you met when we tried and won the Iron Mountain case, and Charlie Dickenson, who's worked with me on all your cases for the past six years. Plus our secretaries. Lou, we've done good work for you over the years. Never lost a case. We'd like to maintain that relationship. If we can keep your business, there won't be a beat lost in the Consolidated suits we're defending."

"I've enjoyed our relationship, Tony, and so have the other attorneys in our office," Kleppa said. "But Cal here says that he's prepared to commit Mr. Covington, head of their Litigation Department, to work on our matters full time if we leave the business with Wilson & Thompson. And he says they won't charge us for Covington's time in getting up to speed. That's an attractive offer." Kleppa sat back with a smile and stroked his mustache.

"And a fair one," Cal added. "We value our firm's long relationship with Consolidated Steel, and are willing to make that commitment. Wally Covington's our top litigator, and he's prepared to make your matters his number-one priority. Everything else he has goes on the back burner or gets reassigned."

"That's a pretty good trick if he can do it," Tony answered. "Wally," he said, turning for the first time toward Covington, "I hope you haven't forgotten the Roosevelt case that you'll be trying. As I recall, it starts a week from Tuesday and is expected to run for at least three weeks. I'll be surprised, Lou," he said, turning back to Kleppa, "If he'll have a free minute to look at your files in the next month. In the meantime, there's a lot going on in your cases - hearings, motions, depositions. You can't afford to have a whole new team try to step in and learn the files, especially a team with an absentee leader."

"Oh, come on, Tony," Covington said, "That Roosevelt case is probably going to settle. Those medical mal cases always do."

"This one won't, Wally, and we both know it." Tony answered. "Don't get me wrong, Lou." He looked back at Kleppa. "Wally Covington's a fine lawyer, and Wilson & Thompson is a fine law firm. But in terms of handling *your* cases, the ones that my team has been handling for you, *we're* the ones who are the best equipped to see those cases through to completion. You've invested a lot of time and money getting us up to speed in those files. Two of them are set for trial this fall, as a matter of fact - the *Loring* suit in October and the *Kim* suit in November. And we're ready. We can win those trials for you, Lou, just like we've won every case we've tried to verdict for you over the past ten years."

Kleppa looked at him for a long moment, and nodded. "I agree. It would be foolish for us to change lawyers in the middle of those cases, especially since we've been very pleased with the way you've been handling them to date, Tony. Alright, you can keep the cases you've been working on. With new matters, we'll decide on a case-by-case basis which firm to assign them to."

"Thanks, Lou," Tony answered, trying to suppress a smile. "You're going to be happy with this decision, believe me."

"Is there anything you'd like me to sign to formalize the transfer of those files?"

"Well, as a matter of fact, I do have something here," Tony answered, pulling a piece of paper from his briefcase "It's a letter to Wilson & Thompson directing them to turn your files over to us and advising them that we're your counsel in those cases from this date on." He handed the letter to Kleppa, who scanned it, signed it, and handed it back.

"Actually, Cal, I can tender this to you right now," Tony said, turning to Cizma. "Might as well save the postage."

Cal looked at the letter briefly, sneered, and stuffed it into his side coat pocket. "We'll turn the files over when we're paid in full for our work to date," he snapped to Kleppa. "Not a moment before."

Kleppa looked surprised. "That's not a very friendly

gesture from a law firm that five minutes ago was court-
ing our business."

"We don't regard this as a very friendly gesture on
your part, either, Mr. Kleppa. And frankly we're disappointed. Disappointed with Consolidated Steel and
disappointed with you, after all the work that our firm has
done for you over the years."

"Mr. Cizma, fax me your final bills by noon tomorrow, and I'll wire you payment before the sun sets,"
Kleppa said as he stood up. "And don't expect another
file from our company in the future." Cal rose and stared
at him for a moment, then wheeled and strode out of the
room. Covington and Vance, looking a little embarrassed,
nodded to the others and followed him out.

Tony watched his former partners file out, then turned
to Kleppa. "Thanks, Lou," he said. "I appreciated that."

"No, you earned that. But those assholes sure didn't
help their position with their highhanded approach.
Especially that bullshit about your being laid up. When I
saw the way they lied about that, frankly, I lost all respect
for them. And I sure didn't care for their attitude at the
end."

Kleppa stepped over and slapped Tony on the shoulder. Pain stabbed into his gut. "Good luck with the new
firm. You're definitely our man in Chicago, Tony."

Tony thanked him and excused himself, turning down
an offer of drinks at Kleppa's club; he had to get back
to Chicago, he said. When he got downstairs and into a
cab he unbuttoned his suitcoat for the first time since he

had walked into Consolidated's headquarters. The lower portion of his shirt and the top of his pants, were soaked with blood.

"Get me to the nearest hospital," Tony said to the driver, leaning back and shutting his eyes. "And hurry, please."

mm

Pete Spanos read the letter again. The U.S. Department of Labor was conducting an audit of Wilson & Thompson's pension fund and was requesting a conference. They wanted to review the fund's account books and inventory of investments, as well as the firm's actuarial projections of its pension fund obligations.

That shouldn't be a problem, Pete thought as he put the letter to one side. He'd just send this down to Wanda and let her take care of it. Then it occurred to him that perhaps he should take a look at the pension fund records before they just turned them over to the feds; maybe they weren't complete or up to date. Better find that out now and fix it, rather than be embarrassed later.

Thirty minutes later all the records were on his desk. Wanda brought them up in two large file folders, one neatly labeled "Beneficiaries Data" and the other, "Investment Data." Pete decided to look at the investment records first. Their investment portfolio was conservative; forty percent in blue chip equities and sixty percent in triple-A corporate bonds. He was eager to see the current balance in their account; the market had been good, and the last time he checked, the pension fund was approaching $20 million.

The monthly reports from their brokerage house were all clipped together, with the most recent one on top. He flipped to the last page of the latest report to see the month-end balance. He looked at the figure, blinked, and looked again. The last reported balance was $8 million. *How the fuck... Where did the money go?* His eyes shot up the sheet to see the latest transaction. It read, "Funds transferred to Trustee: $12,000,000.00."

Funds transferred? What the hell is that all about? He quickly turned back to the first page. The trustee was the firm's chairman, Calvin Cizma. Then it struck Pete like a thunderbolt. *That's where Cal got the twelve million he used to humiliate Tony Jeffries! It wasn't a huge fee from Essen Re at all. Cal cleaned out most of the firm's pension plan in order to make his grandstand play.*

Bertha Roosevelt sat at the table in the courtroom, with Attorney Greene on her left and Robert on her right. She felt comfortable between them. It was awfully nice, she thought, for Attorney Greene to offer to pick them up in his car every morning during the trial. Their new apartment in Maywood was very comfortable, but it was a long way downtown.

The judge was black; she liked that. His name was

Carver - or was it Carter? Bertha wasn't sure. He had white hair, wore glasses, and had a kind face. He looked like he'd be fair.

The people on the jury were mainly working folks, like her family. Three or four of them were retired. One didn't look that old, and she wondered if he'd just said he was retired because he was unemployed. There were a couple of ladies in their thirties; they looked like they were secretaries or something like that. One of the men walked with a cane and said he was on disability. The others were the kind of people Bertha saw on the street every day, and about half of them were black.

The lawyers were all white; that didn't surprise Bertha. The main lawyer for the hospital was Mr. Covington. He was a handsome man with long blond hair that was carefully combed back. She had seen him on television a couple of times and recognized him as soon as he walked into the courtroom. She felt a surge of pride that a famous lawyer was going to be involved in her case, even if he was on the other side. He had an assistant sitting next to him: a young man who looked very busy with all his books and pads of paper and everything. A woman from the hospital was sitting with them too: thin, a little on the plain side, and about Bertha's age. She was addressed as "Sister," but Bertha didn't catch her name.

Her own main lawyer was Mr. Granaldi - Michael Granaldi. Attorney Greene told her he'd brought him in to handle the trial because he was a specialist and very good at what he did. That was fine with Bertha. Whatever

Attorney Greene wanted to do was all right with her. Mr. Granaldi was thin, but athletic and also handsome. He was sitting at the end of their table by the aisle, on the other side of Attorney Greene.

The judge was talking to the jury now; it was hard for Bertha to hear exactly what he was saying. Then he turned toward the lawyers and asked Mr. Granaldi if he'd like to make an opening statement. Mr. Granaldi slowly stood up, and said that he would.

He walked around their table, stood in front of the jury, and began talking.

"Ladies and gentlemen of the jury," he began. "Let me tell you about Sam Roosevelt. He was a good family man and had always proud of the fact that he took good care of his wife and son." Bertha reached over and squeezed Robert's hand. These things were all true.

"Sam always kept himself in good health." He continued "In fact, Sam Roosevelt had been an athlete when he was younger; played football at Crane Tech. Some of them who've been around Chicago a long time might remember Sam Roosevelt. He was an All-City guard for Crane in the early seventies." One of the older men in the back row of the jury nodded. "And Sam was still in good shape, until the day he had a medical problem and went into Blessed Trinity Hospital for help."

"The evidence will show," Mr. Granaldi went on, "that Sam Roosevelt had a minor blood clot on the surface on the right side of his brain when he was admitted to Blessed Trinity Hospital. You will hear expert testimony that blood clots such as that can be easily located and re-moved, and that in eighty to ninety percent of the cases, if proper care is administered, the patient ends up making a full recovery. In other words, when Sam Roosevelt went into Blessed Trinity Hospital that evening, he and his family had every reason to expect him to be back on his feet within a couple of weeks. And he should have been."

"Amen," Bertha whispered.

"The evidence will also show," Mr. Granaldi said, raising his voice, "that Blessed Trinity Hospital and its staff committed a series of stupid blunders and outrageous mistakes in treating Sam Roosevelt. Those mistakes, in the aggregate, amounted to nothing less than an atroc-ity. A technician who didn't even know how to operate the CAT-scan machine that was supposed to pinpoint precisely where Sam's blood clot was. And, as a result, the machine had the right and left sides of the X-rays re-versed. A radiologist who didn't catch that mistake. An emergency room physician who refused to admit that a mistake had been made even after it had been pointed out to him by a senior nurse. A neurosurgeon - another doctor - who cut open the wrong side of Sam's head and poked around in Sam's brain with his medical instruments for half an hour, trying to find a clot that wasn't there,... and then shrugging and saying that they could wait until the morning for another CAT-scan to be taken to see what the problem was, since their CAT-scan machine wasn't work-ing right then. A hospital that hadn't made arrangements to have emergency CAT-scans taken at a neighboring hospital only ten minutes away. And a hospital staff that just sewed up Sam's head and left him uncared for all night while his situation deteriorated dramatically. And in the morning, when they finally got around to taking another CAT-scan, finding that the blood clot, which had always been on the right side of Sam's head, had grown and essentially destroyed half of his brain in the process."

Mr. Granaldi stepped back and looked at the jury. They were all watching him closely. "None of that should have happened," he said quietly. "None of it."

"Amen," Bertha whispered, louder this time, nodding her agreement.

"And as a direct result of that negligence, that terrible conduct, Sam Roosevelt was deprived of all his capacity to move, to think, to understand, even to love. He lies today permanently comatose in a county nursing facility. Before this trial is over we're going to bring Sam Roosevelt into this courtroom so that you can see for yourselves the horror that has been done to him. And his devoted wife and son." Mr. Granaldi turned and pointed to Bertha and Robert. "Who will never again know him as the husband and father that he was."

Mr. Granaldi paused again. "And that, ladies and gentlemen of the jury, is what this case is all about."

"Amen!" Bertha repeated audibly, tears rolling down her cheeks. Attorney Greene leaned over and squeezed her hand.

Cal stepped back to admire his new Leroy Nieman over the fireplace. It was the America's Cup painting: two boats running with the wind, surging through the surf. It had cost him a pretty penny, but was worth it. Everyone recognized that scene. It also fit perfectly here, with the sound of the waves crashing against the beach outside his windows. It was dark now, and you couldn't see the lake, but it never let you forget that it was there.

The bonus that Cal had extracted from the firm enabled him to get his affairs nicely in order. Pete Spanos had winced at the idea of a two-million-dollar bonus, but then, how often in the past had someone brought in a twelve million dollar fee? Never. And it was all profit, to boot. Cal chuckled as he thought about that. It had been so simple to have Citibank issue the certified check, payable to the firm, and then to manually type in the words "Remitter: Essen Re." He'd been able to settle his divorce with Sandy and buy this house on the lake in Evanston all at the same time. Yes, things had improved dramatically.

As he pulled back the fireplace screen and tossed in another log, Cal wondered what Pete wanted to talk to him about, and why it was so important that he see him right away. He'd called about a half hour ago and said he was driving up from the city. It was almost ten; he'd watch the news until Pete arrived. He poured himself some scotch, clicked on his new hi-def television, and sat down on the couch in his den. The picture crackled to life just as the news began.

"Topping today's news," the anchorman announced, "is the complete collapse of the British Imperial Insurance Syndicate. As reported earlier this month, the two top executives of the Imperial Syndicate, Gordon Hawke and Ronald Dasher, disappeared at that time with over three hundred million dollars." Two familiar faces flashed onto the screen. "Hawke and Dasher were rumored to have fled to the Caribbean with their wives, although no word of them has been reported since. Today, the British Ministry of the Interior reported that Imperial's losses were much greater than originally reported, and that it was unable to keep the giant insurer afloat. Imperial has been declared insolvent and ordered liquidated."

"Those sons-of-bitches!" Cal said aloud, shaking his head. "They've probably got half a billion stashed away somewhere." He was glad now that he had posted a reserve to cover their accounts receivable.

The bell rang and Cal turned off the TV. He walked up three steps, then down the long hallway to the front door. When he opened it, Pete Spanos stood in the swirling wind and the mist from the lake with an oversized briefcase in his left hand. Behind him, the steady roar of the waves crashing against the beach filled the night.

"Come on in, Pete," Cal said, stepping back and holding the door open. "Whatever you want to talk about must be pretty urgent, to bring you out this late at night."

"It is," Pete answered as he walked in and shut the door behind himself. "Damn important." He dropped his briefcase and wiped the mist from his hair and face

"Let's go back to the den," Cal said..

"I suppose you heard about Imperial," Pete said as he picked up his bag, walked down the hall behind Cal and stepped down into the large pine-paneled room.

"Yeah, just saw it on TV. Frankly, I'm not surprised. Saw it coming as soon as Hawke and Dasher disappeared. That's going to impact us. We're probably going to have to let some people go. Was that what you wanted to talk about?"

"No, it's more serious than that," Pete said, stopping and turning toward Cal. "Although that's pretty serious stuff. No, what I want to talk to you about, Cal, are the firm's pension funds. Most of them are gone, cleaned out."

"I'm not sure I understand." Cal, of course, understood all too well, but he wanted to see how much Pete had learned.

"I've gone through the records," Pete said as he raised his briefcase slightly, then stepped closer. "The majority of the funds were transferred to you. Twelve million bucks. And I've got a hunch that's the money you claimed was a fee from Essen Re. Am I right, Cal?" He let the bag drop to the floor as he finished.

Pete had him, no question about that. *Damn!* Cal turned away, shaking his head. He'd intended to fix the records to indicate that the money had been invested in a dummy company, but he hadn't yet had the chance to put that together.

"You're right, Pete," he answered, turning back. "Sorry I didn't tell you, but I didn't want to get you involved. It *is* a little dicey, I know, but the money *did* go back to the firm."

"A little dicey?" Pete exploded. "It's a goddamn federal felony! I've got an inspector from the Department of Labor coming in to check our records, and all you can say is that it's a little dicey? Jesus! I've been hauling the damn records around in my car, just so no one will find them."

Cal started to reply, but Pete cut him off. "And you used that so-called fee to get yourself a two-million-buck bonus! You bought *this* place with that bonus," he said, pointing up with his thumb. "Cal," he said, shaking his head, "we've got to replace that money. We just have to."

"For Christ's sake; Pete, that's impossible! We're talking about twelve million bucks. We just have to finesse it somehow. Don't you forget, though, that I used that money to bury Tony Jeffries. If I hadn't completely discredited him at that partnership meeting, he was ready to lead a revolt. And he might have pulled it off--don't forget that! We're still running the firm today because I had the guts to use that pension money smartly."

"But, my God, Cal... ."

"Don't you 'my God' me!" Cal shouted back. "If it wasn't for me, you wouldn't even be on the goddamn management committee! None of us would have been!"

"What the hell are you talking about?"

"The thing that set it all in motion was our esteemed senior partner Henry Gilcrist being arrested for insider trading, fraud, and tax evasion. The killer evidence against Gilcrist was in his own private files. How do you suppose the feds found that?"

Pete was silent for a moment, then spoke. "I don't know. I've always wondered about that," His voice was quieter now and he was staring at Cal.

"Let me tell you how they found it. I copied it late at night and mailed it to them, anonymously - the bank accounts in fictitious names, his handwritten records of his profits, everything. I knew that with that evidence they'd nail him, and that when that happened, he'd be out of here and the management of the firm would be up for grabs. And that's exactly what happened! It worked perfectly. And *you* benefited along with me," he said, jabbing his finger at Pete. "We ended up taking over the whole goddamn firm!"

"Jesus Christ, Cal...you're even more of a cold-blooded son-of-a-bitch than I thought."

"When I have to be, yes," Cal replied evenly.

"But it's not smart to commit a goddamn federal felony, especially with pension money!" Pete was pacing around the room. He turned and pointed at Cal. "You've gone too far, Cal, too damn far. The feds are going to assume that I was involved in your damn stunt. But I'm not going to go to prison over this!"

Cal picked up the briefcase, put it on his desk, and opened it. "Let me see what these records show," he said, pulling out one of the thick folders.

"And as far as I'm concerned all bets between us are off!" Pete went on, his voice rising. "If you're goin' down, Cal, you're not taking me down with you. Maybe I should tell the feds everything I know. Maybe that way I can salvage something."

"And set up your own firm?"

"What?"

"The American Union files. They're all gone. I've checked. You've been slipping them out a few at a time, haven't you? You're setting up shop somewhere else, aren't you?"

Pete laughed at him. "American Union? If you only knew how stupid that was! That's crazy!"

"No, I'll tell you what's crazy, Pete--you going to the feds. Remember, *you're* the chairman of our finance committee. *You're* the one who's always had custody of all the firm's financial records. If you turn on me, I'm going to say that everything was *your* idea - *you* engineered it. I may have gotten a big bonus out of that deal, but remember, you got one too. A hundred grand, as I recall. You approved everything. If I go down, we both go down--partners to the end!"

"But that's not what the records show," Pete said, pointing to the folder in Cal's hand.

"These records? I'll tell you what these records show." Cal turned, strode over to his roaring fireplace and flung them in. "They show nothing!"

"Jesus Christ, Cal! Don't do that!" Pete lunged forward but stopped as Cal grabbed the fireplace poker and raised it toward him. They stared at each other for a long moment as the fire behind Cal quickly devoured the dry papers.

Cal could see desperation in Pete's eyes, then fear. "What the feds are going to find, Pete," he said as he slowly walked back to the desk, lifted the other folder of financial records from the briefcase, and eased back toward the fireplace, keeping the iron poker poised, "is that the firm's pension plan records are terribly screwed up. Probably the fault of that guy you fired, Luke Smith. He was always a fuckup. It'll take them years to figure out what happened, and by then we'll be able to replace the money. Say it had been deposited in the wrong account...something like that. They'll be madder than hell, probably fine somebody. But nobody's going to jail, Pete - if we stay together, that is." With that he half-turned, emptied the contents of the file into the blaze, and tossed in the brown folder.

"And I'll tell you what you're going to do tomorrow, Pete. You're going to walk into the office at nine-fifteen, like you always do, have your cup of coffee, go through your mail, and do your business as usual. Except for one thing." Cal's voice hardened suddenly. "You're going to arrange to bring back all those goddamned American Union files from wherever the hell you've been storing them. I want them back!" he shouted. He took a deep breath, then continued, lowering the poker and his voice. "We can survive this, Pete, if we don't panic. I sure as hell don't intend to panic, and I don't want you to, either, partner."

Pete slowly retreated, almost stumbling over an ottoman. He backed up the three steps to the front hallway without saying a word, his eyes transfixed on Cal. Then he turned and ran toward the front door, pausing only to open it and run out. When the door slammed shut, Cal took another deep breath, walked over to the fireplace, and poked some papers on the hearth into the blaze.

That was close--too close. Pete's scared to death. But he's basically a coward. He won 't go to the feds now--he'll be afraid he'd go down too. And goddamn it, he would! He'll do whatever I say. He's too afraid to do anything else. Tomorrow those American Union files will start coming back and it'll be business as usual.

Chapter Twenty Two

~~~~~

"Ladies and gentlemen of the jury, have you reached a verdict?" Judge Julius Carver leaned forward as he asked the question, watching the jurors' eyes.

"We have, Your Honor," the tall black man in the front row responded as he stood and buttoned his jacket.

"Would you give your verdict form to the bailiff, please."

The judge watched as the foreman handed a folded piece of paper to the bailiff, who unfolded it, looked at it for a moment, and handed it up to him. Their eyes met his as the judge took the verdict form. There was something unusual about this one. He looked at the completed form and understood. He glanced up at the filled courtroom. Everyone was watching.

"We the jury," Judge Carver began reading, stopping for a moment to clear his throat, "find for the plaintiffs Sam and Bertha Roosevelt and against defendant Blessed Trinity Hospital, and award compensatory damages in the amount of two million dollars."

He glanced up again. Everyone was whispering to each other, and the young attorney at the defense table was grinning to Wally Covington. "And further," the judge continued reading, "We award punitive damages in favor of Sam and Bertha Roosevelt and against Blessed Trinity Hospital in the amount of *one hundred million dollars.*"

The whispering stopped. The enormity of the verdict had frozen everyone in the packed courtroom in place. The judge had never seen that reaction to a verdict before. But then he, too, was pausing to consider the immensity of the decision he had just read. It was the largest verdict that had ever been returned in his courtroom.

Suddenly, the stocky old man at the plaintiffs' table stood up. It was Max Greene, the small-time personal injury lawyer who was co-counsel for the plaintiffs. - probably the referring attorney, the judge assumed. He hadn't spoken a word during the trial. Every eye in the courtroom was on him as he stood there with an odd smile on his face.

"One hundred million dollars," he whispered with a grin, staring vacantly at the wall behind the judge. Then Mike Granaldi stood up beside him, put his hand on his shoulder, and pushed him down into his seat.

"Your Honor," Wally Covington called out, "we request that the jury be polled."

"Of course," the judge responded. He then proceeded to ask each juror in turn if the verdict read was in fact their decision. They all responded in the affirmative, some very emphatically. The Judge thanked the jurors for their service, dismissed them, adjourned the court, and asked all the attorneys and the court reporter to meet him in his chambers.

As the courtroom was clearing, and the attorneys were gathering their papers, a teary-eyed Bertha Roosevelt stood hugging her son. Max Greene remained in his chair, dumbstruck, a silly grin on his face.

A few minutes later the attorneys convened in Judge Carver's private chambers. When he saw that they were all there, he asked his secretary to close the door. He took off his black robe, hung it in the closet, and sat down behind his desk.

Mike Granaldi, the plaintiffs' counsel, was there; so were Wally Covington and his associate from Wilson & Thompson, representing the hospital, along with a silent Max Greene and Sister Mary Ann Currier, the hospital's General Counsel.. The court reporter had set up her steno-type machine next to the judge's desk.

When the court reporter nodded to the Judge that she was ready, he began. "Now that we have a verdict there are a number of post trial matters that we need to deal with."

"That's gotta be a mistrial!" Wally Covington said, gesturing over his shoulder toward the courtroom. "A verdict like that is totally preposterous. Couple that with the other errors that occurred during the trial, that we objected to, and it's a mistrial for sure."

"No way," the judge answered, shaking his head. "You might not like the verdict, Mr. Covington, but that's no mistrial."

"Well, I certainly intend to file a motion… ."

"Be my guest, counselor," the judge interrupted. "But your motion's going to be denied."

"Then we'll file a motion for a remittitur," Covington shot back, his face reddening. "Your Honor, you have the authority to reduce the amount of the verdict if it's unreasonable or excessive, which that verdict certainly is."

"That motion's also denied, counsel. Now," Judge Carver paused to shuffle through the papers on his desk, finally finding what he was looking for. "We have the matter of the hospital's motion to resolve. The hospital filed a motion prior to trial that its insurers be held responsible for the full amount of any verdict entered against it. You've all filed your various responses, which I've considered. There doesn't appear to be any doubt that the case could have been settled prior to trial for two-and-a-half million dollars, which was well within the hospital's policy limits. That was a reasonable settlement demand, in my opinion, and the hospital asked that it be accepted. The insurers declined to settle, for reasons that are unclear but in the final analysis irrelevant. Therefore, it's my ruling that the hospital's insurers in this case are fully liable for the judgment returned by the jury: one hundred and two million dollars. The hospital's motion is granted."

"Thank you, Your Honor," Sister Mary Ann nodded to him. "It was our position all along that the case should have been settled."

"I know, Sister. That's why I've granted your motion." The judge glanced to the side to be sure the court reporter was taking this all down.

"I'm also ruling," Judge Carver continued, "based on the documents submitted to me, that the law firm of Wilson & Thompson is the hospital's principal insurer in this matter. They accepted that responsibility in the March 15th, 2003 letter agreement between Gordon Hawke of the Imperial Insurance Syndicate and Chester Melrose, a partner in the firm. Therefore, judgment is entered against the firm of Wilson & Thompson in the amount of one hundred and two million dollars."

"Wait a minute!" Wally Covington shouted, jumping to his feet. "That's outrageous! The most we're responsible for is the first million - everything over that is the responsibility of Imperial and its reinsurer."

"That's not the way I read the documents, Mr. Covington," the judge replied evenly. "Your firm accepted full responsibility, and the Imperial Syndicate agreed that they would undertake to obtain reinsurance for everything over a million per case. If they didn't," he shook his head, "that's unfortunate, and perhaps a breach of contract on their part, but the insuring obligation is still yours. In any event, that's my ruling."

"But Imperial's gone under!" Covington pleaded, desperation flashing in his eyes. "And the reinsurer, Essen

Re, won't respond to our messages. It seems to have vanished. You *can't* rule that way!"

"I'm sorry, but I have. Have your liability carrier post your bond and take it up on appeal if you wish."

Wally Covington turned away, his face twisted in agony. Judge Carver had never before seen any attorney so distressed. Covington turned back to him, shaking his head.

"But that's another problem," he said. "If the full amount of the judgment is entered against us, we *can't* post an appeal bond. You see...," he hesitated a moment, "we don't have any liability insurance right now."

"You're not serious!" The judge couldn't believe what he had just heard. Sister Mary Ann and the young associate from Wilson & Thompson stared open-mouthed at Covington. Mike Granaldi leaned back, smiled, and began stroking his chin. Max Greene's eyes had widened to their limit.

"I am, Your Honor," Covington answered, leaning forward with both his hands on the Judge's desk. "We can't post a one-hundred-and-two-million-dollar appeal bond. Bonding companies want double the amount of the judgment in cash or securities before they'll issue an appeal bond. There's no way we can raise that kind of money. Do you understand? You just can't do that!"

Judge Carver took a deep breath. He knew what he had to do, and what its impact would be. He also knew he had no choice. "I'm sorry, Mr. Covington," he said, "but that is my ruling. I've entered judgment for one hundred and two million dollars against your law firm. And in view of your comments about your firm's lack of insurance and inability to post an appeal bond, I'll entertain a motion to enjoin your firm and all its equity partners from transferring or selling any of their assets without the express approval of this court." Judge Carver glanced at Mike Granaldi.

"I so move, Your Honor." Granaldi said, grinning broadly.

"Granted. I want the record to reflect the fact that the time is now four-fifteen p.m. on September 21, 2004. Each and every person who is an equity partner in Wilson & Thompson as of this moment is jointly and severally liable for the full amount of the judgment and is bound by the injunction I've just entered."

Covington was ashen. He stepped back uncertainly and dropped onto the couch. His young associate, sitting at the other end of the couch, just stared at him, his mouth still agape.

"There's one final order of business." The judge turned to Granaldi. "What is the fee arrangement for plaintiffs' counsel?"

"The usual," Granaldi answered, pulling two pieces of paper from his inside coat pocket and handing them to the judge. "One-third, plus expenses. Of that, my offices is entitled to twenty-five percent, and the remaining eight and one-third goes to Mr. Greene here. We'd ask the court to approve it."

"Actually," Greene said, standing slowly, "that's not

the current fee agreement. That was the *original* agreement between Mrs. Roosevelt and myself, but it's been," he paused, "modified. Actually, modified four times. Here is the existing fee agreement, and all the prior modifications, Your Honor." With that he laid a handful of papers on the judge's desk. "You'll find," he continued, "that my office is actually entitled to the entire amount of the judgment, subject to the twenty-five percent that goes to Mr. Granaldi. And I ask that you approve *this* agreement."

"What?" Mike Granaldi shouted, leaping to his feet. "Max, that's outrageous!" Then, turning to the judge, he said, "Your Honor, we had no idea that was the situation. And we certainly wouldn't have taken part in this trial if we had known that the real party in interest was in fact Mr. Greene."

"You'll find that those modifications to the fee agreement are all in order," Greene asserted. "All signed and notarized, and all given for fair consideration. They're valid and enforceable."

"If that's true, Mr. Greene, I'm going to have you disbarred for grossly unscrupulous conduct," the judge replied, his voice rising. "You used your position of trust to take terrible advantage of that women and her son."

"Well, maybe I'm ready to retire, anyway, Your Honor, especially after my good fortune today," Max said with a comically mocking shrug.

"Alright, everyone, sit down," the judge ordered. "Let me take a look at these documents."

Judge Carver took the latest fee agreement and stared

at it; after a moment he began focusing on the signature. "Your client has terrible handwriting," he said without looking up.

"Yes, I know," Greene replied. "Can hardly read it myself. But, believe me, that's her signature. I saw her sign it and notarized it myself."

"Wait a minute!" the judge exclaimed. "Is this some kind of a joke?"

"What do you mean?"

"The signature on this fee-agreement amendment, if you look closely, reads 'Martha Washington,' not 'Bertha Roosevelt!' It's scribbled, but it definitely reads 'Martha Washington.' And in fact," the judge said, looking at the other documents, "they're all signed 'Martha Washington'... except the first one--it's signed 'Bertha Roosevelt.'"

"That can't be."

"It definitely is, Mr. Greene." The judge stared hard at him, "I'm not sure who was conning who in your relationship with your client, but all these amendments to the original fee agreement are null and void. They're worthless! So I'm going to disallow all of them, and approve only the original agreement; but with one modification. Because of your unscrupulous conduct, I'm barring you from collecting *any* fees on this case. An attorney who acts unethically, which you certainly did in this case, is not entitled to any legal fees for that work. Mr. Granaldi will receive the twenty-five percent that he bargained for, but you, Mr. Greene, will get nothing, nada, zed! And that's my order."

Chapter Twenty Three

"Another cup of coffee, mister?"

Pete Spanos nodded, pushed his empty cup a couple of inches across the counter, and stared vacantly out the window. If the traffic outside the coffee shop on Jackson was moving any better than it had been all morning, Pete didn't notice. The waitress, a gaunt gray-haired woman in her fifties, refilled the cup, and looked at him.

"Say, are you all right?"

"Yeah, sure," he answered, pulling himself together momentarily and forcing a smile. "I'm fine, thanks."

She shrugged and walked away, toting the coffee pot to the far end of the counter and her only other customer, an off-duty CTA bus driver who was slowly working his way through the morning *Sun-Times*.

Pete turned and looked back out the window. He was ruined. He knew that. The judgment in the Roosevelt case was unbelievable... a catastrophe. He'd been up all night trying to find a way to avoid bankruptcy, but couldn't do it. What was he going to tell his mother? Lucy? The boys?

Cal told him that he had a plan that might work. *What bullshit -- another one of Cal's stupid plans!* Whatever it was, it would probably just draw them deeper and deeper into this black miasma that was enveloping them. *God damn Cal!* His "plan" for dealing with the pension-plan investigation was to simply stall the Department of Labor until the firm could replace the missing funds. *With what? What funds? What firm?* Pete slowly shook his head, desperately groping for something to grab on to.

How had this all happened? Things had been going so well. He and Cal had had it all figured out – except that Pete's idea of the plan didn't include stealing the firm's pension funds! *Damn! I never agreed to that! Stupid!* And now this Roosevelt judgment had come totally out of left field; taking away all their options. . . .

Bankruptcy is one thing; a felony conviction is something else. So is prison time. Whatever else I am, I'm not a felon. But this is my last chance to prove that, or even to say it. He sat up and took a deep breath, then another. *Yes. I want to be able to say that, at the end, I did the right thing. To my mother. To Lucy. To my sons. Whatever the cost--and there will be a cost-- I did the right thing.*

A sudden sense of peace came over Pete Spanos. He glanced down at the bill on the counter, covered it with a five, eased off the stool, and stood up. He took his hat and suit coat off the nearby coat rack, turned and nodded to the waitress, then walked out the door and across the street toward the Dirksen Federal Building and the office of the U.S. Attorney.

—*mm*—

Sergeant Luis Alvarez pulled his Cook County Squad Car into the driveway along the Hancock Building's south side and stopped in front of the canopied front door. It was a crisp, cool fall morning with the sun just rising, and he zipped up his blue jacket before he got out.

Alvarez was serving attachment notices for the Sheriff's office. He did that a couple of early mornings a week, for overtime, and found it pretty easy work. This was a little different, though, he thought as he walked around the front of his car. He'd never served an attachment on a law firm before. *Must be a real bunch of sleazebags, if they can't even pay their bills.* He looked down at the attachment notice as he walked through the building's revolving door. *One hundred and two million bucks!* He couldn't help chuckling. *That's one hell of an overdue bill.*

He flashed his badge to the security guard in the lobby and walked back toward the elevators. As he turned the corner into the corridor for the elevators to the eighties he saw an old friend already waiting: Angelo D'Antona, who'd served with him as a vice-cop years ago.

"Hey, Angie!" he said. "What brings you to these august surroundings?"

"Serving paper, Louie," D'Antona answered, stepping up and shaking his hand. "Working for the U.S.

Attorney's office these days. They found a law firm here that's skimmed a ton of dough out of their pension plan, can you believe it? The feds don't take kindly to that. They're going to put some people in the slammer on this one." He held up the papers he was clasping in his left hand. "We put a lien on their bank accounts yesterday afternoon. One of their lawyers walked in and spilled his guts. Gonna lay this paper on their managing partner."

"Did you say a law firm?"

"Yeah." D'Antona looked at his papers. "Wilson & Thompson. Ever hear of them?"

"Ever hear of them?" Alvarez laughed. "That's the same outfit I'm laying paper on. Sounds like those guys are going down in flames!"

The elevator bell rang and they turned to walk toward the door with the light above it. Before they reached it, however, two other men in dark business suits turned the corner and approached them from the opposite direction. Alverez knew they were law-enforcement types - something about their swagger. They all met in front of the elevator door and looked at each other.

"You boys aren't going up to Wilson & Thompson by any chance, are you?" Sergeant Alvarez asked.

"It just so happens that we are," the older, taller one replied. "Official business."

"That's true for all of us. I'm Alvarez. Cook County Sheriff's Office. I'm here with an attachment notice."

"My name's D'Antona," his friend said. "U.S. Attorney's Office. I'm serving a notice of lien and a subpoena for a federal investigation."

The older man in the dark civilian suit chuckled. "Jeter. FBI. I'm afraid you boys are going to have to wait your turn. I think we've got priority on this one."

"What the hell kind of case you guys have?" Alvarez asked.

"International insurance swindle. These guys," he gestured upstairs, "acted as the middleman in scamming half a billion bucks from an English insurance company and transferring it to the Caribbean. The Brits have gone under cover, but their records implicated these guys big time. We've got a warrant for a guy named Cizma. Should be easy to ID him; got a photo here." He tapped his coat pocket. Then he gestured to the open elevator door. "Gentlemen, shall we?"

—*mm*—

Cal Cizma loved walking around the firm in the early mornings before most of the staff arrived and while many of the lights were still off. It gave him a sense of immense satisfaction to know that this was all his. He had fought, and won, dozens of battles leading to this. And now, he controlled it all.

He walked down the darkened corridors past the offices of some of the people he had vanquished on his road to the top. Their name plaques weren't there anymore, but Cal remembered all their old offices - mental reminders, or trophies, of what he had accomplished.

Rasheed Collins... Chester Melrose... Carol James... Henry Gilcrist. They were all gone. He had driven them all out, one way or another. Curly Morgan... George Lazenby... Tony Jeffries... Ralph Stritch. They couldn't take the pressure - none of them. Barton Thompson... Sara Wexler... Charlie Dickenson. They had all failed where he had succeeded. He loved it, absolutely loved it.

Other people were drifting in now, turning on lights and coffee pots. The office was stirring into life, slowly at first, and accelerating rapidly as the clock passed eight.

Cal knew that there were investigations going on, as well as the problem with the Roosevelt judgment. But he could deal with them all. He'd finesse them, just like he'd always been able to do.

He walked up their broad interior staircase to the eighty-eighth floor, admiring the English lithographs that lined the way--artwork he'd personally selected.

In the large lobby on eighty-eight a number of people had gathered, most carrying cups of steaming coffee or tea.

"Good morning, Mr. Cizma," someone said. Others nodded as he strolled into their midst, smiling, acknowledging and returning their greetings. The room was filling rapidly now, as he had expected. He'd sent an e-mail to the entire staff at the end of the day yesterday, telling them not to be concerned about the adverse result in the Roosevelt case and advising them that he'd have an important announcement about the future of the firm to make at eight the next morning, before anyone's meetings or court appearances. He would give them the assurances they wanted to hear.

"Good morning, everyone," he said, raising his voice. "I appreciate your being here." The room quieted as everyone turned toward the chairman. "As you know, we had a little bad luck in the Roosevelt trial the other day. The case was tried well," he nodded to a grim-faced Wally Covington, "but it was a classic runaway jury, compounded by a judge who obviously doesn't know the first thing about insurance law. It was an unfortunate result, but one that, I guarantee you, will be reversed on appeal. We'll be posting our bond in the next few days, and I can assure you that that judgment will have no adverse impact on the operation of this law firm or anyone's job. That's a promise!" As Cal paused, applause broke out on one side of the room and quickly spread into an ovation. Tears rolled down the cheeks of several of the secretaries.

Cal stepped back, savoring the moment. They loved him. He had no idea how the firm could post an appeal bond, but this was what they wanted to hear. He'd figure something out; he always did.

Suddenly elevator doors opened and four men stepped out. Cal saw them immediately. One wore a deputy sheriff's uniform; the others, none of whom he recognized, were all wearing dark suits. Their eyes caught his, and as they began walking toward him the crowd slowly parted. *These guys don't belong here.* He felt a gnawing discomfort as they approached.

"Mr. Cizma? Calvin Cizma?" the tall, older man in front asked.

"Yes. That's me," he answered, clearing his throat, trying to sound confident.

"Jeter, FBI." He flipped open an ID that Cal didn't look at. "We have a warrant for your arrest."

A spike of horror drove through Cal's heart. He opened his mouth to speak, but couldn't. He saw the people around him fall back, some with hands over their mouths in shock. He felt his arms being pulled back and the cold steel of handcuffs clamp around his wrists.

"Wait a minute!" he protested. "Let's go to my office to talk about this, please. There's been a mistake."

"You have the right to remain silent." he heard someone intone. "Anything you say can and will be used against you in a court of law."

"No!" he shouted, trying to pull away. "You can't do this!" Twisting to his left, he lost his balance and fell to the floor. He tried to rise, but stumbled again with his hands behind his back. They pulled him to his knees and began dragging him toward the elevators.

All around him he heard people shouting and yelling. Above the din one deep voice boomed out: "Everything in this office is hereby attached and is under the custody of the Sheriff of Cook County. Nothing can be removed--nothing!"

Then the elevator doors shut and it was quiet. They were going down. He was lying on the floor, surrounded by boots of men he didn't know, sobbing uncontrollably.

441

—*mm*—

Tony Jeffries raised his glass of Champagne to the others around the table in his dining room. The candles were lit and he and Karen and their guests had just sat down to dinner.

"To the future," he proposed. "And to us, the survivors!"

"More than survivors, Tony," Carol James said. "Escapees."

Charlie and Chris Dickenson raised their glasses, as did Brandon Keyes, whom Tony had asked to join them that evening. They were taking their first sips when a car door slammed outside. Moments later, the doorbell rang.

"I'll get it," Karen said, putting down her glass.

They heard laughing from the front hallway; then Karen returned, leading a smiling Curly Morgan.

"Curly, you got my message!" Tony said exuberantly, rising to greet his old friend.

"I sure did! I sure as hell wouldn't pass up the chance to have dinner with you guys." Karen offered Curly a glass of Champagne, but he shook his head. "Coffee for me, Karen," he answered with a wry smile. "I've gotten older and wiser the last few months."

"Have a seat," Tony said, leading him to the one empty chair at the table. "But hey - I invited you to more than dinner, Curly."

"I know. And I appreciate that. And I also wouldn't

pass up the chance to pick up the remnants of the old shop and build a new one, bigger and better than ever - especially if I'm working with you guys." He paused and looked around the table. "A law firm, this time, with a heart and a soul."

"To a law firm with a heart and a soul!" Tony proposed, raising his glass. "Is that possible, Curly?"

"I don't know, Tony. But I guess we'll find out, won't we?"

Epilogue

"Good morning, dear." Brandon Keyes smiled as his wife entered the kitchen of their brownstone on north Astor Street. He put down his *Tribune*, pushed aside his half-empty cup of coffee, and extended his right arm.

Carol walked over, let his arm embrace her, and gave him a soft, lingering kiss. "Good morning to you too," she replied. "Ready to go to work?"

"Yes, it's a beautiful day. Why don't we walk?"

"Great idea."

Carol and Brandon often walked to work on nice days from their home in Streeterville. It was less than a thirty-minute walk to Catlin & Coogan's office in the IBM Building.

Brandon had decided to move to Chicago after establishing the firm's office there with Tony Jeffries as its managing partner. A major factor in that decision was his growing relationship with Carol James. In less than a year they were married.

They strolled south on Dearborn, enjoying the warm spring weather and the soft breeze off the lake, only a few blocks to the east. "By the way," Brandon said, turning to Carol, "what ever happened to those two assholes who so screwed up your old firm? You haven't mentioned those guys in ages."

"Oh, I try to put them out of my mind. Wilson & Thompson was a great firm for a while, until they took it over, and ruined it. And they ruined themselves along with the firm. If they hadn't been so ruthless with everyone else, I might feel sorry for them. But I don't."

"Didn't Cizma get some serious jail time?"

"You bet he did. Ten years for embezzling the assets of the firm's pension plan, and an additional ten to fifteen for his role in Imperial's scheme to defraud its investors and insureds by diverting over a billion dollars to unknown locations in the Caribbean." She turned to Brandon, adding, "He's currently a resident of the federal penitentiary in Marion, Illinois. Got what he deserved."

"Was that money ever recovered?"

"None of it. Cizma swore he didn't know where it was, but nobody believed him."

"What about Pete Spanos?"

"He had to file bankruptcy, of course, as did most of the firm's remaining partners, in the course of Bertha Roosevelt collecting her huge judgment; but he was able to dodge jail time by cooperating with the feds in their prosecution of Cizma. He's dropped out of the practice of law, and the last I heard he's gone into the wholesale produce business with an uncle."

"Well, he may not have gotten hard time," Brandon said, shaking his head, "but it sounds like he really screwed up his life, big time."

"That's for sure. But they both deserved what they got. They hurt an awful lot of people with their greed."

They stopped for the light at Chicago Avenue. Brandon bought a single red rose from a sidewalk flower vendor, pinned it to Carol's blouse, and gave her a kiss.

The light turned green and they crossed Chicago Avenue, hand in hand.

—*mm*—

"Hey, mama! I made first trumpet! I made first trumpet!" Robert shouted as he pushed open the big front door of their home in Evanston, and ran down the hallway to his mother.

"Oh, that's wonderful" Bertha said, throwing her arms around her son, who was now almost as tall as she was. "I'm so proud of you!"

"They said it was the first time that a freshman ever made first trumpet in the Evanston High School orchestra." He said, leaning back with a grin.

"Oh, Robert, I'm so proud. And your dad will be too. Now, let's get ready to go and see him. I'll let you tell him yourself. I'll be just a minute – let me change my clothes."

Bertha turned to walk up the ornate curved stairway to the second floor of their lakefront home – the one that had been once owned by Cal Cizma, and that she had obtained, with the aggressive help of Mike Granaldi, in collecting her hundred-million dollar judgment from the partners at Wilson & Thompson. She especially enjoyed the nice painting of the racing sail boats in the den overlooking the lake.

———

Max Greene was disbarred for his unscrupulous conduct in the Roosevelt case, based on the complaint filed by Judge Julius Carver. He had a paralyzing stroke the day he received his Disbarment Order by certified mail, and was hospitalized in the same Cook County public aid facility that Sam Roosevelt had been housed in. In the year he had been there he had not had a single visitor. Sam, in the meantime, was transferred to a first class treatment center on the North Shore, where Bertha continues to visit him daily.

———

Tony smiled as he hung up his phone. Curly Morgan had just won a month-long jury trial defending a railroad in a wrongful death case in downstate Madison County, notoriously plaintiffs' turf. A couple of drunks in a pickup tried to beat an Amtrak train to a crossing, smashed through the lowered gate, and almost made it. Almost. Their families turned down a modest settlement offer from the railroad, held out for the expected bonanza, and wound up with nothing. It was the third major trial that Curly had won in a row. He was back.

The Chicago office of Catlin & Coogan had flourished the past few years and Tony was proud of its growth as well as its successes. He'd hired several of the former associates of Wilson & Thompson who he knew were good lawyers and had been left high and dry when the firm collapsed, including Sarah Wexler, who Cal had unceremoniously thrown out when the Acorn Insurance work was lost.

Carol James was an equity partner, of course. That was one of the conditions that Tony insisted on when they joined, and Tony had recently appointed her Chair of the office's Long-Range Planning Committee.

—⁓⁓—

Rasheed Collins smiled as he read the e-mail message that had just come up on his computer. It was from the president of the San Francisco Chamber of Commerce and informed him that, in his role as General Counsel of the city's Gay and Lesbian Civil Rights League, he would be honored as the Chamber's Citizen of the Year at its annual awards banquet in the fall.

He had been in San Francisco less than three years; had decided, after a great deal of soul searching, to be proud of his sexual orientation, and had become a force in establishing and expanding the civil rights of gays and lesbians, not just in California but nationally. He had won multiple lawsuits against moribund national corporations and insurance companies, forcing them to recognize and honor the rights of partners of gays and lesbians previously reserved only for hetro couples, and was both proud and at peace.

He picked up the phone on his desk and punched the bank's autodial button. After a moment he said, "Ron, hon, we've got a great reason to celebrate tonight. Why don't we have dinner at that new Italian place on the corner. How's six sound?"

mm

"Roxanne, my dear, would you be so kind as to refresh my gin and tonic while you're up." Gordon Hawke smiled as he handed her his glass, then turned back to Ronnie Dasher, sitting across from him on the veranda of Hawke's home overlooking the lush forest leading down to the Caribbean.

"As I was saying", Dasher said, "The Costa Rican government is fully on board and will guaranty our underwriting for at least the first five years. Of course, it helps to have friends in high places," he chuckled.

"It certainly does, especially when he's the Insurance Commissioner." Hawke returned his smile. "When do you anticipate that we'll be in a position to roll out our new program?"

Dasher swirled his Pims in his glass for a moment,

then looked up. "I'd say the first of the year. We'll have our agents in place by then in every country in the region, and should be in a position to take the Caribbean insurance market by storm."

"Wonderful. Then I'd like to propose a toast to the man who made this all possible. The one without whose help we couldn't have moved all our funds here and pulled this off."

"Right," Dasher replied, raising his glass. "To our dear friend Cal Cizma."

"Indeed."

CPSIA information can be obtained at www.ICGtesting.com
Printed in the USA
LVOW08s1628160114

369508LV00004B/1/P